ALAINA T. LEE

Tantalized

To my mom, who has constantly asked me, "Why can't I read it?" Well, you know what? You can finally read it but don't say I didn't warn you. I promise I'm still your "sweet" baby girl.
Grab you a glass of wine and proceed with caution.

Contents

Dedication #2

iv

Be a good girl, and think about how good you feel when praised, spanked, and choked. Now turn the page, open those pretty fucking legs, and enjoy the ride.

Trigger Warnings

Before proceeding, it is important to know that this book contains stalking, bondage, breath play, biting, spanking, CNC, non-con (with an object), light breeding kink, faked pregnancy (briefly mentioned), child abuse, and mild degradation.

I strongly recommend you do not move forward if you are or could be triggered by any of those things. I trust that you know your limits. Read at your own risk.

With love,

Alaina T. Lee

Playlist

Dangerous Woman-Ariana Grande
Lose control- Teddy Swims
Crazy in love (remix)- Beyoncé
Way down we go- KALEO
Salted wounds- Sia
Someone you loved- Lewis Capaldi
Love is a bitch- Two Feet
Go F*ck yourself-Two Feet
I see red-Everybody loves an outlaw
No Mercy- Austin Giorgio
Like Villain- Bad Omens
Breakeven- The Script
Stay- Rihanna
Gonna Love You- Parmalee
Under the Influence- Chris Brown
I wanna be Yours- Artic Monkeys
High- Stephen Sanchez
River- Bishop Briggs

1

Liza

It's dark, and I can't breathe. Something is constricting my airway. No. Someone is. The person is too heavy, and I can't move. I can't move!

Please help me. Someone help me.

He's crushing me. Why are dots all around me? And it's dark, so dark.

I can't open my eyes; they're too heavy. I'm trying so hard.

But I'm tired. I'm tired of running. I'm tired of fighting. I'm tired of him. He finally got me.

"Fight, Lizzie." Daddy?

"I can't." I don't want to anymore.

"You can. Remember what I taught you." My brain is finally silent. This is it. It's all over. "Now, Lizzie, do it now!"

I ram my knee into his groin, and I fight. I breathe. But I can't open my eyes. Even with the yelling. Who is yelling?

The weight is gone, and I can breathe. Why the fuck can't I see?

"Liza! Open your fucking eyes! Jesus!" My eyes spring open, and I'm confronted with my redheaded best friend, worried, with her hand on my shoulders, shaking me.

"They're open! Fuck sakes." She slumps down on the bed and stares at me.

"You've been here for two weeks, and you've had a nightmare all fourteen days."

"I'm sorry, Em. It's just because I'm in a new place. Did I scare you?"

"Yes, bitch. You did; now, if you're done with your late afternoon nap, sleeping beauty. I want to go out tonight."

I'd been staying with my best friend Emily for the last two weeks in the university apartment until I found one of my own. I had just transferred to the University of Washington as a second-semester senior. Why? Because my mother doesn't want to lose hope in me finding love. She also doesn't want to lose me *again*. She hovers; that's what she does. Especially after my accident, but she met my father here and lived this life she doesn't stop talking about and thinks that Seattle holds some magic healing power. Secretly, I hoped, too, that I'd find someone to keep me safe and that they would show me how to move on. More than anything, I hope that I'll find myself feeling *normal* again. The problem is that my life is anything but normal. Running? Yeah, that's not normal. Stalkers? Not normal. Almost being killed? *Definitely*, not normal.

I stretch and check my phone when she clears her throat.

"Nope, not going. I'm tired."

"You just fucking slept for four hours. Up now, bitch. We've only gone out twice, and you still haven't met Travis. He got back today from his trip with his boys." Travis is her boyfriend; they've been dating since freshman year. I hadn't met him besides on FaceTime a few times.

She ignores my protest and pulls me by my arm into her closet. The loft lacks doors, so privacy isn't really an option. There is only one wall between our beds, but that can barely be called a wall.

Emily's apartment isn't that bad. She got a full scholarship, and the two-bedroom apartment came with it. Luckily, she loves me enough to let me use the spare room. I haven't started looking for an apartment because we have always wanted to live together. But things changed once she moved, and I practically fell off the face of the earth.

My mother hated the thought of me staying with Emily instead of having my own apartment. She didn't understand why I was so determined to do things independently when I was financially well cared for.

She shuffles through her clothes, throwing various pieces over her head. I pick them up as she dishes them out, and she scowls at me.

"Okay, wear this." She picks up a short dress that I'm sure will barely cover my ass. "Fuck no."

"Just try it on; it's longer than it looks, and it'll look fucking great on you."

"I hate you."

I take the dress from her and pull it over my head. She's right—it looks good on me and perfectly hugs my body.

"You look fucking delicious; let me change, and we're out of here."

I grab my makeup bag and pull my mascara out as she yanks dress after dress over her head. I laugh when she trips over her shoes, and she glares at me. I'm fixing my hair when she finally pops her head around the corner of the closet.

"Okay, how do I look?" She twirls around and pops her hand on her hip, flipping her hair over her shoulder.

She has a slender body and is a 5'4 ginger with a killer smile; she's also a senior and one of the most gorgeous women on campus. She wears a blue and white striped halter top, a light blue mini skirt, and brown wedges.

"Hot. Let's go, or I'll change my mind." She laughs, grabs her keys, and we walk toward her white Mercedes. "I'm so happy that we can finally hang out." She exclaims. "I know; I'm finally here, so we will be hanging out a lot more now," I say, noticing a group of guys staring at her. I giggle to myself at how oblivious she is to it. She hits the key to unlock her car, and we climb in.

"You do realize that group of guys was staring at you, right?" She grabs her shades and throws them on.

"What?"

I nod in their direction, and she tilts her sunshades down, looking over at them. "Ugh, freshman, they always stare, but, babe, I'm pretty sure they were staring at you." I roll my eyes, and she pulls the car out.

"I can't believe graduation is coming so quickly." She exclaims, pulling her visor down.

"I know, it's insane."

"I'm still going to the Caribbean after, for probably a month."

"I'm sure you'll have fun."

"I don't understand why you don't come with me."

"Yeah, and be the third wheel with you and Travis? No, thanks."

"Who knows, you might meet your Prince Charming before then, then we can make it a foursome." She winks at me, and I gag.

"Yeah, right...where are we going?"

"It's right up here. We won't stay long, promise!"

"Lies. This isn't my first fucking rodeo with you. Don't fucking leave me."

We arrive at the white two-story frat house around 9:30 p.m. It's exactly as I expected: people everywhere and solo cups in every hand. A guy named Cayson hands her two beers and smirks.

"Have fun and get drunk." I'm too invested in the group playing beer pong to acknowledge him. Em shoves the beer in my face, and I take it.

"I'm going to find Travis; I'll be right back." Just as she's about to leave me to find him, we see him weaving through the crowd with a wide grin.

"Liza, this is Travis," Em says, sitting beside me.

"Finally, see you in person. I thought for sure that'd never happen."

He pulls me in for a hug, and I laugh.

"Yeah, I know, three years later."

He's handsome, and I don't know why I'm so surprised; I wouldn't expect anything else when looking at Em. He's perfect for her, and after talking to her and looking at them, I know they are completely in love. They constantly touch one another, and Em smiles whenever I catch a glimpse of her. I chug the beer in my hand and take them both in.

The music picks up, and they get up to start dancing. I let out a low sigh and begin feeling sorry for myself. I'm a runner; it's what I do. I ran from the demon who tried to ruin my life, telling myself I deserved to be happy and start over. I ran when my mom and stepdad paid off my—*no*, I'm not going there. But I am a runner, and no matter how much I want to be loved and cherished, it'd be dangerous. I'm a walking fucking hazard, and so is my life.

A few hours have passed, and I've had about six beers, completely glued to my phone, looking at old pictures of myself and my brothers. The party is boring, and there's nothing here but drunk boys who keep throwing up because they can't hold their alcohol. *Pathetic.*

I'm setting my beer down when the front door opens. I turn to look, and my mouth turns dry. Standing in the doorway, with every eye on him and a smile that could bring you to your knees, is the most beautiful man I'd *ever* laid eyes on. He's tall, about 6' 2 or 6' 3, with dark hair, almost black, but it's a deep brown that comes to his shoulders.

I look at the dance floor where Em and Travis were a while ago, and of course, they're gone. I scan the crowd again until I finally see her standing in front of the kitchen island, her arms wrapped around Travis.

I lean into her and whisper, "Em, who is that?"

"Graham Salando. He's very rich, important, and fine as hell. He's Travis' best friend. Remember the trip? He was with him." Biting my lip, I try to act as if I'm uninterested, but who am I kidding? I'm practically screaming that I want him to notice me. I'm sure as hell seeing and wanting him without even knowing a thing about him. *No, we're wrong for anyone, but especially him.* I internally thank my conscience for the unneeded reminder.

"He's a senior too; google him," she suggests, shrugging her shoulders. She watches me as I watch him, and her shoulders sink after she realizes what she said.

"Or not..sorry, babe." I don't acknowledge anything she's saying because I can't keep my eyes off this fucking man.

But I would *not* be googling him because the last thing I would want is for him to google *me*.

"You're hot for him, aren't you? Tell me you aren't fucking him in your mind right now." I swat at her arm and cover my face, knowing that it's probably beat fucking red.

"It's okay; they all look at him like that, even my girl," Travis snarls.

"I don't know what you're talking about." I push my hair over my shoulder, and Em elbows me.

"Here comes your Casanova."

"Shut up, Emily."

"Trav," he grins.

"My man, what's up?" He gives him what I like to call a "bro hug."

"What's up, Em?"

"Hey, Graham." She speaks, looking at me. He stares at me while talking to her. No it's like he's burning a hole in my face with how entranced he looks.

I swallow audibly. He finally lifts his hand toward me.

"Graham."

I take it and shake it gently.

"Liza."

He holds my hand a little longer than necessary, and I give him a quick smile that I'm sure looked awkward before pulling my hand back.

"I saw you in that magazine, bro. What the fuck is wrong with people? We just got back six hours ago. How'd they get some shit already? Any broad in your face, and they automatically assume you're fucking her." Travis states, raising his beer to his mouth. Magazine? Who is this man?

"Comes with the territory, man."

Emily clears her throat, grasping my attention. She stands close to me, pulling her cup up to her lips.

"Talk to him."

"No. Absolutely not."

"Did you see how he stared at you? He practically devoured you with his eyes." She nags me, pinching and shoving until I elbow her in her stomach to stop. That's her; she is always pushy and straightforward.

"I need another beer."

"No, you don't." Fine, she's right. I don't, but I *do* need to pee.

"Where's the bathroom?"

Travis opens his mouth to speak, and Emily nudges him and lifts her eyebrows.

"Why don't you show her Graham?" Emily cuts in, and I scowl at her.

"I'm sure I can find..."

"I'll show you," Graham replies in a dark, stern voice, giving me that piercing stare again. My body freezes like it's under a fucking spell. I bite my lip and nod as I follow behind him, and I murmur "bitch" to Emily as we walk past her. She giggles and pushes me.

We're halfway across the room when Emily yells, "Would you wait for her too?" Embarrassment shoots through me, and I pick up my pace to the bathroom.

I lift my dress and use the restroom quickly, washing my hands and touching up my face. I fix my mascara and use my new mint-flavored lip gloss. Graham is sexy as hell, and I do not plan to pass this opportunity up if given to me. Even knowing the rumors and reputation of men who looked like that, he seems to have a different aura about him, and I want to learn firsthand.

He waits for me with his back leaning against the wall. His black fitted shirt shows every muscle in his arm, while his jeans have slight rips at the knees, showcasing his tan skin. I have never been so attracted to someone. I barely know him, but I cannot keep my eyes to myself, regardless of how hard I try. I walk over to him and clear my throat; he glances up at me and raises his eyebrow.

"Thank you for waiting for me." A tall blonde walks up to him and pulls him into a hug. He embraces her as I watch, his eyes on me as he hugs her. She stands next to him, eyeing me up and down.

"No problem," he responds, looking back at her. She places her hand on his bicep before turning back to him. I ignore them and storm back into the party. As I reach the end of the hall, I swear I hear him chuckle. Asshole.

Time to go. My conscience is right. I look around for Emily at the party. Where the fuck is she? I pull out my phone and call her. Voicemail, great. I try again. Voicemail.

"Everything okay?" A dark voice speaks behind me. Graham. His voice is one I know so well already.

"I can't find Emily anywhere; I think she's gone."

"They left already; they usually do. Those two cannot seem to keep their hands off each other," he says with a sly smirk on his face.

She left me. I *knew it.* What the fuck! How am I supposed to get home? Do I even want to go home? She and Travis are probably ripping each other's clothes off by now. I pull out my phone and text her.

Liza: "You left me?!"

I plop onto the couch and wait for a response.

Em: Have fun with Graham; he'll take care of you ;)

Unfuckingbelievable.

Liza: Are you fucking kidding me?! Emily!

Em: Oh, come on! Live your life a little; you like him!

Liza: I don't know him, Em!

Em: Exactly, now you will.

I feel his glare again, so I gather my courage and look at him, raising my eyebrow.

"Are you ready to leave?" he asks, sitting beside me.

"I am, but my ride is gone, and so is a quiet time in my apartment, apparently."

"Oh, you're her roommate."

"Yeah, I am."

"Damn, I feel sorry for you," he utters. "I don't know when you'll ever have the apartment to yourself; Travis still hasn't found an apartment and is there every day; you should consider getting your own place." I ignore his comment, and I start to wonder where I'll go.

"I'm just going to walk back to campus and figure it out from there," I say, throwing my hands up and sliding my phone into my back pocket. *No, we aren't.*

"No, you're not; you will stay with me tonight."

I raise my eyebrow at him because what?

"Excuse me?"

"Oh, I'm sorry. You strike me as the type to want choices. Choice one, my place. Choice two, sit here," he spits out nonchalantly, with his hand tucked in his pocket.

"That's *very* funny. You don't know me."

He turns to walk away, and I clear my throat. "But, since I don't have any other choice, I guess I'll be staying with you for the night."

"After you," he says, waving his arm toward the door to leave. Graham opens the door to the frat house and leads me out. I walk towards the parking lot across the street when Graham grabs my hand.

Warmth and an electric shock pulse through me. I stop and look at him.

"Is something wrong?"

"Don't you know never to walk behind a man? Protecting what you can't see is impossible. In front of me, Liza." I look around at the chilly April night's emptiness, then back at Graham, only to realize he is serious.

"Who is out here for you to protect me from?"

"Just do it."

I shrug my shoulders and walk in front of him. Some battles aren't worth it.

"Which car?" I say. He points to a beautiful, shiny black G-class SUV, and I catch myself before my mouth hits the floor. I've always loved those SUVs. My stepdad always offered to buy me one, and I always declined. Why? I'm not sure. Looking at it now, it's a beauty. But I will not be some car whore that falls at his feet. No matter how badly I want to.

2

Graham

The ride to my house was quiet for the first few minutes. She climbed into the truck and looked out the window, her small hands on her knees.

"Thanks for checking on me."

"No problem; I wouldn't want any of these drunks trying to pick you up. And I don't want you walking back to campus late at night, looking like... " I rake my eyes up and down her body.
I couldn't keep my eyes off her at the party, and I didn't try to. She looks at me with her head cocks to the side.

"Looking like what?" She snaps back.

"Like that. That dress is too damn tight and short."

It is, and if she were mine, I would've bent her over the moment she put it on to show her just how short it was.

"I didn't realize you were the boss of what I wore. But luckily for you, I'll remember that for the next party I decide to go to. Besides, I would've thought you were too busy to notice what I was wearing." She winks at me and rolls her eyes. I know she's referring to Ashley; no, maybe Amber or whatever the fuck her name was that she saw me with at the party.

11

"Meaning?"

"Your little girlfriend was back there; hers was much shorter than the dress I have on."

"She's not my girlfriend, and I'm not talking about how short her dress is. I'm talking about how short *yours* is."

"Don't worry about me. I'm a big girl."

Feisty would be an understatement to describe this one; it was apparent she took no shit from anyone. I liked that; it was different from every other woman I'd encountered, always trying to please me and agreeing with everything I said and wanted. It was exhausting.

Liza's beautiful; she has an attractively fit body and long brown hair. It's also obvious she is into me, even though she thinks she is hiding it. I meant what I said to her; I didn't want anyone hitting on her. I want to be the one to do it myself. I could tell she was nervous at the party when we met; I could practically hear her swallow her saliva, and that alone went straight to my dick.

She's still nervous and afraid to talk to me. Just when I thought there would be more silence, she speaks again. Her voice is soft and small, contrary to her personality.

"So, tell me something about you, Graham."

I almost missed what she said. I pause because the only thought on my mind is how desperately I want to taste her and bite that lip. I contain myself and glance at her.

"What do you want to know?"

"When's your birthday?"

"My birthday?" I frown. "That's what you want to know?"

"Well, yeah, you asked what I wanted to know. You can't go wrong with the basics."

I hate small talk. Looking at her, I can tell she wants to know something specific.

"That just isn't what I expected you to ask; I can tell you want to know something specific, so ask it, pretty girl." I glance at her and then continue to drive.

"And *I* can tell you don't want to talk about yourself."

"If you're not going to say what you want, then I want to know about you; I'm not interesting anyway."

"How about I be the judge of that? Besides, there's nothing *specific* I want to ask; if there were, I'd ask." She folds her arms and rests against the passenger seat door.

"Right, so you and Emily just met each other? Or were you friends before?"

"We've known each other since 8th grade. How do you know Travis?"

"We went to high school together and just kind of never separated; we ended up going to the same college, and that's pretty much it."

"What are your plans after school?

"Just the business I'm in."

"Okay, what else can you tell me about you? Outside of work and school."

"Nothing; I'm boring." She shakes her head but doesn't ask anything else.

Running her away is the last thing I plan to do.

I pull into my five-bedroom, four-bathroom house. It is made of tan stone, with white window frames and white trim around the entrance to the three-car garage. I watch as she looks out the window and reaches for her door handle. I put my hand on her thigh and squeezed it.

"Stay put." She opens her mouth to protest as I climb out and circle to open her door. "You were saying?"

"Sorry," she mutters, putting a piece of her hair behind her ear. I grab her hand and direct her to the front door. "You're very touchy."

"Not usually. Come on in."

Truthfully, it would be nice to have someone in the house with me, especially since my parents no longer live here. My dad is a retired surgeon and the past CEO of Salando Industries, and my mom is one of the top lawyers in Seattle. They live about three hours away, so I bought the house from them when they considered selling it.

"Your house is beautiful; whose cars are those?" She walks in, looking over her shoulder.

"Mine... Are you hungry?"

"Of course they are," she whispers under her breath. "No, I'm fine. Thank you." She looks around the house and runs her hands over the white couch before sitting.

"I hope you didn't spend too much on this couch."

"It's just a couch." She looks over at me, and I pull out pancake batter.

"Pancakes at 3 a.m.?"

"That's the best time to eat them, babe."

Her face softens as she slightly smirks. Her cheeks pink up, and she puts her head down. I smile, realizing she enjoys it when I flirt with her. I pour some syrup over my pancakes and sit next to her.

"Are you ready to tell me about yourself? Or do you want me to ask the questions this time?"

She sighs, but she begins to talk. I stick a forkful of pancakes into my mouth.

"Um, okay, well, I'm majoring in psychology with a minor in human development, and I hope to be a psychiatrist. What about you?"

"I own Salando Industries and do a lot of contracting work. Salando is involved in about every business." I say this with the fork hanging on the side of my mouth.

"Isn't that your father's company? What's your major here?" she asks.

"My father gave me the business; my major is Pre-Med, and I'll probably never use it." I shrug and continue eating my pancakes.

"Why not?"

"You ask a lot of questions for someone who doesn't like giving up answers to anything involving herself," I say, smirking at her. "I understand people and this business; I've been around it my entire life. The money is also a plus. But *you*, being a psychiatrist, looking at and talking to that face all day while you tell me how to manage my problems, well, that'd be *interesting*, to say the least."

I sit back and watch her tense up as the words roll off my tongue. I can already tell that Liza isn't the best at receiving compliments. I have no intention of letting up on them, so she will have to get used to it.

"Let's get to the one question all you women like to discuss. Have you ever been in love?"

She looks down as a crease forms right above her brow. She parts her lips to say something and then shakes her head.

"No." I wait, thinking she will say more, but she doesn't. There is no detail, no story, just a straight-out "no."

I understood that she said no, but I could also tell by the look on her face that there was more to the story. Without trying to seem too pushy, I dive in for more information. Either she will tell me herself, or I will have Ellis give me the necessary information. Ellis is the head of my security and is always close behind me wherever I am. Anyone that I encounter on any level gets a background check. My parents are well-known, and I have a lot of money, so I must constantly watch my back, even when having hookups.

But then again, will Liza be a hookup? Would I go that far with her?

I want to be the dominant man in her life—the man she listens to and obeys. We'll eventually get there.

"Why that face? You might as well tell me because I don't believe you if we're being honest."

"I just had a bad experience and turned against it; it isn't my thing. And honestly? You're kind of mean and a dick."

Isn't her thing? Love isn't her thing? I laugh, not because she's been hurt, but because I have met women like her. Women who claim they've built this wall up because of some old fling or past breakup that destroyed them. Sitting here and looking at her, this beautiful woman has "save me" written all over her.

"Are you laughing?"

"No, not at you; just at the fact that the moment I met you, I could tell you were a romantic, someone who is waiting to be saved. The way you stare off at Emily and Trav, or you'll try to avoid them altogether completely. There's no in-between. I've known you for what? Two hours? You wear your emotions on your sleeve. It's not the best trait to have, sometimes. So, I don't buy it. And pretty girl, I never pretended to be nice. You don't get where I am from being *nice*."

"You're nice to Travis."

"Don't change the subject."

"Fine, I guess you're right. I am a romantic, but I'm a senior in college and still haven't...

"Still haven't what?"

"You know what? I'm pretty tired; I think I'm going to call it a night."

"Liza...come on." She yawns.

"Maybe we can talk more tomorrow."

I quickly glance at the clock; it's nearing 4:30 a.m. I can tell she doesn't want to talk further, so I don't push her.

"Okay, I'll show you to the guest room." I walk toward her and gesture for her to walk up the stairs.

"I love this staircase."

It's made of dark wood and spirals to the top of the stairs; it was one of the reasons my mother fell in love with the house.

"Ladies first." I watch her walk up the stairs in front of me, her body perfectly figured, her ass switching from left to right. Man, I so badly want to grab her and take her any way she'll let me. She gets to the top of the stairs and looks at me.

"I don't have any night clothes."

"It's fine."

I point her to her room and walk down the hall, two doors down, to my room. I grab a gray T-shirt from my dresser and bring it to her.

"Here you go; you can sleep in this tonight."

"Thanks, Graham."

The way my name rolls off her tongue is electrifying. But I've never been off my game for *anyone*, and I sure wouldn't be starting now.
I pull my shirt over my head as I walk into my room. The only thing I need right now is a hot shower. Turning the water on, I still can't believe she's here despite pushing her out of my head. I want her in this shower with me so badly. I want to see her body because using my imagination for the past few hours has become exhausting. My cock isn't thinking straight; that's my excuse. I should've fucked that girl they had me pictured with today, but I didn't. Why? Because no one has come close to satisfying me lately. No one has gotten my attention, and if they do, I barely stomach ten minutes with them before I turn them away. So yeah, my cock isn't fucking thinking straight.

I shed the remainder of my clothes and hop in the shower. I usually never masturbate, but man, I desperately want to for the first time in my life. I fist my cock and start pumping it until it spills into my hand. Thinking about Liza being in here with me and me fucking her until she screamed, it didn't take long before I came. I hear a soft knock at my door as I lather soap in my hand.

Quickly rinsing off, I grab a towel, wrap it around my waist, and walk to the door.

"Oh, sorry, I didn't know you were showering."

"What do you need?" Standing there, I notice her perfectly parted lips beckoning me, causing my cock to stir. *I have to get laid.* I hide behind the door, making sure to cover my cock. She's completely frozen. She doesn't answer me at all. I raise my eyebrow at her.

"Liza. Liza. Li—"

"Yes, I'm sorry. I was wondering if you had an extra blanket; that room is a little cold."

I walk out from behind the door with my hand hovering over my cock and grab a blanket out of the linen closet; she reaches out for it, and I let our hands touch longer than they should.

"Thank you."

"Let me know if you need anything else. Sleep well." I watch her hurry down the hall and close the door. How am I supposed to *not* fuck her when she looks at me like that? Fuck, this is going to be a long night.

3

Liza

What the fuck was that! I froze before him because he was in his towel, water dripping down from his perfectly sculpted arms and defined abs. My mouth felt fucking numb, and my pussy throbbed as he commanded it to want him. I couldn't register words to come out of my mouth. Of course, he'd figure out I was a virgin if I kept acting like that around him. He doesn't seem like the kind of man uncomfortable in his skin. I take the shirt he gave me, pull it up to my nose, and sniff it. I inhale his scent; the musk and the shea butter soap are heavy on his shirt.

I'm being weird. Go the fuck to bed, Elizabeth.

I slip into the shirt and lay on the bed, looking around at the decorated room. I close my eyes and try my best to fall asleep, hoping that with how eventful it was, I'll skip the nightmares and sleep well. Instead of falling asleep, I toss, turn, and think about how well the night was going until he decides to analyze me on love. I didn't do an excellent job of hiding how much I still wanted a happy ending, as I thought I did.

I take a deep breath and squeeze my eyes shut. Graham's perfect fucking face with his dick of an attitude pops into my brain *again*. My belly feels warm, and sleep isn't an option unless I come. I take my hand and grip my sex, pleasuring myself to climax.

* * *

The next morning...

I wake up in a king-size bed, with my deep brown hair all over my face and the sun seeping through the tan and white curtains. I hear the TV on downstairs and roll over to check my phone. It's 7:15 a.m.

I'm suddenly hit with the smell of pancakes and bacon. Stretching my arms wide, I walk to the door and peek my head out to see down the hall. Afraid it might be someone else downstairs, I tiptoe down the hall and into Graham's room. I knew he wasn't in there; I could feel his absence. I see his black t-shirt lying over the stairs from the night before and reach for it. I stop when I realize just how fucking creepy I'm being. The bathroom is a few doors down the hall, so I quickly head over to brush my teeth and fix my hair.

I see a new toothbrush and a note that reads,

You didn't have any night clothes; I'm sure you'll need this too.
-G

I laugh a little and fix myself up. Graham is just how I imagined him to be: sexy, demanding, and sweet—at least to me. Well, he's not, but he also is, when he wants to be.

Maybe when you see him next time, you won't freeze. For your pathetic sake, I hope he's dressed.

I shake my head to clear my thoughts; I can't keep letting my desires get the better of me around him. As I look for clothes to change into, I stop and look in the mirror. Who am I kidding? He'd never be interested in a girl like me, anyway. So I don't change; I have no reason to impress this man.

I get downstairs, and Graham is shirtless in the kitchen, standing over the stove with a cup of coffee. He has a huge tattoo that covers the left side of his back and snakes around to the front of his chest. I might pass out, but I quickly snap out of it.

I clear my throat, indicating that I'm in the room.

"Good morning," I say softly.

He turns around and leans against the countertop, bringing the coffee mug to his mouth with a smile. A smile? Is that a goddamn smile?!

"You wear that shirt better than I do; good morning."

Another compliment: I'm glad I didn't change; I would have been overdressed. I smirk slightly and walk further into the kitchen beside him.

"What are you cooking?" I peek over the stove, eyeing each pan.

"Pancakes, bacon, and eggs; I enjoy cooking; I hope you're hungry."

"Yes, starved," I smirk and go into the living room, suddenly feeling too exposed. I grab the remote and pull a blanket over my bare legs. I glance over and see Graham eyeing me. I ignore his stare and flip through the channels. If it were up to me, I'd be watching the Hallmark channel or horror movies.

Graham scts two plates down on the table and looks at me. "Water, juice, coffee?"

"Coffee, please," I say.

He pours me a cup of coffee, setting the sugar and creamer before me. He points to the empty chair and orders, "Sit, eat, and talk; no TV during meals."

"What?" I say, almost choking and giving him a side-eye.

"You heard me, so up, pretty girl, now." I stand up from the couch and walk over to the breakfast nook. It's a medium-sized tan tiled table with a chair on the outside and booth-like seats around the rest.

"So demanding," I say to him in a faint voice.

He stares at me intensely, and his look is intimidating. I can tell it's meant to be subtle, but it makes me feel *submissive.*

"So, is it true that you're this big-time womanizer in Seattle?"

No, idiot, why would you say that?

My conscience was right; I should not have said that. Out of all things, why did that come out of my mouth? I bite my lip intensely, focusing on pouring the right amount of creamer into my coffee. He reached over and steals a piece of my bacon, which lightens up the mood a little.

"Who said that?"

"No one in particular; I've just read about you." I'm good at taking conversations and making them seem natural, but I just can't with Graham; for some reason, I'm just too nervous.

"I've had my share of women, and I usually get them to do what I want, and then I leave. Unfortunately, most people are not in my life for the right reasons."

He gets up and grabs the gray shirt lying on the kitchen island, pulling it over his head, before he comes and sits back down.

"I don't have the best track record with women here because I don't date them. I fuck them and move on. They're never around for the right reasons anyway." I continue to eat, acting as naturally as I can. I can feel him staring at me, waiting for a reaction. "When you have the life I have and the amount of money I have, you don't take chances. None of them were worth the chance. There was one committed relationship, and it didn't end well." He has an unsympathetic expression when he says that, and it scares me a little.

"And you're okay with doing that to women? Using them to get off?" Graham shrugs, picks up his fork, and starts to eat.

Okay, so a dick and serious trust issues. He is a walking red flag.

"Is there a guy in your life, Liza?"

"No, no one."

"Shocking."

I can't tell if he means that in a good or bad way. His face and expression remain the same. I decide that his opinion doesn't matter either way.

"Eat your food; it'll get cold." I aggressively shove another forkful into my mouth, and he leans over and watches me chew.

"Good girl." I audibly swallow as he continues to watch me eat. I've never made myself eat so quickly in my life.

Good girl? *Holy. Shit.*

Once we finish eating, he takes my plate and starts washing our dishes.

"Do you need any help?"

"No, go shower or relax. I got this."

When I get upstairs, I turn the shower on, noticing it's just as gorgeous as the house, with its marble stone and detachable shower head. I wait for the water to get as hot as I can withstand and step underneath the shower head. The water rolls off my hair and onto my shoulders. I let out a sigh of pent-up stress. I didn't have a dream last night, but I'm sure that's because I barely slept. I was so stressed that I'd have a dream that sleep was a much scarier thought than the dream would be.

After 20 minutes, I cut the shower off, wrapped myself in a towel, and wandered back to the room. As I fix my hair, I hear him on the phone down the hall. I tiptoe to the door and listen.

"I don't care what needs to be done, do it. I don't want any stories surfacing about me and her. Being linked to her makes me sick to my fucking stomach."

Linked to who? He's not talking about me, right? He's not the nicest to me, but I thought he liked me. I don't have time to dwell on my thoughts before I hear a knock at the door. I jump back and act like I'm fixing my hair.

"Can I come in?"

"It's your house, Graham; you can do whatever you want," I say sarcastically. He comes in with a shirt and pants in his hands.

"You and my sister look like the same size; she doesn't live here, so I'm sure she won't mind," he states, handing me the clothes.

"You have a sister?" I say, grabbing the clothes.

Ask about the phone call.

I look at him as he answers, barely hearing anything he says. I want to ask about it and make sure he wasn't talking about me, but even if he was, would he tell me? I decide it's not my place and ignore the gnawing feeling in the pit of my stomach.

"Yeah, 21 years old and a pain in my ass." I laugh and start changing into the clothes as he continues to talk. "She lives about three hours away from here with my parents; she's in design school. I don't see them as much as my mom would like."

"Why not?"

"I love my family, but my father and I aren't always on the same page. Our interactions usually end in an argument, which upsets my mom."

"Why don't you guys get along?" He turns and looks at me as I pull my shirt over my head, revealing my laced bra.

"Oh, I'm sorry," he apologizes, turning his back to me.

Hmm, maybe he's not a prude after all.

"It's fine; I'm pretty sure you've seen girls in their underwear and bras before; you can't see a thing."

He surprises me when he turns to go into his room. "You can come in when you're done getting dressed," he says over his shoulder.

I throw the shirt over my head. I want to know more about why his relationship with his father isn't good, but I also want to know who he doesn't want to be linked to. I pick up my phone and open the Google app. I quickly type his name in, my finger hovering over the "search icon." I stop, closing the app and stuffing my phone into my back pocket. I owe him the benefit of the doubt; he's done nothing to make me think he isn't into me other than not giving me much about his life.

I shake my head at myself and head toward his room.

"Graham?" I say while gently pushing open the door to his room.

"I'm here." He exclaims, merging from the bathroom.

"Your room is nice."

He stretches out on his king-sized bed. "Sit down and relax unless you're ready to go." Oh, I'm ready, all right, but not to go home. I want to be wherever he is, which clearly says something about my judgment of men. He's shown me two things, one, that he's a fucking asshole, and two, that he's a fucking asshole to women, especially. But he's also sweet; can you even be both? Fuck, it doesn't matter. I need to stay away from him.

"No, I'm fine. I'm not really in a rush to walk in on Em and Trav. We can finish talking if you'd like—you know, about your dad." I walk over to his bed and sit down beside him.

Bitch, we are supposed to be staying away.

"I'd rather not; it's not important. He's my dad, and I love him, but he needs to understand the importance of telling the truth."

I wonder if that means he's honest and will tell me the truth if I say I overheard his conversation. I have the words on the tip of my tongue, but I back down and swallow them instead.

"I'm sorry..."

"It's not a big deal. How about we watch some TV? It's not something I get to do often."

I watch Graham as he lies down to watch television. Even when he's peaceful and calm, he still looks dominant and, honestly, *dangerous.*

It's Saturday, and the Syfy channel is showing a "scary movie Saturday marathon," and "Jeepers Creepers" is on. I have tingles all over my body. I want to lie beside him, but I don't. I sit crisscrossed on his bed and watch the movie.

He glances at me. "You can lie down; I don't bite." Okay, I guess I can add "mind reader" to the very short list of things I know about him.

"I'm sure you don't." I lay back on his bed, my legs stretched out. About 45 minutes into the movie, I yawn, and Graham eyes me.

"Someone needs a nap?"

"What time is it?" I yawn again. He picks up his phone, and it reads 10:46 a.m. I didn't realize how early we'd woken up. "Still so early; why did I wake up at 7 a.m. again?" He turns the TV down.

"Lay down, Liza."

"No... I'm fine; I'll nap later." I yawn again mid-sentence. "I want to watch this movie."

He doesn't say anything when he turns back to the TV. As the movie continues, I find myself sliding lower and lower, with my eyelids getting heavier and heavier.

4

Graham

Liza's breathing shallows, and I see her fast asleep. I mute the TV and grab a blanket off the edge of my bed. I pull it over her, kiss her forehead, and lay beside her. She's beautiful, and seeing her as she sleeps, her beauty radiates from her skin. I push a piece of her hair out of her face, and she briefly wakes up, shivering.

"Are you cold?"

"Hmm?" she mumbles, half asleep. I pull her closer to me and wrap my arms around her. *Since when do you cuddle?* I've clearly lost my fucking mind.

"Come here, Liza." She nuzzles closer into my chest, wrapping her arms around my midsection, and falls asleep.

About two hours later, her phone rings. She groans against my chest and then jumps up, noticing her arms tightly wrapped around me.

"I'm sorry; I must've fallen asleep. I didn't mean to. Um, lay–" I raise my hand to stop her talking.

"It's fine, Liza. I put you there because you were shivering and making it a bit hard for me to sleep myself."

"Oh. Sorry." I smirk at her, relishing in her shyness.

"Don't be; you feel better after your nap?"

"So much better; I guess I needed it." She stands up and stretches.

"I guess I should get you back." If I'm honest, the last thing I want is for Liza to leave, which says something for me. Being around anyone for more than 2 hours is too fucking much for me these days.

"Yeah, that sounds good," she responds, rubbing the back of her neck. We both get up and head out the door. This time, I grab the keys to my Audi R8 and hit the garage button. I hit the unlock button, and Liza smirks at me.

"R8, huh? How about I drive this time? And Graham, do you really need three cars?" she asks sarcastically.

"First, I have four—all parked in the driveway. Second, yes, I like having options. Third, you are absolutely *not* driving. Now get in." She rolls her eyes, and I open her door as she enters the passenger side.

"How is it possible to be an asshole *and* a gentleman? You need to pick one." I bend down and lean into the car.

"*Options*, pretty girl."

Okay, so maybe I need to tone down the assholeness because, in all honesty, there's something about Liza that intrigues me. I know I've been burned before, but maybe I should give her a chance; maybe she's not like her. I climb in, start the engine, turn the music on, and drive the 25-minute drive to campus.

Just past 1 p.m., I get Liza back to Emily's apartment. I can't believe Liza lives on campus; she needs her own space, and she will soon if I have anything to do with it. There's no way I'm letting her stay this far from me. I haven't had her yet, but I already know that once I do, I won't be able to stop. We walk towards the door, and she turns towards me, looking down over herself. "I'll return the clothes when I see you again."

"When will that be?"

"Is it supposed to be soon?"

"I hope so; I want to spend more time with you. When you're not upset about your roommate taking off," I laugh. Was I nervous? I don't get nervous, especially around girls, but Liza was more than that; she was a woman who suddenly seemed worth more than just a quick fuck. I wanted her so badly, in every way.

"I'm not going on a date with you, Graham Salando."

She knew my last name; of course, I'm on billboards and magazines all over, but to hear her say it made me feel good. It was good that she knew me and paid attention to what she saw about me.

"Why not?"

"This was a one-time thing. You helped me out, but I'd be a fool to go on a date with you. You're a walking red flag, and you're mean. I told you that."

"I promise I'm not a walking red flag," I smirk at her and she raises her eyebrow. "What do I have to do to get you to go out with me?"

"Nothing because it's not happening."

She was so cute when she tried to play hard to get, but I always got what and who I wanted. I have no intention of her being any different. She smiles—that damn smile again. Liza's smile is the most beautiful I have ever seen. She has something about herself that makes me want more of her. I need to get away from her quickly.

"At least be my friend."

"Okay. I'm your friend." I pull out my phone.

"Friends give friends each other's number."

"Are you kidding me?" I push it into her hands, and she sighs but types it in.

"I will see you around then, Elizabeth Crambell. And I hope you don't think you're out of this date thing with me."

Shit, why did I say her last name? She'd wonder how I knew it. It wasn't my intention for her to find out so soon that I knew, if not everything, almost everything about her. I had Ellis gather any information on her this morning, but she wouldn't find out. She looks at me confused, so I smirk and walk toward the exit.

"It's not happening!" She yells when I'm almost outside.

When I get back to my car, I see her jacket. I grab it and run back to the apartment. I'm about to knock when I hear her and Emily laughing. I give two knocks, and Emily opens the door.

"Oh..you are *not* Travis." I shake my head.

"I'm certainly not. She left her coat." Liza approaches the door and reaches for her coat. I dangle it in front of her, just out of reach.

"Graham..give it."

"Go out with me."

"No."

"Just coffee." She leans over and tries to grab the coat, and I yank it back. Emily laughs and walks off.

"Just say yes." She groans out, and I smile at her in approval.

"Okay, *fine, coffee, that's it*." She reaches again and takes it this time. I grin at her as she fights to hide her smirk.

"I knew I'd change your mind."

"Uh huh, have a good day, Salando."

"You too, Crambell." I run my eyes up and down her, and she tucks her lip into her mouth. "You think this name thing is pretty cute, huh?"

"How did you know my real name?"

"Shut the door, Elizabeth." She shakes her head and slams it shut.

Was I seriously trying to take her out? I don't date. Now that I think about it, I haven't ever dated. The one relationship I did have wasn't the "dating" kind. It was more like a "you run in the same circle and won't leave me alone" type of "dating," and it went too damn far. Maybe she was better off without me. *Yeah, leave her alone, man; you're no good for her.* Perhaps I'm not, but I realize that, as much as I want to leave her alone, it seems impossible. I want her, all of her; I want her to be mine and mine only. The thought of another man even looking at her pisses me off. I couldn't care less when I was with other women;

I knew I'd be done with them eventually. But not Liza. If I got her, I'd keep her. I just wondered if she'd be able to handle my past and, most of all, take the way I liked to fuck. She looks like a good girl, and I plan to change that. A good girl with a feisty ass attitude, and I want her to obey me once we get into the bedroom. When the night comes, I know I'll get what I want.

Seriously, you're getting ahead of yourself; she stayed over once and is into relationships, not hookups. You, my guy, will have to change. You think you can do that? Hell no. You're used to women submitting to you and doing whatever you say. My conscience, of course. Always right.

My phone then rings, interrupting my thoughts. My mom.

"Hello, mother."

"Hi, sweetheart. I know your classes are starting soon."

"What do you need?"

"Your sister, she's back, but she's moping around. And your father is into God knows what; he's being his weird, distant self again."

"Mom…"

"I would like some time with you, that's all."

"Mom, I know there's more you're hiding, but yes, I'll come down. Classes start Wednesday, but I can miss a few days." I get in the car and drive the three-hour drive to my mom's house, preparing myself for the shitshow of what will happen.

5

Liza

I haven't heard from Graham in a month—thirty-one fucking days. He begged me to agree to a date and then blew me off. Just like I knew he would. *Asshole.*

Classes have started, my schedule is somewhat busy, and I'm still trying to figure things out. I haven't seen him around at all, not around campus or with any of the few guys I saw him with at the party. Was Graham avoiding me? Had he changed his mind about us seeing each other again? I remember the conversation I overheard about him telling someone to kill a story. What fucking story? I caved, and I googled his name last night. I found pictures of him and some blonde; that was drop-dead fucking gorgeous. There is no information about his life, only that he is rich—filthy fucking rich. I searched for past relationships, and again, a picture of him and the blonde popped up, but no information on who she was or the dynamic of their relationship. She was way more his speed than I'd ever be. *Get over yourself; he hasn't been to class in a month of his last semester of college. You had one night with him, and I doubt you're worth him missing class over.* Then I realize the little bitch in my head is correct; there has to be something wrong; I stop myself because, honestly, I have no place to worry about him.

At all. So, I continued my week and the weeks after as if Graham never existed. For all I know, he skips class regularly. It's not like he needs the degree. He already has a successful career.

Emily and I make our way to our 11 a.m. class together.

"Em, have you seen Graham lately?"

"No, neither has Trav. He asked about him, too. I also didn't realize I'm supposed to be your personal private investigator." I roll my eyes at her and push her toward the door.

"Well, bitch, *you're* the one that told me to go on a date with him, and then he fucking ghosted me." She shrugs and smiles at our professor as she signs in. As I sign my name, I can't help but feel that someone is watching me. When I look up, I see Graham.

"I found him," Emily chuckles, whispering into my ear.

"Yeah, no shit." She nudges me and grins, walking to her seat as Graham stares at me. *Ignore him; he didn't call you. Don't be so forgiving; you'll look pathetic.*

I stare at him, giving him a blank look. I head towards him, walk past him, and sit two rows behind him. *Good girl, look at you. Give him a run for his money.* I secretly smile at my inner conscience but catch myself as I see Graham turn around towards me.

"Can we talk after?" *Act nonchalantly; I shrug.*

"Sure."

Em leans over to me, "I wonder what he wants to talk about." I roll my eyes at her. "Shut up." She laughs lowly and turns back to our professor.

The class seems unusually long today, making me anxious and eager about what Graham wants to discuss. As my professor begins discussing a late assignment he was grading, I find myself sitting in my seat, daydreaming as I twist my pen back and forth in my mouth. Lately, my daydreams have been the same thing. Graham and I—what a fool! *Snap out of it; he's talking to you. ELIZABETH! ANSWER HIM!* Oh!

She's right; I look up, and Graham is talking to me.

"Liza?"

I didn't even hear the professor say that class was over. Graham stands before me, smiling and trying to keep from laughing at me. I smile awkwardly at him.

"Sorry, what's up?" I start gathering my stuff, glancing at him, and waiting for a reply. Graham looks like his usual flawless self in a black T-shirt and jeans, and the dark look makes him look even sexier. I didn't think that was possible.

"Sorry, I didn't mean to interrupt. I'm heading out. Text me later," Emily says before she turns around and winks at me, and I shake my head.

"I just want to talk to you about why I haven't been in touch," he runs his hand over the back of his neck. I want to sigh in relief, but instead, I don't. I function as if I have no idea what he's talking about, taking my conscience's advice. I look at him with a raised eyebrow.

"You didn't notice that I haven't been around," he questions with a hurt look. He is clearly going through something; I wonder if I should care enough to ask about it. Screw it.

"Yeah, I noticed."

"I thought you were going to say no. That wasn't nice, Liza," he smiles.

"Well, you went a month without texting or calling when you said you would. That's not nice, either." I pick up some of my stuff and let out a silent sigh.

He puts his head down and starts to squirm a little.

"Where are you heading?"

"This is my last class for the day, and I am officially hangry, so I'm going to get something to eat," I say, putting a strand of hair behind my ear. Graham looks at me, and I can tell by the look in his sweet green eyes that he's waiting for me to offer him to come along. I would be having lunch with the guy every girl on this campus wants, which makes me happy.

"You can come if you want."

Graham smiles. "I thought I would have to invite myself." I nod my head in the direction of the exit sign.

"Absolutely not; get in front of me." He stands to the side to let me out of the aisle. I look at him and shake my head.

"Weirdo," I mumble. He's protective, and it's a pleasant change not to have to look out for myself for once. He cares if something happens to me, and that warms my heart. I approach him, and he puts his hand on my lower back. An electric feeling immediately sparks between us. We walk down the stairs and out the door.

A quick walk later, we reach Shultzy's, a bar and grill near our campus. Graham opens the door for me, and I smile.

"Sit anywhere you want," the server tells us as he walks by. Graham walks in behind me and puts his hand on my lower back, directing me to an open table.

That hand will be why I lose myself and take him where he stands. *Stop.*

I listen to the bitch in my head and force myself to stop. I have never been here before. I heard one of the girls talking about it in my class and decided to check it out; I didn't realize it would be with Graham. His touch sends lightning bolts through my body. I feel a warm sensation, and I long for him to touch me again. While trying not to make it obvious, I gently smile at him, walk to the booth, and sit. I didn't know restaurants were on campus, but then I remembered I was attending a well-funded school.

"Have you ever been here?"

"No, I haven't, have you?"

"Yeah, a few times," he says, handing me a menu.

"Thank you." I reach to take the menu out of Graham's hands, and he makes sure our hands touch as I try to retrieve it. Trying to seem unbothered, I say, "So you want to explain your disappearance?" I cast my eyes down and continue looking over my menu, but I can feel him staring at me. I look up at him and notice that he has this sly smirk on his face.

"I thought you didn't notice." I try to hide the smile I've wanted to release since I saw him when he snapped me out of my daze in class earlier. I open my mouth and speak.

"Seriously though," I say, "is everything okay?"

"Yeah, everything's fine, Liza; I just had to help my mom."

"Help her with what?"

"I just had to help her out with my sister." He's still hiding something, and I can tell he's too fidgety, making me uncomfortable.

"You have a sister?" I say, stopping myself from pushing him to tell me the whole truth. I completely forgot that he had already told me he had a sister.

"Yes, I'm the oldest; it's just her and me. I told you that, remember?"

"Sorry, I must've forgotten."

"So, do you know what you're ordering, Miss "I'm hangry," he challenges, smiling at me.

"For your information," I stop mid-sentence because I haven't paid attention to the actual words on the menu. How could I when Graham is searing a hole through my face?

"No... I don't know yet." He laughs as if he already knew what I would say; he just thought it'd be funny to pick on me.

"Well, I know what I am getting, so I suggest you start choosing, or I'll choose for you." I roll my eyes and ignore the smirk on his face.

Graham waves the server over and orders for both of us. He orders us each a side salad, burgers, and fries. *Did he just order for us? What are we in the 1800s?* Down girl, I say to my conscience, didn't you tell

me to stay "chill." The server that takes our order looks at Graham like she knows him, and I mean, knows him in more ways than one. *Ask her if she wants to take a picture.*
Acting as if I don't hear my conscience, I ignore the server and smile at her.

"Ignore my friend here; I'll have the chicken sandwich with a side salad."

"To drink?"

"Water is fine. Thank you."

Graham keeps his eyes on me the entire time, never looking at her once. She writes it down, walks off, and then Graham smiles at me.

"So, do you have any brothers and sisters, Liza?"

"Yeah, I have a little brother. He's about to turn 21 and is a junior at UCLA, and we're pretty close."

"And your parents?"

"They are okay; they've been divorced for years now. My mom remarried when I was eight and seems happy with my stepdad. My dad is doing well; he's still in love with my mom. He works often, and I don't see him as often as I'd like. His job is interesting, to say the least. Mom is transitioning into moving to New York, but my brother and dad are in California."

"New York... So, you came here to school?"

"Yeah, my stepdad has another office in New York and is moving there to run it as the new headquarters. My parents came here; it's where they met; my mom is hoping the same thing for me; the first college I went to wasn't where I wanted to be."
It was too close to home and too close to what I was running away from. I frown at the raw memory of my brutal past.

"What is it, Liza?" he asks while drinking some water.

"Oh, it's nothing; I'm fine....actually, there is something." I open my mouth to change the disturbing thoughts and ask about the phone call I overheard when the server returns, right at the wrong moment. I bite my lip and look out the window briefly as she sets our food in front of us.

"Do you need anything else?"

"No, Abby, we're good. Thanks," Graham tells her, looking at me again. *Abby* nods and walks off, this time not being so flirty. *That's right, do your job.*

"What were you going to say?

"Nothing, nothing. It's not important." I shove a fork full of my salad in my mouth, and he tilts his head at me.

"You sure?" I nod and give him a small smile, hoping I'm hiding my nervousness. "Hurry and eat."

"Why? Are you tired of me and ready to go already? We just got here."

"You ask a lot of questions, Liza; just eat." I look at him, confused.

"Well, you're very bossy, and you throw out orders like you expect them to be obeyed. I don't do as I'm told unless I know *why* I'm being told to do it. And even then, I typically still won't listen to them." Arms folded, I look at him with a stern look on my face.

"We're going back to my house; you're staying with me tonight… again,"

Like hell I am.

"I'm not staying with you."

"This again?"

"You stood me up. You begged me to go on a date with you but ghosted me. I'm not staying with you."

"I'll make it up to you."

"Yeah, I'm sure. Still not staying."

"Okay, a date?" I roll my eyes. He's persistent; I'll give him that.

After we practically fight over the bill, I return to my car. I finally bit the bullet and let my stepfather buy me one. He'd been asking me for months to let him gift me one.

"Stop following me, Graham."

"Come on, stop being mad."

"I'm not mad; we hung out. Now I'm going back to the apartment."

"Well, I have to get Travis anyway."

"Then I guess I'll see you there." I climb in and take off. Men are insane.

Every day for the next week, Graham has texted me and sent flowers to the apartment.

Monday, there were orange roses and a note that said, ***"Day one of trying to get you on a date with me."*** On Tuesday, there were red roses with a note that said, ***"Day two, how am I doing?"*** Wednesday, the fucking roses were yellow; Thursday, they were white; and today? Today, he decided to hand deliver them himself and is standing before me.

"How am I doing?" He asks me, handing me the purple lilies.

"What happened to the roses? Run out of colors?" I take them and wave him into the apartment. He steps in and leans in to hug me. I inhale his scent and desperately want to touch his arms, but I don't.

"I'm sorry for standing you up. But I really, really want to take you out."

Laughter comes from the stairs, and I look over, remembering Travis and Emily are here.

"Graham, man. You're making me look bad." He gestures to the room full of flowers. Emily smacks Travis' arm and sits on the couch.

"She still saying no?"

"Yup."

"She doesn't have classes until Thursday. If you take her away for the weekend, I'll help convince her."

"Emily! I'm literally standing right here."

"What? You need to get laid. And *I* need to get laid. Go have fun." I cover my face and take a deep breath, willing myself not to kill her. He gently tugs my elbow and walks me into the kitchen. Travis and Emily both turn their heads and try to eavesdrop.

"Stay with me, and I'll make it up to you—unless you want to be a third wheel all weekend. You know Travis is going to be here."

"Hey, I heard that."

"Stop eavesdropping."

I look around at the roses all over the kitchen and roll my eyes in defeat.

"*Fine.*"

"I'll drive, leave your car. Go pack."

"We're doing whatever I want to do. And I'll also need lots of hot chocolate; it's fucking *freezing* here. And I'll need something else, but I don't know what yet."

"Whatever you say, you're the boss, angel." Another nickname? I don't look too much into it, but Emily sure does.

She lights up and looks at me, mouthing, "He calls you angel?" I ignore her. "Do you need me to bring anything?"

"I have everything you need. Relax." I roll my eyes, and he chuckles as I trot upstairs and pack.

6

Graham

Angel, yes, that's what I'll call her because that's what she reminds me of.

"Everything I need, huh? We'll see about that when it's 2 a.m., and I'm deciding I want Oreo ice cream." She mumbles as she goes up the stairs. Emily looks back at me.

"She's not kidding. When she eats too early, she always wants ice cream, but only if it's past midnight."

About 10 minutes later, she comes back downstairs with her suitcase.

"Did you put sexy things in there?" Emily whispers a bit too loudly to her; she rolls her eyes and ignores her. Damn, she's even sexy when she rolls her eyes, but she better not roll them again towards me. Every little thing about her turns me on. She's lucky we have an audience.

I grab her suitcase. "Are you ready, angel? And where's your coat?"

"Sorry, *Dad*. Let me get it." She reaches behind me and grabs a long black parka off the couch. I take it from her and help her get into it.

"I don't have the *daddy* kink, angel. Sorry." Emily grins at us from ear to ear, and Travis laughs.

"Damn dude, I do." Travis adds.

"Let's just go before I change my mind." She cuts in.

I open the door for her, and she turns to lock it. Emily looks at her and raises her fingers as if on a phone. She whispers, "Call me if anything happens." Liza turns and gives me a sly smirk. I tried to leave her alone, but that month of not talking to her didn't entirely consist of me helping my mom. I've been trying to keep the darkness out of her life, but I can't. I can't stay away from her. I want to be in her presence, and I want her to crave being in mine.

25 minutes later...

I round the car and open Liza's door when we reach my house. "You still haven't picked one, I see."

"With you? I prefer just to be a gentleman."

"What happened to *options?*"

I lift her suitcase from the Audi and lead her to the door.

"Options got boring." I stop in front of the door and grab the key to unlock the front door.

"Mhm. Right." I know she thinks I'm kidding, but even though I was sending her shit all week, I was also trying my best to let someone or anyone catch my attention. I failed fucking miserably. Clearly, only one '*option*' had my attention, and I needed to make sure she knew that.

"My mom is supposed to stop by with groceries; she may already have, but if she hasn't, prepare yourself. She's never seen me with a woman before, other than the last shit of a girlfriend, and that was unwilling."

She'll be the first woman—the first woman—that I actually want to meet my mom. I don't have time to comprehend what that means or why I have a feeling in the pit of my stomach at the idea, but I don't dwell on it. I open the door with a part of myself, hoping she's there but also hoping she isn't. The one thing I do know is that I like Liza. What I don't know is how long I will like her.

Forever.

That's what the voice in my head keeps telling me. I've never chased a woman in my life, and I can't figure out why I feel this way.

I'm unsure if the feelings are mutual, but I still want time with just her.

I look around and thank God. My mom hasn't been here yet.

"She hasn't been here yet; if she had, the stuff would be everywhere."

"Your mom does your grocery shopping?" She looks at me.

"It's either her or hire someone else to do it."

"And why exactly can't you do it?" She reaches for her stuff, but I shake my head.

"Sit, I can take this up for you. Why would I do it if someone else is already doing it?"

"She's your mom, and you're an adult. You know you can even have groceries delivered to you."

"It gives her an excuse to see me, so I let her do it, if you must know."

"Fair enough."

"Glad my answer was up to par for you. Now sit." She coughs asshole under her breath, and I hesitate before continuing up the stairs. If this were any other woman and they said that, I'd have them over my knee, ass in the air, and turning it red. But I'm barely on her good side; I'll play nice for now.

I drop her things in the same room where she slept the last time she was here. I'm taken aback because the thought of her sleeping with me pops into my head. No one *ever* sleeps with me. I don't allow it. I don't like people in my space; the only time anyone has ever slept with me is my sister after our attack. So why am I thinking about her sleeping with me? Never knowing when a dream would happen, I knew I couldn't risk it anyway. I'm not necessarily violent *during* the dreams, but my sister said that I'm pretty "vocal" when they happen. When I wake up, I'm a slither of myself. I grab the first thing I can and practically squeeze the life out of it, just like I did the attacker.

I shake my thoughts and walk down the stairs. Liza has her arms wrapped around her body.

"You cold, angel?"

"A little bit; why do you call me that?"

I grab the blanket from behind the couch and wrap it around her.

"Better?" I ignore her question.

"Yes, thank you."

I kick off my shoes and lean back on the couch, watching her. She starts to squirm, adjusting the blanket around her.

"I can feel you staring, Graham."

"So, what? Is that a problem?" I hope not because I'm planning to stare at her until I figure out what the fuck I'm going to do with her.

"Seeing that you're still doing it, I don't think it matters if it is a problem." *You're right, it doesn't.*

"I enjoy staring at you."

"Then I'll start doing it to you too." I laugh and slide up to her.

"Do you think I don't already know that you stare at me?"

She bites her lip and then turns towards the TV, picks up the remote, and flicks through the channels.

"Stop biting your lip, Liza."

"I can't help it; I do it when I'm nervous."

"Why are you nervous?" I scoot closer towards her.

"You make me nervous every time I'm around you. And you stare like I'm *tantalizing* you. Then your compliments and... " I approach her while moving closer, this time with our thighs slightly touching.

"My compliments, and *what*, Liza? Finish your sentence."

"Your, your compliments, and your demands."

"My *demands?* You are a free woman; you can do as you please, angel." *Not true.*

She exhales deeply and turns away from me, settling her eyes on the TV.

"Great, then I will find something on TV to watch. And I'd like you to stop calling me that if you can't tell me why you call me that." I lick my lips and lean back on the couch. The girl has fucking self-control. That's for sure.

"Do as you'd like, but I would *really* appreciate it if you learned to take the compliments and, well, the demands, do as you wish with those. Oh, and *angel*, the name stays."

"You have to stop. At least the demands." Good, she's leaving the name thing alone, and I'm glad because that is *not* changing. She is my angel, sent from heaven.

"And why on earth would I do that?"

"Because I like it when I have the option to do things, not when I'm *demanded* to. Do I give you the vibe of someone who likes to be demanded?"

"I don't know... you *did* call me daddy."

"Gross. Just *stop*."

"I enjoy getting my way. You'll get used to it. Trust me, the *demands* will make us both happy."

Smooth, smooth.

At this point, my conscience and I both know that I am talking about sexual demands, but does Liza know?

"Well..."

"Well, what?" I grab the remote from her hand. She looks down and intertwines her fingers together. She's nervous—extremely nervous—but I'll fix that soon. I turn her towards me, pull her hands apart, and hold them in mine.

"I think we'll work on the demands and keep them to a minimum; they could lead to things."

"Things like what, angel?"

She opens her mouth to reply, but nothing comes out. I can hear her heart pounding; she wants me to kiss her. It's obvious, and I plan to do just that. But not yet. I want to get more out of her. Both of our consciences are screaming at us. Mine clearly says to *take her upstairs and show her what she's missing.* This was the perfect moment: it was the perfect setting and the perfect woman. I had to play this right.

I don't want her to think I worked my ass off for her attention just to fuck her.

She opens her mouth again to say something and finally responds, "Just things."

Her voice is so faint that it's almost silent. I raise my eyebrow at her, stroking her cheek slowly with one hand.

"We'll see," I reply lowly.

She opens up to say something more, and I smash my lips against hers. She pulls away, looks at me, and I smirk at her. She puts her head down and bites her lip again.

"What did I say about biting that lip?" She shrugs. She's doing it on purpose, so I kiss her again, this time harder and more urgently when she opens up for me. I entwine my tongue with hers; her lips are as soft as cotton, and she tastes like cinnamon. This is the kiss we both want and have been longing for.

A kiss that has taken far too long to happen—so long that I instantly get hard when our lips touch. I slide my tongue in and out of her mouth. She opens it for me repeatedly, allowing my tongue to intrude into her mouth. She doesn't mind it; she wants it, and she wants me. I put my hand behind her neck and pull her closer until the sound of a doorknob turning and keys jingling rings in the distance.

I slowly remove myself from her presence.

"Mom's here."

I kiss her on the forehead and walk towards the kitchen. She clears her throat, smiles, and trails behind me.

I walk around the corner to hear my mom saying, "Graham, come tell your mother hello."

"I'm here, mom." I hug and kiss her cheek.

"Oh, honey, you smell like cinnamon." I pull back and look at her, only to see her face as if she has seen a ghost.

"Who might this be?" she practically stutters with a smile as she walks towards Liza.

"This is Liza, mom. I think I'm going to make her my girlfriend," I joke with a smile, but I'm not really kidding. I'm done running away from what I want with Liza; it's only been a few weeks, but it feels like it's been longer. She belongs to me, whether she knows it or not.

"Girlfriend, huh? I've never heard my Graham talk about a girl before, well, not in the way of, never mind. Don't mess this one up," she states, looking at me with a sly grin.

I'm glad my mom doesn't mention Madison; it's not something Liza needs to know yet. Liza laughs and smiles at me, raising one eyebrow. I need my mom to leave quickly. I have unfinished business to handle with Liza.

My mom turns and points to the bags on the countertop.

"I just stopped by to bring you food for this house because Lord knows you won't do it yourself." She smiles at me and then turns to Liza.

"Oh, honey, by the way, my name is Madeline; I imagine he didn't tell you my name." She walks past me briskly and mumbles, "He never introduces people."

"Thanks, Mother. I appreciate the nice comments." I roll my eyes and start putting the groceries away. Liza laughs and sits on one of the bar stools in the kitchen.

"So, sweetie, how'd you two meet?"

"We met through some mutual friends at school," she tells her, tucking her hair behind her ear. I wink at her and put a carton of milk in the fridge.

"Oh! What are you majoring in?"

"Psychology."

"Oh, that's lovely. Graham, sweetheart, how is school going for you?"

"Fine, staying ahead of assignments."

"I keep telling you to focus on—"

"Mom, don't." She looks at me in pity before glancing at her watch.

"Well, I have a meeting to get to, but it was a pleasure meeting you, Liza. I hope to see more of you around. We have breakfast or brunch every other Sunday. Please come."

She pulls her in for a hug, and I walk her to her car.

"Sorry, honey, I hope I didn't upset you. I worry about you and that you're putting so much stress on yourself with the company and school. I want you to take time for yourself." I kiss her on the cheek.

"Drive safe." I shut her car door and head back inside, sighing.

I continue unbagging groceries, and Liza starts taking things out of the bag to help me.

"Your mom seems nice."

"Yeah, she is." I try to adjust my mood; I don't want Liza to notice the stress my mom adds to me. She *is* right; running the company and being in school is a lot. But she is right about one thing: I need to focus on myself more, and I plan on it. Starting with my happiness, and Liza is a crucial part of that.

"Goodness, this is a lot of stuff for one person."

"Yeah, she shops once or twice a month. This place is three hours away from her and dad's house."

"Graham..."

"Hmm?"

"Are you alright?"

"I'm fine." Liza nods and continues to help put the things away. She knows it's not the truth, but she doesn't pry. As we put the last few things away, I stare at her.

"Is there something you want?"

"There's that attitude."

"Attitude?"

Liza is so spunky and sassy. I love it. I smile, and after putting the last few things away, I walk over to her.

Wrapping my arms around her, I lower my head and let my lips brush her ear. "Mhm, attitude... did you think I was kidding about the girlfriend thing?"

"Were you?"

"Not even a little bit; I can't get you out of my fucking head."

I tilt my head down to her, planting more kisses on her, and like last time, she instantly opens for me.

I lift her and take her to the couch, her legs wrapped around me.

As I deepen the kiss, I lick and kiss her neck, making her moan softly. My cock stiffens, and it is already ready for her. I put my hand under her shirt, rubbing her back. I continue to kiss her, reaching to unbutton her pants when she says the words I don't expect her to say. The words that explain why I can't leave her alone and why I knew all along that she is different, that *something* is different. Liza whispers into my mouth.

"Graham, I'm a virgin."

I decide right there and then that I know what I'm doing with her.

I'm keeping her.

7

Liza

What a way to tell him, bitch.

I step back from Graham and leave the words hanging in the air. Shocked—that's all I can tell he feels by the look on his face. "Graham, say *something*."

"I knew there was something, but I couldn't figure it out. I wouldn't have thought that, but you're what? 22? And held out for this long?"

"Mhm."

"But you've done things, right?"

"Just the basics, but I want to. I'm not going to fight my attraction for you."

Just sex. I can do that.

"Your first time will not be on a couch, Elizabeth." Graham puts his hand on my cheek and kisses me softly. "We'll wait until the time is right; you've waited this long and dodged God knows how many men, I assume." He looks at me for confirmation.

"Quite a few."

"Sit by me; relax. Sex can wait; I'm sure you know that you're worth it."

He's being so understanding, but I don't want that right now. What

I want is him—all of him—preferably, inside of me. I grab him and kiss him again, defying his words.

"Elizabeth, no."

Don't call me that.

"Fine, but you'll regret it."

Graham gives me a mischievous smile. "I already am."

He grabs the blanket he's sitting on, wraps it around him, and opens it. "Now, come here."

I cuddle up as close to him as I can. My eyes have become heavy, so I must be tired. He plants a kiss on my forehead and closes his eyes.

It's about six o'clock when I wake up from my nap. We're on the couch, and the TV plays some old-time movie. With Graham still asleep, I finally have time to attempt to wrap my head around what is happening. Am I going to lose my virginity this weekend, *finally*? Does it bother Graham that I am still a virgin? *Should've thought about that before you blurted it out mid-kiss.* I ease my way from the couch and into the bathroom. I pull my phone out of my pocket and call Emily.

"Oh, you little slut, *now* you call me?"

"Shut up; I'm in trouble here."

"Spill it"

"I like him a lot, but I'm not sure if I'm ready to be all in with someone."

"Stop letting your past haunt you, Liza. He's into you; what's the harm in having some fun?" Emily knows about my past and how I was tormented, and she's right. I need to live in the moment and enjoy my life.

"You're right..."

"I know; now go. He has shown you how much he's into you; it's okay to be into him, too. You've known him for almost two months. It's not like you both just met a day ago. Who the fuck cares? Call me later." I look at myself in the mirror and fix my hair.

Just have fun and go with the flow. We got this.

"Did I wake you?" I say as he stretches as I sit back down.

"No," he tilts his head towards the TV. "The TV did come here; you were keeping me warm." He smiles, and it's a genuine smile, and my stomach bottoms the fuck out.

He's always smiling around me, and I realize that there isn't another sight I'd rather see in him. I don't want the nonchalant Graham or the Graham who used women. I want the 'Graham' who shows me how happy he is and how much he enjoys being around *me*.

"What do you want to do for the rest of the day?" He asks me, running his finger through my hair.

"Honestly? Nothing. Unless you have something?"

"No, I'm good here." He picks up the remote. "What's your favorite movie?"

"I don't think I have one, but I like scary movies." He raises an eyebrow at me and hovers over *Halloween*.

"*Classic.*"

A few moments go by before I look up to see him asleep again. I pause the movie and cuddle up with him, letting myself fall back to sleep.

* * *

Am I being lifted? I feel like I'm moving. WAKE UP!
My eyes flutter open, and realize that I'm in Graham's arms; he's carrying me up the stairs. I groan as I start to wake.

"I've got you, pretty girl. Go back to sleep." He walks into the room I stayed in a week ago.

"No, I'm sleeping with you."

"Not tonight."

"Why not?"

"Get in bed. I'll see you in the morning." He pulls the covers back

52

and lays me in bed. Too tired to put up a fight, I roll over and fall asleep.

A few hours pass, and I wake and tap my phone to see that it's 3:45 a.m. I get up to use the bathroom and walk back to my bed. *Get in bed with him.* I stop; the little bitch of a conscience is right. Yawning, I walk down the hall. Graham's door is halfway closed but open enough for me to walk right in. His TV is on, and he is tossing and turning his head from left to right. Is he having a bad dream? I start walking towards him, and just then, he cries, *"No, get away from her. Piece of shit. GET OFF OF ME."* I quickly get to his side.

"Graham, wake up; you're dreaming." I nudge him, and he grabs me.

"Angel?"

"Yes, it's me." I guess that's my new name.

"What are you going in here?" I look down at his grip, which is tight.

"You were having a bad dream; I could hear you."

Liar, you were about to get in bed with him when you heard him. Tell the truth; who cares?

He looks at me, confused, as if he doesn't remember the dream. He loosens his grip, rubbing my arms.

"I'm sorry for grabbing you." I shake my head.

"Forget about that. Are you okay?"

"I'm fine; let's just go back to bed."

Now is not the time for me to try to get my way. I turn away from him and start to stand. Graham pulls me back to him.

"No, Elizabeth, back to bed in here. Sleep with me."

"But I thought..."

"Lie down here with me, *now..*"

Do what he says; we're getting our way.

I listen to my conscience and Graham and do as I'm told. I climb over Graham, get underneath the covers, and lie beside him.

He rolls over, kisses me, and wraps his arms around me as tight as ever, placing his head on my stomach.

"Goodnight, beautiful."

"Goodnight." Before I know it, he's sound asleep, and I follow suit.

After yesterday, I know I have a lot to take in; everything I'm more than happy about happened.

Waking up, I feel rejuvenated. I slept like a rock and now feel so refreshed. Today is Friday, the second day of my stay with Graham, and for some reason, I can't wait to see what the plans for the weekend are. I honestly don't care, and I'll surely enjoy whatever it is. I haven't felt this free in a long time, and with how short of a time it's been, that scares the *shit* out of me.

I feel his cock on my butt, stiff as a board. I feel movement on my backside, and I turn over, and see him starting to wake up. He opens his eyes, looks at me, and smiles as he does his morning stretch.

"Good morning."

"Good morning," he yawns, kissing me on my forehead.

I look at him and smile even more, taking in how young he looks in this moment.

"Did you sleep well?"

"I slept—" stopping in the middle of his sentence and smirking, "Liza, you are something to wake up to."

"Thank you." I can't help but look away and bite my lip.

"That lip, angel, stop biting it. It makes me crazy."

"Does it?" He nods as he rolls off the bed, taking one side of the cover as I take the other.

"Lift and lay on three," he orders, smirking.

"One...two...three."

We lift the spread and lay it over the bed. I sit down and watch as he moves across the room. "Why are you staring at me like that, Crambell?" I snap out of it and giggle.

"Just enjoying the view, thank you." I put my head down and brush my hair back towards my shoulders. "I think I'm going to have a shower."

He points to a closet right outside his room. "Everything you need is in that closet; I'll shower too." He winks at me and heads for the bathroom down the hall.

"You can use your bathroom; I can use that one; I don't mind."

"You're fine; I'll use the other bathroom."

Save water. Shower together.

Finally, my conscience and I are on the same page. Down, girl, not yet. I grab my stuff and then head to the shower.

When I get out, I hear Graham's music and him singing quietly. *Of course, he sings.*

I continue with what I'm doing and dress for the cold, rainy weather outside. I wear a long-sleeve white shirt, light blue jeans with knee rips, and light brown high-heeled boots. I brush through my hair, apply mascara, and return to Graham's room.

"Graham?'

"Beautiful?"

"I was just checking if you were still in the shower."

"I'm finished." He strolls down the hall and kisses me on the forehead.

"You smell like cinnamon."

"It's one of my favorite scents," I respond, smiling.

"Hmm, well, now it's one of mine." I can feel my face heat.

"What do you want to do today?' I ask.

"How about brunch and then a little shopping?"

"I don't have a job yet; all of my money is being saved; shopping for me is out of the question, but we can window shop."

I'm exceptionally well off, well my parents are, and because they graciously supplied my savings and bank account since I was twelve with a ridiculous amount of "allowance" every two weeks, I guess I can add myself to that category.

"Shopping is on me. As my *girlfriend*, I must show you exactly what you'll be walking into."

"If you want me to be your *girlfriend*, then you will have to get to know me, *not* spend money on me."

"Of course, I'm going to get to know you." He takes my hand and directs me downstairs. "Get your stuff; I'll start "getting to know you better" over brunch, then even more while we're shopping."

"We still need to work on those demands, I see." I grab my phone, purse, and jacket, then walk out the door.

We arrive at a place called Portage Bay Café.

"I'm glad you picked this place. I wanted to try it, and Em keeps saying how good it is."

"Yes, it's pretty good; my mom always brought my sister and me here."

"Well, I'll trust you have good taste in food places." I wink at him as he parks the car. I open my door and hear Graham let out a groan.

"Something wrong, Casanova?"

"Don't you know not to open your own door?" He badgers.

"Uhhh, sorry," He's shaking his head and starts directing me inside.

"We'll work on it." He winks at me.

That fucking *wink*.

When we walk in, two hosts are waiting patiently with smiles.

"Just two?" The blonde one says.

"Yes."

"Follow me this way."

We follow her to a table by the window with a clear view of the Seattle streets and buildings.

"Your server, Anthony, will be right with you. Enjoy your meal."

"Thank you," I say, she smiles and returns to her post.

Graham looks at me, and I grin. He's always staring at me, and feeling his stare on me makes me unusually hot.

"I can feel you staring at me."

"Sorry, I can't help it, even when you're doing something as simple as looking at a drink menu."

I look up at him and bat my eyes sarcastically. He raises his eyebrow, and I pull the menu in front of my face.

"I'm getting a mimosa—actually, apple juice."

Alcohol will not mix well with how attracted I am to this man.

The server comes up and greets us. "Hello, my name is Anthony, and I'll be your server today. What can I get you to drink today?" He questions, looking at Graham. "Two apple juices...and two mimosas," I smirk at him. Is he taunting me?

"Two apple juices and mimosas coming up; I'll be right back to take your orders unless you two already know what you want," he says, looking at us both.

"I'm ready if you are," Graham declares, and I nod.

"What can I get you, sir?"

"French toast, bacon, and potatoes," he utters, still looking at me. I tilt my head to the side and watch him, almost missing the waiter speaking to me.

"And for you, ma'am?"

"Ah, I'll actually have the same, please, with strawberries."

"All French toast will come with strawberries, blueberries, and whipped cream; would you like me to put it on the side?" I look at Graham and raise my eyebrows in excitement; he beams.

"Nope, all of that sounds delicious." He leaves to put the order in.

"You haven't taken your eyes off me since we sat down. It's weird." I utter to him with pursed lips. He puts his elbows on the table, leaning in.

"Come here." He declares in a low, deep voice. I narrow my eyes at him and mimic his actions.

"Yes?" I whisper. His jaw tenses a bit, and he reaches his hand out to graze my cheek. He pulls my face toward him and gently kisses my lips. When he pulls away, I groan lowly at the absence of his lips.

Anthony walks over to the table, placing our mimosas and apple juice before us.

"Your food should be out shortly."

I lift the mimosa to my lips, taking in a small sip. It's the perfect amount of sweetness and is one of the best mimosas I've ever had.

"This tastes so good."

"And to think you were going to defy yourself of it." As he says that, Anthony drops our food on the table, and my stomach growls as if on cue.

"Let me know if you guys need anything else." I smile at him.

"Thank you... How the hell did they make that this fast? It's been like 10 minutes."

"I don't typically wait very long for service, angel."

"Oh, I forgot I'm with this big-time celebrity or something." I take my first bite of the French toast, which melts in my mouth. Graham leans back in his chair and takes a sip of his mimosa.

"Is it good?" I nod and take another bite. He smiles and starts eating his meal.

"Good, now it's time to get to know you." I swallow hard and quickly down my mimosa. Fuck, I am in trouble.

"Relax; I'll be nice," he says and I roll my eyes.

"Okay, I'm ready."

"Favorite color?"

"Blood orange."

He raises his eyebrow in question.

"Interesting, Birthday?"

"Nice try, but no. My turn."

He leans back in his chair and grins.

"Fine."

"Longest relationship?"

"Not important. Next question."

"Why isn't it?" I ask.

"Because, as far as I'm concerned, *you're* going to be my longest relationship," I smirk at his reply.

"Fine, your turn."

He's such an easy person to talk to, which frightens me. I've always thought my mom was crazy for thinking I'd fall in love in college. Even though it seemed cliché to me, I was still hopeful. But I'll be damned if that isn't happening right in front of my eyes.

"You okay?"

"Yeah, yes, I'm fine. Sorry, I just got sidetracked a bit."

"You do that a lot," he states as he continues eating. I glance at him and shrug, finishing my meal.

"So, what's this about you not being my girlfriend again?"

"Why is that title so important to someone like you?" I punch myself internally after the words leave my mouth.

"Someone like me?" He raises his eyebrow. "I know you've read about me, and I've always been open with the press when they ask about relationships. I won't apologize for my past. You. Are. *Different.* You're making me do things and want things I never thought I'd want. I can't explain it, but it's impossible for me to leave you alone."

"I haven't read much, but I don't know how I've done all that for you... How I've made you think we could work."

"Just a feeling I have; trust me on this one." I look at him, thinking that I'm going to see a hint of amusement on his face, and to my surprise, he looks me directly in the eyes and says, "Just say yes; I promise it'll be worth it."

I swallow spit, hoping he can't hear it, and wonder what I should say.

"No. It's too soon. You barely know me." I sit back in my seat, fold my arms, and smirk while saying.

He leans forward. "Crambell, are you challenging me? Because if you are, I always win challenges." I lean forward and get close to his face.

"Not a challenge, just a rejection. I'm *not* going to be your girlfriend," I propose with a mischievous look. Graham smiles and gives me a quick kiss—so fast it's almost enough for me not to see it coming.

"We'll see about that."

Graham continues to question me about everything, from family to childhood to the future. He *is* trying to win me over to be his girlfriend.

"What's your favorite childhood memory?"

"Fishing with my dad and brother every summer in California."

"Where do you see yourself in five years?"

"In my own practice, I hope."

"Not married?" I shrug my shoulders, taking a sip of my drink.

"I'm not sure if that's in the cards for me. If it is, then great; if it's not, then great. What about you? Where do you see yourself in five years?"

"Honestly, being so successful so young, five-year plans become a bitch to think about. I'd say a wife and a family, but realistically, I want to be happy. I don't want to look back and think to myself, "I wasted my entire life working my ass off and forgetting to find someone to share the success with." That's what my mom was badgering me about; it's what she always badgers me about."

"I'm sorry, but I get what you're saying. I guess ultimately, we all just want to be happy and to have someone to share that happiness with." He nods and gives me a low, sad smile.

"So, your mom and stepdad are in New York, your brother is at UCLA, and what exactly does your dad do?"

"I can't necessarily say. Umm, he's in the *security* business." My dad is into way more than that, but that isn't something I am telling Graham.

When Anthony drops the bill on the table, I quickly grab it; Graham raises his eyebrow as I stuff my card in the black card pocket.

"You got it last time, it's my turn." I hand it to Anthony and quickly shoe him away before Graham can fish out the card he's currently searching for. "Let it go, he's already gone."

Anthony brings it back, and Graham stands up, kissing me on the cheek as we walk out of the restaurant.

"So, you and your sister are pretty close?"

"Yeah, we've always been super close to each other." He starts the car and looks at me. "Ready?"

"Where are you taking me?"

"Shopping—there's this boutique my sister always goes to. Her stylist knows we're coming." I shake my head. I haven't had a stylist since I left my mother's, and even then, it's her being my stylist. We finally pull up to this sleek boutique.

Graham rounds the car and opens the door for me. I follow him into the store, where a lady with long, curly, chestnut brown hair approaches us with a smile and two glasses of champagne.

"Ahh, Mr. Salando, Giselle said you'd be stopping by. And with such a beautiful girl. Don't you worry, I'll take great care of her." She winks at him, then loops her arm around mine.

"There's a new line that *just* came in. You'll love it. My name is Francesca." I turn around and mouth the words "thank you" to him as she whisks me away.

My phone vibrates as the lady makes me try on many things, from skirts to jeans to dresses to pants.

Graham: *You're welcome, baby.*

Liza: *Baby, huh? I thought I was angel. Can you come see this dress on me and tell me if you like it?*

"You can come out, Elizabeth," Francesca squeals, and I feel the smile on her face as I pass through the door.

I push the curtain back and step out. Graham puts his phone down and glares at me, finally smiling after what feels like an eternity.

"She's beautiful, isn't she?" Graham nods and continues to stare at me.

"So, what do you think? Do you like it? Is it too much?"

"No, it's perfect, and you can wear it to dinner tonight; we have reservations at 7 p.m." I nod at him and smirk.

"Do you see anything else you want before we go?" He asks me, looking down at his phone.

"No, this is just enough."

What's so interesting about that phone? He has been fixated on it for the past thirty minutes. I return to the dressing room to change while Francesca asks Graham, "Do you need anything? I've got her all squared away. What about you?"

"No, I'm fine; I have my attire already." I change out of the sparkling blue sequined strapless dress, which stops a few inches above my knee, and put my clothes back on. I down the glass of champagne before heading out of the dressing room.

Graham's waiting at the register for me. Francesca smiles. "You've got quite the man here, you know?" My eyes widen a bit. "And you have a beautiful girlfriend, Salando." She winks, and he stares down at me.

"I do, don't I?

All I can think is that I haven't even agreed to be his girlfriend yet, and he's already claiming that title.

Hell, who am I kidding? I think I might like to be his girlfriend.

8

Graham

I can tell Liza looks tired by the look on her face and how she keeps responding with "hmm" or "mhm" to my questions.

"Enjoying our day together?"

"Mhm, so much fun." Her eyes are barely open.

I put my hand on her thigh, and she takes a deep breath, sinking into the seat.

On the drive home, I think about how I have no intention of waiting a few months to make Liza mine; I already want to do it. I plan to do it as soon as we get to my house. This is unconventional, especially for me. She's the first woman I don't want to use for just a fuck. The first woman I would *willingly* want to be with. I look over at her, and she looks so beautiful.

Moments later, I pull the car into the garage, lean over, and kiss her cheek.

"Wake up." Her eyes flutter open, and she looks around. "Come on, we're back."

I grab her bags and walk to her side, kissing her again. I can't stop finding moments to kiss her; it's all I want to do. I hold my hand out for her, and she takes it, climbing out of the car. I put my hand on her lower back and guide her towards the front door.

Do it now; don't be a bitch about it.

I stop her and turn her toward me.

It's either yes or no; say the right things. Whether I want to admit it or not, my conscience is right. Once I ask this question, everything is going to change. I think of the right words to say to her—the words that can make her say yes.

I put my hands on her face, with the palms of my hands on her cheeks and my fingers tangled in the back of her hair. I look directly into her eyes. Obviously, I'm not the only one nervous; she is, too, trying to figure out what I want to say. I stroke her cheeks.

"I told you I wanted you to be my girlfriend; you said I had to get to know you better. I know it's crazy, and you feel like you don't know me and that I don't know you, but I need to ask you something."

Oh *shit, no backing out now.*

"Okay, what's that?" Her voice is so low I can barely hear it.

"Be mine. I don't want to go another night without being able to call you mine or without knowing I have you. I know it's fast, but I don't usually wait on things I know are right."

I'm trying my best to read her, but it's impossible. She's quiet. Too quiet.

Tick tock, tick tock.

She opens her mouth, and my throat tightens—*the moment of truth.*

I want to scream at my conscience, telling him to fuck off and let me be.

"Hmm....no." She smiles as she wraps her arms around my waist.

"Don't joke with me.."

"I absolutely will *not* be your girlfriend..not unless you tell me *I was an asshole when we first met, and I'll spend our entire relationship making it up to you.*" I chuckle and clear my throat. She laughs and covers my mouth as I start to repeat her words.

"Wow, you were going to be such a good boy, weren't you?"

"Elizabeth.."

"Okay, okay, ask again."

"Be mine. Please."

"I better not regret this."

"I know it's soon and impulsive, but trust me."

"I trust you." I grab the strand of loose hair hanging in her face, tuck it behind her ear, and pull her close to kiss marking her as mine. "Come on, let's get you inside."

When we get into the house, she grabs the bags from me.

"Here, I'll get them. I want to sleep with you, not in your little sister's room." I raise my eyebrow at her.

"Yeah?"

She walks off towards the stairs. "If you'll let me this time," she teases. Noticing she's been gone longer than she should, I walk upstairs. She's in my room, looking at the tuxedo I had delivered to the house while we were gone.

"How did you get this so quickly?"

"I made a few calls while you were shopping. Come here." She walks over to me, grabs my hands, and wraps my arms around her.

"Hm," she looks up at me, I kiss her forehead.

"I'm glad you said yes; if you had said no, the surprise would have been awkward."

"What surprise?"

"Well, if I tell you, it's no longer a surprise." I walk downstairs with Liza following me, tugging on the back of my shirt.

"Tell me, tell me, tell me."

"You'll see soon enough."

We walk over to the couch and sit down. I turn the TV on, and the movie 'Rogue' is playing. She sits with her legs crossed and is fixing her shirt. Realizing that I'm staring at her, she smiles, as usual.

"What is it?"

"Come away with me for the rest of the weekend."

"Sure, where to?"

I expected that getting her to come away with me would be a little more complicated. I expected her to give me an excuse for why she shouldn't go, but then I remembered that she was mine now. Of course, she wants to go away with me.

"That's another surprise, but we will head there before dinner."

"Before?"

"Yes, dinner will be around there. I hoped you'd say yes to the getaway, so I planned ahead."

I push her back on the couch and hover over her. "I guess you should get packed then."

Her breathing quickens, and she laughs. "Maybe I will if you get off me."

I roll off her and point to the stairs. "Alright, you're free; get a move on it."

I smack her ass, and she jumps, running towards the stairs. She stops and turns towards the TV.

"Can we finish watching this? I like this movie." I throw her over my shoulder.

"No, we'll be late; I'll record it for you." She squeals.

"Put me down; I can walk!" I ignore her, swat her on her ass again, and walk up the stairs.

I throw her down on my bed and kiss her.

"All you need to pack are your essentials."

"Essentials only got it."

"Toothbrush, toothpaste, nightwear—nothing more. Once we get there, we will buy you clothes."

She side-eyes me. "No more shopping, Graham; that dress was expensive enough."

"It isn't something that's up for debate." I look at her and watch her move across the room, grabbing her bag. Her face finally settles when she realizes she has no say in this.

"Fine, but not too much. I mean it." I nod; she zips up her bag and sits on the bed.

"We have to go; we can't be late; we have to stop by the shops and get you some clothes before we drop our things off and head to dinner. You have everything?"

"Yes, everything I'm allowed to bring,"

"Let's go."

"Bossy..now, are you ready to tell me where we're going?"

"No."

We get outside, and I put the bags in the truck and walk around toward her door. She tries to open it herself, and I put my hand on her back.

"Elizabeth, I got that,"

"Elizabeth, huh?" She gets in, leans over, and opens my door.

The car ride feels smooth and natural as if we belong here together. I have my hand on her thigh, tightening my grip around it, and Liza has her hand over mine. She goes on and on about wanting to know where we're going.

"Please, *please* tell me where we're going. Oh pleaseeee."

"I'll give you one hint, and that's it."

"Two"

"Angel..."

"Fine, make it a good one."

"It's close to a beach." She holds my hand tightly. "A beach?!" Liza's voice gets a little higher in pitch, showing her excitement. I look at her and smile.

"Now, sit back and be patient." She sits back at ease and doesn't ask another question about it.

The drive to Leavenworth takes about two hours. When Liza sees the sign showing where we are going, she squeals.

"I've seen pictures of this place; it looks so beautiful!" We stop by the shops, and Liza quickly picks a few outfits for this weekend. As we got closer, we passed the lake that my sister and I used to play in every summer. It's beautiful at night.

"This looks *romantic*." I look at her, and she smiles so beautifully. I rub her thigh.

"I'm glad you like it so far; we're almost there."

A few minutes later, I pull into my family's summer lake house, which I recently bought. The house was big and had huge glass windows all over.

"I love the tall double doors, the windows, this driveway, and that fountain right there."

"Is there anything you don't like, angel?" She laughs and answers, "No, I love this house; it's perfect and gorgeous, so whose is it?"

I don't believe Liza is that naive about me having money. There's just no way she doesn't know the extent of how much I have.

"Liza, it's my house." Her eyes widen. Wow, she didn't read up on me like I thought. If she did, she did a damn good job at hiding her awareness. "It's just a house."

"This is not just a house; this is like a mansion."

"Just enjoy this weekend; don't think about the house. Just think about us. This is our getaway from the world." I shake my head and grin at her.

I want to make her feel comfortable. I have a lot of money, and she doesn't care about it, even though her parents are just as wealthy. She is an independent woman, and I love that about her. I love that she is determined to do things on her own. I want this weekend to be unique for her. She did drop a bomb on me the first time we had gotten close to fucking each other. And learning that she is a virgin was a shock, but me being her first will be something she will remember forever. I'll make sure of that.

9

Liza

Graham's lake house looks like it belongs in a magazine. The outside is entirely made of this perfect stone brick. I try to contain my excitement, but I fail. I don't know why it was such a surprise when he said this is his house; I know how well-off he is, which usually means he owns multiple houses. But I get the feeling it's more than I realize. While money isn't new to me because my family has a ton of money and various houses, it's never something I display and never will. I've chosen to attempt to support myself financially. Money or not, this house is breathtaking, and this weekend will be nothing less.

Graham rubs my cheek, and I lean toward his touch.

"Focus on us this weekend. Nothing else, okay?"

"Mhm."

"Ready to go inside?"

"Damn right."

He smiles at me and gets out of the G-Class. I remember the last time I tried to open my own door, and he rushed to tell me not to.

"I see someone is learning to sit and wait."

"Well, the last thing I want is for you to yell at me again and hurt my feelings." I pout with a pitiful frown. He grabs me by my waist. "Wipe that frown off; you'll wrinkle that pretty face, and I can't have that." I squeeze his ass and say, "Come on, horsey, let's do this."

"Ass grabbing is not for you, only me. Got it?" I stifle a laugh and squeeze his ass again.

"Yes, sir, I got it."

"Go ahead; I'll get our stuff for dinner tonight."

As soon as I get into the house, I am in awe. It smells of strawberries and cinnamon—mmm, cinnamon—my favorite. I try to turn on what I think is the light, but it's the fireplace. I jump at the sound of the fire crackling.

"Wrong switch, angel."

He reaches around me and hits the left switch, and the house lights up.

"Look around; we need to be ready for dinner in about two hours." My feet move on their own, and my eyes begin wandering.

"How many bedrooms?"

"Six."

It's spacious and clean, and somehow, it has just enough masculinity for Graham's taste. I look above me in awe of the lights.

"I love this chandelier."

"I figured you would," he teases. As I walk around the house, Graham trots behind me with his hands in his pockets, watching my every move.

The first place I stumble upon is the living room, right down the hall, just off the front door. It was a nice size, with wraparound couches, a glass table in the middle, and a black ruffled rug underneath. The white stone fireplace gives the place a modern look with a twist, and the 75-inch flat screen takes the cake.

After the living room, I walk to the other end of the hall, which leads to the kitchen. It's huge. There are two ovens, and the refrigerator is see-through.

"Very fancy." I walk past it, run my hands over the island, and then turn to Graham. "And our room? Where is it?" He points up, "Upstairs."

I start walking toward the cherry-brown U-shaped stairs.

"These stairs are beautiful."

"I figured you'd say something like that."

I walk up the left side of the stairs, and Graham walks up the right.

"You know, this is a big house to have to ourselves; it could get you in trouble."

"Oh, trouble is what I'm hoping for."

We meet at the top, and he wraps his arms around me. "Finish your house tour; we need to get ready."

"You shouldn't have picked such a big house."

"The movie room is three doors down on the left, the bathroom is the first door on the left, and the guest rooms are on the right side. Our room is right behind you. Tour over."

"So we're going with asshole today?"

"Not quite."

"Just extra bossy, then?"

"Yeah, something like that."

He throws demands out smoothly, and now I have no problem obeying them. He tightens his grip around my waist and whispers, "I'm so happy you're mine, Liza." He kisses me, and I open for him like I always do. Graham releases me, takes me by the hand, and walks to the double doors behind us. He slings open the door and stands beside me, letting me walk past him. The room is beautiful; it has a balcony overlooking the trees and the beach. The beach looks so much closer than it is. There's a king-size bed with champagne-colored drapes over the top. The stone bathroom shower features two shower heads that come from above. The tub is so big that it can cover my entire body if I sit in it. I grab his arm and plant a soft kiss on his bicep.

"Thank you for this."

I walk to the bed, with Graham walking behind me. I sit down and pat the spot next to me. He sits beside me and lays back on the bed.

"I'm just glad you didn't tell me no. I don't know if I would've survived another rejection from you."

"Shut up. You barely worked for it."

"Yeah. Right." He looks at the clock and rubs my back. "We should start getting ready for dinner tonight. Come on, let's get up."

Instead of pouting, I get up and get my stuff ready to take a shower. "What time is dinner again?"

"It's at 7 p.m., but I want to get there at 6:30 p.m.; there's somewhere I want to take you first." I playfully roll my eyes. It's just surprise after surprise with him today.

Shut up and enjoy it. The little bitch of conscience is back. I like it better when you don't have an opinion.

I walk into the bathroom, and it looks like another room. There were gray, marbled granite countertops with a massive mirror across his and her sinks. The shower had the same marbled granite, with a few specks of black mixed in with the gray. There are holes on the sides and top of the shower.

"Is this one of those fancy showers I won't know how to work?"

"Just use the keypad; it's easy. Watch the temperature, though; it can get hot quickly."

He's richer than my family is. Wow, this is a lot to take in.

I leave the door cracked just enough for Graham to see me if he looks in.

Slut.

I hope he looks in. I want him to watch me undress and shower. I want to please him and turn him on. He took me being a virgin better than I expected him to, and I hoped he knew that I planned to lose it this weekend. I glance at him as he faces away from me.

I fiddle with the keypad and set the water to the perfect temperature.

I start to undress, secretly hoping he's looking; he has only seen me in a bra and underwear so far, but for some reason, I feel that will change this weekend.

10

Graham

I can hear Liza turning the water on. I want to join her so badly, but I refrain, listening to my conscience.

She's a virgin; relax.

Fuck, I have no idea what she's done or hasn't done. I need to stay subtle and calm until the right moment comes. This time, regardless of where we are, I'm not stopping until her virginity is mine.

Instead of giving in to my inner desires, I shower in one of the guest rooms. My mind is still wandering, thinking about how Liza is wet and naked right now. I instantly get hard. Ignoring what I want to do, I quickly finish my shower and head back into our room. Liza is still showering, the steam pouring out into the room. I get dressed and walk towards the bathroom. *Stop; don't do it.*

I snap at my conscience to shut the fuck up and I push open the door.

"Liza?"

"Yes?"

"It's 6:05 p.m. unless you want me in that shower with you; I need you to wash your body quickly."

"Graham, it's your house; if you want to get in here, you can." My cock immediately stiffens. See, I *should've waited.*

She peeks out of the shower to see me in the bathroom, fully dressed, with a grin on my face.

"Good to know that I can shower with you."

"Anytime you want." She winks at me and sticks her head back in the shower. "I'm almost done; I'll be out in two minutes! You look nice, by the way."

I grab my cologne from the sink and apply a few drops to my wrist and neck.

I tidy up the room a bit, suddenly feeling like my life is under a microscope for her to judge. Impressing her is at the top of my list; I finally got her to agree to be mine, and now I need to make sure she knows what that entails.

I hear the shower when it cuts off, and after a few minutes, the door swings open, and Liza is standing in her matching black lacy underwear and strapless bra.

"What are you doing?" I gulp, sitting on the bed.

"Getting my dress, I left it out here." She walks towards me, standing in front of me. My cock is still hard, from what she said earlier. She bends down and begins to put her arms around my neck, and I place my arms around her waist. This is it; I can't wait any longer. When I reach for her, she leans over and grabs her dress behind me.

"Well played," I smirk as she walks back toward the bathroom.

"I just want to clarify that you aren't the only one that can leave people wanting more."

She's so fierce, sexy, and *mine*. I rub my hands on my thighs and look down at my still–hard cock. Down boy, false alarm.

She finishes and walks out. Stopping me in my tracks. "Elizabeth."

She twirls. "How do I look? Is it too much? I feel like it's too much."

"No, it's not. You're beautiful. Let's go."

"Or we could just stay in; I'm sure we can find something to do."

She walks over to me and puts her hand on my cock. How is this woman a virgin? How is it that she can provoke me to want to fuck her at any moment so effortlessly?

"Keep your hands to yourself; now let's go." She pokes her lips out, and I kiss her before we head out to the SUV.

I take her to the lake we passed earlier; my boat awaits us. She frowns and looks at me when I park the car.

"What is this?" I unbuckle my seat belt and open my door.

"Get out and see." She doesn't wait for me to get her door this time; instead, she flings the door open and walks to the front of the car.

"Wait, we're eating here?" I walk over to her and place my hand on her lower back.

"Well, I told you I wanted to show you something first." She looks up at me and smiles. I lightly push her, and we start walking toward the dock.

"Hello Graham, nice to see you again."

"How have you been, Troy?"

"I've been well, thank you." Troy smiles and unropes the boat's entrance, allowing us to walk on. I help Liza up onto the boat and follow her.

"This is Liza, my girlfriend. Liza, this is Troy, a family friend and our captain for tonight." Liza gives Troy that beautiful smile of hers and shakes his hand.

"Nice to meet you, Troy."

"The pleasure is all mine; welcome aboard. Are you both all set and ready to go?"

"Wait, it's only us on this boat?" She looks at me in disbelief and asks, "Is this your boat, Graham?"

"Yes, this is my boat."

"Of course, you have a boat; you probably have a jet too."

"Two, actually." She scowls at me.

"Let's get this dinner started."

I take her hand and lead her into the boat. I have instructed the crew to make this boat look romantic for Liza. There are candles everywhere, and low music is playing in the background. They did well. I look at Liza to see her reaction; she appears over the moon. That's all that matters. A crew member approaches me and asks, "Is everything looking okay, Mr. Salando?"

"Yes, thank you." She's a young woman with blonde hair pulled back into a ponytail. She turns on her heels and walks back into the kitchen area.

"This is beautiful, Graham; you sure know how to make someone feel special."

"Not someone, just you...I know you want to see the entire boat, so let's quickly get this tour over."

She laughs, and we start walking around the boat.

"Does she have a name? The boat, I mean."

"Her name is Giselle."

"After your sister, how sweet."

I direct her to the kitchen, which has granite countertops, an island in the middle, and two chair stools in front of it with light brown seating covers. The boat has three rooms. The first room has a king-size bed, a gold comforter, silk sheets, and four big fluffy pillows. It also has black and gold curtains surrounding the room. The next room I show her has a queen-size bed with champagne curtains and a blue and white striped comforter; the last one has the same thing. Those are my guest rooms. I used this boat for the wrong reasons, and these rooms have seen a thing or two.

"This boat is nice; my dad and stepdad would love it. They both have one, about the same size."

Interesting. This is the first time Liza has hinted that her family has money; maybe she'll tell me, after all, not that it matters.

I walk over to Liza, move the long strand of hair out of her face, and kiss her. I didn't plan to, but her lips always look fucking perfect. She closes her eyes, and I deepen the kiss, lifting her from the ground. She opens her eyes and places her nose against mine.

"I think I'm starting to love your kisses."

"They are all yours, angel." I put her down and close the door to our room. "Now come, let's get you fed."

I lead her to the balcony on the boat's top level. It's winter, but it's not too bad of a night for us to still eat outside. White twinkle lights are draped all around a candlelit table set for two. The table looks exactly as I instructed them to set it up, and a bucket of champagne sits in the center. I steer her toward the table and pull her chair out so that she can sit on it.

"Sit, relax; the chef should be out here soon with the food."

"No free will tonight, huh?"

"Oh, you have no idea." I open the bottle of champagne and pour a glass for both of us. She smiles at me, and I sit at the table with her.

"What?"

"Nothing; you're just… This is just a nice surprise."

"Get used to it." I raise my glass, and she tilts it towards hers. Our glasses clink, and we both drink.

"This is good; more, please."

"Don't go getting drunk now, angel." I tease, then pour her another glass.

"Why not? Won't you take care of me?"

"I'll always take care of you." She raises her glass.

"Well, cheers then."

A few moments later, the chef comes with our food—steaks with sautéed shrimp over them, broccoli, a baked potato, and a side salad. Liza has no problem eating in front of me or anyone else. The food is top-of-the-line and tastes perfect. She finishes her dinner, and I move my chair beside hers. She must have loved it because she's licking the sauce off her fingers. Oh my, how I wish she was licking something else.

"Did you enjoy your dinner?" I grab her hands and plant two gentle kisses on them.

"Yes. Delicious."

She leans over and gives me a warm, soft kiss on my cheek.

"Come here."

I pull her arms toward me, then onto my lap. My right arm wraps tightly around her waist; I kiss the back of her head, and I rub her thigh with my left hand. Liza leans back as I shift kisses from her hair to her lips. When she starts kissing me with force, I open for her. She stands and straddles me as she takes her seat on my thighs, deepening our kiss. Our tongues slide in and out of each other's mouths. The kiss becomes so violent and intense. She extends one of her hands, tugging at my hair and the other resting on my neck; she pulls me into her. I wrap my arms around her so tight, making her gasp.

Get a room. You have three.

I pull away from Liza, my hands entangled in her hair.

"We're on a boat; you need to stop." Ignoring everything I say, she pulls me back to her. "Elizabeth, I want to fuck you; hard, and if you keep this up, I won't be able to stop myself."

"I don't want you to stop yourself." She wants this just as badly as I do.

"*Stop.*" I breathe into her mouth.

"Sorry, I'm done taking orders from you. Pick me up, take me into that berth, lie me down, and fuck me." Her normal soft eyes have turned dark.

"Who's the bossy one now?" We both smirk at each other, our foreheads touching. *You heard her; what are you waiting for?*

I look her right in the eyes and say, "It'll be your first time; are you sure you want to do this?"

Please say yes. I'm so close to busting out of my pants.

She nods at me. "Use your words," I tell her.

"Yes, yes, I am sure."

I pick her up and walk towards the room with the king-size bed.

"Wrap your legs around me." She does as she's told, and I start kissing her. We pass the kitchen crew, and the blonde girl smiles at us and turns away.

"Oh my god," Liza laughs. I forgot people were here." I open the bedroom door, kick it shut, and lay Liza on the bed.

"Now, since it's your first time, I'll be gentle, but know that I make the rules in the bedroom. Understand?" With her eyes gleaming, she holds herself up on her elbows and nods again.

"Words, angel. Always, words."

"Yes, I understand."

I undo my tie and hover over her. "You tell me if I'm hurting you, it'll be uncomfortable for the first few moments, okay?"

"Yes, okay." Liza rubs my face softly. "I want to undress you." That's my Liza; she always wants to care for others first.

Let her.

I listen to my conscience.

"Fine, but quick. I don't want to wait another minute before being inside of you." She rolls on top of me and unbuttons my shirt, doing it in a sexy, gentle way. She starts biting her lip, then unzips my pants. I'm hefty in size; I know it. I've always been confident in my size. Through my briefs, my cock pops out toward her. Her face glows; she reaches for him, and I grab her.

"No, tonight is about you." She grabs my cock anyway, this time more forcefully. "*Angel*"

"Please, I want to please you, Graham; let me." She stands up and pulls me along with her. Liza has experience in this; she has too. My body is on fire for her, and as much as I want to be selfish with her, I have to stop, reminding myself that this is all about her tonight.

"Turn around."

I unzip her dress, and it falls to the ground, and she steps out of it. I turn her around to face me, and Liza pushes me down on the bed, gets on top of me, and starts kissing my neck. I try to stop her, and she shakes her head. She licks my neck and chest and slides down on her knees. She unzips my pants and reaches her hand inside, firmly grabbing my cock. Is she going to... Before I can finish my thought, she takes my cock out and shoves it in her mouth, sucking hard. I tilt my head back and jolt at the force she has.

"Angel," she ignores me and continues sucking, taking all of me in her mouth and her head in a bobbing motion. I put my fingers in her hair and shove myself deeper into her mouth. She doesn't stop, but she needs to. *Stop her.*

"You have to stop; I don't want to come in your mouth." She ignores me and seems to suck harder and faster; she starts using her hands and swirling her tongue around my shaft. I grab her and pull her against me.

"That's enough; it's your turn. Lay down."

I stand and kick off my briefs. Liza, still in her bra and panties, looks so beautiful. The light from outside the boat is hitting the side of her face. I climb on top of her, my fists clutching the comforter, and start planting gentle kisses all over her chest. She moans a little. I reach a hand behind her back and unlatch her bra. Her perfect breasts spill out, and I caress them. I kiss and suck her neck and trail my hand down to her pussy.

"Mine." She leans back and lifts her left leg a little.

"Yours."

I put my hand in her underwear and circle my thumb around her clit, causing her to jump.

"You, okay?" She nods in confirmation.

"Yes, keep going." I take my thumb and push it inside of her; she squirms and lets out soft, low moans. I take another finger and thrust it in and out of her, deeper and faster. She grabs my neck and starts kissing me.

"I'm going to come," she whimpers into my mouth. No sweeter words could come out of her mouth. I want her to come. I want her to be satisfied and wet for me before I take her virginity. Most of all, I want her to trust me with her body.

"Come on my fingers, angel." She pushes my fingers deeper into her pussy. I lose control and continue thrusting my fingers in and out of her faster and faster, milking her for everything she has.

"Please, Graham, I want you now."

"Not yet; you're not ready."

She wiggles underneath me, becoming impatient. I pull my fingers out of her and put them in her mouth.

"Suck, *now.*" I demand firmly. She opens her mouth and pulls my fingers into her mouth. She licks all around them, tasting herself before removing them.

"How do you taste?" She then pushes my fingers into my mouth. Ah, she tastes so good. I need more of her. I want more of her. I move down, positioning her right in front of my face. I look up at her and give her clit a couple of long, deep licks. She closes her eyes. I insert my tongue, fucking her slowly, taking my time to stop and spit on her clit. Her body tightens, an arch forming in her lower back, pushing her off the bed. She grabs my head, and I hold her waist down. She's going to come again, and this time right where I want her—in my mouth.

"Come for me. Let me taste you." She moans louder, and I feel her release. I lick her up as she comes uncontrollably into my mouth.

"Yes, that's it." I lick the rest of her come, and her body relaxes. All of a sudden, something hit me, making me realize that I would have to wait to fuck her when we got back home. I won't be able to do what I want with her in this small room. I won't be able to have her as many times as I want with people right out front; she would be embarrassed, and she'd try to control her sounds. No, not for her first time; I want her to scream as loud as she can, to show me every emotion she's feeling. I hover over her, kiss her, and smirk, "That's enough. Get dressed."

11

Liza

Get dressed? Was he serious? I wanted more. I needed more. Why does he keep leaving me unfinished? I look at him in disbelief as he grabs his clothes and starts to get dressed.

"Guess I better get dressed then," I say as he looks at me and flashes me a sly smirk.

"Yes, you better," he growls, fixing his tie. I love that tie, and when he took it off, it was obvious that he had every intention of taking my body and making me his.

I stand up and grab my dress, and neither of us moves from taking our eyes off the other.

"Zip me?" I turn around toward him, and he walks over to me. He lays his hand on my neck and uses the other to zip up my dress. Graham was so gentle with me when I wanted him to be rough. I understood that I was a virgin, but I wasn't fragile. He kissed my neck and said, "All finished." I watch him in the mirror as I fix my hair.

"You ready?" He's sitting on the bed, watching me put the finishing touches on my hair.

"Yes, all ready." I walk over to him and stand between his legs, wrapping my arms around his neck.

"Don't you start again; I'll bend you over on this bed right now." I swallow and smirk.

"I think I'd like that," my voice barely over a whisper.

"Yeah, I bet you would. Let's go. It's time to go home."

Graham stands up, waiting for me, as he opens the door. We walk back out to the deck. I look over the water, and he walks over to Troy. They're talking when I hear Graham's genuine, gorgeous laugh. God, it's...*perfect.*

I turn away and look out over the beautiful, reflective water, thinking about how different my life was a couple of days ago. Now, I am sitting here on a boat on my first *actual* date with Graham. I feel Graham's hand wrapping around my waist.

"You, okay?" He speaks in my ear, gently kissing it. I turn my head and gaze up at him.

"This is beautiful." I secretly hope he doesn't realize that I dodged his question. My inner consciousness is starting to make me doubt myself. I want to stay present and enjoy our date, but self-sabotage is beginning to show.

"Angel," he whispers, turning my head toward him and rubbing my cheek. "What is it? I can tell something is bothering you. Are you regretting what we did?"

"God, no, definitely not. I'm just wondering why all the magazines have you as this bad guy who uses women every day. I mean, I know you do; you haven't been subtle about it, but you're so different with me. I'm just getting in my head, I guess. "

Lie.

"Liza, the magazines aren't lying. Finding someone who is for you and only you is hard when you have a lot of money. It's hard to tell if they're after you or the money, so I always avoided the issue. I told you before that I have fucked, *a lot.* I never said I was a saint, and I hope you don't expect me to be. My past is just that—the past. *You've* made me want more; *you've* made me want to change. So, ignore the tabloids; they've been trying to figure me out for the past five years when you've figured me out in a matter of months." He picks my hand up and kisses it. "What you've read isn't me anymore; I don't want it to be."

I slowly slide my hand out of his grasp, taking a deep breath as I tell myself to let it go. But I can't, I have to say it.

"But why would you intentionally use women?"

"I was younger, and when I became number 1 on the list of the youngest millionaires, I got a lot of attention."

I look away from him and look out at the water. I didn't expect him to have a good reason, but I also didn't expect him to tell me he acted like a piece of shit to any woman he wanted to because of *attention*, either. "I did it because they were naive, and they let me. I took advantage, and I shouldn't have, and I am sorry, but that won't happen to you; you have to trust me."

This is it. This is the moment I must decide, trust him or run—like usual.

You have to give love a try, honey; not everyone will hurt you like he did.

My mother told me that before I left for school. She told me to trust myself, let myself live, and love hard.

Fuck. It. Turning to him, I search his eyes, speaking only when I know I'm making the right decision.

"I do trust you, Graham, but *don't* fuck me over; don't hide things from me."

"I won't; you have my word," He kisses my forehead and wraps me in his arms.

When we return to the dock, Graham and I thank Troy and say goodbye, with Graham handing him two one-hundred-dollar bills.

"Come on, angel, let's head home." He opens my door for me, and I hop in. This was a great night. Had I lost my virginity? No. But did I intend to do so? Hell yes.

While driving back, I stare out the window, thinking about the night I just had and planned to have once we got back. *Yes, if you can stay awake.*

Graham reaches over and grabs my hand, brings it to his mouth, and gently kisses it. I turn my head toward him and give him a warm smile. With his usual tight grip, he rests his hand on my thigh. My inner conscience cries out; this move is the only thing that can instantly turn her on. I try to calm her down by thinking about how crazy Emily will be when I tell her everything that has happened this weekend. She has been the one person I can't wait to tell things to, it's always been that way. I always knew she cared about me, which was more than enough for me. I need people—friends—who care about me and my safety in my life. I pull out my phone and send her a quick text.

Liza: *"I think we'll need a full Friday night girls' night with lots of wine before I tell you everything that has happened this weekend. Scratch that; we'll need tequila"*

I hit send, and we are back at the house before I know it. My phone vibrates, and I see Emily's message.

Em: *"Oh shit, I can't wait; please get laid tonight "*

He parks, quickly rounding to open my door. It's around 12 a.m., and as tired as I am, I still don't want to sleep. I have a plan for how I want this night to end, and it's with Graham inside of me.

"How about we run you a bath and get you into bed? You look tired." With a tight grip, he puts his hands on my shoulders and rubs my back.

"I'm awake." My voice is dry, and I don't even believe the words when they leave my lips.

"Right, you can barely keep your eyes open."

"Hm?"

"Up, now." I roll my eyes but do as he says and slug up the stairs.

"Lay down; I'll come get you when your bath is ready."

When I lay down, I don't remember my eyes closing. Moments later, I open my eyes when I feel his touch. He's kneeling in front of me, removing my 5-inch pumps. Restless, I lay my head back down as he removes the other. He picks me up and carries me into the bathroom, sweeping his lips across my forehead as my feet find the ground.

"Open those pretty eyes." He stares at me, and suddenly I'm awake.

"Turn around," I turn, and he unzips my dress, unhooking my bra in one swift motion. I try to cover myself, and he grabs my hand, pulling it back down to my side.

"Don't hide from me. Ever." I'm sure I'll bite a hole in my lip as hard as I'm digging my teeth into it. He's sliding my panties down my legs, and I'm trying my fucking hardest not to tremble. I take one foot out at a time, my right then my left, putting my hands on his shoulders and using him as a crutch so I won't fall over. The bath is warm and refreshing when he slowly settles me in and smells of sweet cinnamon and lavender.

"Better?" His hands push a piece of my hair behind my ear.

"Mhm. Thank you."

When he turns to leave, I reach up and grab his hand.

"Get in with me; I don't want to be away from you." His smile is low, and I know he doesn't know if it's a good idea. I can see him battling with his decision.

After what feels like an hour, he reaches for the hem of his shirt and removes it slowly.

"Whatever makes you happy." He settles behind me, pulling me to him. I close my eyes and lean into his chest when he kisses my neck.

"Thank you for an amazing night."

"No, thank you."

I find his eyes and tilt my head up for him to kiss me. It's quick and innocent, but somehow, it sends shock waves through my body.

"Let's get you cleaned up and put to bed." He grabs a loofah and puts soap all over it. I've never had a man wash my body before, but I've never known how sexy and intimate it could be. But as he washes my back, I let out a small moan, immediately embarrassed when he chuckles and washes the rest of me.

I'm never washing myself again. He will gladly have that honor.

The bed is soft and comfortable, and the room is at the perfect temperature. He climbs into bed and opens his arm so I can cuddle with him.

"So, you had fun today, right?" He's looking down at me and playing with my hair.

"Yes, I did; the extra "activities" were my favorite part."

"I'm glad you're happy; that's all I ever want to do."

12

Graham

Not another one. My dad looks at my sister, shaking his head as he turns for the door. My sister is blocking the door, and I raise my voice at him. "A liar is what you are, and your reasons don't justify shit. We weren't lying for him; if Mom asked, we'd tell her. "Don't marry one of the top lawyers in the world if you're going to hide dirty laundry right under her nose." My sister says, her strong-minded and stern voice booms loudly. "For fuck's sake, you two, I'm not a monster or a liar; I didn't hide it; it just never came up." My sister pushes him: "Who the hell is he, and why was he following us?"

I wake up in the middle of the night from a dream that I am tired of living. Looking at the clock, it says 2 a.m. I roll over, and I'm instantly soothed. My girl is lying so peacefully beside me. I carefully put her underneath the comforter. I guess we were both more tired than we thought.

"Graham?"

"Ssh, go back to sleep, pretty girl." Nudging her neck closer to the covers, she lets her eyes fall back shut.

Piano, I must play the piano. These dreams have become something that will never go away. I leave the room and walk downstairs to the piano. I start playing, still figuring out what to play. I let the music flow out of me, and the stress instantly fades.

Thirty minutes have passed, and I hear footsteps coming down the stairs. Damn, I woke her up. She's standing in the hallway, rubbing her eyes.

"Did I wake you?"

"No, you didn't; I realized you weren't in bed." She yawns. Wow, she felt I wasn't in bed with her. This woman is going to be the death of me.

"Are you okay?"

"Yeah, yes, I'm fine. You should go back to bed. I'll be there in a few."

"No lies, remember?" She waits for me to tell her the truth.

But what am I supposed to say?

Maybe start by saying it was just a bad dream.

He is right; I should tell her. When I reach for her, she puts her small hand in mine.

"Elizabeth, I'm fine. I just needed to play for a little while and clear my head. I never get to play when I'm home, but when I am here, I enjoy doing it. That's all, okay?" She moves her hand and stands up straight.

"Okay, Graham." Is she upset? Abandoning the piano, I crowd over top of her.

"You are beautiful." I caress her cheeks, her eyes still hazy from sleep. "What are you doing to me?"

"Whatever it is you're doing to me." I hover over her perfectly plump lips, kissing her with urgency and aggression.

Her body tightens, and I know what she wants and needs.

You need it, too.

I kiss her neck, both of our breaths quickening. "I want you so bad, Elizabeth, all the time."

She grabs me by my shirt and pulls me closer to her. Fuck it; first time or not, I need to be inside of her. *Now.*

I lift her and sit her on the grand piano, standing between her legs. She wraps her legs around me as I touch all over her body, grabbing her breast and rubbing my hands over her pussy.

"Graham, please, no teasing tonight," she pleads with me as I kiss all over her neck and mouth. Teasing is the last thing I plan to do. I lift her and carry her up to the room. My body is filled with adrenaline, and my erection is as thick and hard as its ever fucking been.

"Please, Graham, I don't want to wait."

This is it. Her virginity is about to become mine. I pay close attention to her reactions, remembering the spots that would drive her crazy. She grabs me and pulls me down with her as I lay her on the bed, wrapping her legs around me tightly. So tight that I can't move. She's shoving her tongue in my mouth and taking my breath away before I can wiggle free of her.

"Dammit, how can I tease you if you're doing this?" She giggles and continues to kiss me. She wants to play that game.

I roll her on top of me and sit her on my lap. I have to make sure she is ready for this.

"You're staring; what is it?'

"I want to make sure you are ready to do this. There's no rush."

"Keep kissing me and find out."

That's the green light I needed, and when I pull her down to my mouth, she lets out a sigh of pleasure as I tug on her bottom lip. That sigh goes straight to my cock, and then her scent hits me like a Mack truck. I'm fucked.

I flip her over, planting myself on top of her.

"Mm, cinnamon."

My body is ready for her, and I can tell she's ready for me. I need my cock in her. I need to fuck her for the rest of the night. I've longed for that control over her. I want her to submit to my needs. I know that this first time needs to be all about her. But after that, she'd do as I say.

I pull the shirt she's wearing over her head and unclasp her bra. Grasping one of her breasts in my mouth, sucking it, and toying with the other one, Liza moans as she tugs my hair, and it ignites me. I make my way down and lick her belly button.

"Remember, you tell me if I'm hurting you." Her head nods up and down.

"Words."

"Yes, yes, I know." Watching her get so impatient makes me thicken even more. I kneel and take her panties off with my teeth. When I give her pussy a good, deep lick, her back arches, and I silently combust at how deep that angle pushes her pussy into my mouth.
Get it over with.

I stand and drop my briefs to the floor. She looks at me, her face full of want and need.

"I want you inside of me but fuck. I...I don't think you'll fit. Is that thing normal? Jesus Christ," she tenses, looking at every inch of my cock and wondering how she's going to take me.

"It'll fit, don't worry. Feel it." Yanking her by her feet to the end of the bed, I put her hand around my cock. Groaning at her touch, she squeezes it tightly. When I bite my lip, she does it again. I watch her as she calculates her next move, but when she puts her hands on my waist and shoves my cock into her mouth, I curse. She's trying to suck every inch and fuck me if she isn't an overachiever.

"Look at you, your pretty fucking mouth stuffed with my cock." She slurps up and down, wrapping both hands around my shaft. "You look so fucking good with your lips around me." I push her head deeper, and even though she gags, she continues her assault on my dick. When I see those pretty fucking eyes beam up at me, I know all bets are off.

I lean over, grabbing a condom out of the top drawer. She watches me as I yank her up by her hair, slamming her lips into mine.

"Filthy fucking girl." I rip open the condom's wrapper and slide it on.

"Are you ready?"

"Slow, just go slow first."

"Of course," My tip is rubbing against her clit slightly before I make my way to her entrance. She shifts and moans as I place my hand around the back of her neck. I slowly slide the tip of my cock in her entrance, causing her to gasp. Her body tenses, and I let her get used to my size for a second.

"Relax, breathe." As I push deeper inside her, she continues to hold on tightly to my arms. Her breathing quickens as she feels the pressure and pain. I am entirely aware of how big and thick I am. I know it's going to hurt her to take all of me, but I'd make sure she'd take it.

"I'm almost all the way in; just breathe." She inhales, and when she does, I slide the rest of myself into her.

She's moaning softly, "You're so big; I feel so full." My cock is pulsing inside of her; I've been waiting long enough to feel her. The tight fit of her virgin pussy is making me want to come on the spot, but I shift, sliding in and out of her slowly. I feel her relax around me; she sinks deeper into the bed.

"How does it feel?"

"Good, so good. Please don't stop." I wrap her legs around me and thrust in and out of her. Her moans get louder and louder.

"Mm, let me hear you cry out for me, angel."

"Go harder." She wraps her arms around my neck and bites my ear. *Don't lose control.*

"Are you sure?" She starts pushing into me, mounting herself on my cock.

"Yes, it feels so good; please, harder." I move my body with hers, fucking her harder and faster. It's still not as hard as I want, but it'll do for her first time.

"You feel so good; I could fuck you all night, be inside of you all night, and love you all night. You're mine, angel, mine." I wrap my hand around her neck, slightly cutting off her air supply as I push deeper into her. "Say it."

"I'm yours." It comes out in short gasps, and I tighten my hold around her neck. When I start to feel Liza's pussy tighten around me, I flip under her, pulling her on top of me.

"Ride me; I want you to ride me." She looks apprehensive, like she's doubting herself.

"I...I don't know how.."

"Try." She adjusts herself over my cock, lining it up with her pussy. She slowly sinks onto my shaft, writhing her way down inch by inch. She's determined to take all of me, and I can't help but watch in awe. Her motions are short as she finds her rhythm. It doesn't take her long before she's completely sitting on my cock, fucking me.

"Good girl." She's a natural, and when she gets more comfortable, she starts moving back and forth faster with more confidence and force, moaning and biting her lip.

I smack her ass, and she starts bouncing up and down over and over again, crashing down harder each time. Her pussy tightens and squeezes my cock, and I know she'll come soon.

"Don't come yet; you wait for me."

"I can't. Please"

"Yes, you can." I pull her down on my cock as hard as I can, thrusting myself deep inside of her. She raises and slams down each time with me, fighting for control. She's trying to fuck me, and she is doing a damn good job at it. My cock pulses, and my body tightens.

"I'm going to come; come with me, angel." As fast as I can, I move her up and down on me. I let out a moan, with Liza following after me.

"Say my name, Elizabeth; always say my name when you come."

"Graham...Graham"

It's like a beautiful symphony, hearing her scream my name. She explodes all over me; all I can feel is her warmth. She lays on top of me, our bodies sweaty and sticky, and just like that, Liza and her virginity belong to me.

13

Liza

I continue kissing Graham slowly as I remain straddled on top of him while he's still inside me. My head rests on his chest, and he mindlessly runs his fingers up and down my side.

"That was amazing."

I feel a rumble in his chest and know he's chuckling at me. He slides out of me and disposes of the condom in the bathroom.

"Let's get you cleaned up." When I walk into the bathroom, my legs feel like noodles. I barely have enough energy to walk. He was gentle but rough at the same time, and it was exactly what I wanted. I always feared that my first time wouldn't be enjoyable, but fuck me, I was wrong.

"Feeling okay?"

"Yes." I rush out and close my eyes, not meaning to reply so fast. When his eyebrows arch a little, I reach for his arm. "I'm fine."

"What is it?."

"My blood is all over..." My face turns darker when I think about the evidence on his sheets. When he smirks, I glance away, hiding my own smile.

"Your blood coating my cock, while you screamed, begging me not to stop was the highlight of my fucking life, angel."

"Oh no, do you have a thing about virgins?"

"The complete opposite; I hate it. You have to be gentle, slow, and sweet. And I'm none of those things in the bedroom. You, my pretty girl, were the only exception to that. But don't get used to it."

I know something is wrong with me; it has to be because there should be no reason why that is such a fucking turn-on. My legs are clenched so tight that if I open them, the puddle between them will soak the bathroom floor.

"I wouldn't dream of it."

I welcome the hot water beading down my back. Graham's presence is overwhelming; even when I'm not looking at him, I can feel him looking at me. I submerge myself under the shower head, wetting my hair, buying myself time to gather the courage to make eye contact with him. When I open my eyes, I see that he's washing and rinsing his hair.

I bite my lip and walk up behind him, wrapping my arms around him and kissing his back. I want more of him. Now that I've tasted him, it's all I want.

The pressure between my legs is a clear sign of that.

He turns around and pushes me to the wall, the water dripping from his hair down to his back. Graham shoves his tongue into my mouth. I raise my leg and pull on his cock, and he groans.

"Liza, a condom; I don't…" I pull him into my pussy, ignoring his protest. I don't care about a condom; I want him inside of me.

I should set a reminder to get on the pill when I get back to the apartment. As he repeatedly presses me against the wall and pounds in and out of me, all I can think about is how much I have been missing out on. With each thrust he makes, the water splashes harder and harder.

"Fuck, you're going to be the death of me, aren't you?" When he completely pulls out, I throw my head back before he's filling me up again.

"You don't act like a virgin. You act like a needy little slut."

I didn't think I'd like degradation, fuck, I didn't think I'd like dirty talk, but my god, the words coming out of his mouth are enough to make me come without his intrusion. "Say it..tell me you're needy for my cock."

I've never talked dirty, but I know that'll change. I block out my thoughts, turn my brain off, and do what he says.

"I'm needy...for your cock." When he slams me back against the wall and shoves himself deeper into me, I know I've made him lose control.

"Good girl, now come for me."

I come violently, moaning in a scream and digging my fingers into his back. "Say my name, Elizabeth."

My unintelligible moans turn into his name as he kisses my neck. He follows soon after, and his thrusts become short and staggering; his come splatters over my inner thighs.

Our bodies are still as we finish our climax. He runs his hands over my wet hair, his lips find mine, and I hum in satisfaction.

"Wash up."

When I get dressed, I only wear a bra and underwear. I still feel him staring at me as we climb into bed.

My pussy craves more, but I don't think she can handle more. Graham's cock is going to have power over me; I can already feel it. Even with my pussy throbbing, all I can think is how I can't wait to have him in me again. He wraps his arms around me, tugs me into his side, and kisses my forehead.

"Sleep, angel."

***

The next morning...

When I wake up, Graham stares at me.

"Good morning, gorgeous."

"Good morning. I'd kiss you, but I have morning breath and probably look like the girl from the ring." His laughs bellow through the room before he grabs me by the neck with one hand and the other tucked behind his head, pulling me to him.

"I don't care about your morning breath, got it?"

"So I do look like the girl from the ring?" He pinches my side.

"Okay, okay." I press my lips against him; they're soft and sweet. It's natural.

"Good girl, I have breakfast downstairs; meet me there." He kisses me on the forehead and goes downstairs. I get up and stretch; I look over and see a red silk robe and a note that reads,

I saw you eyeing this when we were shopping.

- G

I wear the robe over my laced panties and bra. When I get downstairs, I see Graham sitting at the table, reading something on his phone and drinking his coffee.

"Red suits you well, Crambell." I shake my head.

"You didn't have to do this; I didn't need this."

He waves his hand. "Sit."

I do as I'm told, with my elbows on the table and my hands tucked under my chin. I stare at Graham, taking him in.

"I can feel you staring; what's wrong?"

"Nothing, just admiring you."

"Come here," he pulls me into his lap.

"Is this a better view for you to admire?"

"Yes, it definitely is."

"Eat your food, and let's figure out what to do today other than get you on fucking birth control." I think back to the shower, and I get hot all over again. He's standing, watching me, his eyebrow quirking up.

"Reminiscing?"

"Shut up." His smile is intoxicating, and he doesn't do it enough. "Sit. I am perfectly capable of fixing a plate for both of us. And I was going to make an appointment to do that when I get back." I push him back down in his seat as he tries to stand.

He puts his hand under his chin and looks at me.

"Yes, if you say so." I walk over to the countertop and see that he's made his usual breakfast spread: pancakes, bacon, eggs, two fried and some scrambled, and coffee.

I look at him and say, "Fried or scrambled?" He replies, "scrambled," without looking up from his phone screen. What is distracting him? Is it his business, his school, or his friends? Or that conversation I never mustered up the strength to ask about. I won't know unless I ask him, but I don't want to seem like a nosy girlfriend. Who cares? *Ask.*

I sit his plate in front of him and look at his almost empty coffee mug.

"Refill?" I ask, and he looks up.

"I'm sorry, what was that?" I pick up the coffee. "Do you want more coffee?"

"Sit, I got it; eat." He gestures, I sit in front of my plate and watch him pour my coffee, making it exactly how I like it.

"Graham."

"Yes, Elizabeth."

Why is he calling me Elizabeth? What happened to angel? As much as I wondered why he called me that, I've grown to expect it now. Something is off.

"Are you okay? What has your attention this morning? You aren't yourself."

"It's just things for graduation and ensuring everything is taken care of. Nothing to worry about." *He's lying.*

I nod, ignoring my instincts.

"Okay."

We eat our food in silence. I shove my food down so fast so that I can get up from the table and away from the uncomfortable silence. It's the most awkward I have felt in a long time, and I never thought I'd feel it with Graham. I know there is more to the story about why he's so off, and it bothers me that he's lied to me about it.

"I'm going to shower if you need me or want to have an actual conversation today." I storm off, realizing that I am more pissed than I thought. He's lying to me; something else is up, and instead of telling me the truth, he lied.

"Liza, don't do that." I ignore him and continue walking up the stairs to the bedroom.

I can hear his footsteps as I turn the shower on. I know he's behind me, but I refuse to look at him. When I don't, he clears his throat and leans against the door frame.

"You're upset with me?"

"Yes, I'm upset with you; you broke your promise. You lied to me."

"What? Stop. I don't want you angry with me, Liza; I cannot take it on top of everything else."

"See! On top of what? Tell me, talk to me; that's why I'm here. Don't brush me off and tell me some story about it being about graduation; I'm graduating, too."

"I'm sorry, I shouldn't have done that; you're right; I just don't want to talk about it right now, not this weekend, please."

He places his head against the door. I can see the hurt in his eyes, and I can tell that he really doesn't want to talk about whatever is bothering him right now. But I need to make sure he knows he can when he is ready. I walk over to him and rub his cheek.

"Then just tell me that, and I'll understand." His head shakes in acknowledgment.

"Words, Graham." I tease, using his line against him; I stand on my tip-toes and kiss him. "Come shower with me."

I pull him over to the shower, pulling off his shirt and sweats, surprised to see that he has nothing underneath. I undo my robe, remove my bra and panties, and enter the hot, steamy shower. He wraps his arms around me, resting his chin on my shoulder.

"Don't get mad at me often; I can't bear it."

"Don't lie to me, and I won't. Now wash up."

"Who's the bossy one now?"

"Just do as you are told." Being in charge is fun. Graham washes up and turns towards me.

"I can see now that you will live to defy me and ignore my orders purposefully." I raise my eyebrows and give him a side smirk.

"If a submissive girlfriend is what you're looking for, I'm not your girl." His stare turns dark, and I swallow the lump that formed in my throat from it.

"I expect you to submit to me in the bedroom. I've learned that otherwise, you do as you please." Submit to him in the bedroom? What did he mean?

"And angel, you're exactly what I am looking for." Ahh, angel. He called me angel again. I dab a little bit of soap on his nose and continue to wash up. After finishing and stepping out, he throws me a towel.

"Thanks for understanding."

With his arms around me, I turn around and look up at him with a frown.

"I will never push you to talk to me when you're not ready. Just don't think keeping your feelings away from me is okay." He grabs my chin, pulls my face closer to his, and kisses me.

"Alright, angel, just give me a little time."

It's finally a little warmer than usual outside, so I put on a long-sleeved, low-cut white T-shirt with a plaid flannel wrapped around my waist, dark-washed ripped jeans, and brown boots.

"As always, you look as beautiful as ever," he compliments me. I know I don't amount to the women he has been with, but Graham makes sure to make me understand that I am exactly what he wants.

"You don't look too bad yourself." I look at Graham up and down. He is wearing black jeans with a few rips, a black, red, and orange striped flannel, and a white T-shirt under it.

"I'm sure you're copying me with the flannel, though."

"I guess I just want to be like you today."

"So, what's up for today? We only have one more day left here. I'll need to go into town. I'm pretty sure I need to get a plan B pill." He raises his eyebrow and nods, giving me a slight grin.

"I absolutely need you on birth control. There is no way condoms are an option anymore after feeling you bare. I'll call our physician and have him fill out a prescription for the pill for you." I drop my head and pull my lip into my mouth, biting it as a distraction.

"That fucking lip…" He growls at me and pulls me towards him.

"Nope, it's our last day; let's go." I wiggle my way out of his embrace.

"Let's not think about how much time we have left; I'm sure this won't be our last weekend getaway."

"I hope not; I'm enjoying myself."

"I am too, angel, and I hope you understand how much you mean to me already. It scares the hell out of me."

"Why does that scare you?"

"I'd rather not talk about that. Just know that I am doing my best with this and us. I don't get into relationships, and I don't trust others." I look at him, then sit down on the bed.

"Well, after what you told me on the boat, I understand why, but I also assume there's an actual reason why or an actual person of why."

"Come on, let's not talk about this; let's go out and enjoy our day."

"Graham, unless you want me upset twice in one day, I expect you to tell me why." He looks at me and realizes what he's said has made me nervous. I get in my head enough as it is, questioning my own decisions. The last thing I need is to wonder if he will do the same.

"Listen, I just haven't had the best of luck. I trusted two other women besides my mother and sister, and I didn't have a great experience with that."

"So does that mean you don't trust me either?" I wait for what feels like an hour, and when he inhales and exhales deeply, I know the answer to my question.

"Never mind. You answered that for me." I get up and head out the door, but he grabs me by the arm.

"Stop storming out when I don't talk; I told you already I haven't had luck with this shit." *Game. Fucking. On. Because me neither.*

"Let go of my arm. Now!"

"Stop, please."

"I should not have to pay for those women, and I should not get treated as if I am paying for what they did to you."

"Okay, you're right. I'm sorry; I trust you, okay?"

"Graham, you don't trust yourself; how the hell can you trust me? I need some air." I turn away from him and head outside, slamming the door behind me. I start walking the trail I saw when we first came here. It leads to a pond with a small boardwalk and a sitting area in the middle. The couch gives you the perfect view overlooking the water. I think about how stupid I was to believe he could actually trust me. I trusted him, and so quickly, too quickly. I never did that; my life didn't allow me to trust people. People are evil, and they want what benefits them. That's what I witnessed growing up. But Graham? I want him to open up to me. To tell me what's going on in his life. He said he'll let me know when he's ready; I must be patient. But why is it so hard for me to do it? Why do I feel like I won't be able to handle waiting?

Just then, my phone started to ring. It's him.

I hit the ignore button. Right after I hit the button, the phone rings again. I answer.

"What do you want?"

"You, Liza, I want *you.*"

The words spill out of me before I can stop them.

"We can't be together if you don't trust me. We can't be together if you're going to make me pay for your past. I've had my shit in the past, very ugly things, ugly people that only wanted to hurt me, and you don't see me making you pay for it. It isn't fair." I can hear his breathing as if he's right beside me.

He's walking down the boardwalk towards me, and I watch him as he approaches.

"I'm sorry."

"I need you to trust me, Graham." He nods, and I stand to face him. "And I can't be left out of the loop." He nods again. "Because if I am, I'll leave." He sits on the couch and pulls me in between his legs, burying his head in my stomach.

"You can't leave me, Elizabeth; you can't ever leave me. I wouldn't know what to do. This has been couple of weeks of my life. I saw you when you moved in and knew I had to have you. I knew I had to make you mine. I haven't been the best guy and have a terrible reputation for myself, but you've changed me in a month, and I never thought that was possible. You can't leave me; I'm sorry." I cross my arms and look down at him. I hear my inner self saying, *you're already growing to love this man, and it's clear he is, too. Don't mess this up.* I ignore my inner conscience and keep my arms folded.

I sigh and look down at him. "Get up." He looks out at the water, avoiding my eyes. " Get up and look at me." He still doesn't.

"Graham, look at me." I cup his face in my hands and pull his face up so that he's looking at me.

"Talk to me. Trust me. I'm not here to hurt you, and I won't hurt you."

"They all say that." He claims, standing and pulling away.

"What do you mean?"

"My mom. Elizabeth, she left me. I was a year old when Madeline adopted me; my biological mom didn't want me."

Fuck, I screwed up. This whole time, I imagine he meant a girlfriend. I'm horrible. *Fix it.*

I wrap my arms around him and hug him as tightly as possible.

"Yeah, cat got your tongue, huh?"

What the fuck do I say to that?

"I'm so sorry; if you had just told me, I would've understood; I'd given you space and time." He's quiet, and I squeeze him a little tighter.

"Say something."

"Elizabeth.."

"Don't. I'm sorry. Please say something."

"You are not allowed to leave. You leave, I follow. Every time."

14

Graham

I told Liza the truth about being adopted. The only people who know are my family. We kept it out of the press and concealed it for my entire life.

We sit on the couch, and I continue telling the truth. My angel almost left me; it's been a few days, and she was already about to leave me. I don't want to take any chances, not on that.

"I know everything about you, and I think you've been figuring that out."

"Yes, I have, but I can't figure out how."

"I have a security team, and every person I encounter runs through our system. You may not have noticed, but a black SUV was following us all weekend; that's Ellis, head of my security. He's here now, at the end of the dock." Ellis is tall, about 6'4, with dark hair and blue eyes. Liza sits on the edge of the couch in disbelief.

I purposely leave out the part where I already know her stepfather and mother; to my defense, I didn't even know they had a daughter. My father and I have been in business with her stepfather for quite some time. But I never felt comfortable enough to ask about his personal life; that conversation was reserved for him and my father. They were close friends with each other.

"You're telling me that you know everything? Like about my family and my personal life?" Her face turns up in disgust and what looks like worry.

"Yes, all the way down to your parents' addresses and banking information." She tilts her head and gives me a defiant look.

"That's their business; don't ever look into their personal lives." I didn't plan on it; it just happened to pop up.

"Of course."

"Is there anything else?" I raise my eyebrows in question. What did she mean was there anything else? Clearly, I need to do more digging.

"What else should I know?"

"Nothing, just weird, is all."

"I'm not going to ask you why exactly you're lying to me right now because this trip isn't about us arguing. And because I'm going to assume you're just not ready to divulge whatever the fuck it is you're keeping from me."

"I just.." I shake my head at her, and she stops speaking.

"Anyway, I know I should've told you sooner, but I didn't want to scare you or make you think that I run checks on our waiters at the restaurants we eat at."

"You didn't," she snarls, glaring at me, a hint of humor in her eyes.

"Of course not, but I need you to understand that I could if I wanted to. It's important that you know I'm powerful, and I have a lot of resources."

"Just don't dig into my life again without me knowing; if you want to know anything, you can just ask. Okay?"

"Deal, now let's go." I stop and kiss her first. I wonder when her kisses will stop making me feel like a helpless child needing attention.

I pull her down the dock, her hand interlaced with mine. "Where are we going?"

"You'll see. It'll be fun; Ellis will drive us." I look around at all the white lights lined down the pathway and the bushes full of bright-colored flowers. My sister decorated this trail last summer, and it shows.

When we reach the front, Ellis is there waiting for us. He opens the door for us both and greets us with a nod. I put my hand on the small of her back, gesturing toward the SUV.

"Ellis, is it?"

"Yes, ma'am."

"Liza, but I'm sure you already knew that." He grins, and she slides into the back of the SUV. I reach for her hand and kiss it.

"Don't start it, Salando; I'm still mad at you." I should be mad at her; I know she's hiding something, but I won't push her because I have no room to talk.

"What if that's all I want to do, Crambell? Are you going to stop me? I've got some making up to do."

She bites her lip and leans her head to the side, watching me. Pulling the privacy screen up, I beckon her to come closer to me.

She slides towards me, only an inch or so. Not close enough.

"No, Liza. I want you here." I pat my lap as she hides her grin. I wait to see if she'll obey, but not even a second later, she climbs onto my lap.

I wrap my arm securely around her waist and say, "I can get used to this view."

"Yeah?"

"Mhm, come here." My hands tangle in her hair, pulling her in for a kiss. She doesn't fight me. Instead, she relaxes into my hold.

"I'm going to fuck you until we get to our destination. Understand?" She starts to nod but then opens her mouth.

"Yes."

"Good girl." I flip her over onto the seat and kiss her on the neck;

she lets out a low moan.

"Lift your arms." She raises her arms as I take her shirt off and cup her breast in my hands. My mouth fills with one of her breasts, and I tug on her nipple with my teeth. She's growing increasingly impatient. She grinds her pussy over my pants, panting breathlessly. When I pinch her nipple, she groans, and she reaches for my cock.

"Keep still; I'm not done."

"Graham, please, let me."

"Let you what? Tell me what you want. Tell me what you want me to do to you." I unzip her pants and stick my hand in her panties, gliding my finger against her clit.

She tilts her head back and gasps, "Fuck me, please."

"Oh, I plan to, angel, as hard as I can." I make quick work of her clothes, throwing them on the seat next to us.

"Open your legs and hold them there; don't move them. Understand?"She opens her legs, adjusting herself in the seat. I take my fingers and soak them with saliva, then slide my middle and index fingers inside of her.

"Fuck, you're wet already." I stroke my fingers in and out, moving faster. Her moans become erratic, and she tries to push my fingers away.

"Please, no more, just you."

"Not yet; you're not ready for me."

"I'm ready; please, I need to feel you." I continue pushing my fingers in and out of her violently. I grab her hands and place them on my rock-hard cock.

"You feel how hard you make him; how hungry you make him for you." She reaches for me, and I push her hands over her head, using my knees to move her legs back open. "I told you to keep your legs open."

"I can't; I just want to taste you. Please"

I unbuckle my belt, unzip my pants, and shove them to my ankles. Shoving myself inside her mouth, she wraps her hands around my waist and pushes me harder into her. She gives the best head. I can already feel myself ready to burst. No way; if I'm going to come, it's going to be in that cunt of hers.

"Now. Please." As I lower her onto the SUV floor, I remove the condom from my back pocket and slide it over my cock. Within a second, I'm shoving myself inside of her, thrusting deep and hard with everything I've got.

"The next time I tell you to keep your legs open, do it."

"Yes, yes, I'll do it."

"Tell me you'll submit to me during sex." I say this as I push her legs back further, allowing me to fuck her deeper.

"Yes, I'll submit to you." She pulls me down to her and moans quietly in my ear. She claws my back and wraps herself around me. After this, I know I'll wear the evidence of those marks. I slow down my assault and push into her deeply. She loses it; she bites my ear and moans uncontrollably.

"Fuuuuck, you feel so good." I keep pumping her.

"Harder, fuck me harder, please." Oh, she wants it rougher. I intend to give it to her as rough and hard as she wants it. I give her a devilishly sly smile and start to pump into her as hard as I can, pushing her against the glass with her legs wrapped around me. With my hand against the window next to her head, I continue to fuck her, milking her just like she asked. Every muscle in her body tenses, and I know her orgasm is only a few seconds away. My legs are restless, but I don't stop.

"That's it; come for me; you're gonna be coming this whole ride." I feel her clenching around my cock, suffocating it.

"Fuck Liza, so good, so tight around him." I didn't know I could fuck as fast as I was or be as deep as I was. But when she matches my pace,

I know I don't have much longer before I come.

"Stop, I'm going to come, and I don't want to yet." She ignores me, wrapping her legs around me and pushing against me as fast as she can. She flips me over and climbs on top of me. She takes every inch of my cock. I wrap my hand around her waist and push my load into her, spanking her ass as she moves up and down my shaft. My body is stiff, but Liza is still bouncing, her pussy swallowing my cock as she reaches her orgasm. She screams loudly, and we come smacking against each other. She plops down on me, catching her breath.

"Oh, Elizabeth, we're far from done."

15

Liza

We go two more rounds, and Graham fucks me with everything he has each time. My pussy is swollen, and there's a dull ache. I lay my head on Graham's chest, listening to his heart slow to a normal rhythm. "Alright, angel?" he asks, running his fingers through my hair.

"Mhm, great. Where are we going?"

We are in one of the most romantic little towns I have ever seen, and I still don't want to be anywhere but in bed with Graham.

"Just into town. I want you to see the shops, and there's a park I want to show you; we drove through quickly yesterday. I want you to enjoy some of the scenery here."

"The scenery looks just fine from where I'm sitting." He kisses my forehead and nudges me up. "Get dressed."

We get dressed just in time to hear the SUV come to a stop. I fix my hair and glance over to see Graham watching me.

"Got something on my face?" He grins and holds his hand out to me. Ellis knocks on the window and then opens the door. I turn red, knowing he might have heard what happened in the short driving time here.

Graham stops and exchanges a few words with Ellis; they laugh, and

I can't help but smile at them—two men who could stop a room full of conversation.

"Alright, how about we do some shopping?" He smiles and then looks down at his vibrating phone. "I have to get this; go to one of the shops, and Ellis will be behind you. I'll be right back." When he walks off, I hear his firm voice answering the call.

"Alright, Ellis, just you and me, huh?"

"After you, Ms. Crambell."

"Liza is fine. Please." He nods and walks behind me as I enter one of the clothing shops. I start looking through the skirts and then wander to the lingerie section. Aware that Ellis is never too far behind me, I look up at him and shoot him a wink.

I wonder if Graham would like lingerie, or would it just get in his way? I look at a red all-lace one-piece and think to myself how easy it would be for him to fuck me in it. I get turned on instantly by the thought of him pulling the crotch buttons to the side for him to insert his fingers in my pussy the way he seems to love to do.

Remember where you are, Liza. **Snap out of it.**

My inner bitch is right, but I am absolutely going to find out if lingerie is his thing. As I walk toward the dressing room to try it on, I notice a guy with a camera. It seems like he's taking pictures of me; I must be mistaken. Who in the hell would want pictures of me? Unless... maybe he found me again. When I pick up my phone and call my mom, I see Ellis walking toward him.

I feel a warm hand wrap around me. I jump in fear. "Whoa, it's just me."

I still haven't told Graham about Tim, my stalker, or my abuse. After seven years, I still feel like someone is constantly watching me. My mom and Brantley did everything they could to keep it out of the press, and they paid him off very well to leave me alone.

"I'm sorry, that guy was..."

"Taking pictures of you? Yeah, I'm sorry, paparazzi; you'll get used to it." He kisses me on the cheek and pulls my hands away from my chest to see the lingerie. "What's this?"

Still worried, I shake my head and enter the dressing room.

Of course, they were taking pictures of me, but not because of my past, but because I'm are with one of the most wanted men on this planet.

Duh, idiot.

Shut up.

No, you shut up and invite him into the dressing room.

Absolutely not.

Boring bitch.

She's right, again; Graham has had his share of women, probably more exciting than me. I pull on the lingerie and text him to see it. I button the two crotch buttons and lace up the back; within a few moments, he's pulling back the curtain.

"Need help with that?" He speaks with a low, hungry voice.

"Actually, I just need your opinion." He comes up behind me and looks at me through the mirror. He moves my hair to the side and begins to kiss my neck, pulling me closer to him—so close that I can feel his cock pulsating through his jeans.

"I think…" he kisses my neck again, "That you…" He takes his hand and rubs it over my clit; I inhale in surprise. "Need to keep it on under your clothes… because I plan on taking it off of you myself."

"Oh, okay." I try to slow my breathing, realizing I am suddenly out of breath. He unbuttons the two buttons that cover my pussy, tilts my head back, wraps his hands around my neck, and tugs on my ear a little.

"Watch me finger your pussy," he whispers. I swallow intensely and prepare myself. I'll have to keep quiet and contain myself.

Graham places two fingers in his mouth, covering them with saliva.

Little did he know, I'm already wet for him; I always am. Graham then rubs his index finger and middle finger around my clit, pushing them around in a circle. He watches me diligently, noticing how I react to him. I moan, and he puts his hand over my mouth.

"Shh."

"I'm sorry, it feels so good." I whimper. He smiles and inserts his fingers into my pussy. Speeding up as he goes in and out. I squirm and bite my lip. It's the only way I know how to keep myself quiet. I watch him as he watches me. I can tell that being helpless turns him on. I can tell he has me exactly where he wants me, and I can't say I'm mad about it. Just as I'm about to come and can't take anymore, he stops. He pulls his fingers out of me and kisses my cheek.

"Rip the tag off and get dressed; you'll come for me at home—from my cock, not my fingers." He whispers roughly. I rip off the tag, and he takes it. I get dressed, with the lingerie under my clothes. I look at Graham, and he gives me an evil side grin. He puts his hand on my back and leads me out of the shop.

"That wasn't nice, leaving me on edge like that." He brings my hand to his mouth, kissing it gently. The guy from earlier, lurking on the sidewalk with his camera, is still taking a picture of us.

"I'm sorry; I'll make it up to you later. How about we get some lunch and have a picnic? Would that make forgiving me a little easier?"

"Fine, but only because I ate my breakfast so fast that I'm starving right now." I stalk ahead of him, putting my hands on my hips. I'm so focused on trying to prove a point that I forget that I have no clue where the fuck I'm going. I turn around and see Graham and Ellis looking at me in amusement.

He points to an Italian restaurant across the street. "Italian good?" Ellis and Graham laugh, and I hear Ellis say, "Your life will never be boring, that's for sure." Graham shakes his head, and they walk behind me.

"I was thinking we could get it to go and have a picnic at the waterfall, or we can eat here and go to the waterfall afterward. What do you want to do?" I encase my arms around him.

"How about we get this to go and then go back to your house?"

"We can do whatever you want. But don't you want to shop a little more and see some stuff?"

"Well, how about we shop, get this to-go, and *then* go back to your house?"

"May I ask why you are rushing to get back?"

"Did you forget what I have on under this?"

"Mm, how could I? I can still taste you on my fingers." His words make me blush.

I turn and look at Ellis, who is looking around. "He's pretty cool to have around." Graham follows my gaze to Ellis and nods. "Yes, he is "cool" to have around. Let's look at some more shops."

Throughout the day, as we go from store to store, I try on multiple things, with Graham giving me his opinions on which things I should buy. We stop at a pretzel stand and an ice cream stand afterward. Before I know it, it's around 6 p.m.

We return to the Italian restaurant and order two lasagnas, two salads, mozzarella sticks, and a bottle of wine to go. We wait in the SUV, and soon Ellis returns with our food. "I hope he got something for himself, too,"

"Trust me, I'm sure he did."

***

About thirty-five or forty minutes later, we arrive back at the house. Ellis opens our door, handing Graham a bag of food.

"Thanks, El."

I enter the house in front of Graham, putting the bags down at the door. I turn towards him and lean my back against the wall. He looks at me with his brow furrowed.

"What are you thinking about?"

"I'm thinking about how I have no interest in eating anything right now."

"Oh yeah? Then what does interest you?" He sets the bag on the end table next to the door and walks towards me.

"Hmm? Tell me. What interests you, pretty girl?" He towers over me, with his arms pulling me close.

Would I ever get used to the way he grabs me? To that hold? I can tell that Graham has tricks up his sleeve that he can't wait to use on me; he made it clear to me that he's in charge in the bedroom. While I'm not sure what made me do what I did in the dressing room earlier, I know he liked it. I know he left me wanting more, which was his plan all along. He needs that control; he craves it, and I'll happily give it to him. I'd please him, even if it meant losing my sanity in the process.

16

Graham

Liza's breath quickens as I hover over her. Curiosity covers her face, and I know she's wondering what I'm going to do next—where I'll touch her, where I'll kiss her—and she can't wait to find out. That's my girl, always eager. She parts her lips, and nothing but air comes out.

"*Speak*, what are you interested in?"

"You. *You*, Graham, I'm interested in you."

"Me, and what else?"

"Your touch, your... feel. Please. Please, Graham, touch me," she begs me. She doesn't need to beg me to touch or feel her; that's precisely what I plan to do.

"Be patient."

I cup her face in my hands and drop my mouth on hers, devouring her and making her open for me. Our kiss turns violent, and her hands move up to my hair.

"You make me crazy when you stare at me like that."

It's true; I've caught her staring at me throughout the night—a stare that says, "Fuck me." That stare that shows me how much she wants me.

"That look is going to get you in some serious trouble." I put my hand on her ass and give it a tight squeeze, causing her to jump in surprise.

When I let go of her, she sighs in disappointment. I grin internally, knowing I have that kind of power over her. I pick up the food and head to the kitchen, stopping to grab two plates and two wine glasses. Liza doesn't move, still standing against the wall. I walk up to her and place a gentle kiss on her mouth. "Eat first."

"You're the boss." Yes, I am the boss, and tonight, she will find out just how bossy I am.

She walks into the kitchen and grabs the bottle of wine. I approach her from behind and take it out of her hands.

"Sit...did you have fun today?" I pour her a glass and another for myself. She tucks her hands under her chin, a smile radiating at me. "I'll take that as a yes."

"Yes, thank you for taking me shopping, *again*. It's clearly your thing." I pick up a forkful of lasagna and bring it towards her mouth.

"Open." When she does, I slide it into her mouth. She closes her eyes, savoring the flavors of the perfectly cooked goodness.

"That is perfect, mouthwatering, and it melts in my mouth. More, please," she begs, tilting her mouth toward the fork. After taking another bite, she grins and picks up her glass of wine, gulping it down.

"Mmm."

"Slow down." I smile at her and start eating my share of the food. She's right. It is good.

"I should ask, should I expect paparazzi everywhere we go? I've worked very hard to make sure they forgot I existed."

"Elizabeth, you can never be forgotten. But why do you want to be?"

She looks away, finishing off her wine. When she reaches for the bottle, I grab her hand.

"Look at me... What are you hiding?"

"Nothing; there's just someone from a long time ago who I don't want to remind of my existence."

"Does this person have a dick?"

"I don't want to talk about this... really, it's fine." I pull her toward me, and she stands between my legs. I run my hands up and down the back of her thighs lightly.

"Then we won't talk about it, but understand this. If someone hurts you or so much as fucking looks at you wrong, I will end them."

"It's been taken care of."

"Probably not to my standards, but I'll choose to take your word for it." I decide right then and there that El will need to do some serious fucking digging. Whatever she was hiding from me was still taking a toll on her.

"Thank you for dinner; that was probably the best lasagna I've ever had," she states, changing the subject. I take her in, and she's flustered. Our conversation must be one she wants to avoid.

I engulf her, putting my arms around her and inhaling her delicious cinnamon aroma.

I kiss her cheek, and when I glide my tongue up her neck, she tightens her hold on the plate in her hands.

"I won't bring it up again, okay?"

She lets out a low moan as she puts the last plate in the sink.

"Okay." She whispers, and I turn her to face me, pushing my mouth against hers. "Graham..."

"Upstairs, *now*," I command. Liza quickly turns for the steps, taking them two at a time.

I need more control, and I need to show her that I have to have her trust in the bedroom.

She stands by the bed, her long, beautiful brown hair flowing just below her shoulders. She has that fucking stare again, practically starving for me. Starving for my touch.

"Take off your clothes." I circle her, watching as she desperately tries to control her erratic breathing. She's nervous, but she does as I say. Underneath her clothes is the sexy lingerie I bought her earlier.

"Do you trust me?"

"Ye– Yes, I trust you," she speaks softly, almost in a whisper.

"Good, we're going to try something. I'm going to tell you what to do, and you're going to do it. You understand?" She nods, and I shake my head at her.

"Words."

"Yes, yes, I understand."

"I'm going to strap you to the bed with your wrists above your head, and you're not going to move. Understand?" I command as I look straight into her beautiful brown eyes.

"What?"

"You heard me."

I take her to the bed and lay her down, securing her arms above her head. Her gaze bounces back and forth between her arms and me.

"Don't be nervous; you'll like it." I spread her legs quickly, lingering above her pussy. I unbutton the two buttons attached to the delicate panties and circle my finger around her pussy, gathering her wetness. I take two fingers and insert them inside of her slowly. She tenses, pulling her arms from the bed and letting out a sigh of pleasure.

"I told you not to move."

I stick another finger in her, milking her. Her desperate pleas and heavy breaths are music to my ears. I quickly replace my fingers with my mouth, shoving my tongue in and out of her.

"Graham, please. I want to touch you," she whimpers. I continue to devour her, watching as she comes while trying to keep herself still.

I sheath myself quickly and prepare to sink myself inside her. I need to be inside of her just as much as she wants me inside. Spreading her legs wider, I plunge into her hard, causing her to scream out.

"You're mine, angel."

"Yours!" she gasps.

"Clench your pussy, angel. Make it suffocate my cock." She tenses around my cock, and I pull out and quickly slap the folds of her pussy. She screams, her back arching. When she starts to come a second time, I force myself back into her, the force causing her air supply to cut off as I rip through her pussy.

"I'm...I'm going to come." Thank god; usually, my stamina is unmatched, but fuck these last two days, it's been the polar opposite.

"Good. Give it to me."

"Oh, Graham. Yes, baby," she moans breathlessly. I grunt as I come shortly after her.

She catches her breath while I untie her from the bed. Her wrists are red and raw. I kiss each of her wrists, and she cuddles up next to me.

"I like the marks."

Holy. Shit. This woman is perfect.

17

Liza

The next day goes by in a blur. We stay in for the morning and have breakfast, cuddling up to each other before we have to leave. I think back to the things that took place over this weekend and, of course, last night. He's only given me a glimpse of his dominant side, and I want more. He asked me if I trusted him, and I froze, aware that he would show me a more demanding side of him. I never knew that being tied to your bed, legs spread, and teased could make you so crazy. I rub over the marks that are now left on my wrists. I know I shocked him when I said I liked the marks, and I wasn't lying because, for some reason, I do. I like looking down and knowing he's the reason they mark my skin. I adjust in the seat, realizing how hot I've gotten by thinking of the night before.

Graham's phone rings, snapping me out of my trance. I accidentally grip his hand tighter as it rests firmly on my thigh. He looks at me with a furrowed brow.

"You alright?"

"Yes, sorry." I look out the window, intertwining our fingers. He brings my hand up to his mouth and gently kisses it before hitting the steering wheel's talk button.

"Salando."

I wonder how it feels to be so young and powerful. I know that he is older than me, but it has never dawned on me that I don't know his exact age. There is no way he is my age; no man my age can fuck like that at 23. I tilt my head against the window and watch him bark commands smoothly to his assistant on the other end.

"Move my meetings from today to tomorrow. I don't plan on coming in, if it's emergent, call Andrew first. If he needs me, he'll call me."

"And what about the phone call with the New York office?"

"Ang, unless the building is on fucking fire, no one bothers me today. Andrew can manage the call."

"You've never taken a day off, let alone a week from work. Is everything okay?"

"You've badgered me to enjoy my life. That's what I'm doing. Goodbye, Angie." He ends the call and catches my eye.

"What is it?"

"I've just never seen you in action; it's sexy. Who's Angie?"

"My secretary"

I shrug my shoulders and lean over, kissing his cheek, and I whisper in his ear, "I like hearing you tell people what to do; I like it when you tell me what to do." He grins and looks back at the road.

"You know what I just realized?"

"Hmm?"

"I know everything else about you, but I don't know your age or birthday."

"I'm 25. I'm not telling you my birthday because you'll want to celebrate it."

"So does that mean it's soon?"

"Not telling you."

"Whatever, that's a battle I'll fight later. Well, I'm—you already know this about me, huh?

He winks at me when I shake my head. My phone chirps, and I pick it up, receiving a text from my mother.

Mama*: Hi, sweetheart, I haven't heard from you. Everything okay?*

That's my mom; she's always worried about me. I love my mom, but she sometimes needs to focus on her own life. Ever since the incident, she has hovered over my every move. My stepdad is a wealthy business owner in Seattle and owns some businesses in New York and California, so he is usually busy. But he's always available for her; they go on trips or important publicized events. It's just the times that he is away that she hovers even more. I let out a sigh that I wasn't aware I was holding, and Graham glances at me.

"Who is that?"

"My mom. I should call her. She's not used to not hearing from me for more than three days."

I pick up the phone and put it to my ear, waiting for my mom to answer.

Should I tell her about Graham? Maybe not such a good idea; I'll wait.

"Hi, honey! Where have you been?"

"Hi mama, I'm sorry I've been, um, busy."

He whispers, "That you have been."

I smack his leg and put my finger to my mouth, telling him to stay quiet.

"How is school? Not much longer before my sweet girl graduates and is all grown up."

"School is fine, Mom; I'm not there much. I only have classes on Thursdays, remember?"

"Of course, I remember. Oh, honey, I found you a nice apartment; you should not be living in that tiny loft." she says silently. There she goes, over the top and high-maintenance.

"Mom, I've already started looking for apartments; you don't have to find me one."

"Well, honey, I'm sorry, but I've already signed everything for you! Your movers will be there tomorrow to move you in. I've had the place decorated and-"

I cut in, raising my voice.

"Mom! Stop it. Tell me you did not do that. I appreciate the gesture, but I can find and fund my own apartment."

I realize how harsh and ungrateful I sound, so I take a deep breath. She's silent on the other end. "I'm sorry, Mom; I didn't mean to yell. I just wish you had talked to me first. Text me the address, and I'll stop by and look at it. I don't need movers; my friends can help me move." When she starts to speak again, I can hear her lighten up.

"That's great, honey! I should have asked you. I'm sorry, but Brantley and I just wanted to reward you for your hard work. I'll text the address right now. I love you, honey. Call me when you get there."

"I love you too, Mom." I hang up and roll my eyes. Graham clutches my hand, bringing my attention to him.

"Why didn't you tell me you were looking at apartments? I could've helped you." I don't answer, reading my mom's text about the address and saying how excited she is.

Mama: *You'll love it! It's beautiful, and it has so much space! Let me know what you think. It's practically a brand-new building!*

"Because I just started looking and wasn't sure if it would just be me or if Emily was moving in, too."

"So? Where is it?" I show him the address, and he grins.

"What? You know the place?"

"Something like that."

"Oh, *fuck*, does an ex-girlfriend live there?"

"I don't have any ex-girlfriends, but no."

"Then how do you know the place? I thought it was relatively new."

"I own the place."

I shudder in my seat; he owns where I'll live. *Of course, he does; he's*

Graham fucking Salando. He owns half of Seattle.

18

Graham

I saw her face when I told her I owned the building she would live in. She had no idea I already knew she'd be moving there.

Usually, my assistant handles all of the details with new tenants in that building. However, when Brantley and Beth called and asked for a favor for their daughter, my assistant knew exactly who Liza was. She sent me an email confirming if it would be okay to give her the only apartment left, which just so happened to be on the floor of my office apartment. That floor is usually off-limits, but not anymore.

She stayed quiet the whole way to the apartment building. I park the car in front of the valet, he opens the door for me.

"Evening, sir." I nod at him, rounding the car to open Liza's door.

"You okay?"

"Just fine. Let's go see my new place."

She'll love the place. It's one of our best apartments; I'm unsure what she will do with the extra bedrooms. If Emily didn't move in with her, she would be in a three-bedroom apartment. If I'm completely honest, I didn't want her to stay anywhere other than with me. But I know it's too soon. We walk into the building, and her face settles. She looks around and smiles at the receptionist at the front desk.

"Alicia, this is Liza. She needs the keys to her place. Penthouse floor, apartment B." Alicia nods, "Right away, sir."

"How did you know what floor it was?" I ignore her question and take the key from Alicia, leading Liza to the elevator. I'm not telling her I know her parents in front of my receptionist; it won't go over well. She'll be pissed at me for keeping that a secret; and for not telling her that I knew her mom and stepdad planned to buy her a place here.

She walks into the elevator and glares at me. I hit the P on the pad and relax on the elevator wall. "Answer me, Graham. How did you know what floor and what apartment?"

"Because I own this building. I know everything," I say, closing in on her, my hand softly touching her cheek. In perfect timing to slow her questions down, the elevator opens, showing the penthouse floor. I lead her out of the elevator and show her to her door. "Open it," I exclaim.

"Leave it to my mom to get the most expensive apartment she can find." She quickly scans the room. "How can I be mad at her when she makes this place look as beautiful as she did? Damn it."

"Angel, there are worse things your mom and stepdad could do."

"You have a nice building, Salando."

"You have a nice apartment, Crambell." She looks around, checking out each room and the decorations her mom has put together. I watch her wander around her new place. She's excited, and I am thrilled for her as well. I've never stayed here; I only come here maybe once a week for an hour or two, give or take. This is just an extra business I took over about a year ago; my assistant mostly runs this entire thing.

"She does realize it's just me, right? Why would I need three rooms?" She sits on her couch, tucking her feet under her.

"Oooohh, this couch feels good." She pats the seat so I can sit next to her. I plop down and wrap my arms around her. She pushes against my side.

"Do you like your new place?"

"Yes, I love it. I should call my mom and Brantley and thank them."

"You should, but it'll have to wait. I have something to show you." I grab her hand and direct her down the hall to office space. She stops in front of the door and looks at me in confusion.

"What's this?"

"This is where I work when I'm here." I open the door, and she walks in. I study her to see what she's thinking, and her face is blank.

"Graham..." She turns to me, wrapping her arms around my waist.

"Angel."

"I need to know the truth." She wraps me tighter. I look down at her, raising my eyebrows. I knew she would ask again eventually. I knew she wouldn't let it go.

"How did you know which apartment it was? And why weren't you surprised when I gave you the address? It was like you knew. You knew, didn't you?"

"You—" She pulls away from me and cuts off my words.

"Tell me now; tell me how you knew." She's furious, pissed off, and really fucking angry with me. She turns on her heels and heads for the door, her signature fucking move when I don't answer her.

"Don't walk away from me," I bark, walking after her. The same thing happens every time: I chase after her whenever she walks or, worse, runs away. She keeps walking and reaches the knob of the door, and I slam it shut just as quickly as she opens it.

"I know your parents. Well, your stepfather. I know Brantley."

"How do you know him? Does he know about us?" She barks, anger breathing through her voice.

"No, he doesn't know about us. And I didn't know he was your stepfather until I did your background check and saw his name." Tears well up in her eyes. Fuck, she's going to cry.

"You've known who I was for at least two months; you said you got that file on me the moment you met me. That was two fucking months ago, Graham." I grab her hands, and she yanks them away from me. "No, you told me about everything besides that. How is that *not* important? Tell me."

I open my mouth to explain, but she interrupts me. "You know what? I don't want to be around you; I don't want to look at you." She turns and grabs the door handle again; this time, I move in front of the door. It's my fault; she's right. I should've told her that night that I knew her stepfather and often collaborated with him on business plans. I should have told her everything; instead, I lied to her face.

"Please. Stop and let me explain."

"There's nothing to explain. I told you trust is important to me. You should have told me. You know how important my personal life is to me. What were you going to do when I introduced you to them? Pretend you didn't..." I silence her, placing my mouth on hers. I violently kiss her; it's the only way I know how to communicate with her when she's like this. She doesn't immediately open for me, so I bite her lip, causing her to open her mouth.

"I'm sorry, Elizabeth. I should have told you, but don't ever try to run out on me." A tear slides down her face, and she puts her head down. "Don't cry. Please. I'm sorry. It's my fault; I never should've kept it from you. I didn't think it would be a big deal." She sinks into my arms.

I walk her to the couch against the wall in my office and sit her on my lap, running my fingers through her hair. I wipe the tears from her face as she looks up at me and bites her lip.

"I overreacted; I'm sorry."

"And I'm a dick and should've told you."

She sits up, facing me. "I have to tell you something." She bites the inside of her cheek, staring everywhere but at me.

"I didn't just leave UCLA because I didn't like it. I left because of an incident, and California reminded me too much of it.

"What kind of incident?"

"I umm... I had a stalker in high school and college. His name was Tim, and we were pretty good friends throughout high school. But in college, it got bad. He did things to me." Her eyes water, but she pushes through. "Brantley had to pay him off, and he took off. This is why I need to know everything you know about me. I need to know that you know my parents. I need to know."

"This stalker? Where is he now? Why wouldn't you tell me this?"

"He's gone. I am just paranoid. The incident happened this time last year; now, I'm always on edge. Brantley paid him a million dollars to leave me alone and never show his face again. He took the money and left. Since then, I haven't heard from or seen him. I still feel like someone is watching me sometimes. Lately, I feel like I've been seeing him. Like I'm being watched, which is why I freaked about the paparazzi guy."

"I'll always protect you; mark my words if he ever shows his face again- I'll fucking kill him."

No one touches what's mine, threatens what's mine, and lives to tell about it. He got lucky once; there won't be a second time.

19

Liza

I nuzzle into Graham's arms, settling myself down. I told him about my past—the past that my stepfather and mother worked so hard to help me through. I should have known he knew my stepfather; I have been photographed with him and my mom a few times. It bothered me that Graham kept this secret from me, but who was I kidding, trying to walk away from him for a second time? He wouldn't let me go, and I didn't want him to.

"Stay with me tonight. I have to go into the office tomorrow for a few hours, but..." I put my finger to his lips.

"You don't have to convince me, you know?"

"Let's grab you some clothes." We abandon his couch and head to campus.

When I get to my room, I'm not surprised it's empty. I throw some clothes in my bag and reach for my phone to text Em.

Liza: Hey Em, staying with Graham tonight... Oh, mom found me an apartment. It's so nice, and I can't be pissed at her for getting me one without me knowing.

Em: Bummer, who am I gonna binge with? So happy for you. Call me later.

Liza: *Well, I hope you'll come over and binge with me at my place!*
Em: *Oh, count on it, bitch! ;)*

It's starting to feel like second nature to stay with Graham. We quickly fell into a routine, with me showering and him preparing for tomorrow's work meetings. After we had dinner, somehow, I mustered up enough strength to have sex again before falling into a deep sleep. My body was sore and exhausted from everything I'd been putting it through. Graham cared for me afterward, but I still needed the sleep.

I wake up to an empty bed and a note from Graham.

Be back in a few hours; I scheduled a massage for you at 12 p.m. Behave, angel mine. -G

I check my phone and see that it is 7:45 a.m. I have my doctor's appointment for birth control at 9 a.m. After I shower and get dressed, I step outside the house and see Ellis waiting for me.

"Ms. Crambell."

"Please, just call me Liza. I can drive myself to the doctor. I'm sure you have other things to do." Graham had my car driven here last night for me, and I didn't know how I'd feel about a driver. I hadn't had one since I moved out of my mom's house.

"I'll drive you."

"Oh...Okay, well, thank you."

"Pleasure."

Once in the car, I look for Em's contact on my phone and hit call. It only rings once before she answers.

"About time you called me."

"Shut up; do you wanna hear about my crazy life or not?"

"I'm listening."

"Okay, so we went to his lake house, which was completely breathtaking. We shopped a little and had some nice dinners. It was perfect."

"You lucky bitch." I giggle at her and brace myself for what I'm about to tell her next.

"Oh...and he asked me to be his girlfriend."

"What?!" Her voice goes up an octave. "That was quick... He must think you're really special."

"I guess so. I know it's quick, and you probably think I'm crazy for saying yes."

"Not at all; Travis and I only knew each other for about a week. I'm so happy for you. But if he hurts you, I'll kill him."

"I know; I'll let you get the first hit. He also apparently knows my family. Although, he kept that a secret from me, and that ended in me completely losing my shit."

"Seriously?"

"Oh, and get this... he owns the fucking building I live in now. He knew I was moving in before I even knew."

"Liza...that's fucking intense."

"Yeah, well, he's pretty intense. I told him about Tim."

"I'm sure he wanted to claw his skin off."

"He said that he'd kill him if he ever showed his face." That makes her laugh, and I laugh with her.

"Fucking ruthless! I love it but tell him he'll have to get in line for that. You were my girl first."

"I don't think he'll care about that for some reason. He's a bit, um..."

"Possessive? Crazy?"

"Shut up, Travis is that way too."

"Ditto."

"Listen, I'm at the doctor; call you later."

"Yup. Love you!"

"Love you, bye."

My appointment went by quickly and easily; she told me to refrain from unprotected sex for a week. Graham will most definitely be *happy* about that.

When I return to Graham's house, I quickly change into yoga pants and a T-shirt. I stretch out on the couch, closing my eyes for a nap before my massage. My body is seriously playing catch-up. I toss and turn before giving up and grabbing my phone.

Liza: *Your antics are destroying my body.*

Graham: *I told you I wasn't gentle. I'm in a meeting, see you soon.*

The doorbell rings, and I slide the phone into the side of my pants as I open the door. "Ms. Crambell?"

"Yes, that's me. Call me Liza."

"My name is Zelda; I'm going to do your massage for you. I need a few minutes to set up, and then I'll be all set. If you want, you can go ahead and undress to your level of comfort." She takes her equipment to the accessible area in the living room.

I remove my clothes, leaving my panties on as I shyly hold my boobs in my hands.

"All set?"

"Yes, Ms. Crambell, if you could lay here." I stretch out over the massage bed, putting my face through the hole.

She puts a sheet over the bottom half of my body, covering it as she works on my shoulders. I lay down and drift in and out of consciousness as Zelda massages my shoulders and back. I relax and settle into the massage, and before I know it, I drift off into a light sleep.

I shift lightly as I feel the hands on my back are different. They are no longer small, tender hands; they are large, calloused but soft. I know these hands, the way they touch me, the way they nurture my body, and how they worship it.

"Turn over, pretty girl."

"Hi, baby." The look on his face takes me by surprise. He is wearing a navy blue suit with a charcoal gray tie. He is even sexier in a suit. This is something I could get used to.

"Mmm, I like business, Graham." He massages my front shoulders.

"Hush, you're supposed to relax; now close your eyes." I close my eyes as he massages me.

"You have such a beautiful body," he whispers in my ear, and my eyes flutter back open. "I told you to keep your eyes closed and to relax."

"How am I supposed to do that when you're talking to me?"

My eyes close, and I struggle not to look at him. He pushes the sheet back, revealing my breasts, and when the air hits me, I shiver. I inhale, holding my breath when he lifts my breast into his mouth.

"No teasing, Graham, please."

"Hush," he orders, trailing his fingers down to my pussy. My hand shoots out around his wrist as he inserts his fingers inside me, groaning in my ear. He slides his fingers in and out of me, making me come on his fingers in an embarrassingly short time; he sticks his fingers in my mouth, and I suck.

He lifts me from the massage table, and I encircle my legs around his torso. Our tongues begin to fight to gain dominance.

"You make me crazy, so fucking crazy, Elizabeth."

"Good."

He takes me upstairs, carrying me with such ease. He kicks his door shut with his foot and throws me onto the bed.

When he loosens his tie, and his stare turns dark, I know I'm in for it. I should be scared and nervous, but I'm not. I'm in awe of how he moves and how it makes my body feel. My lips will be bruised tomorrow from how hard I bite them as I watch him move towards me.

"What did I tell you about biting your lip? Do you like turning me on? Making me crazy?" I nod in response, and he smirks. "Bad girl. Now you are going to get punished."

Finally, my body craves his punishment.

"Yes, please. I think I'd like that," I say quietly. He wraps his tie around my eyes, blindfolding me. I can feel my pulse becoming tachycardic.

What is he going to do? It honestly doesn't matter. I want to show him that he can fuck me the way he needs to; my body is his to do whatever he wants.

"Lie back." Not being able to see him excites me when it should scare me. I know Graham won't hurt me, and after the night at the lake house, I've learned that he knows my body better than I do. He knows what I'll like and what I'll get pleasure from. I tell myself to relax, and then I feel the pressure of his hand on my pussy. Something cold pushes into me; it vibrates and sends my body into shivers of pleasure.

"What is that?"

"Relax, you'll see soon enough." I wiggle under him, the pressure between my legs building. "Turn over."

I flip myself over and let out a moan, the feeling between my legs getting more intense and vibrating faster. Graham then kisses my back and whispers, "Does it feel good?"

"Yes...yes... It feels good."

"Good, I'm going to spank you, and you'll like that too." My eyes probably double in size when I process what he says, my mouth to protest when Graham's hand firmly lands on my ass. I jump, and with the combination of the smack and the vibration in my pussy I think I might explode. Graham's hand comes down again, this time harder. I whimper, wiggling my body and pushing my face into the bed.

"Two more of these; you're turning red for me." I bite into the bed sheets, waiting for my last two strikes. I didn't think I'd enjoy this. I thought it would hurt. Being spanked is a cruel punishment, right? Wrong. I love it. I love every blow to my ass; it makes my body pulsate, and I want more. How can I enjoy pain? How can pain lead to pleasure? I'll never understand it.

When I hear him take a deep breath, I know he's enjoying this, too. He's itching for that release, and having control of my body is exactly what he craves.

He smacks my ass harder, gripping my ass with the last blow.

"On your knees and hands, now."

I try to move, but the vibration between my legs kicks up a notch, causing me to sink back into the bed. He pulls me up on my hands and knees. I feel his hands inside of me, and then suddenly, the vibration is gone. He took it out; whatever the object was, it caused me so much intensity between my thighs. I whimper at the sensation of it leaving my body, not having much time to miss the feeling before it's replaced with Graham's cock plunging into me.

He fucks me with hard, deep thrusts.

"You're always so wet for me." *Thrust. Thrust. Thrust.* I reach for him, and he slams my hands down, pushing my face deeper into the bed. "Don't" *Thrust.* "Move" *Thrust.* "Do you understand?"

I bite my lip and whimper, "Yes, yes, I understand." I need to touch him; I need to see him.

He violently flips my body to him, encircling my legs around him, and moves in and out of me with so much force. The slapping sound of our flesh hitting each other is louder than my moans. I cry out his name, my body filling with pleasure. He kisses my neck, and I practically scream.

"I'm going to come."

"Good, I want to feel that pussy tighten around me." My body shakes, releasing everything built up inside of me. He loves teasing me, and I love the outcome of finally getting what I need from him. I feel his cock pushing deeper into me.

"I'm going to fuck this little pussy anyway I want; you feel so fucking good." He puts my arms around his neck, and I bury my face against it and place soft kisses up and down.

"Fuck. Fuuuck, I'm going to come." I feel his body jerking, and he stops for a moment before thrusting a few more long pumps. His breathing quickens as he pulls me closer to him. He takes his tie off my eyes and looks at me.

"Okay?" My eyes adjust to the light, and I look him right in the eyes and nod. I am more than okay.

"Angel..."

"Yes, I'm okay. What was that? In my... what did you put inside of me?" He points to a pair of balls on the bed's side table. "What are those?"

"Ben Wa balls, did you like it?"

"Ben, what?" He silences me, giving me a soft kiss.

"Go shower; I have a phone meeting in a few minutes." When he stands, I notice he's naked; I'm instantly annoyed that I missed him stripping. I love watching Graham get naked. He disposes of the condom, puts on a t-shirt and a pair of gray sweats, and trails down the hall to his office.

I get up and climb in the shower, taking my time to wash my hair.

I start thinking about my upcoming assignments that are due soon, and I smile at the thought that my mom is right; after this semester, I'll graduate and jump into my career. I hope that I'll be able to land a job quickly. I worked so hard throughout college, ensuring I got the best internships and training. It's hard to become a well-known psychiatrist, but it is something I plan to do.

20

Graham

Amid me barking orders to my staff, I see the door creeping open. She peeks her head around the door, and I wave her in.

"Andrew, what am I paying you for if you're not going to listen to the shit I tell you to do? We've hosted it for the last fifteen years, and I'll be damned if we miss it the first year my father leaves the company."

I watch Liza as she glances around, stopping before the bookshelf and looking through the books. I continue with my conversation.

"G, all I'm saying is that if you're going to trust anyone with security, it should be me. Not some fucking idiot you found online. This is the biggest fucking event of the year. If something happens, your father will blame *you*, and you *know* that. And if you're letting someone else do it, then you might as well cancel it because it'll be a shit show."

Andrew is one of my closest friends; he always keeps it straight with me and does his job. I never have to question him or his work ethic, which is important to me. I've had my fair share of "friends" who never really had my back; they just wanted to be able to say they were friends with a fucking billionaire.

I run my fingers through my hair, grinding my teeth.

"Fuck sake. Don't make me tell you things you already know." He says, annoyed.

Liza walks over to me and kisses my cheek. I pat my lap, and she practically jumps on me with excitement. She leans back into me and traces her fingers over the tattoo on my wrist. "Andrew, look, I don't give a shit who runs security; just double it. Many important people will be there, and you know what happened during the last event."

Liza looks up at me and mouths, "What happened at the last event?" I read her lips and kiss her forehead.

She looks at me and frowns. What is going through her mind? Is she feeling neglected? I've only been on the phone for thirty minutes; I thought she'd want to shower after the fuck I gave her. I blindfolded her, expecting her to stop me, but she didn't; she gave me her body.

She stands up and pushes my chair back. I mute the phone.

"What are you doing?"

"Don't mind me; you won't even know I'm here. Continue your call, Salando." I narrow my eyes at her in question. She drops to her knees and tugs on my sweats, my cock springing free. She is not going to suck me off while I am on a fucking *work call*, is she? She looks up at me as she places her mouth on my cock, only taking half of me in. I lick my lips and watch as she bobs her head up and down on my cock, collecting her saliva each time. I let out a low groan; damn, she's good at this.

"Graham, Graham, dude, fucking answer me." Shit, Andrew. "*What?*"

"So, does that work?"

"Does what work?" I answer, never taking my eyes off of Liza.

"I'll double security and designate paparazzi to one area instead of them everywhere like last year."

I grab her head and push deeper into her mouth, fisting her hair in my hand. She sucks me in faster and harder, toying with my sack in her hands. I lean my head back as she deep-throats my cock.

"Fuck...yeah, um, perfect, that works." I have to get off this fucking call; there is no way I'll be able to come with Andrew's fucking voice in my ear.

"What the fuck are you doing right now?"

"Andrew, get the fuck on with what you're saying."

He chuckles and hesitates.

"You need anything else from me? I'd hate to get in the way of whatever the fuck you have going on right now?

"No. I'll see you in the office tomorrow." I hang up and yank Liza into my lap, and she giggles.

"You think that's funny?"

"You didn't seem to be bothered by it... and besides, I wasn't finished."

I raise an eyebrow, pushing her up. I gesture with my hands at my cock, and she slips her lip in her mouth.

"Then finish." She sinks to her knees, pulling my cock into her mouth. This time, with so much force, I nearly come the moment her mouth touches my cock. I fist her hair in my hand and maneuver her head up and down, pushing her down to the shaft of my cock. She takes all of it—every inch of me in her mouth. My body tenses as she quickens her pace.

"That's right, be a good girl and make me come." When those brown eyes look up at me, I explode in her mouth. She takes every drop of me, swallowing it all, making sure she doesn't miss a drop. She leans back on her heels and runs her tongue over her bottom lip.

"Now I'm finished."

"Stand up."

She stumbles as she stands. "I think it'd be selfish of me not to take care of you, don't you think?" I place one hand on her hip, steadying her while I slip the other down her sweatpants. I notice that she has one of my sweatpants and T-shirts on.

"Hmm."

I take my hand and rub her clit, replacing it with my finger. She leans into my hand, never taking her eyes off me. Her beautiful hair sprawls over her back. She wraps one of her hands around my neck and moves her pussy with my fingers. They move faster and harder inside her until she wraps both of her arms around my neck and sinks further onto my fingers. Her body shudders, and she cries out. She comes in a sudden rush, clawing my neck. "Fuck, angel. You're so beautiful when you come."

She presses her forehead against mine and tries to catch her breath. I rub my hand up and down her back.

My feelings for her intensify in this moment. Holding her feels right; she feels like she's meant to be mine. How is it that I feel like I have known her for longer than a two months? How is it that I feel like I couldn't live my life without her? The sound of her stomach growling snaps me out of my inner thoughts. I raise my eyebrows, and she giggles.

"Hungry?"

"Starving." I rest my head on hers. "Do you want to go get some lunch?" She snuggles deeper into my chest.

"Can we order in? I don't want to go anywhere. I have a few assignments to do." I have some work things to deal with and assignments due myself. We'll be graduating soon, and balancing school and running a company has been taking its toll on me. Adding Liza to the mix has me forgetting my duties and responsibilities.

"Chinese?"

"Yes, please."

"Go do your homework. I'll order us some stuff, and I'll be down after a shower."

I call our local Chinese restaurant and order beef with broccoli, shrimp with broccoli, chow mein, and two shrimp egg rolls. I walk down the hall and into my room; it's clean—way cleaner than it was. She cleaned up, and that, for some reason, makes me smile. I enjoy having her here, and if it were up to me, she'd never get to leave here. After graduation, I'm unsure of her plans, but I hope they include me. She may not know it now, but she'll be here whether she wants to or not. If I have to tie her to the bedpost and lock her in my room so that she'll never leave, then I will.

I shower quickly and throw on a gym shirt and running shorts. I retrieve my laptop and phone and head downstairs. She's stretched out on the couch with her laptop resting on her legs.

"Hi, baby." She greets softly as I sit by her. I pick her feet up and set them on my thighs. "Food should be here in twenty minutes. I'm sure I ordered enough for all of your cravings."

"Yeah, right. You love it as much as I do." She goes back to her assignment, eyeing me over the top of her screen.

I look over my assignments for the next few weeks. The only way I can balance work and school is by getting ahead. Even though I'm a large shareholder at the college we attend, I still like to do the work and earn the grades I receive. I'm sure every professor would pass me even if I didn't do the work, but my work ethic is vital to me, and I need that to show in everything I do.

"What are you working on?" She asks, staring up at me. "Work?"

"No, I'm finishing my last assignment. What are *you* working on?"

"Same; it's surreal that we only have a few months left of school." I hit submit on my last assignment and move my laptop. I pick her foot up and begin to massage it.

"You know we have to go to your apartment at some point today, right? I sent movers over this morning, and you're all moved in." I say to her, continuing to massage her foot.

"You didn't have to do that; I didn't need movers, but thank you. Can we go later? I'm almost done with my last assignment." I acknowledge her, and the doorbell rings. I get up and walk over, looking through the peephole. A guy is standing there with a big brown bag.

"Salando?"

"Thank you." I grab the food and tip him, shutting the door in time to hear Liza in complete bliss.

"Finished, thank God." She stands up and walks over to me, sniffing the bag. She snatches it from my hands and returns to the couch.

"I am starved."

"Well, eat up. You'll need your energy, pretty girl." She tucks her bottom lip into her mouth, and I quirk my eyebrow at her.

"You're incredibly hard to satisfy."

"Are you complaining?" She stuffs an egg roll into her mouth, her smile grim.

"Not in the least."

"Good girl."

We finish the food, and I pull Liza into the cusp of my arm. She yawns and tucks her face into my chest. I mindlessly tangle my hands in her hair as she drifts to sleep.

My phone buzzes.

"Salando." It's my assistant, Angela.

"Graham," her voice cracking; something was wrong, I can tell. I straighten, accidentally waking Liza up. She rubs her eyes and sits up. "What is it, Ang? What happened?"

"Your mom, she's been in an accident."

"How bad is it? Will she be okay?"

"She's in the hospital; they said they don't know much yet, but she should pull through." I stand up, and Liza looks at me, mouthing, "Everything okay" to me. I turn my back to her.

"I'll be there as soon as I can." I hang up and head for the stairs. It's a three-hour drive to my parents' house, but there is no way I'd not be there for my mom. She drives me crazy and hovers, always wanting me to call and see her more. But I love her; I owe her everything.

"Graham," I don't answer her; I keep walking up the stairs.

"Graham! What's going on?" She grabs my arm, and I yank it away. "Answer me!" I stop and turn to her, my eyes red and watery. "Baby, tell me what's wrong. What'd your assistant say?"

"My mom was in an accident; I gotta get to her." She wraps her arms around me, and I stand there with a blank look on my face. I'm not used to people comforting me, but I still manage to wrap my arms around her.

"I'm sorry; I'm sure she'll be okay."

"I know you have to go to your apartment; I can drop you off on the way there." I walk away and start packing a bag.

Please be okay.

21

Liza

Drop me off on the way there? How could I tell him I wanted to stay and be there for him? Maybe he didn't want me to meet his family yet. I mean, it had only been two months since he'd known me. *This isn't about you.* Fuck my conscience for being right once again. This wasn't about me. I gathered my things, quickly changed into jeans, a T-shirt, and booties, and walked downstairs, waiting for Graham.

"Do you have everything?" he asks me, grabbing the keys off the counter. Graham had changed into a casual V-neck shirt with jeans and a pair of black chukka boots. I bow my head, and we walk to the SUV. Ellis is standing there, waiting for us with the door open. I smile at him.

"Ellis."

"Ms. Crambell." I glare at him in annoyance and climb into the SUV. I told him to call me Liza, but of course, always professional, and he hasn't deviated from that plan. He pats Graham on the back. "She'll be alright; I'll get you there." Graham clenches his jaw and nods, sliding into the seat beside me. He picks up his phone, and his fingers start moving rapidly. I look out the window and wonder what to say to him. He seems so distraught; I understand it; it's his mother, and he has no idea what is happening. His phone rings, and he answers quickly.

"How is she? What happened?" There's chatter on the other end of the phone before he responds. His jaw clenches, and he tightens his hand around the phone.

"I'll be there in 3 hours... Love you too," he says, ending the call. I reach for his hand, and he takes it, looking at me and managing to crack a small smile.

"How is she?" I ask softly.

"Still unsure."

"What happened?"

"Some asshole ran a red light and slammed right into her." He tells me, looking out the window. I bring his hand to mine and kiss it, whispering.

"She'll be okay."

Before I know it, we reach my new apartment building. I unbuckle my seat belt and grab my things. Ellis opens my door, and I slide out. Graham gets out and stands at the door, waiting for me. I walk over to him and kiss him on the cheek.

"You don't need to walk me up. I'm okay. Keep me updated on your mom. I'm here if you need me." His brows furrow as he looks down at me in confusion.

"What are you talking about?" I look up at him.

"I know you're going to take my bags from me and walk me up to my door, but you don't need to do that. Get to your mom; that's more important."

"Elizabeth, you're coming with me. You're only here to get clothes. What did you think was happening?"

"I thought you were dropping me off, I thought—" he cuts me off.

"You thought I was going without you? I'll need you there. I need you more than anything right now."

He *needed* me there. I hadn't expected that. I smile and hug him.

"Give me five minutes, and I'll be down."

"I'm coming with you."

"Graham, really, I just have to grab a few things. It won't take me long." He ignores me, grabs my hand, and leads me into the building.

I took what I needed from my new apartment, noticing that the movers had put everything away for me. Trying to find everything I needed was confusing, but I'd learn where everything was when I got back. Graham sits on the couch, waiting for me.

"Okay, all done." He stands up and takes the bag from me.

"Got enough to last until Thursday?"

"Mhm!"

"Angel, why did you think I didn't want you to come?" I look up at him and put my head down. He tilts my face back up to face him. "Answer me."

"I thought you… um, that you didn't want me to meet your family."

"Of course, I want you to meet my family. I just had to get everything straightened out and tell them it wouldn't just be me." I give him a reassuring smile, and he places my bag down and cups my face.

"I need you, and I'll always need you. You not coming was never an option for me." I faintly smile.

"I'm sorry. I shouldn't have assumed the worst. I tend to get in my own head sometimes." He kisses me, grabs my bag and hand, and leads me back to the SUV.

3 hours later…

When we arrive at the hospital, Graham tightens his grip on my hand and inhales a deep breath.

"It'll be okay, baby. I'm here, and she'll be fine." He exhales and opens his door. Ellis opens mine and gives me what I think is a smirk.

"You're good for him, you know?" I quickly hug Ellis, taking him by surprise.

"Thank you; so are you," I murmur. I run to Graham's side, taking his hand. He looks down at me.

"What was that?"

"Just thanking him for taking care of you." He grins, and we walk into the hospital.

We walk to the front desk, and Graham gives the clerk his mother's information.

"Madeline Salando, can you tell me where she is? She's my mother." She types quickly on her computer before responding.

"Third floor, Mr. Salando. The elevators are right around the corner." She points to the sign, and we follow it until we reach the elevators.

Once we get to the third floor, we follow the signs to the waiting room, and a younger girl runs towards us. She looks about eighteen, no more than twenty years old. Graham drops my hand and opens his arms as the girl runs into them. She cries, and he hugs her tighter. She releases him, and he wipes the tears from her eyes.

"Selle, what's going on?"

Selle? That's his sister; she is fucking gorgeous. What is it with this family? Do you have to be flawless to be a part of it? Fuck's sake. She looks about 5'8 tall with long hair and beautiful eyes.

"I thought you weren't coming," she cries, and he rubs her cheek.

"Of course, I'd come." She wipes her face and smiles. It's small but still makes Graham happy; he directs her to face me. "I want you to meet someone." She turns to face me, wiping the last tear from her face. "This is Elizabeth, my girlfriend. Angel, this is my sister, Giselle."

She walks closer to me and smiles, hugging me instantly. "Hi! You're beautiful!"

"Oh, um, thank you. It's nice to meet you. I hope your mom is okay," I say back to her.

"She's tough; it's where we all get it from," she states, winking at

Graham.

"Here, let's introduce you to everyone." She grabs my hand and takes me over to a group of people sitting in the waiting room. I turn and look at Graham. He stands there with his hands in his pockets and raises his eyebrows with a grim smile.

"This is our dad, Joe." She points me toward a tall man with dark hair and chestnut-brown eyes. He stands and extends his hand to me.

"Joe Salando. It's a pleasure to meet you, Ms..."

"Crambell, Elizabeth Crambell."

"You're Brantley's daughter. I've heard a lot about you over the years. It's so nice to put a face to the name." He puts my hand up to his mouth, kissing it.

"That's enough, Dad; give her her hand back." Graham cuts in, putting his hand around my waist. Joe chuckles and releases my hand.

"So, you finally picked a worthy one. Good for you, son." Graham's jaw tightens, and he moves past his dad, introducing me to Angela, his assistant, and her husband.

"This is Angie and her husband." She gets up and hugs me. Goddamn it, is everyone here, huggers?

"So nice to meet you. This is my husband, Cal." I shake his hand, turning when I see the doctor walking out.

He's speaking with Graham, Giselle, and Joe, giving what I presume is an update.

Angela comes and sits by me and pats my lap.

"I don't know what you've done to this one, but he's crazy about you." She's staring at Graham.

"Really?" I said softly, "I hope so."

I still had no clue what he was doing to me. I felt like I couldn't breathe when he wasn't near, and I nearly broke down when I thought he didn't want me to come with him here. Knowing the feelings are mutual would be a plus.

"It seems you are, too; he's a good one, sweetheart. Don't let him push you away. Trust me, he'll try."

I look at her and remember how closed off he was on our weekend trip, and I know she is right. He would try to push me away, but I wouldn't let him. I knew we belonged together, but I could also tell it wouldn't be easy. I give her hand a reassuring squeeze.

Our heads both turn quickly when we hear shouting.

"You're a piece of a shit." Graham spits out in his father's face. Giselle is in the middle with her palms on both men's chests, pushing them apart.

"Dad, G, not here, please," she pleads, looking back and forth between the two firm men.

"Listen to your sister; you have *company*. I don't think you want to run this one off like you did the other one." Graham clenches his fist, and I stand up. Angela grabs my arm and shakes her head at me.

"Don't," she pleads.

"She's not *company*; she's my fucking girlfriend. And she isn't going *anywhere*," he barks back.

"We both know that's what you're good at. She won't love you. Your mother didn't." Giselle gasps, yelling at her father and pushing him back.

"Why would you say that to him?" she sobs.

"You know it's true; your brother loves fucking thin—"

Before I know it, Graham's fist hits Joe directly in the nose. He's on his father in a heartbeat, and Giselle is on his backside, pleading with him to stop.

"Stop, get off! GRAHAM! " She yells, pulling on his shirt.

I try to go after him again, but a stronger hand takes hold of my arm this time. *Ellis.* I turn to him and plead.

"You have to stop him, Ellis."

"My job is to keep you where you are, Ms. Crambell. He will stop on his own." I try to pull away from Ellis, and his grip tightens. I see Graham plunge another fist into his father's face. I look back at Ellis with tears in my eyes.

"Please, he'll listen to me. Ellis, please." His face softens, and he releases my arm.

Giselle is still pulling on Graham; he turns and looks at her. "Selle. Fucking Move. *Now.*"

She moves, running directly into me.

"Please, stop him. You have to stop him." I turn, looking at Ellis. He reads my mind and grabs Selle.

I get to Graham just in time to catch his arm as it goes up for another swing. A nurse yells that she will call security if they don't stop. Graham turns to me, opening his mouth to scream at me, thinking I'm his sister.

"*Stop it.*" He has fire in his eyes; he's boiling with rage. His father's comment about his mother sent him over the edge. I pull him up from hovering over his father and make him face me. I take a glance at Joe and grimace at the sight of him. He'll need stitches. I'm sure Graham broke his nose, and he has a gash above his eye.

He sits up, holding his nose, and speaks through his blood.

"You better run while you can, girl; this one is tough to love."

Graham shrugs from my grasp, and I lunge myself in front of his dad.

"Graham, look at me." He raises his fist, ignoring my pleas. "Look at me!" I scream at him. I step forward when he finally looks at me. His dad mumbles words behind me, and I glance behind me.

"Joe, if you know what's good, you'll stop fucking speaking." I bark at him before turning back to Graham.

I enclose his face with my hands, blocking everyone and everything else out. His focus is solely on me, and when I see him take a deep breath, I know he's in the right head space to hear me.

"Remember why you are here; this would destroy your mother if she came out and saw this. Look at your sister." He looks at her and back at me; his eyes soften, and he relaxes his fist. He looks past me, directly into his father's eyes, and says, "You don't fucking talk to her."

He grabs me, and we walk off. He looks at his sister and says, "Get him a doctor; I broke his fucking nose." She wipes her tears away, peaking over his shoulder to get a view of her father.

"Call me when mom gets released." She throws herself into his arms. He rubs her hair and whispers, "I'm sorry, he just doesn't care about her." She sniffles.

"I know. I'll call you when she leaves." He lets her go and grabs my hand. We're almost out of the hospital when I hear my name.

"Liza! Wait." I turn around and see Selle waving me down. I look at Graham and push him forward.

"Go. I'll only be a second." I jog my way to her. "What's wrong?"

"I just wanted to talk to you, to thank you... No one has ever been able to stop him."

"Wait, this has happened before?"

"Yes, my dad is a dick, and Graham doesn't stand for it." I hug her, and she hugs me back.

She looks me over and speaks, "You're good for him, and he loves you. I can tell." I'm stunned at her words, but I try my best to hide my reaction as she goes back into the hospital. Did he love me? It'd only been a month, and I knew I loved him from the week at the lake house. How could I not love someone who constantly and undoubtedly made it his task to make me happy and keep me safe? I pull out my phone and shoot off a text to Em.

Liza: *My life is officially fucking nuts.*

Em: *Duh, bitch, that's what happens when you fall for a billionaire.*

I smile at her reply and close the message.

Ellis pulls the SUV up, and Graham and I get in. The drive to his place in Leavenworth took about twenty minutes. I had no idea that his family lived here. We were just here for the weekend at his lake house, and he didn't mention it. It was only maybe forty-five minutes away from where we were. The drive is entirely silent, with Graham looking out the window. I want to hold his hand, examine him for bruises, and make sure he's all right. I can't do that now; he looks angry, and I have to wait until he needs me. *He needs you now.*

I shake my head and glance over at him. The SUV comes to a stop, and he opens the door. I have never seen Graham angry, and while I hate that he's so upset, I can't help how his rage turns me on. I'm clearly fucking crazy. The way he handled his father at that hospital ignited something in me. My door flings open, and Graham pulls me out of the SUV.

"Graham, what are you—"

"No more questions, Elizabeth." Elizabeth? He was angry with me. Why?

"You're hurting me; let go of my arm right now." I back away from his grip, and he glares at me.

"Go inside; I need to talk to Ellis." I stand there with my arms folded. Who the hell does he think he's talking to?

"Elizabeth, now. For fuck's sake, just do one thing I tell you to do." I roll my eyes as I storm into his house.

Graham's house is beautifully decorated, just like his other two. Damn, how many houses did this man have? I wander around the house, looking at old photos of him and his sister. He loves her so much; seeing them together at the hospital melted my heart. How gentle he was to her; how good of a big brother he was to her.

I walk up the steps, checking out each room. I land in the master, knowing this one is Graham's. Pulling my phone out, I kick my shoes off and sit on the floor. I call my mom.

"Hi, mama, the apartment is beautiful. Tell Brantley I say thank you."

"Oh, honey, we're glad you love it. You know your mama is always looking for an excuse to decorate. How are you?" I let out a sigh and tears well up in my eyes. I have to tell her.

"Sweetheart? Are you okay?"

"I'm okay, mom. I have to tell you something. I'm with someone, um, romantically." She pauses for a few moments and then finally speaks.

"Yeah? Who is he?"

"Graham...Graham Salando." There's another brief silence on the other end of the call. "Oh! He's such a catch. Good job, honey! Is he treating you right? Are you happy?"

"Yes, to all of the above. I feel bad for keeping it a secret from you. We went away for the weekend, and the paparazzi saw us. I freaked out because I thought it was "*him*," and he found me again. Anyway, I figured you'd want to hear it from me first. He also told me about working with Brant."

"Oh, honey, he is long gone. We paid him, and we never heard anything else from him. He had a price, and we dealt with it. Don't let him make you live in fear; I won't have it. But Graham and Brant—yes, they work together on a few projects; I've only ever heard wonderful things about him. We'll all have to get together soon." As I open my mouth to respond, Graham strides in and snatches my phone from my ear.

"Hi Bethany, how are you?" I glare at him. Why was he being such an asshole to me?

"Yes, we'll have to set something up soon. You too, goodnight. I'll tell her." He hangs up and pulls me up, but I push him away.

"What is your fucking *problem*?"

"Don't *ever* get in my way during a fight; what if I had accidentally hit or hurt you? I would've never forgiven myself. Next time, stay the fuck out of—"

Before he can spit the rest of the words in my face, I slap him. When I draw back to hit him again, he grabs my hand. I'd never hit anyone, yet I hit the man I've grown to love so quickly. I tried to help him at the hospital. There were people everywhere; his sister was screaming, the nurse was screaming, and he wasn't listening to anyone. I thought he was going to kill his father, and I knew I could stop him. I tried to help; I *thought* I was helping him.

"I'm... I'm sorry; I don't know what overcame me."

22

Graham

She slapped me. I know I deserved it, but I'm still fuming. I'm pissed with her and my dad, but mainly with myself. I should have never let him get me to that point. The last time it happened, I almost didn't stop; if it weren't for my mom, I'm not sure I would have. But this time, Liza was my comfort; she was the only one who could stop me.

I was furious that she threw herself in front of my father, protecting him. Deep down, I knew she protected me from myself, but I didn't care then. My dad always brought my mom up during arguments; it shouldn't still shock me. The issue was that he said it loudly enough for Liza to hear. How could he tell her I was hard to love? I wasn't hard to love; I just carefully chose who I allowed to love me. I'd let Liza love me. I expected her to bolt after that. After she saw how I acted in front of her, I realized how distant she was.

I wanted her to grab my hand on the way back here, but she didn't; instead, she gave me stolen glances. I scared her; that wasn't shocking. But I needed to fuck her, and I needed to do it *my* way. I didn't have time to be gentle with her, and I didn't want to be gentle.

"I don't know what overcame me," she apologizes. I did; I was being an asshole to her, but she was being so cold towards me. "I'm so sorry;

I should have never…"

I release her hand and pull her tightly to me, crushing my mouth over hers and kissing her so violently that she gasps for breath. She opens her mouth to speak, and I push my tongue inside, seeking entry. Running her hands into my hair, I quickly grab them.

"I want to touch you," she whispers.

I shake my head, growling, "Not this time."

I pick her up and take her into the bathroom. I sit her down and glare down at her. "Undress. Now."

She steps back from me, turning her back to me. I see her eyebrows furrow in the mirror. I turn the shower on and start to undress myself.

"Look at me and undress." She stops as she reaches for her bra and turns around to face me. Her face is bloodshot red; she's either nervous or mad. Hell, maybe a little of both.

"Don't ever hide your body from me. It's mine." She bites her lip and unclasps her bra, her beautiful breasts tumbling out. She bends over a little and pulls her purple lace panties off. I quickly pull off my pants, shoes, and socks and get into the shower. She stands there with her eyes squinting.

"Get in here, Elizabeth, now." She inhales a shaky breath and enters the shower. I reach out, grab her by her neck, and push her into the wall. She puts her hands over mine, and I move them again. "What did I tell you? No touching."

She rolls her eyes, and I tighten my grip around her neck. She narrows her eyes in surprise. I lift her leg over my hip and plunge into her. Of course, she's already wet; she always stays wet for me. She has no idea how crazy she drove me today, not listening to anything I told her to do. Ellis had specific orders to keep her away from me if things got heated. He had specific orders to keep her away from the fire and not to fuel it, and instead, she ignored him, telling her to stand back. I didn't particularly appreciate it when people did the opposite of what I ordered them to do, but it made me more upset when that person was Liza.

I give her everything, fucking her so hard that she hits her head after each thrust. I tuck my hand behind her head, always protecting her. I turn her around and bend her over, spreading both of her ass cheeks open enough for me to push as deep as I want into her. She screams out, and I exhale a breath as I come into her pussy, unloading all of my anger on her. I quickly pull out of her, noticeably leaving her unfinished.

This wasn't about her getting off; it was about me. I smack her ass, and with the combination of the water and the weight of my hand, her ass turns red immediately. I give her two more slaps on the ass and watch her as she grabs for my hands. I stand her up and turn her toward me. "Don't ever put yourself in harm's way to protect me. Do you understand?"

"You're... punishing me?" she questions, confused. Had she not understood what she did? Then, she was so cold with me afterward, making me think she couldn't handle what had happened. I glare at her.

"Yes, I am. And now I'm *done* with you. Wash up." I walk past her out of the shower when she grabs my arm. I almost release myself from her hold until I see her face. Her sweet, innocent face, tears in her eyes finally releasing.

Fuck. At that moment, every piece of my anger melts away, and regret takes its place.

What had I done to her? She lets go of my arms and wraps her arms around herself. I had been so rough with her and so angry with her. It was my job to take care of her, not hurt her. I caused her pain, not sexually but mentally, and that was worse.

"Angel." She looks at me, and I wipe her tears away, another one replacing the last. "I was too rough; I'm sorry."

"No, you were cruel. You were mean. You wanted to hurt and leave me undone, and you did." She cries, shaking her head at me. "Get away from me." She turns her face away from my hands and pushes against my chest.

"You didn't stop me. Why?"

"Because I like to please you, Graham, to do what you want and what you need. But you're so stupid, and you don't see that."

She's right, and I have no response. I wrap myself around her, the water beading down on us. I take the loofah and lather it with soap. I start gently washing every inch of her curves. I take my time washing between her legs, knowing that her pussy is still throbbing. She leans into me, spreading her legs a little wider, allowing me to clean her better. I put shampoo in my hands, rub them together, and softly start to wash her hair, repeating the same motions with some conditioner. She turns to me and buries her face into my chest, the hot water rolling off her back. I kiss the top of her freshly washed hair.

"I'm sorry," I tell her again. She sinks into my chest, kissing my pecs.

"Can I wash you too?" she asks softly. Even after being so rough—no, "cruel" to her—she still wanted to cater to me.

I hand her the loofah; she grabs my body wash, covering it with soap. I stay still, letting her wash my body however she pleases. She's just as gentle as I was, nudging me to sit so she can wash my hair. She smiles at me and puts the loofah down. "All finished." I kiss her forehead and turn the water off.

I wrap a towel around myself, and she does the same. As I dry off, I keep my eyes on her; she must feel me staring, and she looks back at me.

"What did my sister want?"

"Oh, nothing... She just said that you love me, is all."

My sister could figure things out with just one glance. I told her about Liza the moment I laid eyes on her, and she pushed me to go after what I wanted. I guess, in a way, I owed her. I did love Liza. I loved her so fucking much and so fucking quickly. It made my head spin when I thought about how quick it had been.

I raised my eyebrow at her.

"Oh, she did, did she?" I say back, Liza's cheeks flush, and I smirk at her. I throw on a T-shirt and sweatpants while Liza grabs one of my shirts. She sits on the bed and picks up her phone.

"My mom says she's glad I found you. I'm not sure how she already loves you, but I'm sure she's expecting you to be at Sunday dinners from now on." She teases sarcastically.

As I stop standing in the room's doorway, I reply. "I'll be at whatever dinner you want me to attend, angel. Come here."

She walks over to me, putting her arms around my waist.

"Sir?" she flirts amusingly.

I chuckle at her and say, "Thank you for coming here with me. My mom will be happy to see you."

"Have you heard anything about her?"

"Selle says that she'll be home tomorrow. We'll head over early in the morning to see her, then go back to school instead of staying. She has enough help." I place a fly strand of hair behind her ear and search her face, kissing the top of her nose. She smiles and hugs me, this time a little tighter than usual.

"Angela told me I couldn't let you push me away." She finally states in a whisper.

I look at her. "Angela is a wise woman, but she's right; sometimes I can be closed off. Most women can't handle it."

"I'm not most women." I press my finger over her mouth.

"Let me finish," I say to her. "I know you're not like most women; that's what I love about you. You didn't run away when you saw my anger come out with my father today. You didn't run away when you saw how the paparazzi liked to be in my business; you didn't run away when you found out I was adopted, and you didn't run away when you found out I kept a secret from you. I can't promise it will be easy; I've never been good at this, but I'll try, I swear. Promise me you won't leave me." I look her in the eyes, and she kisses me.

"I'm not going anywhere."

The next morning...

I wake up wanting Liza. She's still sleeping soundly, and I can't stop myself from doing what I'm doing. Her breathing is slow and shallow, and her lips are perfectly parted.

I shove my boxer briefs down and place myself in between her legs. I run a finger through her folds and damn near come on the spot when she's drenched.

Fuck. Me.

My cock is at attention, begging to be devoured by her pussy. I run the tip through her folds, using her wetness to slick my cock, and then I slam into her. She groans when I pull back and do it again, placing my hand around her neck.

She's sleeping but still welcomes me into her warm hole so perfectly. I sink myself in her, bottoming out when she finally moans my name. Her eyes flutter open, and instead of pushing me away, she wraps her legs around me to push me deeper inside her. She closes her eyes again as I milk her even more.

"Rise and shine, pretty girl. Wake up and come all over my cock." She tightens around me, and I yank her face to me.

"Let me see those beautiful eyes."

She opens them, focusing them on me. She clenches around my cock so hard I physically feel incapable of moving. I give her a long, deep thrust, and she moans.

"Oh God..."

"Not God, angel. Me. My name. It will always be my fucking name."

She arches her back and digs her nails into my back when I increase my assault on her pussy. *Thrust. Thrust. Thrust.*

She's shaking uncontrollably, and I know she's coming. The look on her face, when she comes, is unfuckingmatched. It's like Christmas morning. I fucking live for it.

"Do you feel how your pussy suffocates my cock, how it holds onto it for dear life?" I pump in and out of her, filling her with my come. I sure hope that fucking birth control works because there's no goddamn way I'm using protection with her ever again.

The thought of a brown-eyed, long-haired baby girl pops into my head. I push the thought out just as quickly as it comes. When I pull out of her, she groans from the absence.

I grab a wet washcloth and wipe the inside of her legs. She sits up on her elbows and watches me, her eyes still clouded with sleep.

"What time is it?" I glance up at the clock.

"8:17 a.m."

"No, I need more sleep; you fucked me too hard. I'm not complaining, though; that was one hell of a wake-up call."

I chuckle. "Up, we're having brunch with my family before we head back. My mom got home this morning and wants to see you."

"She doing okay?" she asks, sitting up.

"Yes, just one hell of a headache, but she's fine. I think I want one more round with you before we go."

She groans and covers her body with the blanket.

"Stay away, you broke her. She's out of commission."

"Turn over." She looks at me suspiciously as I lean over to retrieve a flogger.

"Graham..."

"Turn over, Elizabeth." She slowly flips onto her stomach. "Will you be a good girl and keep your hands above your head, or do I need to handcuff you?"

"Y–yes, sir. I–I'll keep them up."

"Mmm, of course you will, pretty girl." I stand up and run the flogger across her back. She arches and moans a tiny but glorious moan. I watch as she squirms from the sensation of the flogger on her skin. I quickly lift it and slam it down on her back, causing her to yelp. Before she can stop screaming, I slap her ass again with the flogger as she whimpers.

"Fuck, you look so good taking this like a good girl."

"More," she begs through gritted teeth. I raise my eyebrow and give her three more blows across her back, and then I flip her over and slap her breasts with it quickly. I throw the flogger to the ground and yank her up to me by her neck.

"Wrap your legs around me."

She wraps them around me, and I push her against the wall. She sinks onto my cock so easily it feels like heaven. I feel like I'm high on ecstasy when she runs her tongue over my lip. I bite her neck hard until I'm met with the taste of copper in my mouth.

"You'll wear my marks for everyone to fucking see. Now bounce on my cock, angel." She gives me an evil grin and wraps her legs tighter around me, adjusting herself before she bounces up and down on my cock deliriously. The sounds of our skin slapping together fill the room. She increases her speed, and I push her further to the wall. When she lifts herself, I hold her there for a second, and then I thrust my cock into her so hard she screams.

"Graham! Fuck!"

I do it again, and she sinks her teeth into my shoulder. I tangle my hand into her hair, wrap it around my fist, and yank her face toward me.

"Look at me, angel... who do you belong to?"

"Mmm." I pound in her pussy harder, and she gasps.

"Answer me." *Thrust, Thrust, Thrust*

"Oh my fucking God…mmm."

"Last warning, before I turn you around and fuck that tight ass of yours." A part of me hopes she doesn't answer me just so that I can fuck the one hole I haven't claimed.

"You, I belong to you. Always you." I slow my pace and kiss her forehead.

"Good girl. Now come for me." On command, she releases her climax all over my cock. I thrust in her once, twice, and a third time before I fill her sweet cunt with my come.

I slowly lower her down until her perfectly painted toes touch the ground. I watch as my come leaks out of her, and before I realize what I'm doing, my hand shoots out and pushes it back into her pussy. She stares at me in astonishment.

"We're not wasting a fucking drop. And don't think you're out of the woods. I'm still fucking that ass. Just not right now because we unfortunately don't have time."

"Aren't I just frenzied over that?" She groans sarcastically, her hips swaying as she brushes past me. I give her a smack on her ass, and she bellows out in laughter.

This fucking woman.

We wash up quickly and head out the door.

I meet Ellis at the SUV; he greets me as usual.

"Good morning, you two." Liza smiles at him.

"Good morning, Ellis!" she exclaims.

"I didn't get that much excitement; how come he does?"

"I happen to like him a lot more than you," she chuckles, leaning into me. I raise my voice, "El, you're fired. My girlfriend here likes you more than me."

23

Liza

We drive up to Graham's parents' house. It's beautiful, but I didn't expect anything less after seeing Graham's house.

Ellis opens my door, and Graham approaches me, grabbing my hand.

"Be nice today, baby. Promise me." I say to him.

"Don't worry."

I narrow my eyes at him. Don't worry. Was he serious? He broke his nose the last time he and his father were in the same room. I need him to control himself. "I promise."

Selle comes out, beaming.

"Liza!" Graham frowns and looks at me.

"What is she? Your bestie now?"

She playfully pushes him. "Jealous?"

I laugh and hug her. "Hi, Selle, ignore him. He's grumpy. He didn't get much sleep last night." I look over my shoulder as she guides me into the house. Graham winks his eye and follows behind us.

"Elizabeth, honey, I'm so glad you came with Graham."

I turn around and see pure grace approaching me. Madeline looks stunning—not like she's just been in an accident. I smile at her.

"Hi, Mrs. Salando. I'm so glad you're okay." She opens her arms to hug me.

"Honey, please don't call me that, call me Maddy... I'm fine; those doctors made it sound much worse than it was. Ahh, my Graham, hi, sweetheart. Come here." Graham strides over to his mom, planting a kiss on her cheek.

"How are you feeling, Mom?" he asks, scanning her body. She steps back and waves at him.

"I am fine. Now, let's get you kids fed, shall we? Oh, and honey, for the love of God, keep your hands to yourself today," she orders, winking at him. Graham puts his head down and chuckles.

"Yes, ma'am."

Selle grabs my hand and tugs me down the hall.

"Wait until you see what G did to Dad. The fucker deserved it; it'll bring G some joy seeing him."

I look around just in time to see Joe walking into the dining room with a nose splint and a bruised eye. I look at Graham, and he glares at me with amusement. I gesture my head toward his dad, and he chuckles and grabs two mimosas.

Selle nudges me, "Told you. Let's sit." I follow her to the chairs, leaving one for Graham. Joe walks over to me, picks up my hand, and brings it to his mouth.

"So sorry for the scene at the hospital; glad to have you here today, Liza."

"Thank you, Mr. Salando."

"Please, call me Joe." I hear Graham clear his throat from behind, and Joe moves to the side, turning to face Graham with his back to me. Selle turns to them both, sitting behind me. She nudges me again, making sure I'm not missing a thing.

I raise my eyebrow at Graham; he catches my look, and his face settles.

"Son," Joe speaks, walking closer to Graham.

"Dad."

Joe reaches out to shake his hand, and Graham looks at it.

"Sorry, hands are full. Later."

"Ooh, burn," Selle whispers in my ear from behind. I shake my head and turn toward the table. Joe shakes his head and sits at the head of the table, leaving Graham sitting beside me. His mother sits at the opposite head of the table, looking back and forth between her husband and son.

"We are not starting this brunch until I hear both of you apologize to each other." Silence falls at the table; I pick up the mimosa Graham set in front of me and chug it. If she plans to make them apologize to each other, I'd need alcohol. If there was one thing I knew, no one was getting an apology from Graham. He wasn't sorry.

I kick Graham under the table, and he looks at me. I clear my throat, and he rolls his eyes. "Mom, can we just..." she raises her hand to him.

"If yesterday showed either of you stubborn men anything, it's that life is short. Stop bickering; this *war* you two have against each other is just disgusting, and it will end today. *Right now.*" Selle hands me another mimosa, grabbing one for herself as well.

"You'll need another one of these."

Joe cuts in, clearing his throat. "Your mother's right, son; I don't typically enjoy bickering with you. I should have never brought you know who up. It was beneath me; I need to treat you with more respect than that. I apologize." His father sits back in his chair, intertwining his fingers. Madeline leans closer to Graham, who still hasn't looked up from his drink.

"Well, sweetheart, your father is talking to you."

Graham finally looks up at his mother and sighs. He turns to his father and says, "It's not me I want you to respect; it's her." He gestures towards his mother. "I could give a shit if you respect me, but her? You will respect, you will love, and you will honor her. Those were your vows, right? Abide by them, and you will have no pushback from me." His mother puts her hand on his arm, and he gives her a small smile.

Joe drops his head, "Of course, she's your mother, and I expect you want nothing but the best for her. We have issues like any other marriage, but I will always respect and honor your mother."

Graham rolls his eyes; I lean over and whisper.

"Be nice, apologize, and move on for your mother."

"I hope so, Dad, for your sake. I apologize for your nose." His mother sits back down and looks at me with a smile.

"Well, now that that's settled, let's eat, shall we?" Madeline exclaims. I look at her, and she winks at me.

Graham puts his arm around me, pulling me in and kissing my cheek. "Don't make it a habit to tell me what to do, Elizabeth," he warns, speaking low enough for only us to hear. I giggle, and Selle leans forward with us both in her view. "Get a room, you two." My cheeks turn red, and Graham bends over and playfully pushes her.

"Shut up, Selle."

24

Graham

"Get off her. Piece of shit. Don't touch me." The man with the beard hovered over me, yanking at my clothes. I look over and see my sister unconscious. Blood dripped down the sides of her face. My father was a part of the drug cartel, and now we were caught up in his fucking mess. My sister should never have been with me; they were following me; they wanted me, not her. "Sit up, boy." I spit at the man's face.

"Fuck you!" I spit out. Within a second, I get an intense blow to my face. "Keep it up, I'll fuck your sister while you watch." I try to break out of the chains that wrap around my wrists.

"You won't touch her."

The bearded man grins at me, then walks over to Selle. "Wanna bet?"

"Graham, baby, wake up; we're back at your place." I jump out of my sleep, grabbing Liza's hand tightly. My pupils dilate, and I feel rage pouring out of me. She yanks her hand back and frowns.

"I'm sorry, I didn't realize I fell asleep." She gives me a faint smile, but I know I scared her. I reach for her hands and plant a soft kiss on it. "I didn't mean to grab you that way."

"What were you dreaming about?"

The same dream every time, and I can't get it out of my fucking head.

If it's not this dream, it's the dream of my fucking mother, that makes no sense. Every time I fucking close my eyes, I have to pray that I won't have another dream. I never know how I'll react to it. Sometimes I can carry on like it never happened, and sometimes I act like a fucking psycho when I wake up.

"Nothing. Come on, let's go inside."

25

Liza

This was the second time he had woken up like a bat out of hell, the second time he had a nightmare, and he didn't tell me what it was about. I watched as Graham got out of the SUV with a furrow in his eyebrows and ran his hand through his hair. I walked behind him and waited for him to open the door to his place.

"Go on in; I'm going to talk with Ellis for a second," he states, and I reluctantly go into the house.

I pull out my laptop and distract myself by looking for places to do my internship. It's late April, and I must find a place to spend the last twenty hours of my internship before graduation. It's hard for me to believe graduation is a couple of weeks away, but I have been preparing for this for the last four years, racking up all of my internship hours needed at UCLA.

Fifteen minutes later, I put my laptop down and looked out the window to see what was taking Graham so long. Ellis's SUV had vanished, and Graham was nowhere in sight. I opened the front door and stepped out onto Graham's driveway. Walking around the house, I heard music from an outhouse at the back. I opened the door and stepped inside, music blasting into my ears.

I search around and finally see a shirtless Graham lifting weights at the back of the room. I lean against the wall and watch as he gets on the ground in a push-up position. There is something wrong. I could sense it, but I had no idea how to get him to open up to me about it. *Don't let him push you away.*

Angela's words ring in my head; I walk over to the stereo and turn it down. He jolts and looks up at me.

"What are you doing?" he asks harshly. I raise my eyebrows at his curt voice, and his face softens.

"There's something wrong; tell me what it is," I push, walking towards him. He watches me as I get closer to him. He ignores me, continuing with his push-ups.

"Nothing's wrong." I sit before him, crossing my legs and tucking them under me.

"Why don't you and your father get along?" I ask. He ignores the question, increasing the speed of his last four push-ups. He gets up and moves to the punching bag that hangs freely attached to the ceiling.

"He's a dick. That's all you need to know." He spits out as he throws a punch to the bag. I jump at the sound of his fist pounding the bag. I watch him as he begins striking the bag harder and harder.

"That's not all. I need to know... You hit him, Graham." He pauses before hitting the bag.

"Okay, and you hit me." He says through his teeth. I inhale, taken aback by the venom with which he speaks. "I'm sorry. I didn't mean to say that." I shrug my shoulders.

"Tell me... Please," I beg as he picks up his pace and hits the bag faster, making grunting sounds with every punch.

"Elizabeth, my dad..." He stops and stares at me, shaking his head, and continues his punches. "My dad cheated on my mom, worked with a drug cartel, got my sister and me kidnapped, and then lied about it all for years." He hits the punching bag three more times. "Is. *Hit.* That.

Hit. Enough. *Hit.* Information?" He wipes the sweat off his forehead and watches me.

"He what?" I'm realizing I am angrier about him getting Graham kidnapped before I register the drug cartel issue. Graham raises his eyebrow and grabs his water.

"He's a piece of shit, and my mom won't leave him because she still doesn't believe he cheated, or she does and just doesn't care."

"You and your sister were…"

"Kidnapped, yes, years ago, kept it out of the press. It was a ransom kidnapping." Gulping down his water before he continues, "I was 17, Selle was 12." My eyes start to water, and he walks over to me. "Don't cry."

"Your nightmares? Are they of…" I look away, unable to bring the words out of my mouth. He places his thumb on my chin, forcing me to stare into his eyes.

"My nightmares are fine; I'm fine."

"You're not fine. I didn't ask that night, but you were screaming and yelling at someone not to touch you. Did they touch you? Did they touch Selle?" He shakes his head.

"It's not important, angel. Let it go."

"I want to understand and know what happened to you. I want to know why you are so jumpy sometimes, why you zone out and come back to reality *angry*. You promised no secrets. I need to know."

"No, you don't; it won't do anything but make you feel sorry for me and want to fix it. It happened, and I'm fine. Selle is fine. End of discussion."

I leave the conversation alone; I don't want to push him on this. Besides, he is right, and I would want to fix something that is entirely out of my control.

The rest of the night goes by quickly. Graham's shower must have eased his mood because he returned to his usual loving self. We cuddled, ate some food, and slept nuzzling against each other the entire night. I woke up around 2:30 a.m., realizing we never made it upstairs to bed.

I push Graham's hair back and kiss his forehead.

"Graham." he flutters his eyes and flicks them open.

"What's wrong? Was I dreaming? Did I hurt you?" He sits up quickly.

I grab his face between the palms of my hands. "Breathe...no, you weren't dreaming; I was just waking you to come to bed with me."

He lets out a deep breath and softly kisses my lips. Hurt me? Why would he hurt me? What happened to him during those dreams?

"You don't seem to have them when we're sleeping together..." I say softly. He stands up and reaches for my hand.

"I know, come on."

26

Graham

Liza was right; I only had a few dreams during our time together. One was when she was in the next room, and the other was when she was sitting next to me. Angel sounds so much more fitting now. I'm at peace when she's beside me, and I never want to have a night without her.

I've been battling with these nightmares for eight years now. They come and go, but for some reason, lately, they've been occurring more often. They've happened every night for the last month, except when I was asleep with Liza. I hadn't planned to sleep next to her until I could get my nightmares under control, but it didn't happen that way. Instead, she walked in on me having one, and I practically begged her to spend the rest of the night with me.

I lead her upstairs to my room and watch her change into one of my shirts. I loved that she slept in my shirts. I knew she had sleepwear with her, but instead, she opted for my shirt, knowing how much I loved it. I watch her pull the comforter back and climb into bed. She looks at me and pats the empty spot beside her. I stand there with my arms crossed, leaning on the wall.

"Are you planning to stare all night? Come here," she flirts bashfully.

I unfold my arms and walk to the bed, pulling my shirt over my head and pushing my pants to the ground.

"I told you, I enjoy staring at you." I climb in beside her and pull her to my chest, planting a kiss on her forehead.

"Do you have to go into the office tomorrow?"

"It's 3 a.m., angel. It is tomorrow," I say with a smirk. She smiles and nudges me. "Yes, I have to go in and sign some paperwork for this charity event we're having next weekend." She wraps her arm around me, quickly falling asleep in seconds.

I look at the clock and see that only twenty minutes have passed, and I still haven't fallen asleep. Liza's face when I told her about my father, with her look of surprise and hurt, is constantly replaying in my head. *Why do you call me 'angel'?* When she asked me, it was hard to explain. Why was it so hard for me to answer that for her? Why was it so hard for me to tell her why I called her that?

I look down at her, sleeping peacefully on my chest, trying not to wake her. I run my fingers through her hair.

"I know you're asleep, but I'm not ready to say this while you're conscious. I call you *'angel'* because that is who you are to me; my life hasn't been easy, and I'm not the easiest person to deal with. I used to get into fights all the time, lose my temper quickly, and hurt people I loved just because I could."

"When my sister and I got taken... I lost a part of myself and found rage taking over. I finally grew up when I took over my father's business. I want to shield you from that part of my life because, eventually, you're going to see just how fucked up my family is. The nightmares scare me, but I'll never admit that to you. The first night we stayed together, I didn't have one. That's when I knew you were an *angel. My angel.* You don't know this yet, but I love you, Elizabeth...so fucking much." I quickly wipe my tears when I hear a sleepy Liza.

"I love you too, Graham, so much." My eyes widen, and I look down at her.

"What did you say?" Did she say she loved me? Is she dreaming? Did she hear me?

"Elizabeth... What did you say?" She groans and falls back into a deep sleep. She obviously didn't mean it and didn't hear what I said. She was probably sleep-talking; she had to be, right?

* * *

Fuck! My alarm... 6:30 a.m. already?

I roll over and hit the end button on my alarm. I'm tempted to work from home today; the last thing I want to do is get out of the warm bed with the woman I love cuddling beside me. If it had been any other time, I would've easily cut my alarm off and wrapped myself around Liza again, but we have an important event coming up in one week that I need to go off without a hitch.

I gently slide my arm from around Liza's waist and slide out of bed. She groans and readjusts herself.

"What time is it?" She moans, her voice husky.

"Early. Go back to bed, *angel*." She rolls back over and closes her eyes; I walk into the bathroom and start the shower.

The steam fills the bathroom as I strip off my boxers and step in under the water, letting it roll down my back. Another night passed without a nightmare, and I knew it was because of Liza. Last night, I indulged in my feelings and spilled everything to a sleeping Liza. I told her I loved her, and she said it back; she was asleep, but she said it as clear as day. I cut the shower off and wrapped the towel around my waist. I see Liza sprawled over the bed with her arms wrapped around my pillow. As much as I wanted it to be me who she cuddled up to, it would have to wait until the workday ended.

I smile at the thought of me coming home to Liza and walk into my closet. I quickly scanned through my line of suits and finally decided on a navy suit with white pinstripes; I decided to pair it with a charcoal gray tie. I walk downstairs and start a pot of coffee, grabbing an apple and biting into it while I wait for it to finish brewing. The kitchen begins to fill with the aroma of freshly brewed coffee. I grab my mug and fill it to the top. My phone rings as I pick up my mug and savor the smooth taste of vanilla hitting my tongue. *Andrew.* Fuck.

"Andrew," I say annoyingly.

"Sorry, boss, are you almost at the office?"

"No, what do you need?"

"Are you aware that your father moved the event to this Friday?" I nearly drop my coffee mug.

"My father is not the CEO of this company anymore; I am. The event is in one week." I declare sternly.

"Sorry, boss, I'm just the messenger... and that's what he called and told–"

"I don't give a fuck what he called and said. I'll deal with him. Continue to follow the one-week plan. Don't change a thing unless I call you." I hang the phone up and glance at the clock: 7:20 a.m. I walk upstairs and gently kiss the top of Liza's forehead; her eyes flutter open.

"I'm heading into the office; what are your plans for today?" She yawns and rubs her eyes.

"Looking for an internship. You look very sexy in that suit." She compliments.

"Meet me for lunch at my office today? At 12 p.m.?" She pulls me down for a kiss.

"Have a good day at work, baby." She tells me. I kiss her one last time.

"Have a good sleep, *angel*; dream of me." She rolls to her side and drifts back to sleep.

I call my father as I enter my Audi, but he doesn't answer as usual. Who does he think he is? He doesn't run this company anymore; I do. He believes he can move up one of the most important social events one week early. Especially after the fucking disaster we had last year. During the charity event last year, the paparazzi decided to ambush one of our guests and started a full-on brawl. People were hurt, some severely, and it was on our fucking watch. It was the last thing we needed this time around. Not to mention, the fucker wasn't even on the guest list; the guest list my father decided didn't have to be 'strictly followed.'

I parked my car in my usual parking spot, and Ellis followed me. Usually, he'd drive me to work, but Liza was at my house today, so I wanted him at her disposal if she needed him. I walk into my headquarters building and step into the elevator, scanning my palm to get to the top floor, where my office is. To get to the top floor, you have to scan your palm; we updated security a while back due to an incident we had.

Angela is at her desk as usual.

"Good morning, Mr. Salando," she says sweetly; Angela was more like family and was the reason this place hadn't fallen to shit yet. Keeping me on track and not afraid to call me on my shit, she was precisely the assistant I needed; she was my father's assistant for the years he also ran the company.

"Angie," I say. She grins and walks into my office behind me.

"Alright, you're busy this morning, but your afternoon isn't too bad. You have a meeting at 9 a.m. with the company that wants to help sponsor alcohol for the charity event. Then, at 11 a.m., you have a meeting with the contractors for the New York office. Don't forget, you have to decide who you will move or promote to run that place." I bow in agreement. I take off my suit jacket and lay it over the chair. She huffs behind me, grabs the coat off the chair, and hangs it beside the door on the tall brown coat rack. That was Angie—more like a second mother to me than an assistant.

"Do you need coffee before you get settled in?" she asks, holding her computer and looking at me.

"No, I'm all good. Liza will be here at 12 p.m. to have lunch with me. Can you—"

"I'll order you two some lunch and set it up in conference room one unless you have plans to take her out. I can make a reservation."

"Lunch here should be fine. I want to show her around here, and Ang, order something for yourself, too." Angie grins and turns on her heels for the door.

I sit at my desk and pull out my phone to call my father. I don't know why he thought he could make executive decisions when I'm in charge. I put the phone on speakerphone and put it on my desk. I pull up the details of the charity event on the computer.

After a few rings, he answers.

"Son, is everything alright?" I inhale a deep breath and try to keep my composure; the last thing I needed was for Liza to see me later and have my anger taken out on her because of an argument with my father. Regardless of how pissed I get with him, like Liza said, he's still my father.

"Do you want to explain why Andrew thought the event was this Friday instead of next Friday?"

"Well, I assumed you knew about the upcoming events with the other competing companies and their charities, so I made the call."

"You don't get to make the calls on anything; you no longer own this company, I do. I make the calls, and the event is next weekend. We are still ensuring security is top of the line. We don't want the same thing that happened last year to happen, so a few things are different this year. Starting with an invite-only policy, you will not be allowed if you are not on the list. As for the paparazzi, we have a list of those who will be there. We've already done background checks on them. Especially since someone decided to skip that part of clearance last year." My dad lets out a huff and stays silent on the other end.

"See you next weekend, Father." I hang up the phone and check the clock—8:27 a.m.

I pick up the phone and call Liza, she should be up by now. The phone only rings once when her perfect voice answers.

"Hi." She responds softly. I smile at her voice. As pissed off as I am with my father, all that fades when I hear her voice.

"Hi, *angel*."

"Aren't you supposed to be working or something?"

"Or something."

"Slacker"

"I miss you," I say, the words rolling off my tongue. I want to be around her 24/7 and miss her instantly when she's not near. I couldn't see her, but I knew she was smiling. I hear my door open and see Angie standing with the biggest smile. She has never seen me like this with a woman, let alone seen me love a woman. And love is exactly what I feel. I just wondered how I would tell her and when I would tell her while she was conscious this time. I put a finger up, signaling Angie to give me one minute.

She waves me off and comes to sit down in the brown leather chair that sits in front of my desk.

"*Angel*, I have to go. I'll see you at noon."

"Can't wait," she exclaims.

"Me either." I hang up the phone and look at Angie. "You're in my office eavesdropping because?"

She raises her eyebrow and grins, "You love her. I never thought you would love someone; she's so good for you. Don't mess this up."

I ignore her and pull up the agenda for the 9 a.m. meeting.

"They're in the conference room waiting; they arrived pretty early."

"I'll be in there soon," I reply as she exits my office. I take my suit coat from the rack, shrug it on, grab my papers, and head to the conference room.

27

Liza

I walk into the medical building and see the sign indicating the way to the mental health wing. This one was close to the last building I had left to look at. I had been to three other buildings, which were full of interns. This one was at the top of my list, but I heard how hard it was to become an intern here. They had some of the most prominent psychiatrists and doctors in the building. It would be fantastic for my career, and if I did well, I'd be able to get a great letter of recommendation for graduate school.

I get to the second floor and walk through the elegant glass door with a picture of a brain on it. I look around and see it's decorated nicely with a modern twist. There is a glass table with a vase filled with marbles and a row of seats in the waiting area. A blonde sits at the front desk with a phone up to her ear. She looks up at me and smiles, hanging the phone up.

"Hi, can I help you?"

"I'm here to fill out the internship application," I state. She grabs two papers and a pen.

"You can fill it out here or take it with you and mail it in."

I take the papers and pen and sit in one of the chairs. I fill out all the paperwork, then get up and hand it over to the receptionist. She looks over the paperwork and smiles.

"Okay, thank you, ma'am," I say as I turn for the door. She stands up quickly, catching my attention.

"Actually, wait right there. I'm going to give this to Luke, and he may want to talk to you." She indicates, walking toward the back. I stand by the door, fidgeting with my hands, hoping he would offer me a position if he wanted to talk to me. She walks back out smiling; on her heels is a tall man with dusty blonde hair and a perfect smile. He looks over to me, my application in his hand. When he reaches me, I see his cool blue eyes.

"Ms. Crambell?" He asks, extending his hand to me. "Luke Cinkade... I understand you need an internship. Follow me if you have time; a spot just opened on my schedule, and I'd love to talk more with you."

"Yes, absolutely," I say. He turns on his heels, and I follow behind closely. We reach his office, and I walk in; it's warm with shades of red and brown. He waves his hand toward the chair in front of his desk, and I sit.

"So, you're a senior at the university?" He asks, his fingers resting on his knee.

"Yes, I graduate in May."

"Well, I looked over your paperwork, and we'd be more than lucky to have you here in the meantime. I think you'll learn a lot. You can start as soon as Monday." I try to stop my mouth from dropping open. He smiles as I open my mouth to speak, but nothing comes out.

"I take that as a, yes?"

I nod and smile, "Yes, I'd be thrilled." He stands up and walks around where I'm seated.

"Great, I will email you the details, your schedule, and pay...if you have any—"

"Pay? I would get paid?" he frowns.

"Absolutely, this is a paid internship, and I'm sure you will enjoy the pay rate." He smiles and walks over to open his door.

"Thank you so much, Dr. Cinkade." He puts his hand on my shoulder and guides me out. "Please, Luke is fine. I'll see you Monday, Elizabeth."

I walk outside and see Ellis waiting for me.

"How'd everything go, Ms. Crambell?" I glare at him.

"Liza. Please, Ellis, call me Liza. And I guess I will be starting my new internship on Monday."

"Congratulations, *Liza*."

I climb into the SUV and retrieve my phone to call Graham. To my surprise, he doesn't answer. I look at the time and see that it's 10:45 a.m. He must be busy. I scroll to my mom's name instead, and like I knew she would, she answers within seconds.

"Hi, mama."

"Elizabeth, hi honey! How are you?"

"I'm good, mama; I got the internship... I start Monday."

"Oh, honey! That's amazing!" I hear her telling my stepfather the good news and faintly hear him congratulating me. "Brant says congratulations; he wants us to celebrate. Are you free for dinner this weekend?"

As happy as I was that they wanted to celebrate, I just wanted to celebrate with Graham. I hadn't seen my mother since I left for college here, and I knew I couldn't be selfish and continue to put her off. I inhale a breath and respond quickly before I change my mind.

"Yes, I'm free this weekend."

"Okay, great. We'll discuss the details. I can't wait to see you, sweetie. I love you!"

"Love you too, mom." I hang up the phone and look up at Ellis. "Have you talked to him today?"

"No, Liza, I haven't. He told me to bring you to the office at noon for lunch." I look at the clock again. It's 11 a.m., which is only an hour early. Oh, what the hell? I'll go anyway; I can kill time in a little bookstore around the corner from his office.

"Can we head there now? I want to go to that bookstore around the corner from his office."

About fifteen minutes later, we pull up to an antique bookstore. For as long as I can remember, I loved to read and put myself in someone else's life. When I had a stalker, it was the only way to escape my life. I didn't like my life; I wanted anyone else's life but mine. For the first time, I loved my life; I wanted no one else's life but my own.

I walk into the bookstore and look around, heading for the romance section. I look through books, looking at every shelf. I pick up a book from a newly released collection when my phone rings. *Graham.*

"Graham?"

"*Angel.* Hi. I'm sorry, but I was in a meeting when you called. Everything okay?"

"Yes, I just wanted to give you the good news. I got the internship, and I start Monday."

"Of course, you got the internship... hold on one second." I hear a man's voice and a woman screaming. I then hear Graham say, "Get out." I begin to speak into the phone, "Graham, who is that? What's going on?" Silence. "Graham!" He finally responds and practically yells, "I'll see you soon." *Click.* I look at the clock; damn, it's still not time. Whatever. Close enough. I haul out of the bookstore and walk towards Graham's building. I glance to the side and see Ellis following me in the SUV. I get to Graham's building and walk into the elevator. *Fuck.* A hand print scanner? I start pushing buttons, finally resting my finger on the call button.

A man answers. "How can I help you?"

"Yes, my name is Elizabeth, I'm Mr. Salando's girlfriend. Can you send me up?"

"One second, ma'am."

Before I know it, the elevator reaches the top floor. I leave the elevator and see the doors with "Salando Industries" written elegantly. I open the doors and immediately start to hear shouting. I follow the chaos, knowing one of the voices belongs to Graham. The closer I get, the more I realize that the other voice is his father's.

I turn the corner and walk to the end of the hall, where I see Graham's name written on the wall plate. "Graham Salando, CEO." The door is open, and the shouting is getting louder. I quickly walk through the doors and see Graham standing behind his desk. His father is on the other side, and Angie stands in a corner with her hands on her hips. As Graham leans over his desk, he tells his father, "I don't give a fuck what you think you're doing, but I can assure you if you don't get out of this office, I will put you out myself."

"Graham!" I hear Angie shout. I step into the door frame, and Graham freezes, looking directly at me.

"You need to go now. I won't ask you again." His dad turns and sees me.

"Elizabeth, I'm sorry you keep seeing us this way... We were *discussing* the charity event timeline. Even though everything is in order, my son seems to think next week is better." Graham rounds his desk, his mouth flying open, and yells obscenities at his father. I step further into the room, quickening my pace to reach Graham. I rest my hand on his forearm, looking him in the eyes and giving him a reassuring look. He relaxes, closes his mouth, and watches me. I step in front of him and turn to his father.

"Joe, I'm sorry this keeps happening with you two. But, if I understand correctly, you gave this company to Graham, which I'm assuming was because you trusted him to run it." Graham rests his hand on my lower back. "He's been working hard to ensure everything goes off without an issue for next weekend. Besides, we'll be out of town this weekend."

"I assume you'll attend the event; however, let me explain further. This weekend works better for the event."

Graham groans, and I lean back on him, keeping him grounded. "It works better because there is another charity event next weekend, and most of our guests were invited. I did not move this event to spite or undermine you. You were away at the lake house over the weekend. Brant called to inform me of the other event; he said he tried calling you, but your phone was disconnected. So, I went into the office and handled everything. I knew you were enjoying your time, so I did it to help, *not* to take back over the business."

"Why didn't you tell me that from the beginning?" Graham softens, moving me to the side.

"Because you didn't give me a chance to. I wanted to do something nice and help." Angie inches out of the room, and I follow her.

I release a breath and close the door so they can talk. "That was a mess," Angie sighs, sitting at her desk. I lean over her desk.

"How long had that been going on?" I ask.

"He barged in after his meeting, and the next thing I heard was yelling. Anyway, where are you two going this weekend?"

"My mom invited me to dinner to celebrate getting my internship." Angie's face lights up. She rounds her desk and hugs me tightly.

"Congratulations! I'm so happy for you! Does he know?"

"Yes, but not about New York this weekend. I planned to tell him during lunch, but then this happened." I waved towards Graham's door. She grins.

"Well, he knows now. So, when do you leave?"

"I'm not sure I don't have the details yet, just that it's in New York on Saturday. My parents are finally settled into their new house there."

"They'll love New York. It's beautiful, and Graham is working on the contractors for the office we're opening there."

"My mom is hoping I'll move there after graduation," I say, putting my head down as I realize I've never told Graham. How would he react if I moved to New York? Would he come with me?

28

Graham

As I leave my office, I hear Liza telling Angie about possibly moving to New York. Absolutely not. She is not moving to New York—her mother can forget that. The only way she'll go there is if we go together. Feeling uneasy, I walk up behind her. Angie's eyes are on Liza, signaling her to stop talking. I wrap my arm around her small waist and nuzzle my face in her hair.

"You can tell your mom the answer to that will be no, *angel*."

Angie grins at us both and sits back at her desk. Liza turns to me and giggles.

"Eavesdropping isn't nice. And I don't want to move to New York—not yet, at least." Not yet? What does she mean not yet? Did that mean that she eventually would? It wouldn't be an issue; I have an office there. It'd be simple to move there after graduation and run that office instead of this one, and it would also be a smart financial move. *Stop; you haven't known her long enough to think about moving to another state for her.* I ignore my conscience and look over to Angie.

"Could you see if my father needed anything else? And please, get him out," I command.

My father and I discussed everything and concluded it was a big misunderstanding. Before Liza, I wouldn't have heard anything he had to say. But since she came into my life, I have had more patience with my father than ever.

I look back at Liza and tuck a loose strand of hair behind her ear.

"What do you mean not yet? Are you thinking of moving to New York at all?" She wraps her hands around my waist and nudges my chest.

"My mom always assumed that's where I'd go after graduation, but I haven't given it any thought. Maybe after I visit her, I'll decide if I would even like living there. I would also have to consider my father. Even though he's constantly busy working, I'm sure he expects me to head back to California." I kiss the top of her hair.

"Well, can we go after the event? We won't stay long—just long enough to make an appearance, then fly straight to New York. And we can plan to take a trip to see your dad."

She leans back and simpers. "So your dad was actually trying to help you after all?"

"Seems that way. Will your mom mind?" She shakes her head.

"Nope, I'll tell her we'll be there late."

We both look down the hall when Angie and my father approach us. Angie stands beside her desk, and my father rounds me to get to Liza. He brings her in for a hug and kiss on her cheek and does the same for Angie.

"I have some business to attend to. I'll see you all at the charity event on Friday."

"It's on Friday?" Liza asks. My father and I nod in confirmation of her statement. "Dinner with my parents isn't until Saturday."

"Well, perfect. I'll see you all soon." My father nods at me and walks out when the phone rings. Angie sits at her desk, picking it up. "Salando Industries, this is Angela."

I look at Liza and rub my finger across her cheek; her skin is so smooth. She stares at me with a dark, twisted look in her eyes. The look she gives me when she is wet for me and she wants me to fuck her. I raise my eyebrow at her, and she bites her lip. I suddenly realize where I am, and I hear Angie's voice.

"Lunch is here; I'll set it up in the conference room." She looks back and forth from me to Liza. I reach for Liza, and she takes it immediately.

"Send lunch to my office."

She smirks and whispers, "Yeah, in 20 minutes. Sure thing."

I direct Liza back into my office and frost the office windows. She walks in, and before she can turn to me, I push her against the door, locking it in one move. My lips smash over hers, and she opens up for me, letting out a low groan.

"This is your office, we can't." I ignore her and push my hands against her breast. She leans her head back, and I take the opportunity to plant a trail of kisses on her neck.

"I'm the boss; I can do whatever I want here," I whisper in her ear. She shivers and slings her arms around my neck. She bites her lip as I look into her eyes. "That lip..."

"Hmm?"

"You know what happens to me when you bite your lip, *angel.*"

She puts her head down in shyness and bites it again; I palm her cheek in my hand and pull her to me again, picking her up. She instinctively wraps her legs around my waist, and I hold her up with both hands. I carry her to the black leather couch against the wall in my office. It's a pull-out couch, but we don't have time for that. I'll have to fuck her hard and fast.

I sit her down and push her legs open. She's wearing a black wrap dress that hugs her hips and stops above her knees. Her breasts are on display, just enough to show her cleavage. I pull her black lace panties down and slide my finger against her clit. She's so wet for me; that's my Liza, and she's always ready for me no matter where we are.

"Fuuuck!" I groan. Her head falls back, and she settles into my fingers; I slide out, adding another finger.

"You're dripping, Elizabeth."

She tries to sit up, and I plunge my fingers deeper inside her. She lets out a loud moan and places her hand over her mouth to suppress it. I pull my fingers out and move her hand from her mouth. I hover over the top of her.

"You want me to fuck you? Right here?" She nods and reaches for my belt buckle. I catch her hands and smirk at her.

"Tell me that you want me to fuck you." Her cheeks flush, and she opens her mouth to speak, her voice low and raspy.

"Please, Graham, please." Liza is still so shy; she loves it when I talk so dirty to her, but she doesn't understand that I plan to make her talk just as dirty.

"Say it, say you want me to fuck you."

"I want you... I want you to fuck me. Please."

I look down at her and pull the loose string tied to the side of her dress. Her dress falls to each side, exposing Liza's black lace bra. She reaches for my belt buckle again, watching me. I don't stop her this time. She sits up when she realizes I won't do what she wants. She unbuckles my belt and pulls my dress pants down, my cock springing out to her face. She shoves my boxer briefs down and pushes me up to my feet, standing in front of her. She fists my cock and looks up at me with her big, bright eyes staring back at me. She takes my cock in her mouth, licking the tip gently at first. I growl and roll my eyes to the back of my head. I grab her by her hair and push her further down, making her take more of me in her mouth. She opens wider, trying to take as much of me as she can. Quickening the pace, she starts moving her mouth faster and faster, looking up at me as I groan out her name.

"Elizabeth, I'm not coming in your mouth," I protest, lifting her. I sit on the couch and pull her on top of me. She straddles me, resting her hands on top of my shoulders. I rub my hands up her back and say, "I don't bring condoms to work, you know." Not that I've used one the last few times I've fucked her.

"I took the pill on Monday. She said to refrain for a week, but I think it's fine." I do the math in my head. It's Wednesday, and she started it on Monday. Would it be that bad if she got pregnant? Would I even care? I stop thinking further and give her a dark look, narrowing my eyes.

"Ride me."

She lifts herself and positions her pussy over my cock, lowering painfully slow, taking me in inch by inch. She throws her head back and lets out a moan again, covering her mouth. I push myself into her deeper and more forcefully, and I kiss her neck.

"They can't hear you, soundproof walls. Now, let me hear you scream like you're my own personal slut."

She moves her hand from her mouth and bounces on my cock faster and harder as I join in on the momentum pushing all of me inside her. She moans louder, gripping the back of my hair as she pulls me in further with every bounce. I move her and bend her over, spreading her ass, allowing me to push deeper into her.

"Fuck, I can feel every piece of you now. You're so slick around me, fucking me like a little perfect slut." I thrust into her, feeling her pussy and my cock tingling together. Realizing how much I needed to feel her bare, never missing the thin barrier between us, I pushed further into her. I continue to pull her hair and grasp her ass with the other hand.

"Mmm, so good." She moans. I wrap my hand around her neck, bringing her mouth to mine.

"So good, and so mine," I say to her. She bites her lip, and that sends me over the edge; I turn her around and lift her, pinning her to the wall. She wraps her legs around me, and I fuck her to her climax. She pours out over my cock, and I quickly follow behind her, grunting in her ear.

I set her down on her feet, still pinned against the wall. She kisses me, and I push her hair behind her ear.

"Well, now I look like a mess." I grin and point to the bathroom in my office.

"You can clean yourself in there. I'll grab the lunch, and maybe you should call your doctor for another plan B." She pushes past me, giggling, and walks into the bathroom, shutting the door. I grab a tissue and clean up the come left on my cock. When she leaves, I'll need to clean myself up properly. Liza is soaked, and I have the proof smeared all over me. I pick up the phone and call Angie's desk as soon as I finish.

"Hungry? Huh," she proclaims sarcastically. "I'll bring it now."

Within a few seconds, Angie knocks on the door. I walk over and take the bag from her. "Thank you, Angie." She smirks and walks away.

Liza comes out and glares at me.

"I'm starving, thanks to you." I hand her a Southwest chicken salad, and she smiles. It's Wednesday. Technically, I have classes tomorrow, but I'll have to skip those. With the event in two days, I had a lot to take care of, starting with making sure Liza was the most beautiful woman there.

Liza

By Friday, I was exhausted and anxious to have a weekend with Graham in New York. He seemed so busy yesterday, ensuring everyone was preparing everything for the event tonight; I slept in my new apartment and away from him for the first time since we officially started dating. I can't say I enjoyed being away from him, but he stopped by when he left his office and had dinner with me. While I knew I'd miss college, graduation could not seem to come fast enough. I wanted to be available to help Graham yesterday with his event, but instead, I barely saw him because I had class.

It would be May tomorrow, and graduation was only a week and a half away. I still hadn't decided what I planned to do after graduation. My mom seemed adamant about me moving to New York to work. But I still wasn't sure. Seattle was treating me well and seemed to have a lot of opportunities for me, starting with my internship.

I walk into my apartment, lock my door, and throw my keys on the end table next to it. I grab a bottle of water from the refrigerator and scroll through my phone contacts until I land on Graham's name. It rings once or twice before his sweet, masculine voice cracks through.

"Angel..."

"I'm sorry. I know you're busy; I just…miss you."

"I know, I miss you. How was your first night in your apartment?"

"It was fine, boring. What's the attire for tonight?"

"It's a ball. So, ball-like, I assume?" he jokes. I immediately place my water bottle on the counter and run to my closet.

"Calm down. I know you are worried about what to wear. I have someone coming over with dress options for you. Your hair and makeup will be taken care of as well. Just relax." I take a deep breath and flop on my bed.

"What time will they be here?" I say. Before Graham can answer, there's a knock at my door. I chuckle. "Never mind."

"Is that him? I'm sure he brought his backup."

"I think so, umm, black hair, green eyes? Very peppy?" Graham chuckled at me.

"Have fun; I'll pick you up at 7 p.m."

"Bye baby… I… I'll see you then." That was not what I wanted to say; I wanted to express my love for him. I wanted him to know, and I planned to tell him tonight.

I open the door, and the man immediately stares me down. I stop and look down at my wardrobe, suddenly self-conscious. "Hi. I'm Li…"

"Beautiful, you're beautiful. Oh! I'm going to have so much fun with you! I'm Jorge, and this is my partner in crime, Ingrid. My dear, you have beautiful cheekbones." I smirk and step aside, waving my hand and gesturing for them both to enter. Ingrid stops and rubs her hands over my hair.

"She has beautiful hair, too! A half-up style, perhaps. Liza, could you grab that hair stool for me?" I grab the stool and close the door behind her.

Jorge whispers behind me, "With her cheekbones? Hell no. Up, all the way. Maybe some hair pieces dangling."

I look between them both, holding cases of hair supplies and makeup.

"We'll do your hair and makeup first, then my guys will bring your dress and shoe options. Sound good, darling?" I nod, and he grabs me by the hand and walks me into my bathroom. He pulls out the stool and places it in front of my vanity. He gestures for me to sit with Ingrid, standing in the corner, digging through her makeup case. I sit on the stool, tucking my fingers underneath me. Jorge starts with my hair, settling on a braided up-do with a few straggling curled hair pieces to frame my face. Once he's finished, he twirls me around towards him and smiles.

"Perfect, absolutely perfect. Ingrid, your turn, darling."

Ingrid glides towards me with the brightest smile. "I have the perfect look to go with that hair. You're going to bring him to his knees tonight."

I grin and put my head down because that's precisely what I plan to do. About forty minutes later, Ingrid turns me around to face the mirror, and I inhale sharply as I see my reflection. She completes my look with natural makeup, a light smokey eye, and dark burgundy matte lipstick.

"Damn, this may be one of my best looks! BRING IN THE DRESSES, JORGE!" She screams into the room. Minutes later, I hear footsteps coming into the room. Jorge has two dresses in his hand, and someone is following on his heels with three more.

Jorge hangs his option up first. The dress is a red spaghetti strap long satin gown, and dress number two is a dark green strapless gown with a slit up the thigh. The other person, a younger girl, steps up and hangs up the dresses. Dress number three is a black skinny strapped satin dress with a low back and a slit in the front of the dress, with specs of silver glitter throughout the dress. Dress number four is a gray-fitted strapless dress sequined with black and red details. The last dress is effortless: a black halter-top satin dress.

I look at all the options; I inhale, with Jorge eyeing me with curiosity.

"They're all so beautiful. How can I pick?"

"Well, darling, you need to choose so we can make sure your man matches." I look at myself in the mirror, glancing at my hair and makeup, then back at the dresses. I run my hands over them all, stopping at dress number three. "This one—I like this one." Jorge and Ingrid look at each other and give an evil grin.

"Well, darling, you no longer need us." He walks over and kisses me on both sides of my cheeks, with Ingrid doing the same. They gather their belongings and quietly leave the apartment. I slide the dress on, careful not to mess up my hair or makeup. I look at the clock and see that it's 6:45 p.m. Graham will be here soon, so I slip on the black Jimmy Choo pumps right when a knock on the door comes through.

I stand up and look at myself in the mirror one more time. I walk over to the door and check the peephole to see a handsome Graham in a tuxedo waiting patiently. I open the door and smile at him.

"Hi," I say shyly.

"Angel, you look ravishing," he tells me, hunger dripping from his voice. He steps in and pulls me to him, holding me tightly.

"You don't look too bad yourself." I grin at him, and he narrows his head to meet mine, placing his lips over mine.

As he intensifies our kiss, I smile into his mouth. I pull away from him, and he groans with sadness, missing my lips on his.

"We don't have time for this, Graham," I whisper.

"I'll be quick." Before I disagree, his hands travel up my leg where the split is.

"This is quite the dress on you." He kisses my neck and tugs on my ear.

"Graham..." I utter out of breath. We'd have to save this later if he wanted us to get to his event on time. Besides, I'm sure that after I tell him that I love him, he'll want nothing more than to fuck me all night.

I step away from him. "That's enough; there's plenty of time for that later. We have an event to get to right now, don't we?"

He grins and waves towards the door. "After you."

I grab my clutch and head out the door with Graham on my heels. Ellis is patiently waiting in his all-black tuxedo.

"Good evening, Ms. Crambell." I smile and kiss him quickly on the cheek before he can pull away.

"Hi Ellis! You look nice!" I slide into the back seat of the SUV.

"I'm going to have to split the two of you up, aren't I?" Graham teases. I giggle and swat at him as he slides in beside me. Ellis shuts the door, climbs into the driver's side, and pulls into the Seattle traffic.

About thirty minutes later, we pull up to the side of the curb. Cameras are flashing everywhere, and Graham grabs my hand.

"We don't have to stay long, an hour tops, then I want to take you home and get that damn dress off you. Deal?"

"Deal," I gleefully reply as Ellis opens the door.

"I'll park the car and be in right after. You have security at the back and front watching until I get back to you."

"Thanks, El." He reaches his hand out to me, and I grab it once I slide out of the car. Flashes of cameras immediately blind me, and Graham tightens his grip on my hand, pulling me closer to him.

"Mr. Salando, over here, can we get a picture? Over here!" a reporter yells. Graham stops and turns me toward the photographer. He pulls me into his side and whispers, "Smile, *angel*." I swallow and turn to smile at the camera.

"Alright, the quicker we get inside, the quicker we get out." I shake my head at him, knowing why he's so eager to leave and return home. I secretly couldn't wait either.

30

Liza

We walk into the building, and white Christmas lights line the walls. Servers are dressed in white and black tuxedos, some carrying drink trays and some carrying appetizers. A waiter with a drink tray greets us, and Graham grabs two glasses of champagne.

I take a sip and loop my hand through Graham's arm. "Our table should be in the front, and my parents should be arriving soon if they aren't already here." I nod and follow him to the front of the nicely decorated ballroom.

"I see Selle. Why does she look so... worried?" I say to Graham. He frowns and scans the table, his eyes narrowing and cheekbones tightening. "What is it, Graham?"

"Nothing, everything is fine. Let's sit." I frown but don't ask questions. I walk over to the table where his mother and sister are sitting.

"Liza!" Selle yells as she rounds the table and hugs me. She whispers, "Don't be mad at him; he didn't know she'd be here." I look at her in confusion and raise my eyebrow.

"What are you talking about?" I tell her, and she opens her mouth to respond when Madeline moves her aside and pulls me in for a hug.

Graham hugs his sister when I hear him say, "Why the fuck is she here? And why is she at this table?"

"Honey, you look absolutely stunning. I'm so glad you could come. You both will give the paparazzi something to talk about." Madeline exclaims. "Come, come sit."

I notice another woman sitting at the table already; she's beautiful, with blue eyes and long blonde hair, wearing a stunning red dress. I remember the photos I saw online; this is the same woman in the photos. My conscience circled back to what Selle said: Was this who she was talking about? Who was she? Why did Graham seem so upset that she was here? I feel out of place, not knowing the entire story, but I'll be damned if she notices that.

I sit down with Graham on one side of me and Selle on the other. A server comes over with a plate of finger appetizers and offers everyone calamari and something with a cucumber on it. Graham shakes his head no, and the woman at the table tilts her head to the side.

"Graham, aren't you going to say hello?" She grunts sarcastically. He rolls his eyes and throws his arm around me.

He clears his throat and speaks dryly, "Madison. Hello."

"And your friend," she states, gesturing towards me. I clear my throat and smile. "Elizabeth, nice to—"

"She's not a *friend*. *She's* my girlfriend."

She throws her hands up jokingly and giggles. Selle leans forward and puts her hands on the table.

"How about you don't be a bitch for one night?"

Madeline drops her voice so low that I feel like *I'm* in trouble. "Everyone at this table will act like civilized adults, Giselle; you will watch your language. Madison, I expect more from you. Now, Graham, your father is headed this way. Play nice." She demands sharply.

"Am I missing something? I take it you two know each other." I say to Graham. He shakes his head.

"I'll tell you later." I try to ignore the stares coming from the other side of the table.

About an hour had passed, and we finished our dinner.

"Liza, bathroom break with me? Selle offers, pushing up from her chair.

"Yeah, of course, I could use some freshening up." I start to stand up when Graham and his father stand first. It'll take me a little while to get used to the amount of testosterone at this table.

"Hurry back, *angel.* I want to dance with the most beautiful woman here tonight." Madeline smiles and nudges Graham's father. I look over to see them staring in awe at us both. Selle smiles, and Madison rolls her eyes before standing up from the table.

"I think I'll join the both of you."

"Nah, two is enough. Next time, Maddy," Selle declines. Graham chuckles, and I kiss him on the cheek.

"Be right back for that dance, handsome."

Selle grabs my arm and wraps hers in mine, pulling me into the restroom with her. "Selle, who is that girl? Why is she acting so weird? Why are *all of you* being weird?"

"I think you should talk to G about it," she exclaims. I narrow my eyes at her.

"Just tell me."

She sighs and turns to the mirror to reapply her red lipstick.

"She's his ex. That's all I'm telling you. G will not end my life tonight for being the nosey, tattle-tale little sister." I want to ask more questions. She's an ex? He said two women broke his trust—his mother and another girl. Was it her? Were they serious? Was this who he didn't want to be tied to? As I nearly let curiosity get the best of me, Madison walks into the restroom door with a gleaming smile.

"Well, well, well. Graham has a new toy. How nice."

"Shut up, Madison. She's not a toy. He loves her—more than I could say about how he felt about you." Selle snaps back. I step forward and open my mouth to defend myself when she says words that completely rip my heart out.

"Then why did he propose to me? If he didn't love me as you say, why did he want me to be his wife?" She proclaims, her hands on her hips.

"Because you faked a pregnancy, you crazy bitch. Liza, let's go. Don't listen to her."

"He...pro...proposed?" I say in a whisper.

"Yup, sure did, about a year and a half ago. He didn't tell you? Typical Grah—" Selle's hand goes directly across her face before she can finish her sentence. Madison gasps in shock and grabs her face. Selle pulls me out of the restroom and stops me in front of the entrance.

"Liza, look at me; she is a manipulative bitch, who loves to lie. He only proposed to her because he didn't have a choice. Dad *made* him, which is another reason he hates him so much. He found out she lied about the pregnancy and broke up with her. Don't let her ruin you or get to you."

I glance at the dance floor and see Graham dancing with his mother. I look back at Selle and try to crack a smile at her. I can't understand any of the words she's saying.

Graham lied to me. He told me there were no more secrets, yet this was such a big one. This night was turning into one I wanted to forget. I look up and see Graham staring at me.

"I'm going to grab a drink; could you tell him?" She tilts her head and sighs. I walk off in time to see Graham walking toward us. I reach the bar and see Selle talking with Graham. Based on his stone-hard face, I can tell she's explaining what happened in the bathroom. Moments later, Madison emerges from the restroom, her makeup freshly reapplied. She stops at Selle and Graham, and I see Graham spitting words at her. He walks off and heads towards me at the bar, leaving Madison with her arms folded, watching him.

"*Angel.*" I turn back to the bar and chug my champagne. He grips me by my shoulder, turns me to face him, and sees the tears in my eyes.

"Dance with me, and let me explain…please. Let. me. explain." I wipe the tears out of my eyes when I see Madison glaring at us. I refuse to give her the reaction she so clearly wants to see.

"Fine, then I'd like to leave." He nods and grabs me, leading me onto the dance floor.

31

Graham

I spin Liza around and pull her towards me as we sway back and forth on the dance floor. I can feel how distant she is and how she doesn't want me touching her right now. How could I let this happen? Why didn't I tell her about Madison when I saw her sitting at the table?

"Elizabeth...I was going to tell you."

"When, when exactly were you going to tell me that you were fucking *engaged*, Graham?" she snaps. We continue to sway back and forth to the music, and I sigh deeply.

"I didn't know when it was the right time to tell you. I didn't mean to hurt you... I..."

"Graham, I want to go. Now. You kept it from me, I told you no secrets, you told me you had a fucking *ex*—not that you almost married someone!" Her voice raises a bit, and I notice my mother watching us intently, with Selle next to her. I have no clue where Madison went, nor do I give a fuck. If she knows any better, she'll disappear before I permanently erase her from this fucking planet.

"I would've never married her on my own. I had to propose to appease my father. I thought she was pregnant."

"And you felt that I didn't need to know that? Did you honestly think we'd never see her? She's the epitome of someone you're probably used to being with. Who you *should* be with."

"Elizabeth, don't." If there was one thing that made me lose my shit on the spot, it was listening to her make up reasons why we couldn't be together.

"Don't you dare tell me what to do and not to do right now. You both deserve each other." She tries to break out of my hold, and I tighten my arm around her.

"I'm not supposed to be with anyone but you."

"I'd like to leave. *Now*." She pulls away again, and I narrow my eyes at her.

"Graham, let go. I'm not asking again. I want to *leave*."

"Okay, I'll take you."

"No, I want to go alone without you. I'll call Em."

"Elizabeth, I will take you."

"I said *no*." She says again, and I shake my head, knowing I don't stand a chance right now.

"Ellis will drive you, please. I need to know that you get there safely."

"Fine, but do not follow me. Do not call me. Do not visit me. I do not want to see your lying face again. I mean it."

She walks away from me, and I follow her as always. I'm always the one who follows behind her; always following behind the fucking breadcrumbs she leaves.

"Elizabeth, please don't do this," I grit through my teeth behind her. She continues to the door, reaching Ellis. He sees me and heads for the SUV. When she turns to face me, her eyes are dark. Her face is stone, and she's looking at me like I'm nothing. Like, I mean *nothing*. And if a feeling brewing in my stomach from that one look wasn't enough to set the fucking world on fire, her following words were enough to push it there.

"It's already done, Graham."

"So, you're leaving me? For good? That's it; you won't even let me explain? It was a misunderstanding."

"You didn't explain. You made *excuses*. You didn't tell me because you're a *coward*. I don't want anything to do with you."

Before I can respond, she pushes through the crowd and out the door. I stand there, unable to move or realize what has just happened. I lost her; I had her and lost her.

* * *

I left the event shortly after Liza left and headed home. My mother rushed to my side after seeing Liza leave, and she badgered me about it and whether everything was okay. The only thing on my mind was getting to Liza and fixing it. Then turning Madison's life into fucking dust.

"El, is she okay?"

"She's home safe, son." I feel relieved; I have to fix this. I'm going there whether she wants me to or not. She can't just leave me.

"Thanks, I'll head over."

"She was pretty torn up, crying, you know. Maybe not tonight." He tells me. I'm surprised at his comment, but I don't respond. What the fuck have I done?

"I want you to send me any and every fucking thing you can dig up on Madison. She's done. I'm ruining her fucking life like she did mine."

"Consider it done."

Game on.

32

Liza

Ellis dropped me off, and I quickly ran into my building, practically knocking Ellis over to push past him. I skipped over the elevator and decided to take the steps instead. Once I got into my apartment, I kicked off my Jimmy Choos and sank onto the floor, bringing my knees to my chest. Now that he's gone, I feel like my chest is heavy, and I can't breathe. I'm empty and lost.

This is not how my night was supposed to go. I should've been in Graham's arms, telling him I loved him. We should've been getting ready to go to New York for dinner with my... Oh, FUCK! Dinner with my mom! Amid the chaos, I forgot that we were leaving late tonight for the weekend in New York. There's no way I can cancel on my mom, but did that mean I would have to tell her about Graham?

I pick up my phone and search for last-minute flights right when I get an incoming text from Graham.

Graham: *I'm going to call you, please answer.*

Has he lost his mind? The last thing I want to do is talk to him. Seconds later, my phone buzzes, and I hit ignore. I go into my bedroom and quickly change out of my dress, pulling on a pair of jogger sweatpants and a hoodie. Moments later, my phone buzzes again. This time, a text message.

Graham: *The plane is leaving for New York in an hour. Ellis is still waiting for you. I'm sorry about tonight... I'm falling in love with you, Elizabeth. I wish I could've told you that before it blew up in my face tonight.*

I place my hands on my face, wiping the tears that slowly fall from my eyes. *Respond, Elizabeth, don't be a bitch.* The little voice in my head screams at me. I pick up my phone and respond.

Liza: *"Are you going to be there?"*

I hit send and start packing my bag; I pack the last bit of my clothes when I notice a missed alert on my phone that reads "Ellis." I call him back.

"Sorry, El, I'll be down in a second!"

"Do you need help with your bags, Ms. Crambell?" I groan at his comment.

"You've seen me cry. I think you can stop with the 'Ms. Crambell'... I'm all set. See you in a few." I hang up and go to Graham's messages. He still hasn't responded to me. Why did I want him to? Why did I ask if he'd be on the plane? He lied to me, and here I am, so quick to want to be around him again.

I grab my belongings and head downstairs. Ellis is waiting out front as usual. I smile, and he grabs my bag as I enter the SUV. He pulls off, and we head toward the airstrip.

Thirty minutes later, we arrive at the tarmac. I'm slightly disappointed when I don't see Graham on the airplane waiting for me. I buckle myself in and accept a glass of wine from the flight attendant. Before I knew it, I had fallen soundly asleep.

I wake up to the beautiful New York lights. I have to quickly decide what I will tell my mother about why I'm here alone and not with Graham. I could tell her the truth, but then I'd have to face the reality I didn't want to face: that I left him after I said I wouldn't. I still left.

I step off the airplane and check my phone; there are still no messages from Graham. I call Ellis. Something's wrong.

"Ms. Crambell, is everything alright?"

"Where's Graham?"

"He's home." Home, not here, not New York, but Seattle, without me. I sigh and quickly respond, "Thank you, Ellis. See you later."

"Is there something you need me to tell him?"

"No, no it's nothing. Thank you."

"Very well." I hang up just in time to see my mom pulling up in a black Mercedes Benz. She climbs out of the back and runs to me. Without realizing it, tears fill my eyes, and the moment she wraps her arms around me, I sob.

"Oh, honey, what's wrong? Are you here alone?" I cry harder, and she tightens her hold on me.

"What happened, honey? Let's go home."

I wipe my face, leaning my head on her shoulder as she directs me to the back seat of the car. The driver grabs my luggage and drives us off into the streets of New York.

I stay silent for the majority of the ride, noting my mom staring at me with worry. I reach over, tugging her hand.

"I'm so happy to see you, Mom. I missed you."

"I'm happy you're here too, sweetheart." She peeks out the window and clasps her hands together. "Oh! We're here. Brant will be so excited to see you!"

We step out of the car and into the driveway, and I see the front of the beautiful stone-brick estate. "Mom, this is beautiful."

"I told you it was breathtaking; as much as it cost, it better be! Come, let's go inside."

When we enter, a beautiful sitting room is decorated with gray and black furniture. Some of the house is empty, with boxes that need to be unpacked.

"Most of the house already came decorated, but there are a few rooms that I wanted to start on from scratch," my mom says, waving her hand at the rooms still holding boxes. The house was beautiful. There were paintings and family pictures all over, and there were splashes of gold and creme throughout. My mom always loved decorating, and she was good at it. I always told her that she missed her calling as an interior designer.

Finally, after my mom showed me the entire house for what felt like two days, I greeted Brantley and headed for my room. I overheard Brantley say, "He called to make sure she got here safe... I'm not sure what happened, dear." I stop at the door to my room and slowly let out a deep breath. He called. Why didn't he call me?

An hour later, I'm still tossing and turning in bed, replaying the night in my head. He told me he had an ex-girlfriend, but he said nothing about a fucking *fiancé*. I keep trying to remind myself that I can't be mad about it and shouldn't have left the way I did without letting him fully explain. Especially because all I knew was that she fucked him over or, rather, in his words, 'hurt him.' I needed more information; I needed to know the whole story. My heart has a hole in it right now; I know it's because I left. I'm so far away from him.

All I wanted to do was tell him I loved him, and from his text message, he had the same plan. I loved him so much, and it upsets me that he hid that from me. I think I'm more upset that *she* felt she had power over my relationship and I'm even more upset that I gave her that power and played right into her hand.

I pick up my phone and check the time. It's 3:42 a.m. I scroll through my contacts, stopping at Graham's name. I inhale and press call.

Almost immediately, Graham answers.

"Elizabeth? It's late. Are you okay?" I hear music in the background and become increasingly angry before I even realize it.

"Are you at a party? Why is it so loud?"

"Liza, it's not like that. I'm here for—"

"It doesn't matter; forget it. I wanted to check on you, but you seem *just fine* without me. Goodnight, Graham."

"Liza...wai-"

Click.

I hang up and turn on my side, slipping into an unsettling sleep.

* * *

"Elizabeth, honey. Wake up! I have such a day planned for us!"

I wake up to my mother's high-pitched voice. I groan and look at the time on my phone: 9:30 a.m. Yeah, that's sleeping in for me; I was more tired than I realized.

"Mom, do you have to be so loud?"

"Whatever, just get up and get ready. We're having brunch in an hour and a half."

"Do we have to?" I moan, and she comes and sits next to me, rubbing my knee.

"What happened? He called your stepfather, you know."

"Yeah... I overheard." I put my head down.

"Honey, he seemed upset, and *you* seem upset. Can't you work it out?"

"He was engaged, Mom... and didn't tell me." She looks away, unsurprising. I wait for her reaction, for any response, but I fail to get one.

"Mom, why aren't you upset?"

"Honey, I knew about it. It was all over the blogs and magazines; I believe she pretended to be pregnant. I remember Brant saying how she used him for money and fame. She hurt him pretty badly; he didn't love her." I look at her in disbelief as she speaks.

"Do I live under a goddamn rock? How'd I miss this?" She puts her head down and says.

"It was while you were away, getting better…"

I knew what she was talking about. When Tim stalked me, I left for about two months; I shut out the world completely.

"Elizabeth, listen to me…" She grabs my hand. "You graduate in one week. In one week, you will face real-life problems, start your career, and be all grown up. You have to ask yourself, sweetheart… Do you see him next to you in those moments, those memories?" I glance away from her and shrug my shoulders.

"Do you love him?" She continues.

Tears pool in my eyes; I close them, letting them spill over.

"So much, mama."

"Then you take the space you need to get over this, but you have to try. Give him a chance. He *loves* you; it shows. I know he lied to you, and I know he hurt you. But you have to choose your battles." I wipe my face and smile at my mother.

She always knows exactly what to say to me, and she's right. I'll talk to him when I'm ready. If he loves me as much as I love him, he'll wait for me.

33

Graham

I called to check on her the night before, and Brant assured me she had arrived safely. While I knew she wasn't okay, I knew that showing up there would worsen things. Brant and Beth invited me and told me to show up and make her talk to me. I had a feeling that it wouldn't go over well.

Ellis told me she called too, and if she was at least "worried" about me, I knew she was thinking about me. I ignored all her texts, despite every inch of me wanting to respond the second I saw the text message. Knowing she was still worried about me gave me hope that she still wanted to be a part of my life. I needed her to care, and I needed her to want me.

* * *

The next day...

I woke up feeling hungover and stupid. Did I really lose Liza last night? Why didn't I go with her to New York this weekend? Or, better yet, why did she ask if I was still coming? Did she want me there?

I roll out of bed and grab the aspirin and a bottle of water from the refrigerator. I quickly down it and look at my phone; no missed calls from her. A few from my mom, but I know it's only to see if I managed to pick my sister up from that party last night in one piece.

Moments later, Selle walks into the kitchen, rubbing her temples. I give her an aspirin and another bottle of water.

"You were supposed to pick me up, not get there and get drunk with me." She says. I flip her off and pull out eggs and bacon for breakfast.

"Have you talked to her?" She continues, and I shake my head and start whisking the eggs together while the pan gets hot.

"Why don't you just go to New York? I'll come with you. Say it's a business trip." I shake my head again and pour the eggs into the pan.

"She doesn't want to see me, Selle. I need to give her space."

"Mom doesn't think so." I turn and face her, angry with my know-it-all sister. I tried to keep everything from my mother; she saw Liza leave and saw my face. My mother is a lot of things, but stupid isn't one of them. She knew something was up but wouldn't ask questions until she felt she needed to.

"What does she know? Selle, did you tell her?"

"Madison did... your precious ex-fucking *fiancé* that needs to get a life." I slam my fist on the countertop and pick up my cell phone.

"Who are you calling?"

"Madison, I'm tired of her shit. Watch the food. I'll be back." Selle smiles and walks over to the stove.

"Gladly, ask her how her face feels, would ya?" I frown in confusion and walk out.

The phone only rings twice before her annoying little voice answers with excitement. "Graham! I sure didn't expect to hear—"

"Listen to me, Madison. I want nothing to do with you. I never will, ever again. The quicker you understand that, the easier you move on."

"Move on? How can you act like I meant nothing to you? Like we weren't going to be marr-"

"Married because of a fucking lie you started because you wanted to make a name for yourself? You used me for my money and then lied to me about becoming a fucking father. I want nothing to do with you. Leave Elizabeth *alone*. Last fucking warning."

"You love her? You seriously love *her*?"

"I don't just love her... I'm in love with her. Understand? And I may have lost her because of you."

"Well, aren't I just sorry about that-" She says sarcastically. Right then and there, I decided that when her life turned upside down, she needed to know it was me.

"Hear me now, that little business you just started? Dead. The money you've been making from your *investments*. Dead. Your father's company? It is now completely fucked. You should've never come for what's mine. Now I'm going to ruin your perfect little fucking life, just like you ruined mine."

"Graham, you wouldn't dare." I can hear her breathing picking up, just like I wanted. She fucked with the wrong person.

"This conversation is over." I hang up the phone and walk back into the kitchen to see Selle on the phone. She puts the last bit of bacon in the pan and puts the phone on speaker. She glares at me and signals for me to be quiet.

Moments later, I hear Liza's voice on the other end. I reach for the phone, and she mutes it.

"I called to check on her, and she doesn't know I'm here with you. Be quiet if you want to know how she's doing."

"Selle? Selle, are you there?" Liza asks.

"Yes, I'm here. Sorry, I'm cooking breakfast and almost burned the damn bacon. Anyway, I'm sorry she ruined your night. She's such a bitch. I'm not just saying this because he's my brother, but he was going to tell you. I think you two should talk."

"I can't; I hurt him. I need space, and he does, too. I..I don't know;

the space is just."

"Just what?"

"Good for us, I think."

"All I'm saying is don't spend so much time caught up on what he *didn't* tell you and remember everything that he *did* tell you. He's never kept anything from you before; even if he has, he always tells you." Liza is silent on the other end, and Selle looks at me and shrugs.

"He's my brother. I love him regardless, and I'm not defending him, but I think you're being a little cruel."

"Selle, it's just a little space."

"What if space isn't exactly what you need? What if it goes wrong? What if it doesn't work out how you want it to?"

"I...I don't know how I want it to work out."

I put my head down and walk upstairs to my room. She did hurt me, but the last thing I needed was space from her. Being away from her is fucking killing me. My breathing is restricted every time I think about the fact that she's currently in a different state than I am. I hope that she feels a slither of the pain I feel.

I stretch out on the bed, deciding that taking a nap would be better than dealing with the shit that I had going on when Selle pushes through my bedroom door, carrying breakfast in one hand and cupping two cups of coffee in the other.

"Eat. It'll be fine." I shake my head.

"Selle, get out. I'm fine. I'll eat later."

"No, eat now, and I'll leave."

I let out a sigh, sit up and grab the plate. "Fine."

She sits down on the edge of my bed and giggles.

"You fall for anything, so when are we leaving for New York?" I shake my head and pick up a piece of bacon.

"We're not Selle. You heard her on the phone; she needs space." She shrugs her shoulders and turns to me.

"All I'm saying is, you've never had to fight for anything in your life. Now that you do, you won't. Since when do you listen to what people *need*, especially when it comes to Liza?"

Was she right? Should I go to New York? I *did* have business there, and running into her could be a complete *accident*.

34

Liza

After getting off the phone with Selle, I go to lunch with my mom. Wallowing in my sorrow won't change anything; I left Graham and didn't give him a chance to explain. All this time, I bitched at him about trusting me when it was me who ended up not trusting him.

Was he going to tell me? Selle said he was, and I believe he was; I needed space from him either way. I needed space from the constant reminder of how much I felt like I couldn't be without him. In the brief time we were together, I had completely lost myself in Graham; I relied entirely on him and did everything with him in mind. It's time to focus on me again, to remember who I was before him.

Thirty minutes later, I look like normal Liza again. I put on a pair of light blue jeans that hug me in all the right places, a low-cut silk red shirt that my mom bought me, and my nude red bottom pumps.

"Oh! Sweetheart, you look stunning. Let's go."

Once we get to the restaurant, my mom practically pulls me out of the car. As always, there's paparazzi around snapping pictures. She clings close to me, and we smile for the camera. It's always weird to me when people want pictures of someone as ordinary as me; as a kid, we managed to keep my brother and me out of the press as much as possible. Now that we are adults, from time to time, we might see someone taking pictures of us, but it is such a rare thing.

My mom grabs my hand. We walk into the restaurant, where the host tells us our table is ready.

"Oh! Mrs. Gilman, your table is right this way."

"So, sweetheart, I was thinking we can maybe shop or get mani and pedis after lunch."

She grins at me once we are seated, her grin turning into an unsure half-smile.

"Are you okay? Did you think any more about what I said to you?"

I pick up my menu, ignoring her question. That's all I've been thinking about, and I haven't stopped. My mom was right, and I knew she was, but why was it so hard to admit that?

The waiter arrives, and we put in our orders. Over our food, we discuss what we want to do for the rest of the weekend.

"Do you want to go to a movie? Like old times?"

"Sure, mama. That sounds fine."

"How has the apartment been?"

"Well, honestly, I haven't stayed in it much yet. But it looks great. I wonder, though, why you didn't tell me Graham owned it."

Her grin widens, and I raise my eyebrow as she drinks her champagne as a diversion. It's the first time I've enjoyed a conversation and time with my mother; she wasn't badgering me or picking a fight with me. It was nice to have her there with me.

"Alright, let's go get pampered," she exclaims, winking her eye at me.

She always cares about her looks and does not care who knows it. If there were one thing my mom would do, it would be to keep up with her appearance.

I get up and follow her out of the restaurant. When we get to the front, a car like the one Ellis drives rolls past us. I stop when I notice it visibly slows down. My breathing slows, and I try to look through the dark-tinted windows. Nothing. I can't see absolutely anything, but I can feel him.

"Honey, are you alright?" my mom asks, touching my elbow to grab my attention.

I bring my attention back to her. "Yes, mama. Sorry. I just thought that looked awfully like the car Graham has Ellis drive him in."

She looks at the passing car, and I swear I see her lips tilt up in a smile. However, before I can question her more about it, our car pulls up.

Was Graham here? In New York?

35

Graham

It's been a week, a week without hearing from her. I sent her flowers on the first day of her internship and got a 'thank you' text. I asked to have dinner with her and got no response. I went to New York intending to fix things with her, but when I saw her outside that restaurant, I couldn't bring myself to get out of the car. Instead, I told Ellis to get me out of New York, called her stepfather, and told him I would give her the space she needed from me. The look on her face was all I needed to know; she knew it was me and recognized the car. That's what our presence does to each other, even if we aren't within arms' reach. We can feel it if we're in the same vicinity, and I left like a coward.

I lost the one girl I loved because a girl who wanted nothing more from me than my money and to make a name for herself decided to fuck my life up even more. I should've told Liza about the engagement, but it was never the right time to mention it. I'd fix this; she had to miss me. She could dodge me all she wanted, but there's one place where I knew I'd have my chance to plead my case: graduation.

Graduation is this Saturday, and I plan to get my Liza back by then. After speaking with my mother, I figured giving her space was best, and I just hoped she'd come back to me. But I'll be miserable till then.

She called me once, and it was that night. She assumed I was at a party when I picked Selle up from a party she went to after the event. I'd explain all of this to her when I saw her, I would explain everything to her.

I've been drowning myself in work to distract myself from the thought of her. Everyone around me has been walking on eggshells, afraid to mention her or ask if I am okay.

It's about 6:30 p.m. when I finally decide to quit working and head home. I leave the office and instruct Ellis to order dinner at a friend's restaurant, one of my favorite spots. He picks up the phone and dials the restaurant.

"Francis wants to talk to you." I grab the phone from his hand as he continues driving.

"Fran, what's up?"

"You don't want to come here tonight, my guy."

"Why?"

"Because you're not going to like what you see when you walk in—or rather, who you see."

"Just spit it out, Fran. What the hell are you talking about?"

"Your wonder woman is here, and she isn't alone." I grind my teeth together, growing increasingly pissed off.

"I'll be there in ten minutes."

The following ten minutes feel like a fucking eternity waiting to pull up to Fran's Italian restaurant. I grow nervous, my stomach in knots, when I see her in the window, a younger man sitting across from her and another on the right with his arm around her chair. *Was Liza on a fucking date?*

I swing the door open, and Fran meets me at the entrance. "Whatever you do, don't destroy my fucking restaurant." I bypass him and walk directly to her table.

What am I going to say or do? She's single, and she is free to date whoever she wants and do whatever she wants.

I fix my furrowed brow, straighten up, and smoothly glide to her table. She looks up and adjusts in her seat, her face pale. I hear the man next to her say, "Are you okay? What's wrong?"

She clears her throat as I near the table and gives a fake slant smile. "Graham. What are you doing here?"

I force a smile back. "A friend owns the restaurant. I'm just stopping to pick up some dinner. I just wanted to say hello. I'm sorry to be rude to your date."

She frowns and tries to open her mouth, and both men break out in laughter.

"Bro, I'm not her date, and neither is he. I'm her brother, and he's my best friend. You two clearly need to talk." He stands, and I back away, resting my hand on his shoulder.

"I apologize. Graham Salando." I reach out for his hand, and he shakes it.

"I know who you are. I'm Elias, call me Eli. This is Hogan; call him stupid." Hogan punches Eli, and they both laugh.

"Well, I was just stopping by to say hello. Elizabeth, it's always nice to see you. I look forward to seeing you at graduation. Enjoy your dinner, everyone." I turn and head for the bar, where Fran stands with a smug look on his face.

"Well, you didn't punch the fucker's face in, so that's an improvement. You must really be trying to get her back."

"I'm not trying to do anything. That's her brother and his best friend. Put their dinner on my card."

"What has gotten into you? The G, I know, would go after who and what he wants. Stop moping around. Either fix it with her or, for God's sake, get another piece of ass."

"How much longer on the food?" He cocks his eyebrow, and his eyes get big behind me.

"For fuck's sake, what?"

I turn around and see a beautiful Liza standing behind me with her coat in hand and her hair tucked behind her ear.

"Your food should be ready in five minutes. I'll take it out to El." Fran tells me, leaving toward the kitchen behind me. I nod and turn back to Liza.

"Elizabeth. I'm sorry, I shouldn't have assumed."

"You really think I'd be with someone? It's been a week," she grits out shockingly. I put my head down and sigh. "Liza, I don't want to argue with you. I just wanted to say hello."

"Did you know I was here? Did your friend... Never mind; I should go." She turns for the door, and I grab her arm. I look out the door and see Eli and Hogan standing near their car, watching. "Liza..." she stops and turns to me, tears in her eyes. "Don't cry...please. I've missed you so much. Please don't do this."

"I'm sorry. I just... I have to go; I *want* to go." She walks out of the door and onto the street. I run after her.

"Wait, Elizabeth, *wait*." She stops, and I turn her towards me. "Have dinner with me. Please?" She picks at her fingers, and I can tell she's thinking about it. I reach out for her hand. "Please... just dinner so we can talk, then I'll leave you alone if you want me to." She looks down and tightens the hold on our hands, and I smile.

"Is that a yes?"

She shrugs. "I don't know... Maybe, can I think about it?" she whispers.

"Do you miss me? At all?" I ask with my head down, realizing a pool of tears is forming in my eyes. A second later, I feel her hand lifting my head to face her. "So much. Okay? I miss you so much."

"Then why are you doing this? Why are you making this so hard on us? I fucked up; I know. But you have to give me a chance to make it right. She's not a problem for us anymore. Please just forgive..." She cuts me off and removes her hand from my face, leaving me instantly missing the touch that I've been longing for all week.

"I do forgive you. I know you would've told me; I know you would've explained. But you have to understand that when I left you, I realized how much I relied on you, how much I needed you, and how much you consumed me. I had lost myself in you. I have to find myself, Graham. You have to let me do that." I step away from her and look her in the eyes.

"I broke you, didn't I?" She frowns at me and shakes her head. "No, no, that's not what I mean. You did not *break* me. You shielded me from everything—from too much in such a short time. You took away the one thing I've always had to do for myself: watch out for my safety. When I left you, I was back where I had been after the Tim incident. I felt unsafe and hopeless. I worked so hard to build myself back up after that, to show myself how strong I was, and once I met you, you took that from me."

"It's my job to protect you. It will always be my job to protect you, not because I think you're incapable of protecting yourself but because I always protect the people I love, even if they are as strong and fearless as you are." She gasps. I frown. "What's wrong?"

"You said the people you love..."

"You are one of those people. I know I've never said it, but it's true. And that's why it's so hard to let you protect yourself. I never meant to take that power from you, but you took everything from me the moment you walked out of the doors of that event." She puts her head down.

"Why do you love someone who is a hypocrite?" I step toward her.

"A hypocrite?"

"Yes, I told you to trust me, yet I ran out on you the moment our trust was tested."

"My ex told you something big enough to make anyone run out. And

I just assumed you were already on a date, so I guess neither of us gave each other the benefit of the doubt then. But I understand the need to walk away."

The sky gets angry, and it starts thundering.

"Liza! It's about to pour. We're leaving." We both turn and see her brother and Hogan climbing into the car on the side of the street. She looks at them and yells back, "Go ahead. I'll see you guys at the apartment. Love you."

"Yeah, if you make it there. I love you too." Her brother smiles, enters the driver's side, and pulls off.

"Will you drive me home?" she asks. I sigh and grab her hand.

"Of course I will."

36

Liza

"Of course I will," he agrees.

I'm not sure why I didn't go home with my brother. Maybe I was ready to be around Graham. Or perhaps I just needed to see if I could handle being around him again. What I did know was that I missed him so much. I'm hurt that he thought I'd be with someone else so soon. Was that really what he thought of me?

We walk over to his car, and Ellis greets me.

"Ms. Crambell," he states with a slight nod while opening the car door so I can slip in.

"Hi, Ellis." Graham slides into the back seat after me, and Ellis closes the door. I look down, our hands practically touching on the seat. I quickly turn my head and look out of the window. He must've noticed our hands because he sighs and lays his hands over his knee.

"Where to, you two?"

"We're just taking Liza home."

My mother's words ring in my ear the entire drive home. She's right. I have to get over this, and I have to fight for my relationship. It took me so long after Tim to feel like I would be able to give myself to a man that not every man who liked me wanted to hurt me. Graham was a big part of me opening myself up to that. He's the man I have feelings for, and he loves me like I love him. This isn't a relationship I have to be afraid of; this is a relationship I can choose to be in.

"I actually think I'd like to go to your house," I say boldly, quieting myself after the words spill out. "If that's okay with you, I mean." He spins his head toward me in disbelief, and I continue. "I'd like for us to talk."

"I think us talking is a great idea. I can take you home after."

I catch a glimpse of Ellis smiling in the front. He is always rooting for us. He takes so much pride in Graham's happiness, and it warms me to know that he thinks I'm such a big part of it.

"Head to my house, El, and then you're off the hook for the night." He looks down at his vibrating phone.

"Yes, princess, what do you need?" He teases sarcastically, and I hear his sister's voice on the other end. "I'll call you later; I'm busy right now."

"Busy with what?" I hear her yell. He groans in frustration, and I touch his hand.

"Tell her I say hello."

"Liza says hello." I hear her squeal, and Graham pulls the phone away from his ear. "If you're done, I'm going to hang up now."

"Graham, do not screw this up." He hangs up the phone, and his grip tightens.

"I'm sorry. She's been calling me every day since... well since you left," he explains quietly. I'm saved by the bell when we pull into Graham's driveway. Ellis gets out and opens my door.

"Goodnight, Ms. Crambell."

"Night, Ellis." He and Graham wave each other off, and we approach Graham's front door. He stops before it and slowly inserts the key, stopping briefly before turning it.

"Is something wrong?"

"It's just a bit of a mess in here. I've been, um, well, it's just a mess."

Even with the fair warning, I am unprepared for the mess behind the door. Whiskey bottles and beer cans are everywhere, as are pizza boxes and leftover Chinese containers on the kitchen and living room tables.

"Graham, we have to clean this," I'm stripping off my coat and hanging it as he starts grabbing things.

"No, this isn't your mess to clean. I planned on cleaning it tonight, but I ran into you."

I ignore him and get to work.

About an hour later, the house is back to its original condition, and it smells like lemons and cinnamon. I light a candle and place it on the kitchen counter. The hairs on my neck stand at attention, and I know he's watching me.

"What?" I look down suddenly, feeling nervous.

"Nothing. I just missed you, is all...so that talk." He heads toward the couch, and I follow him. One of us sits at each end, and the minutes pass; I sigh and break the silence.

"So, here's the thing..." I stop because I have no idea what to say.

"The thing is, I broke your trust and hurt you. I'm an *idiot* who loves you but doesn't know how to show it. I'm also a sorry idiot who wants another chance to show you how sorry I am and how trusting I can be."

"I know I messed up, Liza, and it wasn't intentional, but this week has been so hard for me without you. I never want to feel that emptiness again. Please don't make me feel that emptiness."

I look down at my fingers and quickly think about my response. This is when I can choose forgiveness for once and know it's on my terms. I can move forward with my relationship with Graham, knowing that it isn't because I'm too weak to turn him down but because I can't take another moment where I'm not his.

"No more secrets..." I say; he slides closer to me and grasps my chin between his thumb and forefinger, tilting it to his face.

"No, no more secrets."

"Were you in New York?"

"Yes."

"Why?"

"Because your parents and Selle thought it would be a good idea to track you down and make you listen to me."

"So that *was* you? I saw you outside of the restaurant then." I tilt my head to analyze him. "Why didn't you stop then?"

"Because I don't do rejection well, and you already did that once, I told El to take me back to the plane and give you space."

"Oh."

"Yeah... I knew you'd notice the car."

"I *felt* you... I don't know how to explain it, but I felt you. I couldn't see you, but I just knew. I knew it was you," I say softly. He places his hand on my cheek and lightly strokes it.

"Isn't it weird how that happens?" I tuck my lip in my mouth, and he nudges me. "It happens to me all the time; you just have that effect on me, huh?" I can no longer contain the smile I'm desperately trying to hide.

"I missed that smile." He lifts my face to his and softly kisses my lips.

"I missed these lips," he whispers, planting another kiss on each side of my cheeks.

"And I missed this face."

"Graham...quit it," I say. He chuckles and pulls my hands in his.

"Fuck Liza, I'm sorry for everything."

When I look at him, I see all the guilt he's been carrying, and I feel sad for him—sad for the week I'd put him through, sad for ignoring him and making him think I hated him.

"I'm sorry too," I say, leaning into him. He leans back on the couch and pulls me into the cusps of his arm. I snuggle tightly against him and inhale the scent I've missed so much. He kisses my head, and I slip into a silent slumber.

<h1 style="text-align:center">37</h1>

<h1 style="text-align:center">Graham</h1>

A few hours later, I wake up to see it's around 3 a.m., and Liza's sleeping in my arms. It's the sweetest sight I could ever wake up to; finally, she's here, back where she belongs. I knew how lucky I was to have her forgiveness and to have her come back to me. I knew how hard it was for her to hear about my past engagement, and it was even more difficult for her to feel like she was losing the person she was.

I slowly slide my arm from under her, trying my best not to wake her. I lift her in my arms, and she shifts; I kiss her forehead.

"I've got you."

She quickly opens her eyes and shuts them once she hears my voice. I climb the steps and reach my room, lowering her on the bed. I turn to my drawer and grab a T-shirt for Liza to sleep in. I turn around to find her sleeping peacefully. I carefully take her clothes off and slide the shirt over her perfect body. Damn, I've missed her.

"Mm, what are you doing?" Liza groans sleepily. I grin at her and kiss her cheek.

"Go back to sleep; stay with me tonight." She looks down and sees that she's already in my shirt. She lifts her eyebrow at me.

"Well, it looks like I have no choice, huh? Just let me text Eli and let him know."

"It's 3 a.m., I think he knows." She nods and lies back on the pillow, her hooded eyes finding mine.

"What?" I ask.

"I just missed you, is all. I'm happy I'm here. With you."

"Trust me, angel, now that you're back, I don't plan on ever letting you go again. That week was torture."

I put my head down, remembering how it felt when she left me. She must sense the sudden change in my mood because moments later, she sits up and cups my face.

"I'm here, and I'm not going anywhere, I promise." She brings her lips to mine and softly kisses me. I deepen the kiss, showing her how sorry I am. Our tongues intertwine; I push my hands into her hair and pull her closer, biting her lower lip. She lets out a gasp and pulls me onto the bed closer to her.

She yanks at my pants and says, "Take these off."

"Are you being bossy?" I pull my pants off as instructed. "What next?" I say, standing in front of her.

"Boxers. They need to go, too." I try to hide my amusement and kick my boxers off. She opens her mouth to make another command, and I pull her up off the bed to stand her in front of me.

"My turn; the shirt and everything underneath it needs to go. Quickly."

"So impatient."

"Damn right, you have no idea how much I've missed seeing your body underneath mine." She gives me a shy look and lifts her lips into a slight smile. She quickly follows my directions and, soon enough, is standing naked in front of me. I pull her close to me, our noses practically touching. Her breathing quickens, and her pulse speeds up.

I nuzzle against her neck, pressing a soft kiss.

"Missed you," I say to her. I move to her ear, nibbling against it. "So much, *angel*." She closes her eyes and leans her head back, her legs weakening slightly. I steady her and pull one of her breasts into my mouth; she reacts instantly, letting out a tiny groan in satisfaction.

I start nudging her backward toward the bed until she falls onto the bed.

"Trust me?"

"Yes."

"Stay there."

I walk to my closet and punch in the code to the bookshelf. It opens up, showcasing an array of whips, chains, paddles, balls, and blindfolds. I grab the spreader tucked towards the back.

When I look at Liza, her chest rises and falls, and she watches me; her eyes widen when she sees what's in my hand.

"What is that?"

"A spreader."

"What does it... do?"

"I'm going to put it on your ankles, and it'll widen every time you move. I want all access to you. I want to be so deep inside of you that I feel like I'm a part of you."

She tucks her lip in her mouth as I apply the restraints to each ankle. I widen it, and she groans; I step back and take in the sight of her spread open for me. Her pussy on full display for me, waiting for me to devour it. I climb on top of her, planting kisses all over her body, beginning with her neck and trailing down to her sweet pussy. She grips the bed sheets when I slowly slide my tongue up and down her pussy lips. She pushes her hands into my hair and tugs.

"Graham," she shrieks breathlessly.

I eat her pussy more aggressively, adding my fingers as I move my tongue and fingers in and out of her. She starts quivering, coming violently into my mouth. I continue to lick her, taking everything she'll give me.

"Oh god," she starts fighting, yanking at my hair as I continue to devour her, her legs getting wider and wider from the fight.

"Come for me, you're going to be coming all fucking night."

I stand up and climb over her. Her eyes pierce through me as she tries to catch her breath. I pull her towards me by her thighs, and she squeals. She tries to sit up face-to-face with my now excruciatingly painful hard cock. I help her up as she struggles. If I don't get inside her soon, I'm going to fucking explode. She grabs my length and licks the tip of my cock, moving her lips and mouth over me. Taking more of me in her mouth until she hits the shaft, I groan in response.

"Fuuuck."

There was no way she was making me come into her mouth; I knew exactly where I wanted to come, and that's what was going to happen. I pull out of her mouth and climb on top of her, rubbing the tip of my cock over her pussy's entrance. I sure as fuck hope she's been keeping up with her birth control because I'm not wasting a drop.

Lies. You want her pregnant so she can't get away from you.

I shake the thoughts from my mind and push the tip of my cock in and out of her pussy; slowly.

"Graham, please." She whimpers as I toy with her clit.

She has no idea how much torturing her tortures me. I wanted nothing more than to be inside of her already, to sink myself so deeply in her that we felt like one.

"Not yet." She lets out a frustrated groan when I pull out of her just as quickly as I push my cock inside her. "Do you know how much I missed you?"

"Show me, please."

I can't resist her any longer. I sink into her, finally remembering how she felt around me—tight and like a fucking glove made perfectly for me. No one else, just me.

"I...oh god, I missed you...so good, you feel so good." She moans into my ear. I deliriously pump in and out of her, adding more force with each thrust. She claws at my back. "I'm going to come." She moans, out of breath. That just won't work for me.

"No, you're not. You're going to wait."

"Graham, I can't. I need."

"What." *Thrust.* "Did." *Thrust.* "I." *Thrust.* "Say?" *Thrust.* "Fucking wait."

I reach my fingers around and plunge them into her pussy, she gasps, and I slap her pussy lips. She's concentrating so hard on not coming, her bottom lip tucked between her teeth, and she's so close to hyperventilating. I watch her fight the urge, landing a slap on her pussy again.

"Come for me, angel. Give me everything you've got."

Her pussy grips my cock, and I tighten around her, losing myself just as she is. It was quicker than I wanted, but I knew I had all night with her. This would be the first of many climaxes she'd experience tonight. I had too much to compensate for and planned to do just that.

I reach down and free her from the spreader, kissing the marks on her ankles.

We lay there, our bodies tangled together, out of breath.

"Don't ever leave me again, Elizabeth."

The words are out of my mouth before I can stop them. She grips me tighter around my waist and nuzzles her naked body into mine.

"I'm sorry. I won't." She kisses my neck, and I run my fingers through her hair, stopping to smell the cinnamon and lavender in her hair.

"Promise me, Liza. Promise me you won't run from me, that we'll work through everything. You can't do that to me again. I know it was my fault, and I should've told you, but..." She puts her finger over my lips, silencing me.

"I promise, and it's not just *your* fault; it was mine, too. We're in this together…I promise."

I kiss her and thank the Gods that she's still naked because I need to feel her again; I need to appreciate her—slow and deep this time. Something I didn't even know I was fucking capable of until my cock made its acquaintance with her pussy. My cock jumps to attention at the thought of being inside of her again, and the only thing I could think was…

Welcome fucking home.

38

Liza

The next day, I wake up to Graham cuddling me. His arm wraps tightly around my abdomen, and his leg is on top of mine. I turn to face him, and he starts squirming a little.

I peek over his shoulder to check the clock, which reads 7:45 a.m. We only slept for about two hours, thanks to us "making up." I should have been exhausted, but instead, I felt more awake than I ever had.

I softly kiss his cheek, and he gives me a sleepy grin and turns on his back. "Don't start, Crambell." I throw my leg over his and lay my head on his chest.

"Why not, Salando?" He looks at the clock.

"Well, for starters, you need your sleep. Once that happens, I will gladly take whatever you're trying to offer me."

I take in the fact that his cock and mind were on two completely different tracks.

"Well, maybe you should give him the memo. He seems pretty eager to take what I want to give right now," I say, brushing my hand over his stiffness. He groans and grabs my hand. I tangle my fingers in his.

"Okay, okay. Let's get some sleep then," I say unwillingly. He kisses my forehead, and I drift back into sleep.

I jump out of my sleep when I hear my phone ringing. It's only been about two hours later; I groan and grab it to see it's my mom. I clear my throat and answer, "Hi, mama."

"Elizabeth, are you still sleeping? Your graduation is tomorrow, and we still have to find you a dress. I want us to have dinner tonight." Graham opens his eyes and rubs my arms.

"Who is it?" he asks in a sleepy voice. My mom overhears him, and her voice escalates a notch.

"Oh, I'm sorry, honey! Tell Graham hello. He'll have to have dinner with us tonight!"

"Mom, as loud as you were, I'm sure he heard you himself," I say, shaking my head in embarrassment and putting the phone on speaker.

"My parents and sister are coming home tonight. I would, ma'am, but—"

"The more, the merrier; we'll have dinner at 6 p.m. I will text Elizabeth all of the details! Oh, this will be great."

"Okay, mom. I need to get ready. I'll meet you in a few hours. I love you."

"Love you, honey."

I hang up with her and throw my head back, repeatedly hitting it gently against the wall. Graham sits up on his arm, tilting his head at me.

"What's wrong?"

"Nothing. She's just been hovering since our breakup, and I know she means well, but she has been driving me nuts."

"Well, tell her I'm back, and she can relax now." I close the gap between us, giving him a small, quick kiss.

"Okay, I have to go home and get ready. If I don't find a graduation dress today, she'll kill me."

I get up and throw on my clothes. Graham rises from the bed and pulls on his sweats, leaving his bare chest for me to see. I stare for a few seconds too long.

He notices and walks over to me, "Don't look at me like that unless you want your mom to find that dress alone." I push my hands against his chest, pushing him away.

"Behave, Salando." I tease as we walk downstairs.

"I'm going to get dressed too. Selle and my parents should be here soon. I'll call El to take you home." I make a sad face, and he pulls me into his arms. "Why the sad face?"

"How about you take me home, and I give you that gift I wanted to give you a few hours ago?" He growls and pulls me into a tight embrace, lowering his mouth over mine. I open for him, trying to pull away, when I hear keys. The door swings open, revealing Graham's family.

"Oops, we certainly didn't mean to interrupt," Madeline speaks, my cheeks flushing, and Selle giggles.

"I. I'm sorry. I was just about to head out. I was waiting on Ellis." Madeline walks over to me with her arms open, and I walk into them, giving her a warm hug.

"It's so nice to see you, sweetheart."

"You too, how are you?"

She whispers her response, ignoring my question. "I am so glad you two worked it out. This makes me so happy; you make him so happy."

Joe walks over and plants a kiss on my cheek.

"Nice to see you again, Elizabeth."

"You too, Joe."

"You are not waiting for Ellis to drive you home; I'll take you. We'll have a little girl's day," Selle suggests, winking at me.

"I have to find a graduation dress today. I'm meeting my mom in a few hours....You know what? You should come with me. You too, Madeline."

Maybe if I brought them both with me, my mom wouldn't pry me about the details of Graham and me. Madeline smiles.

"I'd love to, honey, but I have to check in on a few clients here.

"I'm game; let's go," Selle agrees, grabbing the keys to Graham's Audi. He laughs and snatches them out of her hand.

"Absofuckinglutely not Giselle. You are not driving my car." Madeline smacks Graham's arm.

"Have you lost your everlasting mind? You do not use that language in front of me; I am your mother, Graham Salando." Selle and I burst out in laughter.

"Sorry, mom...Ellis is here; he'll drive you both."

"I don't understand why I can't drive the Audi; you said I could when I turned 21, and that was two months ago." He rolls his eyes and focuses on me as I rub his arms.

"If you guys don't have dinner plans tonight, my mom and Brant would like us all to have dinner together."

"Oh, that would be lovely. We will be there. What time?" Madeline asks, with Joe standing beside her with his hand on her shoulder. I smile at the gesture, realizing I've never seen him show much affection.

"6 p.m."

"See you then," Joe confirms; I turn to Selle.

"All set?"

"Yup, let's go." Graham pulls me to him, and I blush at his affection.

"See you later, angel. Stay out of trouble."

"You too." He kisses me gently; his parents watch us tentatively.

"That's enough, guys; it's just a few hours. Goodness, let's goooo," Selle complains. I pull away, and Graham is reluctant to let me go.

"Bye, everyone; see you soon."

We walk out and get into the car, and Ellis drives us back to my apartment.

When we pull into the apartment, Ellis lets us out, and we say goodbye.

"Thanks for the ride, El," Selle says; he nods.

"Anytime, you ladies, be safe."

"Oh, my brothers are here. Ignore them."

We see Hogan and Eli sitting on the couch as soon as we open the door, each holding a beer bottle.

I walk in and smack my brother on the head. "You still have three more days before you can do that legally." He flips me off and smiles. "This is Selle, Graham's sister. I'm going to get showered and dressed. Do not harass her. This is Eli and Hogan."

"Oh, I didn't know you had two brothers; Graham only ever mentioned one."

"Hogan isn't my real brother; he's Eli's best friend. He's practically family." I say, tussling Hogan's hair.

"Stop, Lizzie."

He's one of the few who call me Lizzie—well, him and my brother—and they only do it to annoy me. My dad has been the one who has called me that since I was five. I walk away, shower quickly, and get dressed.

I can hear Eli and Selle talking and asking each other questions. They are both around the same age and in college, so I figured they'd hit it off well. As I curl my hair, my phone chimes.

Graham: *I miss you, is it 6 p.m. yet?*

Liza: *I wish it were, almost. I think my brother likes Selle.*

Graham: *Don't want to hear about it.*

Liza: *Such a big brother. See you later, handsome.*

Graham: *Looking forward to it, angel.*

I can't help but smile. I missed this. I missed being called "*angel*" by him, seeing his name pop up on my phone, hanging out with his sister, and most of all, how he made me feel when I was with him. I'm knocked out of my daydream when I hear my mother's voice.

"Elias Anthony Crambell, put that beer *down*."

"Mom, my birthday is in three days."

"Then I guess you'll enjoy the rest of it in three days, won't you, sweetie?" Hogan and Selle laugh, and I quickly finish my hair and walk out.

"Hi, mama."

"Letting your brother drink underage, are you?" I shake my head and kiss her on the cheek.

"He's practically twenty-one. It's fine." She spits back and tsks. "Selle, this is my mom. Mom, this is–"

"We've met already, honey. I told you I'm good friends with her parents. I can't wait to see them tonight. Everyone all ready to go?"

I look at my brothers and scoff. "Don't destroy my apartment, you two."

"Can you leave your car keys? We want to go to the mall later."

"As long as you buy me a damn good graduation present."

"I got you, sis."

I bend down and kiss him and Hogan's head.

"Love you guys."

"Love you too, sis," they both shout.

I loved our relationship; Hogan had been around for so long that I considered him my brother. Having them both here meant so much to me. They were both a huge part of me finding myself during the week Graham and I were apart.

We get downstairs, and my mom has a car waiting for us.

"Mom, we could have just driven, you know."

"Oh, honey. You know I like to chit-chat and catch up with you during our drives. Now hop in."

Selle nudges me, and I sigh and climb into the back of the car. They both follow, and the driver pulls out into traffic.

We went to several local boutiques, trying out dress after dress. If this is how long it took to find a graduation dress, I would hate to know how long it would take to find a wedding dress. I stunned myself at the thought of finding a wedding dress. I wondered what planning a wedding and marrying Graham would be like.

"Mom, this is the last store. It's 4:45 p.m., dinner is at six, and I'm tired of trying on dresses. This one is fine." I say, looking at the plunging-neckline white dress, which fits my hips perfectly. I felt confident in this dress, and I loved the neckline. It wasn't too much or too little.

"I agree. This dress is perfect for you. You look super hot in it," Selle gives me a wink. She whispers in my ear, "And Graham will love it."

My mom stands with her arms crossed, examining me in the dress from top to bottom. "You're right, and it is perfect." She turns to the store associate. "We'll take this one, please." The store associate nods, and my mom quickly goes to the register before I can object to buying it myself. I change back into my clothes and exit the changing room. My mom and Selle are standing at the register, chuckling.

"Mom, I can buy this, I don't need-"

"Oh, please, call it a graduation gift." She hands her card over to the associate, and we head out.

39

Graham

When we get to the restaurant, I can barely take another question from my mother about Elizabeth and me.

"Honestly, honey, I know I'm prying, and I'm sorry, but you just don't understand how happy I am for you. You were a *mess*; I know it was just a week, but you weren't yourself. This is the happiest I've ever seen you. Just do whatever you can to keep her and yourself happy *together*."

"I know, Mom, I'm trying to do that."

"You know… graduation is tomorrow."

"Yes, I know…being that it is *my* graduation."

"Did you get her anything?" I stop and look at her. *Shit.*

"Don't worry, son. I'm sure we can find her something before the day ends," my dad encourages.

"I know what I want to get her. Can we get our jeweler out here tomorrow morning?"

"Of course, I'll set it up right now."

My mom's eyes grow big, but I see Bethany and Brant's car pull to the curb before she can ask any more questions. "Thank God," I mumble under my breath.

"I heard that." My mom swats me.

Their driver opens their door, and the family pours out: Brantley, Eli, Hogan, Bethany, Selle, and Liza. Selle walks directly to me.

"I know she looks hot, but close your mouth, idiot." I nudge her.

"Shut up," I say, my voice cracking a bit. I meet Liza halfway and extend my hand to her.

She showcases that beautiful smile, and I damn near turn her around, put her in the car, and leave.

"Pretty girl... You look fucking edible." She looks down over herself and back at me and blushes. She's wearing a black fitted dress with an open low back and shiny black pumps. Her hair tumbled down her back in loose curls. She takes my breath away like she always does.

She intertwines her fingers through mine. I kiss her forehead and walk us into the restaurant.

Dinner goes by quickly. Our families blended perfectly. There was laughter, stories, and memories being made. Throughout dinner, I'd squeeze Liza's leg or plant quick kisses on her cheek.

Brantley and my dad argue about who will pay the bill. I look at the server, quietly waiting, hiding her annoyance.

"I'm sorry, ma'am. Take this." I hand her my card while both men are distracted.

"They're going to get you for that, ya know," Liza whispers.

"Stay with me tonight?" She shakes her head.

"Nope, I have too much to do tomorrow before graduation... I'd love to, though." She declines, wiping her mouth and winking at me.

"Graham, we're going to the bar after this. You game?" Eli speaks, leaning forward. Liza leans forward, too, narrowing her eyes at her brother.

"And how exactly are you planning on drinking? I think I've said this already—three days shy of twenty-one, remember?" I rub her back and look at Eli.

"Since your sister doesn't want to hang out with me, I'm *game*." I lean over the table toward him. "Don't worry about the 21 thing," I say quietly. He laughs and leans back, crossing his arms over his body.

"Hogan, are you drinking too?" Liza asks.

"Damn straight, sis." She shakes her head and smiles. By then, Brant and my dad are handing the server their cards.

"The bill has already been paid, sir." She tells Brant.

"Well, how the hell did he manage to do that?" My dad laughs and raises his hands.

"It wasn't me."

Everyone starts to push back their chairs. And I notice my father stays back, so I push Liza forward and linger behind. He's been acting weird since I saw him this morning with his phone stuck to his fucking hand. He's tucked in between the bathrooms, whispering.

"Look, I'm not a part of this anymore. I don't owe you anything. I paid you."

I inch closer, trying to figure out who he's paid.

"Listen, this is over. I'm not in this life anymore." What life? Tell me not this fucking cartel again.

"I'm hanging up."

I pick up my pace and head back to the others.

"Had to use the bathroom, pretty girl," I say, placing my hand on Liza's lower back. Everyone chuckles. My dad rejoins the group and hangs back with Brant, having a quiet conversation.

"Ellis can drive you home."

"I figured as much." Eli comes up beside and tussles Liza's hair.

"Alright, man. Are you ready?" Liza takes the keys from him.

"Graham drives. Got it?"

"Where are you gentlemen going?" Bethany asks.

"Yeah, where to?" my mom adds.

"Nowhere, just a little bar," Hogan replies.

"Listen to me, Elias. You better act like you have home training, Hogan; you too," Bethany states.

"Okay, Mom," they say, kissing Bethany on the cheek. Bethany, Brant, and my parents all get into Bethany's car.

"We're all going to have a nightcap; we will see you all tomorrow," Brantley announces. Everyone nods and says their goodbyes.

"We'll be at the car," Eli informs; I nod, and he and Hogan both give Liza a quick kiss on the cheek.

"Love you both, stay out of trouble, please." She pleads to her brother, or at this point, *brothers*; it's how she introduces them anyway.

"Love you too, sis." They say and start walking to the car.

Liza yells out, "AND NO FIGHTING!" I chuckle in the background and start walking Liza to the car, where Selle is settled in the back, and Ellis waits on them.

"What's Selle doing in there?" I say, gesturing toward the backseat of the car.

"She said she had plans, and Ellis is driving her there after he drops me off." I frown, and Liza swats my chest. "Leave her alone, Graham. She's a big girl." I pull her in for a hug.

"You just focus on keeping those two out of trouble tonight. Call me if anything goes wrong." I kiss her deeply. Her worries about her brothers are making me wonder if I'm missing something. She turns to get into the back of the car and stops, quickly ending my curiosity about her brothers.

"What is it?"

She turns and faces me again.

"I love you."

My heart stops in its tracks. I knew she loved me, but I'd never heard the words, except that one night she said it while sleeping.

I quickly move my feet to face her. "You tell me that for the first time right before I leave you to hang out with your brother?"

I place my hands on her face, slowly caressing her cheek.

"I love you, *angel*, so much." She kisses me again and climbs into the car.

"Have fun."

40

Liza

I watch Graham get smaller as the car pulls further away toward my apartment. Saying 'I love you' to him was much easier than I made it out to be. I was nervous about saying it, even though I knew he loved me back. I know I should've waited for a more intimate time. There was nothing more I wanted to do than return to his place and show him how much I loved him. But at that moment, it rushed out of my mouth before I realized what I was saying.

"What are you smiling at?" Selle asks, smirking at me. I rub my hands over my knees and smile even harder.

"Sorry, nothing. Just your brother." She makes a gagging sound, and we both laugh.

"Speaking of brothers, I noticed you and my brother seem to have hit it off pretty well," I say, narrowing my eyes at her, showing my suspicion. She waves me off.

"We're just friends. He's pretty cool. I think Hogan lives to embarrass him, though."

"Oh yeah, they live to embarrass one another, but I'm not sure I'm buying the 'just friends' part."

"Yeah, right. My brother would *freak* out, and I'd never put you in that situation."

"What situation?"

"Of being in between your brother and I."

I shrug my shoulders. "Heart wants what the heart wants, and as for your brother, don't ever let him be a reason you don't pursue your happiness. Leave your brother and his overprotectiveness to me." I wink at her; she hums in agreement.

"You're right, but regardless...still just friends."

"Riiiight.....So, where are you going after Ellis drops me off?"

"Oh, nowhere specific, I thought I'd do some bar hopping downtown."

"Yeah, the guys are going to some bar downtown, too." She looks at me with an evil grin on her face.

"You thinking what I'm thinking?" I frown and look around in confusion.

"Umm, going out on a limb here and saying no."

"You should come out with me. You look hot, and we can have a little *girl's* night."

"Absolutely not; I have so much to do tomorrow before graduation."

"We won't stay out late. I promise we'll be out by 1 a.m. at the latest." I let out a sigh of uncertainty. "Come on, it'll be fun. Some dancing, drinks."

"I know I'm going to regret this."

"YES, GIRL, THAT'S WHAT I'M TALKING ABOUT!! Ellis, my love, downtown, please." He looks up in the rearview mirror and nods.

We pull up to the curb about fifteen minutes later, and Ellis lets us out.

"We can meet here at 12 a.m.," Selle tells Ellis. He looks at his clock and then at me.

"Should I let Graham know where you are?" I open my mouth to answer, but Selle covers it with her hand.

"Nope, she's a big girl. I got this." She grabs my hand, and we start walking away when she turns around. "See you later, El." She gives him a slight grin, and he glares at us.

"Let's start with Octopus and end with Kraken," she explains, excitedly squeezing my hand. I check my phone for the time; it's still fairly early. Dinner lasted much longer than expected, but it was only 10:30. We arrive at the Octopus bar when a guy stops us.

"You ladies want some company?" he asks. We both turn toward him, and I say, "No, we're good, but thanks for the offer." I wink at him.

It was graduation weekend, and there were people everywhere. The line to enter the bar is halfway down the street. I go to stop at the back of the line when Selle lets out an exasperated gasp.

"I don't wait in line, and neither do you," she pulls me to the door. The bouncer looks at us, letting us pass by him.

"Have fun, Selly," he tells her. She kisses his cheek.

"Sure thing, Gig."

"You know him?" I ask when we're walking past him.

"Yup, when I'm in town, I usually come here with some friends." We find a spot at the bar and wave the bartender over.

"What will it be, ladies?" We look around at the liquor options behind the bar, both deciding to settle for a beer. A few moments later, the bartender serves us two beers and two tequila shots.

"We didn't order the shots," Selle tells him, but he's nodding toward a group of guys sitting on the other side of the bar stools.

"They did."

We both smile at the group and raise the shots in thanks.

"We haven't been here for 5 minutes, and we're already getting drinks?" Selle hands me the shot and takes hers.

"Cheers to living like we're forever young," she says, winking. *Clink.* We both throw the drink back, the tequila burning my throat slightly.

I put the lime in my mouth and suck.

"So, you and Graham, you two all good now?"

"Yup."

"Good, because he was a fucking disaster and a huge dick while you guys were apart." She picks up her beer and takes a sip. I look at her, and guilt rushes over me.

"I had to find myself again. I know it was only a week and might sound ridiculous to others, but it was the longest week of my life. He wasn't alone, but we're okay now," I gulp down my beer.

"No judging here; love is messy and hard work. My brother is hard to love; I get it. But trust me and hear me when I tell you that he has never, and I mean *never*, cared about anyone this way. I never thought he was capable of the love he's showing you."

"Thank you, Selle." She nudges me.

"Don't mention it; now let's drink!" She orders more shots, which we quickly down. The music gets louder, and she drags me out on the tiny dance floor. We dance for about an hour before she screams in my ear.

"Okay, next spot. This place is boring me." I laugh when my phone buzzes in my hand.

Graham: Your brother is trashed...and telling me stories about you.

Liza: Oh no... don't believe a word.

Graham: I miss you...

Liza: Good.

"What time is it? My phone died." Selle asks, her words slurring a little. Fuck, she's drunk too.

"Almost midnight. How far is the Kraken? I'm afraid if we don't walk there now, you won't be able to make it there," I say, trying to hold my laugh in. She waves me off.

"Oh, I'm fine. Let's go!"

We start walking to the bar, which isn't too far away.

Once we get there, we head straight for the bar. "Two Jack and Cokes, please!" I say to the bartender. She tilts her head in approval and starts making the drinks. Selle and I are talking about what we are going to do after graduation tomorrow when a drunk guy comes and puts his arm around my waist.

"Hey, sexy, want to fool around?" I push him off.

"Unless you want me to break your arm, keep walking, 'sexy.'" He gives a low, husky laugh.

"Feisty. I like feisty."

"Hey asshole, leave her alone," Selle barks. We both roll our eyes and turn back to our drinks. "Let's go dance."

She pulls me out onto the dance floor, leaving the idiot smiling awkwardly in our direction.

"Weirdo," I say to her as we walk away from him.

"I can't believe he grabbed you." I shake my head and start moving my hips to the music; I'm good at dancing, and with the combination of the alcohol, it's even easier to sway to the beat. About ten minutes pass, the DJ starts a slower song, and I smile. Selle and I laugh as we fan ourselves while the song entirely changes over, and just as we are about to find a booth to sit in, I feel a possessive hand wrap around my waist; just as I ball my fist up, I relax it. This hand feels familiar, and I smile to myself.

Graham.

I start moving my hips and ass to his front, and he groans.

I look up and notice Hogan on my side, dancing with a dark-haired girl and Eli dancing with Selle. The two of them are extremely close, with Eli's hand wrapped around her waist and Selle's arms wrapped tightly around his neck as they sway back and forth to the music. They're just friends, huh? I turn to see his face. His eyes are dark and lustful.

"You're here."

"I am, and you're going to get into some trouble. What if I were someone else?"

I continue to rock back and forth with him.

"But you weren't."

He lets out a low growl in my ear, and I bite my lip.

I turn to face him, wrapping my arms around his neck, and he pulls me closer.

"I think your little brother likes my sister, angel."

I look over my shoulder at the two, smiling at each other while they dance.

"Yeah...and I think your little sister likes my brother." He shakes his head and starts to speak while gazing at them. "Me, Graham. Focus. On. Me."

I put my hands on his cheeks and turn his face to mine. He leans down to kiss me.

"As you wish." I didn't know the chances of being in the same bar simultaneously, but I didn't care. This was perfect. This night has turned out to be perfect. The song ends and transitions to an upbeat song. People around us start to come alive, dancing fast and screaming the song lyrics. Graham and I stand there, still entwined with each other. He dips his head down and kisses me, and I smile into his mouth. We finally pull away from each other, meeting the others at the end of the dance floor.

"I'm hungry; let's go," Selle whines as if on cue, and my stomach growls silently.

"I second that," I slur. Fuck, am I drunk too? Graham grabs my hand, and we start for the door. We're almost out when the same idiot from the bar that hit on me is standing next to the door.

"Slut." He spits at me.

"Excuse me?" I say while walking directly to him, and Graham yanks me back.

"Who the fuck are you talking to?" Eli barks out.

"The little slut you have with you, that's who." Eli lunges for him, with Hogan pulling him back.

"Eli, chill."

"Get off me, he just called my fucking sister a slut."

Before he can break away, Graham rushes the drunken guy, pinning him up against the wall with his hand around his neck.

"Say it again, I'll rip your fucking head off." He growls at him. The guy is about 6'0, has a short buzz cut, and a missing tooth. He smiles viciously at Graham.

"Oh, I get it, that's *your* little slut, huh?" Graham slams his fist into the guy's nose, his head swinging back and hitting the wall, drawing the attention of others; I hear the bartender yell.

"Take it out of here!"

"Shut your mouth, you piece of shit." Eli barks out.

"Dude, what the fuck is your problem?" Hogan yells at him.

"Graham, let him go," I say. He releases him and turns toward me. I nudge him out the door, pushing Eli and Hogan out behind him.

"You, okay?" Selle whispers to me. I turn and look at her, "I'm fine. Let's just go."

"I bet she tastes good; that's why you're fighting for her?" We all turn around to see the off-balanced guy exiting the bar. Without hesitation, Graham turns around, and I grab his hand.

"No. Ignore him; let's just go." Graham yanks his hand away from me.

"Fuck no, he's not going to disrespect you."

"Please, let's just go," I beg. While I'm talking Graham down, I hear Selle yell, "GUYS, STOP."

I turn around to see Hogan and Eli charging after him. Selle tries to grab them but only gets a hold of Hogan. Eli draws his fist back and connects it with the guy's nose. *Crack.* If his nose wasn't broken from the hit Graham gave him, then it's definitely broken now. The guy falls to the ground, and Eli rounds on top of him, delivering blow after blow to his face and stomach. I drop Graham's hand, pushing toward my brother. Graham grabs me.

"No. Stay out of it." I yank away again.

"He's my brother! Stop this now, Graham. Please."

Graham quickly approaches the two men and pulls Eli off. "That's enough, Eli. I think he learned his lesson," he tells him. Eli shakes his hand and checks out the damage. He walks toward me, and I grab his hand and check it for bruises.

"Are you okay? You promised no fighting," I retort.

"He called you a slut, all bets were off. I should've broken his fucking face." That's my brother, always protecting me and never backing down from a fight. Selle starts to walk over to us, and I see Graham walking back towards the rest of us. The guy opens his mouth to say something low enough that only Graham hears it. Before I know it, Graham spins around, slugging him in the face. Blood gushes from the guy's nose; Graham says something to him and walks away.

"This is a cluster fuck; when will it fucking end?" I whisper to myself. As Graham gets closer, I see the horror in his eyes. When he gets close enough, he grabs my arm tightly and pulls me to the side of the building out of everyone's view.

"Graham, let go. What are you doing?" He pushes me back to the building and towers over me.

"Did he fucking touch you?" I frown at him, taken aback by the question.

"Wh..What do you mean?"

"He said that he...just answer the question." I shake my head and answer.

"No, he grabbed me around my waist when we were at the bar earlier; I brushed him off. That's it."

"We're going...*now*," he speaks in a demanding, low tone.

"Ellis will drive everyone home," he states. He walks over to Selle. "You, okay?" She shrugs nonchalantly.

"She handled herself, G, and I'm sure she's had enough for a night."

He gives her a quick kiss on the cheek and waits for me at the end of the sidewalk.

"I'll be home later; do you have a key?" I say to Eli.

"Yeah."

"Okay, love you both."

"Love you too," they say in return. I walk over to Graham, and he holds his hand for me to grab. I grab it, and we walk to the car. He opens my door, and I slide in. He rounds the car, climbing into the driver's seat.

The drive is painfully silent for the first ten minutes. I look out the window, wondering how one guy flirting with me completely ruined the night before my college graduation. Graham and my brothers had gotten so angry, defending me. As much as I appreciated it, I wished they'd understand that I could protect myself if needed. I let out a sigh, and Graham glances at me. He sighs before speaking.

"I'm sorry." He mumbles; I look at him and give him a reassuring smile.

"Me too."

I don't know what exactly I'm apologizing for, but I'm doing it anyway. I can tell he feels guilty for fighting and embarrassing me when he questioned me about the guy from the bar. He must read my mind because he frowns.

"You have nothing to apologize for; I'm the asshole who didn't believe you could take care of yourself. I'm also the asshole that made this night go from perfect to a shitshow." I grab his hand in mine and lay it on my thigh.

"It was kind of hot."

He grins and brings my hand to his mouth, planting a soft kiss on it. I look out the window again, trying to hide the little satisfaction I have on my face. Even though I wished the night had ended differently, a small part of me was turned on by the fact that Graham would fight for me. I get a flashback of how angry he got and how sexy he looked when his jawline tightened. I adjust myself in the seat, trying not to show the heat that blazes from my pussy.

"You okay over there, pretty girl? You look...bothered," he teases, rubbing my thigh with a sly grin. I bite my lip and nod, taking a deep breath.

"Yup. I'm fine," I lie.

He laughs lowly and trails his hands under my dress. I swallow and put my head back.

"You're driving," I finally say. He shrugs and pulls his hand up higher, finding my panties.

"Take them off," he orders. I glance at him and see the fire in his eyes. "Now."

I quickly slide my panties down to my ankles.

"Now come here."

"*What?*"

"I said, come here, sit on my lap, back against the window."

I climb across the armrest and position myself on him, my back pressed against the cool window. "Now bend your knees and open them."

He puts two fingers up to my mouth.

"Suck them." I do as I'm told. I suck his fingers; he pulls them out and slides his hand back under my dress until he reaches my pussy. He inserts a finger, and I groan. He pushes it in deeper, inserting another.

"Graham...more," I plead.

He grins and inserts another finger, working them in and out of my pussy. He speeds his fingering motions, taking a moment to glare at me. I feel myself getting closer and closer; seconds later, I explode on his fingers. He fingers me harder and faster, taking every breath out of me. I gasp, my body shaking.

Moments later, Graham pulls his fingers out and sticks them in his mouth, sucking them, tasting me.

"You always taste so good, *angel*." I catch my breath and smirk at him.

"That was–"

"What? It was what?" I pull my panties back in place, willing my cheeks to return to their normal color.

We pull into Graham's driveway; he kisses me and pushes the door open so I can climb out. I realize quickly that Graham still got his way. He wanted me to stay with him tonight, and I told him I had things to do tomorrow, yet here I am. Even though it ended in a brawl, it was still a great night. I danced, laughed, and hung out with the people I loved.

I kick my heels off as soon as I walk through the door.

"Ugh, what time is it?"

"Almost 1:30 a.m."

"I have to wake up early tomorrow... big day, you know."

"I know; I have a few things to get done, too."

He pulls me towards the sofa, and we both sit, letting out a long sigh after we sit down. I lay my head on his shoulder, and he grabs my hand and kisses it.

"Can you believe we graduate tomorrow?"

"Pretty crazy. But I'm ready. It's been a lot to juggle between school and running the business. I'm looking forward to giving the business my full attention now. Do you think you're going to continue interning at the clinic?"

I had been going to the internship every day for five hours. I got the last twenty I needed to complete my graduation requirements, but I enjoyed it so much that I stayed longer than required. I had the pleasure of sitting in on sessions with Dr. Cinkade, taking notes and comparing them with his after each session. He was attentive to my thoughts and interested in my opinion. He told me on my last day that he thought I'd make a powerful addition to his team and to let him know if I wanted to work there. I am still deciding on my after-graduation plans, so I never told Graham about the offer. But that was about to change.

41

Graham

"Well...he actually told me I could work there after graduation." I tilt Liza's head up towards me.

"Why didn't you tell me that? That's good news."

"Because I haven't made any decisions about after graduation yet, where I'll work and where I'll... live."

"What do you mean, where you'll live?" She sits up and turns her knees and body toward me.

"I mean... my mom wants me to move to New York. My dad and brother are in California, and you're here. I don't know where I'll live, so accepting a job offer wouldn't make sense unless... "

"It's fine. You don't have to explain anything to me. I'm going to go to bed," I say quickly. Standing up, she grabs me as I turn for the stairs.

"You're mad?"

"No, I'm not mad. I'm just tired."

No, you're hurt. You're hurt that she didn't tell you right away, and you're even more hurt that there's a chance she'll leave you again.

My conscience was right, but I couldn't tell her that, not right now. I walk up the stairs, leaving her sitting alone. I turn the shower on and step under the piping hot water.

All I can think about is where Liza will go after graduation and whether or not she'll move or stay here. Her move to New York could help my business and make it an easier transition because I could run it myself and appoint Andrew as the new executive for the Seattle office. But if she decided to return to California, we'd be apart. *Again.* I knew I couldn't live without her; one week almost fucking killed me. I knew then that I would do whatever I had to do to stay with her, but this was a decision she had to make. And I would have to adjust to whatever choice she made.

I hear the door creak open. I close my eyes and dip my head under the water again. I feel her arms creep over my waist, and I suck in a breath.

"You can't leave me again, Elizabeth." She freezes from my words. She's just as shocked as I am at saying that. As much as I wanted to open up to Liza and tell her every feeling I had, it was hard. But this was something I needed to do. I needed to let her know how I felt.

"I'm not leaving you, Graham." I put my hands over hers. She kisses my back and turns me around to face her. "I'm not going anywhere." She cups my face, stands on her tippy toes, and kisses my lips.

"Liza..."

"No, hear me. I am not going *anywhere.* I got the offer when we were apart; that's the only reason you didn't know. I wasn't hiding it from you." She kisses me again, and this time, I grab her and plunge my tongue into her mouth.

She opens for me as she always does, welcoming my tongue into her mouth. "I'm going to fuck you fast and hard; do you understand?" She nods, and I shake my head, my breathing quickening. "Words, *angel,*" I growl.

"I understand." I push her back against the wall and lift her leg. I quickly sink into her, pumping her harder and harder with each thrust.

"So good. So good." I say into her ear. She wraps her arms around me, digging her fingers into my back.

"Fuck me, Graham, please." I speed up my pace, picking her up as she wraps her legs around me, moving with me. I push deeper and deeper into her with each thrust.

"Oh, God," she whimpers, and her body starts to shake.

"Come, come all over my cock."

She falls apart, and I follow her, filling her with everything I have. Fucking her into oblivion. She screams as her body convulses, my come dripping out of her as I force more into her. She feels so fucking good, and I'm not ready to stop, even though my body is fighting against each stroke. The more I thrust, the tighter her legs wrap around me. I hold her there as I step out of the shower, not ready to pull out of her, to feel the emptiness of her. I turn her around and slap my palm over her ass.

"Mm, more."

I groan at her response before giving her another, her ass turning red. "Bend over." She places her palms on the wall as she bends down, water dripping down her body. I run my tongue up her leg, pushing her legs open and gliding my tongue over her pussy. She arches her back just right, and it gives me the view I need to push two fingers inside of her. She throws her head back, and I stand, yanking her head towards me.

I stick my fingers in my mouth, tasting her before I circle them around the brim of her ass. She stiffens, and I kiss her cheek.

"Relax, you'll like it." I push my fingers deeper into her. And she sinks back into my fingers with a feral groan. My cock is eagerly awaiting its turn. I move my fingers in and out of her ass, and I lean over, grabbing the lube from the bathroom drawer and slathering it over my cock as she starts to come undone. "You'll come on my fingers, *angel*... and I'll come in your ass."

I push the tip of my cock inside of her, and she screams, her body stilling. She wiggles her hips to adjust to my size, and I fight the urge to push further into her. "Okay?" She tucks her lip, and her eyes are full of tears. I slowly slide more into her, and she grabs my hips.

"Breathe, pretty girl, and let me in." Her breath hitches, and she wills her body to relax; I push the rest of my cock in. She moans as I push in and out of her.

"Fuck, you're tight fucking hole is swallowing my cock."

I fuck her ass harder and harder, digging my fingers into her hips. She pushes back on me as I slam in and out of her. I reach around and stick my fingers in her pussy. "Graham....baby...ahh."

When I feel her pussy clamp my fingers, I know she's there, and I continue to milk her faster and faster. "Give it to me, *angel*, fucking unravel on my fingers while my cock fucks your ass." Her screams fill the bathroom, and her nails scrape down the wall as I dig my cock deeper into her while I come. My come leaks out of her ass, and I groan at the site.

I kiss her back as I pull out, turning her around to face me. I cup her face in my hands.

"I love you."

"I love you."

I gently dry her, being careful with her when she flinches as I lightly touch her pussy. I smirk to myself. Aftercare is about to be my new favorite thing.

* * *

The next day, Liza's alarm goes off around 6 a.m. I know she's tired; I ran her an Epsom salt bath and gave her a massage last night. Even with me using a shit ton of lube, she still stretched and bled from me fucking her ass. I knew she'd be sore, but it didn't stop me from taking her again before she finally fell back to sleep. She begged for my cock, and I couldn't say no, even though I knew she needed to rest.

I roll over and cut off her alarm, kissing her forehead. "Wake up."

"Uhhh, I don't wanna."

"As much as I want to stay in bed with you all day, we both have some things to get done before tonight." Last night, my dad texted me to tell me that the jeweler and he would be here at 8 a.m.

"I know, I know. I'm getting up." She throws the covers back, kisses me on the cheek, and gets up. She calls her brother to pick her up, then heads for the shower. I text my dad, double-checking that the jeweler is still on track.

He quickly responds, even though it's early. My dad was always one to wake up at 6 a.m., no matter what day it was. He firmly believed in the 'early bird gets the worm' saying.

Twenty minutes later, Eli is here for Liza. We're sitting downstairs as we wait for Liza to finish.

"You really love her, don't you?" He spills out. I look at him and grin.

"I do, yes."

"Don't hurt her. She's had enough bullshit in her life. When my parents split up and her being stal-" He stops abruptly, apprehensive about mentioning her stalker. I lean back on the sofa.

"You can say it, her stalker, Tim. She told me about him."

"She did? She doesn't tell anyone that." I nod, and he sits up and looks me directly in the eyes, serious.

"No, Graham, I mean *anyone*... Our father still has no clue." I frown and sit up.

"What do you mean, your fath- "

"Okay, I'm ready. Let's go before Mom kills me," Liza shouts, finally downstairs. She looks back and forth between us and raises her eyebrows.

"What's up with you two? Did I miss something?" Eli shakes his head, and I smile, pulling her into a hug.

"No, you didn't miss anything. I'll see you later." She looks at me like she's second-guessing my response but doesn't push it any further. She kisses me, and I send them out the door.

How did their father not know Liza was stalked? Where did he think she was for two months? And more importantly, how am I supposed to look this man in the face today for the first time, knowing that his family has kept such a vital secret away from him for seven years? I shake off the thought. I wouldn't be the one to tell her father; Liza would never forgive me. I climb the stairs and get ready. The jeweler would be here soon, and the only thing on my mind was picking out the perfect gift for my *angel.*

42

Liza

Graduation is in two hours, and I feel good—so good that I feel better than I have in a long time. Graham will meet my dad for the first time today, and I will see him for the first time in six months. I miss him so much and can't wait to see him. I put the finishing touches on my hair and applied my nude lipstick.

"You look beautiful, baby girl." I look in the mirror and see my handsome father in a black suit standing in front of the doorway.

"Daddy!" I immediately run towards his outstretched arms, and tears fill my eyes. "I missed you so much. I'm so glad you're here."

"I missed you; I wouldn't miss your college graduation for anything in the world. Now let me look at you." He leans back and smiles at me. "All grown up." I smile at him. This man raised me—this man I loved so much.

"Honey, are you all set?" My mom walks in and stops in her tracks. "Axel, I didn't know you were..." She stops and clears her throat, running her hands over her dress. "I didn't know you were here already."

"I got in this morning." This is awkward—extremely awkward—and I want to get out of it.

"Okay, so I'm going to go; I'll see you guys there." I give them both a quick kiss on their cheeks and leave them in my room, with so much tension between them that the air becomes thick.

I called Graham from my car and told him about my parents. I told him they hadn't seen each other in six years and that it looked like my mom longed after my dad. When she walked in, she tripped over her words, and my mother, Bethany, did *not* get off her game—ever.

We line up for graduation, and Graham and I are in different sections. I want to fast-forward to graduation being over so we can celebrate. Moments later, we're all walking in, and the ceremony begins.

I look into the stands and see our families sitting together. I lock eyes with Eli and Hogan, and they both nudge their heads toward my mom and dad. My dad is sitting next to Eli, and my mom is next to my dad. Brantley is on the other side of my mom. They are all talking amongst each other and look comfortable, which is weird, considering how I left them two. I look back at Eli, and he holds up his phone.

I look down at my phone and wait for Eli's text.

Eli: *I think Mom and Dad had sex.*

My heart drops, and I inhale a breath. My parents did what? My mom is *married.* She wouldn't cheat on Brantley, would she? I look up at Eli, and he gives me a small smile. I look back at my parents, and they both wave at me, along with Brantley. I smile back, and I'm saved from this awkward moment when they tell my row to stand and be ready to receive our diplomas.

The rest of graduation goes by in a blur; the only thing I could think about was whether my parents had sex. Did my dad help his ex-wife *cheat* on her husband?

I stopped to take pictures with some friends, and they discussed their plans for tonight as we walked towards our families. I saw my parents, and as I approached them, my breathing quickened. Not only is Graham about to meet my father, but I have to get this thought out of my head quickly before I blurt it out in front of everyone.

"Mr. Salando, would you and Ms. Crambell mind a photo?" *Thank God.*

I've never been so happy to be bugged by paparazzi. Graham places his hand on my lower back, and we look into the camera. The flash goes off a few times, and the photographer thanks us.

"*Angel*, are you alright?"

Should I tell him? Of course, I shouldn't. That'll be the only thing he'll think about right before he meets my father. I'll tell him after.

"Yes, fine. Just nervous."

"Shouldn't I be the one nervous?"

"He'll love you because you love me." He kisses my cheek.

"And that I do," he whispers.

My father smiles at me as we walk towards him and the rest of our families. "If you want to bail, now's the time," I whisper, smirking at Graham. He grabs my hand and intertwines our fingers.

"I'd never dream of it."

"Look at you. My little girl is a college graduate." My dad pulls me into an embrace. "I'm so proud of you." I nuzzle into his hug.

"Thank you, Daddy." I pull back and stand beside Graham, stepping forward a bit. "I want you to meet someone." Graham holds his hand out, and my dad takes it, shaking hands sternly.

"Graham Salando, I'm glad to meet you, sir."

"Axel Crambell. I've heard a lot about you. Our last few phone calls have been strictly about how happy my daughter is lately. I take it that you have something to do with that." I blush and put my head down.

"I sure do hope I do, sir."

"Axel, please. 'Sir,' it makes me feel like an old geezer."

"You are an old geezer, Dad." Eli comes and playfully pushes my dad and gives me a warm hug. "Congratulations, sis. I'm proud of you."

"Thanks, Eli. Where's Hogan?" I say, looking around. My dad,

Graham, Brant, and Joe are all talking. Eli pulls me by my arm to the side. "He's talking to some girl. It's the same girl from the bar last night; she graduated also. Anyway, so, mom and dad. You think I'm right?"

I look around and nudge him. "Ssh, Dad is standing right there." He shrugs his shoulders, and I sigh. "Why do you think they had sex?"

"I know what sex sounds like... They were definitely having sex. Hogan and I left when I realized it couldn't be you in there. We waited in the car, and twenty minutes later, Mom and Dad came out of your building. They looked weird but friendly, and we both know they haven't talked in years."

My brother was right. That was the first time my parents had seen each other in years. My dad was still in love with my mom, and it had been seven years. As much as I would have loved for my parents to stay together, I loved Brantley and how he treated my mother. I may not have been planning to bring it up now, but I'll bring it to both of my parents soon.

"Oh, honey! I am so proud of you! Come, let's take some family pictures," my mom bellows, approaching Eli and the rest of us. We take pictures together for the next fifteen minutes, some with Graham and me and the rest with our families.

"We graduated, bitch!" Em runs up to me and engulfs me in her arms. "Let's take some pictures!" We snap a few of just her and me and then a few of me, her, Trav, and Graham.

"I'm seriously going to miss you while I'm traveling," she says, poking her lip out.

"I'm not coming with you, Em, don't even think about asking *again*."

"Graham! Come on, man, talk some sense into your lady. We'd have a fucking badass time! At least come visit."

"If you plan to stay in one place for over a week, I'll fly her out to you."

"Yeah, as if you'd stay behind," Em mumbles. Graham pinches her side, and she bellows out in laughter.

"Okay, we gotta go. We're not even going to have dinner. We're getting our asses on a plane in three hours! Call you later. Love you!"

"Love you, don't get knocked up out there."

"Never bitch." She whispers in my ear. They're gone so quickly, and my heart breaks a little. She's my best friend, we've done everything together. Not seeing her for the next possible year makes me sick.

"Hey, we'll visit. Don't worry. My best friend is leaving too. We'll see them. I promise." Graham says, planting a kiss on my forehead.

"Okay, one last photo!" My mom yells, and I groan.

"I hope your mom has no plans for you after this," Graham tells me, putting his hand on my lower back. My body tingles at the thought of what that means. I clear my throat, which suddenly becomes intensely dry.

"Why's that?" I say softly.

"Because I have something planned for tonight, *angel*." He kisses the side of my head, and I reddened.

"Okay, Mom. Are we done here?" I ask with a forced smile.

"Yes, honey, we're all done. I thought we could have dinner tonight."

"I already have plans for tonight. Tomorrow?"

"Of course, yes, you go have fun."

I raise my eyebrow quickly at her. "Yeah. Thanks."

Graham looks at me suspiciously, and I ignore his glare. My mom tilts her head to the side and furrows her eyebrows. "Elizabeth, sweetheart, a moment before we all head out." I sigh deeply, leaving the rest of our families mingling. Eli looks at me, and my dad keeps glancing our way.

"Is something the matter?" My mom asks with a worried look. I nod my head.

"Everything is fine, Mom."

"I'm your mother. I know when you lie, Elizabeth. Now spill it, tell me. Did something happen with you and Graham today?"

"No, *Mrs. Gilman.* Nothing happened with Graham and me. How about you and Dad?" Her face goes completely blank, and I let out a low, disappointed laugh.

"How could you, Mom? I'm too disgusted to even look at you or Dad." I turn my back to her and walk past my father, who must have overheard the conversation.

"Are you ready to go?" I ask, smiling at Graham. He nods, and we both say our goodbyes to his parents and Selle. I toss Eli the keys to my car.

"Be careful. I'll see you tomorrow. Love you." He catches the keys and grabs my arm.

"That was a little mean, don't you think?" I shrug.

"I'm not the one who cheated on my husband in my daughter's apartment."

"Lizzie, they are still our parents."

"Elias, I'm not making excuses for them just because they are our parents. I'll see you later."

"Okay, love you." Selle walks over to us, and she and my brother start talking. Graham rolls his eyes, and I laugh a little.

"Let's go," I chuckle.

43

Graham

I lead Liza to the front, where Ellis is waiting for us. We graduated today and accomplished our first milestone together. I just hoped it wouldn't be our last one. Liza still hadn't decided where she would live, and the more I tried not to think about it, the more it was on my mind.

"Congratulations, you two," El says.

"Thank you, Ellis!" She climbs into the back of the SUV, and I follow behind her.

I wanted tonight to be special—a night Liza would remember. I planned to give her a graduation present and tell her exactly how I felt. I knew she had to make a decision, but I didn't want her to make it without knowing exactly how I felt.

"What's going on in that head over there?" she questions, nudging me. I shoot her what I hope isn't a giveaway of a fake smile.

"Nothing; I'm just excited to spend the night with you." She narrows her eyes at me.

"Tell me," she pleads, sliding next to me. I grab her little hands and place them inside mine. I take a deep breath and kiss her knuckles.

"Graham. What is it?"

"I wanted to talk about this later, but I guess I'm not doing as good of a job as I thought I was doing with hiding it, now am I?" I gather my courage and spill it, because if there was one thing Liza always did, it was make me feel comfortable enough to tell her anything. "I'm just afraid that I'm going to lose you. You don't know where you'll be, and you haven't mentioned anything showing that you remotely have an idea." She adjusts herself, turning her body towards me. "You also haven't mentioned what it means for us if you choose to leave Seattle."

She grips my hands tight and puts them in her lap. "Well, I'm not ending us if that's what you think." A wave of relief washes over me. "Graham, I haven't made a decision yet, but I'm hoping that whatever decision I make, you'll support it, and we'll figure out the rest from there."

"Of course, I'll support you, and we will always figure it out."

"Promise?"

"Yes, I promise."

"Sealed with a kiss?"

I pull her in for a soft kiss. "I love you."

"I love you more... Now, you want to tell me what you have planned for tonight?"

"Nice try, but no." I lean back in my seat, and she sticks her bottom lip out. "Tuck that lip back in, or I'll bite it."

"I think I'd like that," I raise my eyebrows at her.

"Oh, would you?" Her cheeks turn red, and she tries and fails miserably to hide them. "Soon."

Moments later, we pull into my driveway.

"Come on, there's something I want to show you...close your eyes," I tell her, guiding her into the living room. A big red box with a white bow sits on the couch. "Okay, you can open them."

"What's this?" She looks at the box, her feet practically glued to the floor. I nudge her towards it.

"Go open it and find out." She walks forward, reaching down to untie the bow. Her face lights up as she pulls out the red-laced lingerie and black Louboutin heels. She looks at me and opens her mouth.

"This-"

"There's more, keep going." She moves the tissue paper to the side to reveal the black velvet box and stops before reaching for it. She grabs it slowly and opens it, revealing a diamond necklace.

"It's beautiful." I walk towards her, taking the necklace out of her hands. I turn her back to me, push her hair to the side, clasp the necklace together, and kiss her neck.

"You're beautiful," I whisper. She leans back into me, and I wrap my hands around her. "Happy graduation, *angel*."

"Happy graduation."

We stand there for a few minutes, and she sighs, sinking deeper into my arms. "Something bothering you?" I kiss her cheek and she sighs again.

"My parents slept together."

"Your parents, as in.."

"As in my mother and father, yup."

"And you're sure of that?"

"Eli and Hogan heard them, then saw them walk out of the building together."

"So that's why you were so "off" with them after graduation?" I turn her face to me and I continue. "I know that sucks, but try not to meddle—let them figure it out."

She frowns at me.

"Meddle?"

"Yes, I've been there. I made it my mission to let my dad know how disgusted I was with him, and in the process, I lost sight of the fact that he was still my *father*."

"I guess you're right; I just can't believe they did it. I know my dad still loves her, but I never would have thought he'd..." I run my hand over her cheek.

"I get it, but even parents can get pulled into a moment. Don't dwell so much on it. Let them work it out. I'm sure they're already disappointed in themselves."

"You're right." Just then, her phone rings.

"Hi, Daddy," she answers softly as she puts her phone on speaker-phone.

"Hi, sweetheart. I know you're disappointed in me, but I wanted to let you know that I will head back to California tonight."

"But I thought you were here for three more days?" There's a long pause before he finally answers.

"I think it's better if I go."

"Dad, don't do that. I want you to stay." I look at the tears in her eyes and rub her shoulders.

"I want to stay too, but I think I should go. Your mother agrees." She looks at me and rolls her eyes at her dad's comment.

"...Okay, Dad."

"Love you, Elizabeth; I'm so proud of you."

"Love you too, Daddy." She hangs up the phone, and tears stream down her face.

"*Angel*, don't cry." I wipe her tears, and they quickly replace one with another.

"I'm sorry; I just wish I could spend more time with him. He works so much, and I was so mean, and now he's leaving." I hated seeing her cry, and there wasn't a thing in this world that I wouldn't do to make her happy.

"How about we go to California for a week? You can spend some time with your dad and decide whether you want to move there or not."

"Really? You'd do that?"

"Of course, I would. I hate seeing you upset."

I was supposed to start going to the office full-time on Monday, but they'd have to do without me for a week. I trust Andrew to manage things for a week.

"Call your dad and tell him. If he's okay with leaving tomorrow morning, I'll get Angie to get the plane ready." She kisses my cheek.

"Thank you so much, Graham. It means the world to me." She grabs her phone and heads upstairs to call her dad. I pick up my phone and call Angie to inform her of the plans. Then I called Andrew, giving him the rundown of each day and instructing him to contact me if any pressing issues arose.

Truthfully, I had plans for Liza tonight; I planned to push her sexually, testing her limits. But this seems more important for her; with such last-minute plans, I take her to dinner to celebrate graduation. Then, we stop by her apartment to pack her bags for our early flight the following morning. As much as I wanted her to stay with me, she insisted that she talk to her mom before she left. I reluctantly kissed her goodnight and went home alone.

44

Liza

After I finished packing, I grabbed my phone to call my mom. Graham and Eli were right. As disappointed as I was with them, they were still my parents. My dad was ecstatic that I'd spend a week with him and was grateful that Graham made it happen for me. But like I told him, I needed to talk to my mother before I got on the plane tomorrow.

The phone rings twice, and soon enough, my mother's fragile voice picks up.

"Elizabeth, hi, honey." I could tell she'd been crying. My heart breaks.

"Hi, mama. I just wanted to say I'm sorry. It's none of my business, and I shouldn't have acted that way."

"No, honey, you're right. There's no excuse for what your father and I did. I told Brant..."

I gasp. She did what? Is that why she's crying? Did he leave her?

"Wait, did he- "

"No, honey. He didn't leave me. He loves me, and he understood that it was a mistake—a mistake that'll never happen again. It'll take some time, but we'll be all right." I feel relieved.

"I'm going to California for a week, I leave tomorrow." The other end is silent for a few moments.

"That's great, honey. I know you haven't spent much time with your dad." We talk for a few more moments. I promised her I'd plan a trip to New York soon and that I'd call her when I got to California.

I climb into bed, noticing that I have only four hours before I need to wake up. I reach for my phone and send a quick text to Graham.

Liza: *It feels weird being in bed without you.*

I expected him to be asleep. It's 1 a.m., and we have to be on the plane at 6 a.m., so I hit send and put my phone down. Moments later, my phone dings.

Graham: *I know. I hate sleeping without you. I tend to have bad dreams.*

This is the first time Graham has mentioned his dreams and been so open with me about having them when I'm not around. That breaks my heart. I want him to open up about them and tell me what happens when he has them, but I know that won't happen anytime soon.

Liza: *Maybe you should come here?*

Graham: *Don't tempt me. Get some rest, angel. I love you.*

Liza: *You have a key if you change your mind. I love you.*

I put my phone on the charger and roll on my side, falling asleep instantly.

Graham wraps his arms around me, kissing my neck. I nuzzle closer to him, then turn around to face him. He smells so good, as always. I wrap my arms around his neck and kiss him. He runs his fingers up my back, sending chills down my spine. I let out a low moan, my breathing quickening. He reaches down and inserts his hands in my panties, quickly running his hand over my aching pussy. "So wet for me," he groans. He yanks on my hair, pulling my head back, exposing more of my neck to him as he places kisses and pushes his fingers in and out of me. My body starts to tense, and I know

I'm right there. "Come for me." *And on his command, my body releases on his fingers.*

My conscience screams this feels real—*too real.* I open my eyes to see that this isn't a dream at all; this is real. Graham is in my bed, milking me for *everything* I have. He really came into my bed in the middle of the night because he needed *me.* I catch my breath, and he drapes my motionless leg over his.

"That was definitely not a dream." I'm out of breath, and he chuckles, kissing the top of my head.

"No, *angel*, it wasn't. Now sleep." I snuggle into his arm.

"I'm glad you came."

He pulls the blanket over our bodies, and I fall into a deep sleep.

* * *

5:30 a.m. comes quickly. I hear the alarm and instantly groan. I roll over and grab the sheets, reaching for Graham, but I find an empty spot beside me. Where was he? I sit up, and I'm hit with the scent of freshly brewed coffee. I smile to myself, realizing that Graham has made himself at home. Technically, it is his home; he did own the building. I walk into the kitchen quietly, passing the rooms my brother and Hogan slept in last night. They both said they planned to stay here another week before starting their summer vacation.

Graham is fully dressed in black jeans, a white shirt, and black boots. My goodness, the man could make anything look good.

"Hi, baby."

He looks up from his phone and smiles at me, setting his coffee mug down.

"Good morning, *angel*." I walk over to him and wrap my arms around him, taking in his scent.

"How long have you been up?"

"Not long. How'd you sleep?" I recall last night when Graham came into my bed and fingered me into blissfulness.

"I had a bit of a surprise but slept great," I say, nudging him. He grins.

"You want your coffee now?"

"No, I'll grab some for the road. I'm going to shower and then I'll be ready in a bit." I quickly shower and do my hair. I thought about leaving a note for my brothers to let them know I'd call, but I figured I might as well just let Eli know.

I knock and quickly enter, stopping when I see him sound asleep with Selle cuddled beside him. His eyes fly open, and he quickly sits up, startling Selle. She shoots out of bed when she sees me standing in the doorway. I signal them both to be quiet.

"Your brother is in the kitchen, and unless you want him to come in here and find you in bed with *my* brother, you both need to be quiet." She puts her head down, and I shake my head. "I'm heading out, Eli. Will you be here when I get back on Saturday?"

"Yeah, I leave Monday. Be safe...and sis?" He says as I turn for the door. I stop and turn around.

"Yeah?"

"I'm sorry for not telling you..." I take a deep breath and then look at Selle, standing in the corner with her arms wrapped around herself.

"For not telling me what?" I wink at them, and she half-smiles. Eli lets out a little laugh.

"Love you, Eli. I'll text you when I land, and for Pete's sake, lock this door."

I shut the door and decide to skip over entering Hogan's room, not knowing what or who I'd find in there with him.

"Ready?"

"Here's your coffee." I grab it and taste it; it's perfectly made to how I like it. I give him a quick kiss, he grabs my bag, and we head out the door.

We get to the tarmac quickly, and I see my dad smiling and waiting.

"You go ahead. I need to call Selle. She wasn't home last night."

I feel guilty for keeping it from him, but I told them I wouldn't say anything. I'd have to text Selle and tell her she needed to tell him. It felt wrong keeping this secret from Graham, especially when I said no more secrets.

"Hi, Daddy!" I say, hugging him. "Hi, sweetheart. Are you all set to go home and spend some time with your old man?" I nudge him. I am excited to show Graham where I grew up, but a part of me is also nervous about returning to California. It's where Tim was—or at least where he used to be until Brant paid him off.

"Axel, Good morning," Graham greets, approaching us.

"Graham, thank you for bringing my little girl to spend time with me." His mouth tilts up in a grin, and he puts his hand on my lower back.

"Of course, we all ready to go?" We all board Graham's jet.

* * *

It was a quick flight to California. Once we arrived, we headed straight to my childhood home, passing familiar hang-out spots and my old high school. We are almost to the house when I think I spot Tim. My mouth becomes suddenly dry, and my eyes blur. I blink to have a second look, and he's gone. I need to get it together. Tim is *not* here, and no one is watching me. I shake off the feeling just in time as we turn to my father's beautiful two-story estate. The house is white with black shutters and beautiful landscaping out front. My dad took pride in the landscaping and always ensured it stayed clean. Honestly, I was surprised he kept the house with just him and my brother here. My brother graduates from college next year, making me wonder what my dad's plans for the house were. After walking in on my brother and Selle, something told me Eli may be returning to Seattle more permanently soon. I'd hate for this house to no longer be ours. No matter where I was, it would always be home. I grew up here. It's where I had my first slumber party, cried my first tears over my first heartbreak, and got ready for my first prom. There were too many memories for me to think my dad would consider selling it. *You're getting ahead of yourself.* She was right, I was.

I walked into the house, and my eyes bounced around, taking everything in again. "I missed this place."

"Your home is beautiful, Axel," Graham says.

"It's a full-time job, that's for sure." He gives Graham a tour of the house, and I go up to my room, not a bit surprised that my dad hasn't changed anything. It's the same room I left a year ago. Growing up, I was always a modern girl—simple and sophisticated.

"I like your room, *angel*," Graham compliments, walking up behind me and wrapping his arms around me. I lean my head back against him.

"Better get out of here before my dad has a heart attack." Right on cue, my dad walks in and clears his throat.

"I'm no idiot, Elizabeth. I know you two spend the night with each other...*often*," he states, and my eyes bulge at his remark.

"Sorry, Dad," I say, slipping out of Graham's embrace and turning to him. "Where would you like Graham to sleep tonight? Eli's room or the guest room?" I say reluctantly. I wouldn't say I liked the thought of him sleeping anywhere else besides next to me, and judging by the blank look on Graham's face, neither did he.

My dad folds his arms and looks between the two of us. "I can't believe I am allowing this; he can stay where he is. I trust that you will behave." My face drops. Where is he, as in... in my room?

"Wait, you mean he can- "

"Elizabeth, I was your age once. I remember how it was not wanting to sleep apart. I trust you and Graham. Now, where do you two want to have lunch? It's 1 p.m." I smile and try not to show my excitement.

"Wherever you want, just nowhere fancy. I'm pretty tired."

"How about we order in, watch movies, and catch up?" That sounded perfect—a Sunday in with my two favorite men.

"I couldn't think of a better day."

"Alright, I'll order; you two unpack and get settled." He kisses me on the forehead and disappears.

45

Graham

Axel allowed me to stay with her, and I'm not sure if it's because I told him about my dreams and how she helps me sleep better while he gave me a tour of the house. Or if it was because he remembered how it was when he was young and in love. He damn near grilled me while we toured the house, asking me about my intentions with Liza and how she would fit into my life while running a multi-million-dollar business. He asked me what I'd do if she moved away from Seattle—the one question I knew the answer to but hadn't told Liza. I told him, "Wherever she was, was where I wanted to be."

He understood that all I wanted to do was take care of Liza, support her, and make her happy—something we both wanted for her. Her father was the picture of how every father should be with their little girl. He was caring, trusting, and compassionate—everything I wished my father was like from the beginning.

We all sat at the table while Axel told stories about Liza when she was a kid. I smiled, picturing a small, headstrong little Liza. We were about to clear our plates and get dessert when the doorbell rang. Liza frowned and looked at her dad.

"Are you expecting anyone?"

"No, I'm not. Are you? Did you tell any of your old friends you were home?" She shook her head; her dad approached the door while I helped Liza clean up dinner. A few minutes later, her dad returned, shaking his head.

"Damn kids, I still don't know how they get through the gate. I get to the door and open it, and there's no one there; it's been happening for about two weeks now; little fuckers are starting to piss me off."

"How do you figure it's kids?" I ask suspiciously.

"I mean, who else would it be?"

"Have you ever gotten close to seeing a face at all?"

"Nope, usually they're gone by the time I get to the door. I have a door cam; that son of a bitch broke right before this started happening."

I start to remember when Liza told me she thought someone was following her; that's when she opened up about Tim. When we arrived, she completely zoned out, looking as if she'd seen a ghost, then snapped out of it. I look over at her with my eyebrows raised; she shakes her head and fakes a smile.

"Okay, who wants dessert?" She squeaks, changing the subject and holding a strawberry cake from the local bakery she's been raving about.

We all ate dessert and watched one more movie before calling it a night.

"Alright, you two, behave yourselves. We're going to the lake tomorrow. Does 9 a.m. sound good for you?"

"Sounds good, Dad. Goodnight, love you." She hugs him a little tighter than usual.

"I love you too, Lizzie; I'm so glad you're here."

"Graham, remember our little talk?" he reminds me, slightly smirking.

"Sure thing, goodnight." Liza glances between us, and I open the door to her room and guide her in.

"What talk?" She asks as I give her a light push into the door while she looks back at her dad.

"None of your business. Now, you're not off the hook. We both know that the door cam did not break on its own. Why did you look like you'd seen a ghost earlier? What's going on?"

She puts her head down, strips off her clothes, and pulls on one of the T-shirts she'd taken from my house.

"Graham.."

"I cannot protect you if you don't tell me things."

"I don't need protection. It's just my imagination playing tricks on me." I also strip out of my clothes and put on athletic shorts. We climb into bed, and I turn to her, sliding my fingers through hers.

"What did you see?"

She sighs and finally tells me, "Not what, who..." I frown at her.

"Okay, then who?"

"Tim, I saw Tim, or at least I thought I did... I blinked a few times, and he was gone. So, I know it's my imagination. There's no way he's back, no way he burned through that money, and there is *absolutely* no way he's the one playing tricks on my dad."

"I hope for his sake, you're right." She cuddles into my side, wrapping her arm around my waist. I throw my leg over hers and run my fingers through her hair, taking in her cinnamon scent. I meant it; if Tim knew what was good for him, he would think twice about coming near Liza again. The first time he messed with her, she was alone; this time, she had me, and I will kill for her.

46

Liza

Graham runs his fingers through my hair, on the verge of sleep when I call to him.

"I'm glad you're here with me."

"Me too, baby." He whispers in a sleepy voice. I look at him and plant a soft kiss on his lips. I know I told my Dad I'd behave, but all I want is for Graham to fuck me to sleep. Graham kisses me back, settling me back on his chest as he falls into a deep sleep.

* * *

An hour later, my pussy still throbs. I know what I want. I look up to see Graham asleep and slide under the covers to attack the task at hand. My mission was simple: make it impossible for Graham to tell me no. I ease his shorts down and free his cock. He shifts under me, starting to wake up. I wrap my lips around the head of his cock, moving my head up and down while stroking him slowly. I glide my tongue over the tip of his cock, licking up his salty juice. I feel a hand tussling in my hair and a low groan coming from Graham's mouth.

He pulls me up, growling, "What are you doing?" I bite my lip and tease him with a sly grin. "No sex, Elizabeth." I kiss the side of his neck, running my tongue across it. I move towards his ear, completely ignoring his protest.

"Tell me you don't want to fuck me right now," I whisper to him.

"Your dad is..."

"On the other side of the house. Please, Graham, I need to feel you." I kiss his neck again; this time, he grabs me and pulls me to face him.

"Fuck," he curses, kissing me deeply this time, and flips me over.

"Can you be a good girl and be quiet for me?"

"Mhm." Hovering over me, he begins teasing me by leaving kisses all over my body. He lifts me, pulling the shirt up, and I lift my arms in response as the shirt slides over my head.

"Lay back."

I do as I'm told, and in an instant, I feel Graham's fingers inside of me.

"So wet, always so wet for me." He toys with my clit moving his fingers in and out of me. I moan in response, biting down on my lip. He replaces his fingers with his mouth, licking all around me and sucking my pussy. I shiver under his touch and can't help it even if I want to. I reach my release so fucking fast I don't even realize it's happening, and he continues licking me, devouring me clean.

"Oh, Graham...Graham." He moves over the top of me, putting a finger to my lips.

"Quiet, or you get nothing. Understand?" I take my lip in my mouth and nod. He raises an eyebrow, and I know what he wants.

"I understand."

"Good girl, now pull your knees to your chest."

I open my legs, lifting my knees as high as they reach my chest. Graham slips into my tight pussy, and I gasp full of sensation. I tense up a bit, adjusting to the fullness of his cock being deep inside me.

"Relax, I've got you. Let me in." My body relaxes before I register what he's saying; that's how welcoming my body is to him. He pumps in and out of me, slowly at first.

"Fuck, you feel good. So good." I reach up to wrap my arms around him, and he grabs my hands, pinning them above my head.

"Keep them there."

Choosing my battles wisely, I keep them there, pushing myself towards him, causing him to go deeper.

"You want me to fuck you harder?" he moans as he slams in and out of me, making me take every inch of him with every gratifying thrust.

"Yes, oh god, yes," I whisper. Graham teases me, sliding in and out of me, resting the head of his cock on my entrance before pushing into me again. I need to come; I need to explode, and he won't let me.

"Graham, please," I beg as he showcases an evil grin; he's enjoying torturing me. I might lose my mind, but he finally gives in and gives me what I want. Graham picks up his pace, wrapping a hand behind my neck and pulling me into him with each thrust, always harder and deeper than the previous.

"Come. Now *angel*. Come," and I obey just like he tells me to; my body shakes with relief, and he follows, spilling into me. My back arches as my climax subsides, and Graham's arms wrap around the small of my back, pulling me to him as he furiously cums.

Graham gets up and heads toward the bathroom, returning with a warm washcloth and cleaning me up. Every time I have sex with Graham, I can barely move after; it is just that good; it takes everything out of me. I focus on catching my breath when I feel the bed dip again; this time, Graham pulls me into his side.

"You okay?" he asks, looking at me intently. I smile and nod, nudging my head into his side. He kisses my head, and we drift off to sleep together.

* * *

Bang. Bang. Bang. My eyes fly open to see Graham pulling on his shorts and shirt. I quickly sit up and throw on his shirt and pajama shorts. I look at him, my eyebrows together in confusion. He opens the door and sees my dad on the staircase steps.

"What in the hell? It's 3 a.m." My dad grits out to Graham. I begin walking behind Graham.

"Dad, why is someone banging on your door at 3 a.m.?"

"I don't know, Lizzie, but I am damn sure going to find out. Stay here." I ignore my dad, following behind him and Graham. The banging continues; I wrap my hands around Graham's arm and tug.

"What if it's…"

"It's not; relax and stay behind me, understand?" I nod, and for the first time, he doesn't make me use my words. We all head down the stairs; the closer we get, the more twisted and unsettling my stomach feels. What if it wasn't my imagination earlier? What if the eyes I thought I felt on me were real? I always felt like he would come back for me. What if this was finally the moment he made his move? I swallow hard from my wild thoughts when suddenly the banging stops.

"Axel, do you have a weapon in the house?" I look at Graham and my dad. My dad shakes his head. "I take it that Lizzie never told you what I do for a living?"

He pats his back and lifts his shirt, showing his gun. I look at the gun in his waistband and don't even flinch. I wasn't a stranger to guns; I grew up around them and went to the shooting range often.

My dad gets to the door and looks through the window next to the door.

"I don't see anyone."

"What do you mean? We all…"

"I know Lizzie, but there isn't anyone out there." He goes to the door and opens it. There isn't anyone there, but an envelope lies on the doormat. My dad picks it up, frowns, shuts the door, and turns to me. "Lizzie"

"What? What is it?" I exclaim, walking towards him. He hands me the letter. *'Welcome home, Elizabeth. I've been waiting.'* I freeze. Graham takes the note from me and immediately picks up his phone.

"What is this about?" I never told my dad about Tim. I never wanted him to worry, or rather, I never wanted him to do something he'd regret. My dad was protective, especially over his "little girl." I never planned for him to find out, especially this way. I can hear Graham on the phone with Ellis. This is the first time he's ever traveled without security, but I'm sure that will change in the next few hours.

"Dad, I—" Graham walks in at the perfect time. I am not ready to tell my dad what we've been hiding from him for the last seven years. It would crush him, and he would never forgive my mom and Brant for keeping him out of it.

"Ellis is sending a team up here." I put my hand on Graham's arm and shake my head.

"No need for a team; Dad already has one." Graham frowns and tilts his head, obviously remembering what my dad said about what he does for a living. I let out a sigh.

"What exactly do you do, Axel?" My dad gives me a sly grin and embraces me.

"If I tell you, I'll have to kill you." I swat at my dad, and he groans lowly.

"I run a security company; I just retired from special forces. I appreciate you putting something together so quickly, but I got it. It's nice to know that my Lizzie will be protected when I'm not around," he states, winking at Graham. He pulls away from me and scans my face.

"Now tell me, what is that letter about, and why the hell was it delivered to my doorstep at three in the goddamn morning?"

"We should probably sit down," I say, walking toward the living room. I wrap a blanket around myself before plopping down on the couch. Graham sits beside me, reassuring me, and touches my knee. My dad sits across from us in his rocking chair, studying both of us. "Do you remember Tim?"

"Yeah, the kid that used to have that crush on you?"

"It was way more than a crush. Seven years ago, Tim stalked me for about a year or year and a half; when I thought he had stopped, he found me in my sophomore year of college." I stop, gathering myself. I haven't revealed the specifics of this incident in seven years. Graham rubs my shoulders. "It's okay." I take a deep breath and continue, afraid to look at my father, so I keep my head down, playing with my fingers.

"He snuck into my room at Mom's and Brant's one night and demanded I explain why he wasn't "*enough*" for me. When I told him I had no clue what he was talking about and that I thought we were friends, he hit me, dragged me out of bed, and tried to rape me."

"I remembered everything you taught me back then; I kneed him and pushed him off. He was stronger; he climbed on top of me and wrapped his hands around my neck, strangling me. By that time, Eli heard the struggle and ran into my room. Eli tackled him, and I yelled for Mom and Brant. After that, Brant dragged him out of my room and told him that if he didn't leave me alone, he'd call the police. Tim told him if he didn't pay him one million dollars, he'd kill me the next day. Mom and Brant didn't want to take their chances on the police, so they paid him, and I never heard from him again. I've felt like someone has been watching me lately, and I keep seeing him everywhere. I assumed it was my imagination, but then you said you kept getting weird knocks on your door and that your door cam was busted. Tim was good with technology, from what I can remember. It would have taken him no time to break into your system at the front and to break your door cam." I glance up at my dad; his eyes are teary and full of rage.

"Why wouldn't you tell me this, Elizabeth? I am your father. I would have killed that fucker with my bare hands." I break down, tears streaming from my face. Graham pulls me into him, his face stone, and I realize this is the first time he has heard the whole story. Fuck. I'll think about that later. My dad stands and begins pacing the room repeatedly, cursing. "Seven years, seven years—you've kept this from me. We tell each other everything we always have. And you thought you couldn't bring this to me?"

I sob through my words, "No, Daddy, I knew you would lose it; I knew you would do whatever you had to do to keep him away from me. I didn't want you to get in trouble. You had just started your special forces position; I didn't want to jeopardize that. I thought I had it under control. I thought I could protect myself."

He kneels before me, lifting my face to his. "No job is more important than me protecting my little girl. You are my world, Elizabeth. You and your brother—that's all I have. You should have told me."

"I know. I'm sorry, I'm so sorry," I say, still sobbing; he pulls me into a tight hug.

"It's okay, Lizzie, it's okay. We'll handle it. You're safe."

47

Graham

I watch as Liza cries in her father's arms, both full of so much regret. She held this secret from him for seven years. It was the first time I heard the details of her attack, and it left me boiling. The thought of anyone trying to harm her made me sick to my stomach. It made me coil with anger.

I pulled out my phone to text Ellis. I knew that he would still want to come even if I didn't need the team. He trusts no one besides himself to watch over me when it is needed. And he added Liza to that list the moment I made her mine.

Graham: *Leave the team. Axel had one.*

El: *I'll be there in the next few hours.*

"I'll make some coffee; I don't think any of us are getting any sleep tonight." Axel moves up to sit by Liza.

"He loves you, you know?" She looks over her shoulder, and I wink at her. "Yeah. He does."

I know how important her father's approval of us is to her; having it makes things easier. Even if I didn't have it, it wouldn't have mattered to me, but it mattered to her. I busy myself in the kitchen and do a mental check of the last few weeks, trying to remember if I had seen anything out of the ordinary.

Graham: *Make sure to have the footage at the apartment checked.*

El: *Already done. He was there twice. Will update you once I land.*

Graham: *Hurry the fuck up. I am losing my footing here.*

El: *She needs you strong.*

I close the messages, and my hand clamps tight around my phone—the frustration leaking from me. I'm trying my hardest to be what she needs, but knowing he's been there *twice* adds fuel to the fire. I want my hands around his fucking neck. I won't be happy unless I'm the one who watches the life drain from his pathetic body. She hasn't been at her apartment much, but my guess is that he followed her brother to Seattle and started watching her from there.

Axel is on the phone discussing the incident and telling them who he wants on the job, and Liza is curled up on the couch. I round the sofa and sit beside her, handing her the cup of coffee.

"Thank you." She tucks her feet under, and I pull her into me. Her hands tremble, and some coffee spills onto the couch.

"You're shivering." I pull the covers over her body, rubbing my hands up and down her arms in an attempt to create heat. She takes a sip of her coffee.

"Mm, perfect."

I kiss the top of her head and ease us back against the couch.

Axel joins us as he sits in his chair; he grabs the cup of coffee I placed on the table for him and stares at Liza. With his eyes tearing up, he shakes his head and sips his coffee.

"My team will be here in fifteen minutes; we can get some rest once they are here. I've checked the cameras on my phone, and he's nowhere on this property; none of the perimeter alarms have gone off. One thing I know for sure is that he can't get inside this house."

After a few minutes of silence, Axel sighs. "I can't believe your mother kept this from me; I ought to kick Brant's ass."

"I asked them not to say anything; you can't fault them." He shakes his head and turns on the TV. We sit in silence until the doorbell rings, startling Liza. I tighten my grip on her.

"It's okay, *angel.*"

About a minute later, seven or eight of Axel's guys stroll into his house.

"I checked the outside perimeter, and we're all clear. The gate is secured as well. I'll keep two of our men at the gate tonight and the rest throughout the house's perimeter. I'll keep watch in the control room." Axel nods as one of his guys speaks.

"Alright, if anything happens, you call me immediately. I won't sleep much tonight, so I'll pop in and out of the control room."

"Roger that, sir." He heads for the control room, saying something to the other men in his earpiece.

"Lizzie, go on and get some sleep. He isn't getting near you."

"I'm staying up with you, Daddy."

I nudge her, and she turns to look at me in protest. I cup her face, running my thumb over her cheek. Her face softens, reading my eyes.

"Fine."

Her father smiles at her and gives me an approving nod. I intertwine our fingers and lead her back up the stairs to her room.

We climb into bed, and Liza cries into my chest for what feels like a lifetime. I play with her hair, calming her until she finally lets go and falls asleep. I slip from under her and out of her door to see her father sitting atop the steps. He turns when he hears the door open.

"Is she finally asleep?"

I sit beside him on the stairs. "Yeah...she is."

"How did I miss this?"

"I think your daughter is good at hiding things when she thinks it protects the people she loves."

"You take good care of her; I appreciate that. It's all I want for her."

"I won't let anything happen to your little girl. I love her too much." He pats me on the back, squeezing my shoulder.

"Yeah, I know you do. She has that effect on people."

"We both should try to get some sleep. She'll go nuts if she wakes up and you aren't there."

"Yeah, you're probably right."

* * *

When morning comes, I am already awake and watching Liza sleep. I would do anything to protect her. Whatever I had to do, I would do it. There was no doubt in my mind. Ellis texted me hours ago, saying he's posted in the front of the house. I relaxed a little more, knowing that he was lingering around. I knew Liza wouldn't want to leave and head back home, but I damn sure still planned to try to persuade her too.

She squirms in my arms, blinking her eyes open. I push her tussled hair out of her face.

"Good morning, pretty girl."

She rolls over, tapping her phone. "Hi. We should get ready for the lake."

"I don't think your dad expects us to go to the lake anymore." She ignores me, pushing the covers back.

"I want to go, Graham; I refuse to let this dickhead make me a prisoner." I give up, realizing I won't be able to tell her anything different. While she's in the shower, I step out and update her dad.

"She still wants to go to the lake. She's not taking no for an answer."

"That's Lizzie; I figured she'd still want to go. I'll be ready in twenty minutes." I scroll over Ellis' number and wait for him to pick it up.

"El, she still wants to go to the lake. I want you and one of Axel's men with us."

"On my way over." I quickly take a shower and meet everyone downstairs. I instantly regret agreeing to this, and we head for the lake.

Once we get to the lake, we gather on Axel's boat, which is almost identical to mine. It's a nice day for the lake, with the perfect temperature and the right amount of breeze.

"Okay, I packed a ton of snacks and food for us!" Liza exclaims as she carries an oversized cooler. I grab her arm and take the cooler from her. She saunters over to the lounge chair on the boat. We are in the middle of the lake when her dad finally says what I've been thinking about since last night's events.

"We need to get you out of here, Lizzie."

She expresses her disapproval, "No. I am not afraid of him."

"I know you aren't, but you need to go back. He shouldn't have been able to get through the front gate, Elizabeth. You are going back tonight, and that is *final*."

"I am not running away from this piece of shit again. He took enough from me, Daddy; he does not get to take any more from me." Axel looks at me for help, and I turn to face Liza and take her hands in mine.

"Elizabeth, you have to think about this. You are safer in Seattle. You know that, and I know that." She looks away from me and into the water, tears forming in her eyes.

"I'm not leaving." I turn her face back to me, leveling our eyes at each other.

"You are; even if I have to throw you over my shoulder and onto the plane myself, you *are* leaving.”

She yanks her hands from me and walks into the berth, slamming the door. I'd leave her alone and let her cool off, but no matter what she says, she's getting on that damn plane tonight.

“She'll be fine; she's just stubborn. But she knows we're right. Don't worry about it.” Axel explains as he opens the cooler, grabs a beer, and throws one at me.

* * *

Three hours later, we returned to the dock. Liza came out of the berth after about 45 minutes of pacing. She still won't speak to us, only talking to Ellis, completely blocking her father and me out. I shake my head and smile at her father, who is doing the same thing.

“Lizzie, what do you say we get food from one of your favorite places?”

“I just want to go home; I don't want to be around either of you right now.”

“Lizzie.”

“Please, Daddy, just leave me be,” she steps off the boat and heads for the car.

His eyes watch her, and he tries to hold his laugh. “She is *pissed*.”

I watch her as Liza circles the corner to the car and stops. She turns around and drops her bags. Axel and I look at her and frown; something is wrong. Before I can get to her, Ellis yells, “Gun!”

“Lizzie, get down...” *Pop.* Axel's words clip when a single shot pierces his side. *Pop.* He takes another to his shoulder. Axel drops to the ground, clutching his stomach. “Lizzie, get Lizzie.”

My body moves before I register what happened. It's at that moment that I hear another shot. I can't pinpoint the source of the shot, so I quickly bark out, “Elizabeth, get down. NOW!”

48

Liza

It sounds like a tire has popped repeatedly. What is going on? Gunshots—it's *gunshots. Oh, my God. Graham. Dad.* As I walked to the SUV after fighting with Graham and my father, I stopped in my tracks when I noticed that the windshield of the SUV had 'I'M HERE' in bold red letters. I turned around quickly. I had to warn them, but I wasn't fast enough. My dad's shirt is covered with red splatters. He's soaked. Why is he soaking? Another shot pierces his body, and he drops to the ground. My ears are ringing. I can't hear; I see Graham. He's running toward me. Am I moving? Why aren't I moving?

I stand there, completely stuck, with my feet melted into the ground.

"Elizabeth, get down. NOW!" Graham, it's Graham. He yells at me to move, but I can't. I open my mouth to talk, but nothing comes out. Moments later, my body hits the ground, crushed by the weight. My head hits the ground hard, and I can't breathe, and then darkness surrounds me.

* * *

"She's waking up. I'll tell her. Thanks, Brant." *Graham.* I open my eyes to Graham staring at me, and the beeping sounds of a hospital monitor wake me completely.

"*Angel.*"

"My dad, where's my dad?" I say, piecing together the events that took place. Laying there, I vividly remember his bloodied body and how I couldn't get to him.

"He's in surgery. How is your head?"

"Hurts," I barely open my eyes.

"Your mom, Brant, and brothers are coming here." He rises from his seat and grabs the water pitcher, and I see his arm in a sling. My eyes fly open, and I sit up abruptly.

"You're hurt!" I instantly feel dizzy. Fuck, my head. Graham turns around quickly, wrapping his free arm around me.

"I am fine; lay down, Elizabeth." I don't even put up a fight, and I lower myself back down to my bed.

"So, it's Elizabeth now," I pout.

He gives me a small smile and softly says, "It's the only time you listen to me without a fight."

"What happened, Graham?"

"What do you remember?"

"I remember seeing the window and seeing the writing. I tried to warn you, and then I heard tires popping. No gunshots, I heard gunshots. I couldn't move, and then it was dark."

"Tim followed us to the lake. He waited until we were leaving and shot your dad. I assume his goal was to shoot all of us and take you." My eyes tear up, and Graham puts his hand on my cheek.

"Don't cry, *angel.*"

"Where is he now?"

"Ellis tracked him briefly, but then he disappeared. The police will want to talk to you in an hour or so." He looks over me. "I'm going to get the doctor to give you something for your head."

"Why is your arm in a sling?"

"It was just a flesh wound." He was shot. My body tenses up, and I'm so full of guilt. This was because of me, my dad, Graham, and their team; all of them could've been killed because of *me*.

"I have to fix this," I whisper to myself. Graham tilts my face to his.

"You don't have to fix *anything*. You need to rest so we can check on your dad and get you out of here."

"This is my fault. He's after *me*."

"This is not your fault. Sit still; I'll be right back." A few moments later, a nurse comes in.

"Hi, Ms. Crambell, I'm Addie, your nurse. Dr. Carmichael is your neurophysician. She doesn't think you need to stay more than one or two nights, depending on your pain level after this medication. How are you feeling?"

"I'm okay. It's just a little headache and some dizziness."

"You hit your head pretty hard when you fell. A headache is normal after a fainting spell, so we will monitor you closely. She may do a CT scan, but she has not decided yet." She hands me two big pills and water. I swallow the pills and the water, my mouth feeling like cotton.

"Do you have any information on my father?"

"Yes, he just got out of surgery. Everything went great. Mr. Salando requested your father be transferred to this room, so they should be transporting him here soon."

"Thank you."

"Of course, if you need anything, hit your call button, and I'll be right in." She slides the call button beside me, within arms' reach, before she leaves.

Graham pulls his chair next to my bed and brings my hand to his mouth, planting small, tender kisses. His eyes water and I feel the tightening grip on my hand.

"Graham, I'm okay."

"What if he had shot you, Elizabeth? What am I supposed to do without you?"

"He didn't, and you won't have to find that out." Just then, the door to the room opens, and two nurses roll my dad in. Graham wipes his eyes and stands, overseeing them.

"Is he okay?" I ask. My dad is fast asleep in his bed, with dressings over the wounds on his shoulder and right side.

"He's fine, he's lucky. He should wake soon from the sedative." I watch as they finish hooking him up to their monitors, one nurse hanging another bag of antibiotics.

"He may be a little groggy when he wakes up; make sure to hit the call button."

"Will do, thank you." The nurses leave, and Graham sits back in the chair. He looks exhausted and is still in the same dirty, bloody clothes.

"Why don't you go home and shower and get some sleep? I'll call you when he wakes up."

"Not happening."

"Graham, I'm okay. Really. Go."

"I am not leaving you while this fucker is still out."

"At least shower; you can leave Ellis here with me." He stands and hovers over me.

"I smell bad, angel?" I try to smile at him, pain searing through my head. It hurts so much, fuck, but I don't care. Graham makes everything feel better. He kisses my cheek and nuzzles against it.

"I'll be back in an hour and a half, not a moment later." He carefully kisses my chapped lips.

"Could you please bring me some chapstick back? My lips hurt." He grabs his keys and heads for the door.

"Love you."

"Love you more."

"Not possible." The door shuts, and I'm left alone with my sedated father and my silent thoughts, thoughts that I don't want to think about as I learn about what happened in the past few hours.

49

Graham

I reluctantly leave the hospital and head back to Axel's house to shower. Ellis stayed at the hospital with Liza and her father, leaving me alone to think about the fucking day I had. I could have lost her *again*. This time because of a fucking loser who couldn't get a grip on something he wanted and couldn't, *wouldn't* have.

I hop in the shower, the steaming water rolling off my hair and down my back. My arm hurts like a bitch, but it's a good thing I just need the sling. It was a flesh womb; I'd pop some painkillers and be good as new. Even though Liza was the one who was hurt in the hospital, she was worried about other people. That was what I loved about her; she was always thinking of others. Except for this one time, I wanted her to be selfish and take the time to rest—the time she needed not to blame herself for her father getting shot. But I knew she wouldn't do that.

I finish showering and throw my clothes on when my phone starts ringing. Ellis.

"Everything okay?"

"Yeah, G, I'm just letting you know Brant and Bethany are here."

"Where are Elias and Hogan?"

"They're here, and so is Selle."

My face turned hard. Why the fuck was my sister here? She didn't need to be around any of this shit until someone caught that bastard.

"I'll be there soon."

"I'll let Elizabeth know."

When I reach the hospital, I go straight to Liza's floor. As I approach her room, I see exactly who I expect: Hogan and Elias. However, who I see next to them is what sends me reeling. My fucking sister is next to Elias, holding his hand with her head on his shoulder. They all spot me, and she drops his hand.

"Too late, Giselle." I look between her and Eli, his eyes red from crying. Realizing this isn't the place to hash this out, I put my hand on his shoulder, squeezing it.

"They're both fine."

He tries to shake it off, and I can tell he's struggling. He doesn't acknowledge my words; he hangs his head low. Eli reminds me so much of myself: hard, strong, and tough. The last thing he wants is to seem weak, so he hides his tears, but I know how he feels. I learned way too well how that felt. I knew too well how much pressure he had on him, and if he didn't release it soon when he finally did, it would break him.

"What happened, G?" Hogan asks, resting his elbows on his knees. I sigh and give him every detail of our shit show.

"Wait until I get my fucking hands on him," Eli growls. I raise my eyebrows and sigh.

"You'll have to wait in line for that one. Your dad awake yet?"

"Yeah, he's up; he was asking for you."

"I'll head in." I head for Liza and Axel's room.

"G, wait a second." I turn to face my sister as she walks towards me.

"What is it, Giselle?"

"I'm sorry."

"Sorry for?"

She puts her head down and plays with her fingers—the one thing she does when nervous. I grow impatient at the silence, turning my back to her and heading for the room again.

"I don't have time for this."

"I like him...okay. I like him so much," she admits, grabbing my arm. I yank away from her and look over my shoulder.

"Good for you. I need to check on Liza. We'll talk about it later."

She folds her arms around herself and stands there, tears forming in her eyes. I'd regret being so mean to her later, but I don't care right now.

I walk into the room and see Brant, Bethany, and Liza laughing around Axel's bed. They all stop and turn, their eyes on me, and Bethany stands, kissing me on the cheek.

"I'm glad you're okay, honey." She tells me, rubbing my shoulders. Liza and Brant both smile at me. I stand behind the chair Liza sits in. I reach into my pocket, hand her the chapstick she requested, and rest my hands on her shoulders.

"Axel, how are you feeling?"

"Lucky. That shot to my shoulder should've been it for me." Liza shutters, and I squeeze her shoulders reassuringly.

"And you, *angel*, how are you feeling?"

"A lot better; the doctor said I can go home tomorrow."

"Hallelujah," Bethany exclaims. "You are on the first plane back to Seattle until your dad can catch this son of a bitch."

"I'd like to take her back, if that's okay?" I look from Liza to Bethany.

"Oh, of course you can. I'm so glad you were there to protect her." She looks from me to Axel and sighs. "I'm glad both of you were there; I don't even want to think about what would have happened if she were alone."

"Neither do I," Brant adds, resting his hand on Bethany's thigh. Liza rolls her neck in a circle, bringing her hand up and massaging the side of it.

"Your neck hurts?"

"Just a little sore is all."

"I think you should get back in bed."

"No, I'm okay. I'm tired of lying down." I groan and start massaging her neck, moving my thumbs around in a circular motion. Her mom smiles at us, and her dad gives us a little grin.

"You two make my heart swell."

"Mom, stop it. Please."

"What? I can't be happy that my daughter is happy." Liza rolls her eyes, and her dad chuckles.

About an hour passed before Brant and Bethany said they were heading out and would see us back in Seattle; they planned to stay in California until Axel was discharged. Hogan, Eli, and Selle walk in shortly after, and a knock on the door startles us all.

"Hi there, I am one of Mr. Crambell's nurses. I'm just going to draw some blood from his IV and then take him for a few tests."

"How long will the test take?" Liza asks.

"He'll be back in a less than a hour; do you need anything?"

"No, thank you."

"Of course. We'll be back soon." She steers Axel's bed out of the room, and they are gone.

"I thought you guys would have left with Mom," Liza speaks as Eli pulls up a chair beside her.

"Nah, I'm going to chill here with you for a while." Selle sits beside him, glancing at me before quickly putting her head back down. Liza narrows her eyes at me and raises her eyebrow.

"We aren't doing this," she states, looking between the three of us. Eli sighs.

"It's not me... it's him."

"Elias, don't," Selle declares.

"No, please, Elias, continue," I say flatly. Hogan plops down in a chair and crosses his feet with a smirk. I look at him and tilt my head.

"Something funny?"

"Just interested to see how this conversation is going to go."

"There is no conversation to be had. They are together, and she is capable of taking care of herself. My brother is a great guy, and they are happy. Let them be," Liza chastises, climbing into her hospital bed. I grab her arm and help her into the bed.

"Why are you talking like you knew about it?"

The room grows quiet, and I frown, stepping back and looking at everyone.

"Are you telling me that everyone, except me, knew that my girlfriend's brother is fucking my little sister?"

Liza smacks my arm, and Selle stands abruptly and heads for the door. Eli stands up to go after her, then turns to me.

"You know, I would think that all you'd want is for your sister to be happy. If you know her at all, the only thing she wants is *your* fucking approval. I like you, G, I do, but keep hurting her like this, and we'll have a serious problem."

He stalks out of the door. Hogan stands, making an "oh shit" face, and turns for the door.

"Have you lost your goddamn mind? Sit. *Now* Graham." Liza snarls, sitting up and pulling her knees to her chest. I sink into the chair in front of her bed. "They are happy, what is the problem? Why would you say those things to her? She is your sister, your *adult* sister."

Liza is right, I was being a dick. I knew the worst part was that I didn't care that they were dating. I cared that she didn't feel comfortable telling me she was remotely interested.

"Are you going to answer me or just sit there?"

"I know. I'm sorry. I'll talk to her."

"What is your issue with this, Graham? Do you think my brother isn't good enough or something?" I slide my chair closer to her bed, and she reaches for my hand.

"She didn't tell me. We tell each other everything, and she didn't tell me about this huge thing that had happened in her life." I look up at her. "*You* didn't tell me."

"They asked me not to... I walked in on them before we left the apartment." I shake my head.

"You've known since we left, and you kept it from me; it's my sister, Elizabeth."

"It wasn't my secret to tell Graham; they asked me to stay out of it. She wanted to tell you, and I told her that she had to tell you soon or that I would. I'm sorry..." Just then, her dad returns to sleep in his bed. The nurse plugs his blood pressure cuff and looks at us.

"He'll probably be out all night, Mr. Salando. If you're staying, please let us know, and we'll grab you some warm blankets and sheets for the cot."

"I will be. That would be great. Thank you."

"I'll be back." She leaves, and the moment the door shuts, Liza talks through strained teeth.

"You don't have to stay here."

"Elizabeth, I'm staying."

The nurse quickly returns with warm blankets, sheets as promised, and a pillow. "Let me know if anyone needs anything." She leaves, quietly closing the door. I walk to the cot, pull the sheet over it, and kick my shoes off.

Liza clears her throat. "Stop calling me Elizabeth."

"That's your name," I tease.

"No, that's my name when you're mad."

"I'm not mad."

I say, lying on the cot. She folds her arms and stares at me. I gaze up at the ceiling, ignoring her death glare. I have no reason to be mad at Liza—hell, I have no reason to be mad at anyone. Hurt, yes, but mad? No.

"Fine, whatever. I'll see you in the morning."

She turns on her side, her back facing me. I feel like an asshole. First, I made Selle cry—not once but twice. Now, I'm letting Liza go to bed, thinking I'm mad at her. What is wrong with me? I could have lost her today; hell, I could have died, and here I am, acting like a fucking idiot.

I get up and glance at Axel, who is still sleeping. Whatever they gave him as pain medication was keeping him asleep. I walk over to Liza, lift the covers, and slide in behind her, wrapping my arm around her. Her body tenses up.

I let out a deep sigh, "I'm sorry. I'm an asshole. A fucking asshole." Her body relaxes, and she turns to face me.

She plants a soft kiss on my lips. "You are an asshole," she agrees, letting out a little giggle in my mouth. I smile at her and pull her closer to me. "Watch it, *angel.*"

I kiss her softly, and she bites my lip. I groan. "Your dad is in this room."

"Yeah, thanks to you," she whispers. I smile at her.

"Tomorrow isn't that far away. Get some rest."

"I love you."

"I love you more," I respond.

"Not possible."

"Mm, don't care angel. Sleep." I kiss her forehead and watch her fall asleep.

50

Liza

The following day went by quickly as the nurse discharged me and gave me an update on how long my father would be staying. My dad was lucky; he could have died from his wounds. He would be staying in the hospital for another three days and then coming back to Seattle with Brant and my mother. I respected Brant a hell of a lot more. I mean to know that your wife not only cheated on you with her ex-husband but now you're going to move him into your house while he recovers. That was a type of strength I never knew any man could have.

Once we got to my father's, Graham had already left our suitcases at the bottom of the stairs. I quickly showered, moving as fast as my sore body let me. Clothes were lying on my bed, waiting for me. I dressed, grabbed an apple from the kitchen, and headed for the jet.

The flight back to Seattle seemed oddly quick. Graham was on a work call but held my hand the entire time. I watched a movie and drifted in and out of sleep until the flight attendant came to tell us we'd be preparing to land. Selle decided to stay in California with Eli and Hogan for a few more days, and she said she would fly back with my parents. Graham wasn't too happy about that, but instead of voicing that to Selle, he hugged her and said he was sorry. That was progress; after last night, I understood why he was so upset.

"Are you okay, *angel*?" Graham asks as we approach his house. I nod and smile at him.

"I'm glad you're okay. I'm sorry, my life is such a mess." Graham cups my face, rubbing my cheek.

"Your life is not a mess; even if it were, it's *my* mess, too. Because *you're* my mess." He plants a kiss on my lips and smiles at me.

We settle into Graham's quickly and cuddle up on the couch. I rest my head on his chest and play with his fingers. This is where I feel the safest and most comfortable.

"I need to go home and unpack my things," I say, hoping Graham will tell me not to. Graham growls, and I mean, he literally growls.

"What?"

"Nothing"

"It's only for a little." He sighs and starts to sit up, moving me away from him.

"Graham, I will come back tonight if you want me to, but I have my own place. It's probably smart that I stay there at some point; otherwise, why are Brant and my mom paying rent?" I could easily get out of this since I was sleeping with the building's owner. My conscience screams at me.

"Okay, Elizabeth, I'll drive you." He walks off, and I stand behind him, throwing my hands up.

"What is your problem? Why are you so upset?" He keeps walking, grabbing my suitcase and his keys.

"Are you ready?" He asks, ignoring my outroar. I tug on my shoes and shake my head at him. He opens the door, and I walk out, climbing into his SUV. I turn my body toward the window and fold my arms. I'm sure I look like a pissed-off child, but I don't care. I replay the event in my head, trying to figure out what I did to upset him so much. He has been giving me clues all weekend that he doesn't want us apart, ever. I want to tell him I am choosing to stay in Seattle, but this went horribly wrong. He climbs in the driver's seat and heads for my apartment.

The ride is silent, and I let out a deep sigh. Graham watches the road, ignoring me. I pick up my phone and call my mom; I haven't checked on my dad, and now seems like the perfect time since my asshole of a boyfriend is ignoring my fucking presence anyway.

"Hi, sweetheart!"

"Hi mama, are you at the hospital?"

"Yes. Your father is doing great; they're going to let him go home tomorrow instead, so we'll return to Seattle in two days."

"Can I talk to him?"

"Of course, honey, hold on." I hear her telling my dad it's me, and I listen to him cough a little before getting on the phone. His voice is still scratchy and raspy.

"Hey, Lizzie."

"Hi, Daddy, how are you feeling?"

"You know me. There's nothing to keep me down for too long. Are you all settled in Seattle?"

"I'm on my way to my apartment now." When I mention that, Graham's hand tightens around the steering wheel. I ignore him and continue talking with my dad.

"Good, but I don't want you alone until we catch this bastard. My team still hasn't located him, and I'd feel a hell of a lot better if you stayed at Graham's house until then." I blink my eyes quickly.

"Daddy, did you just tell me you want me to sleep at a boy's house?" My dad chuckles.

"He saved my little girl's life. He's more than just a boy. I know that, and I think you do, too. He's it for you, Lizzie. And I couldn't be happier." I look over at Graham. This time, he looks at me, and I see his lip curve slightly to smile.

"Look, we're pulling into my apartment; I'll call you later."

"Sounds good. Love you, Lizzie."

"Love you too, Daddy."

Graham parks and grabs my suitcase, and we head towards the door.

"Good morning, Mr. Salando," Alicia greets, staring too hard at him for my liking. Maybe that was just me being anxious right now, not knowing what the hell he was upset about. He nods at her and gives her a small smile.

"Alicia."

"Good morning, Ms. Crambell."

"Hi, Alicia."

We get on the elevator, and when the door shuts, I turn to Graham, who is looking at something on his phone. I clear my throat, and he looks up, raising his eyebrow.

"Something wrong?" he spews in a low, dark voice.

"You tell me, you're the one acting like a dick."

He turns to me, fire in his eyes. Oh, fuck, he is mad, scratch that he is *pissed*.

"Elizabeth, I'm taking you *home* like you requested. You wanted to come *home* and *stay here*." The elevator opens to my floor, and he gestures his hand out. "So, go. To your *home*. It's waiting." *No, home is right in front of my face, I say to myself.*

My mouth drops open in surprise at his words. I yank my suitcase out of his hand and exit the elevator when he speaks again, this time in a small, hurt voice.

"You know what's funny? I thought I was your home. I thought *my* home was your home."

I step forward, ready to plead my case, and tell him he is my home when he raises his hand.

"I'll talk to you later, Elizabeth." Then, the elevator doors close.

I stand shattered as I roll my suitcase to my door, unlock it, and shut it slowly. I put my forehead against the door, instantly ripped from my thoughts.

"Welcome home, Elizabeth." I freeze, knowing exactly who that voice belongs to. Coldness immediately chills my body. I turn around, and it's none other than Tim, and he has a gun pointed directly at me.

"Tim, what are you doing? Why do you have that? How did you get in here?"

"You're asking all of the wrong questions, Elizabeth."

I swallow hard, my instincts kicking in as I reach for the doorknob. Before I can open the door, he yanks me by my hair and takes me away from it. "I'm finally getting what you should've given to me seven years ago."

I punch and kick him, some making contact and some hitting the air. This isn't happening to me again.

"You don't have to do this. Please."

He draws his hand back and slaps the gun across my face when I elbow him in the nose. I can taste the blood immediately, and I don't know if he's bleeding or if it's from my own mouth.

"Unless you're begging for my cock, save it."

"I'll never beg for that. Or *you.*"

I clamp my mouth shut as he grabs me and pushes me onto the couch. I fight against him as he climbs on top of me. I knee him, digging my fingers into his arm, and he slaps me. "Don't fight me, Elizabeth; I can't promise you I won't kill you and fuck your corpse for as long as you've made me wait."

"Don't fucking touch me." I fight and fight, tears leak down my face, and he takes his tongue and runs it up my face, licking the tears up. "I'll tell you what. We're going to play a little game. But first, I'm going to use this gun here to fuck you, then my knife. Lots of objects today, I'm feeling adventurous."

My stomach turns when he rocks the gun back. I feel sick and nauseous, and my vision is blurry. I'm no longer in control; fighting him is impossible because he's stronger. He has a gun and a knife, too. He yanks my pants down, taking my panties along too. I feel the weapon running along my pussy folds, and I gag when he smiles.

"I can't wait to feel this. But in the meantime, this will do."

He plunges the gun inside of my pussy, and I cry out. Tears, anger, and what's most fucked up about this is that some sick way my body wants to enjoy it. Just not with *him*. I feel the vomit rising, and I try my best not to kick him. Knowing that if he made any sudden movements, he could shoot me. I lift my leg to aim for his face, and he glares at me as he tilts the gun upwards in my pussy.

"Don't get creative. Safety isn't on, and I can make it look like an accident."

"You're disgusting. You'll never get away with this."

"I don't see anyone coming to your rescue this time." He pushes the gun out of me and places a knife against my neck.

"Different play? Your blood probably tastes spectacular. He slides the knife down my neck, digging the tip of it into my neck and placing a small puncture. I feel my blood drifting down my neck. He runs his tongue up my neck.

"Ahh, you taste better than I imagined."

"You're fucking sick."

He chuckles so evilly that my skin crawls. He slides the knife down to my pussy and slowly pushes it inside of me. He opens my pussy lips with the knife and plunges the gun inside. I'm terrified to move. He flips the knife to the dull end and pushes that inside of me next to the gun. Adding more force, the harder he pushes, the more I cry and clamp my legs shut.

"Obviously, your pussy wants my cock instead." He yanks his jeans down, and I vomit. I actually fucking vomit, and I purposely ensure it's all on him.

"You bitch!"

"Sorry, I guess looking at you makes me fucking *sick.* "

The tears have stained my face, and I give him an evil grin. I can practically see the steam coming from him. He raises the gun at me, and I shrug.

"Do it. Graham's going to kill you anyway."

My job right now is to keep Tim's cock away from me. If I get killed in the process, then it's fucking worth it.

"Don't speak his name around me. He's an obstacle that I'll get rid of soon enough." He kneels in front of me, covered in my vomit, and he pushes the gun into my shoulder.

"Here's what you're going to do. I'm going to take a shower because of obvious reasons." He looks down over himself and turns his mouth up.

"But first, I'm going to tie you up, and when I get out, you're going to choke on my cock. Then we'll take care of that little obstacle together before we leave for our honeymoon."

"Honey...honeymoon?"

"Yes, our *honeymoon.* Either you marry me tonight, or I'll kill your brother. He's a waste of space if you ask me."

I rear my head back and slam it against his, rolling on the ground and behind the couch as he stands up and barrels after me. My hand reaches the door again, but not before I feel the barrel of the gun at my temple.

Graham, help me.

51

Graham

Once I got home, I fixed myself a glass of whiskey and downed it. After all this time, Liza still didn't understand that my home was her home and that I wanted this to be *our* home. I had been dropping hints all weekend that I wanted her to move in with me, or at least I thought I had been. I knew she hadn't decided where she planned to be, but I wanted us together either way. I'm on my fourth whiskey when my phone rings.

"Hey, Selle."

"Are you okay? You sound weird."

"I'm fine, what's up?"

"I just wanted to say I'm sorry. I shouldn't have kept Elias a secret from you."

I silently kicked myself for making my sister feel bad for who she wanted to be with.

"Selle, you have nothing to apologize for."

"I just didn't know you'd be so against us being together."

"It's not that. If you're happy and being treated well, that's all I care about. I was upset that you kept it from me. We tell each other *everything*. We always have."

"I know; I'm sorry, G."

"I'm sorry, too."

"How's my favorite girlfriend doing?"

"We're not talking at the moment."

"What did you do?"

I explained what had happened to my sister, and for a moment, she was silent. I heard her suck her teeth, and I know she's rolling her eyes.

"Damn, G, you fucked this one up."

"Me? Were you not listening?"

"No, were *you* not listening? Put yourself in her shoes. She gave you the *perfect* opening to ask her to move in, and you took it and turned it into an argument. When she said she needed to go home and unpack, you could have easily asked then. But you didn't. Imagine how that made her feel. Why do you think she was speechless at your rant? Because she didn't expect it."

I run my fingers through my hair, gathering my thoughts.

"I'm a fucking idiot."

"Yes, you are, but I love you, and you can fix it. I've gotta go. I'm having lunch with Brant and Bethany."

"Be safe, love you."

We hang up, and I scroll to Liza's number. I call three times, and it goes to voicemail each time. She always answered my phone calls, no matter how angry she was with me. *Always.*

I grab my keys and bolt for her apartment, which will definitely be gone tomorrow if I have anything to do with it.

I get to Liza's in record time. I park the G–Class and stride into the building. The bellhop is nowhere to be found, and neither is Alicia. Weird.

I pull my cellphone out and call Liza again. It rings twice and goes to voicemail again. Something is off. I can *feel* it.

I go around the counter to use the building's phone when I see Alicia and our bellhop, Martin, against the counter, tied up with their mouths taped shut. I run over and rip the tape off Alicia's mouth.

"Ms. Crambell, you have to help Ms. Crambell."

"Where is she? What happened?" Alicia starts hyperventilating, and I cut the ropes off.

"Alicia, I need you to relax and tell me what happened; Martin is knocked out cold. You are my only hope."

"Someone came and said they were here to visit Ms. Crambell, he got here right after you both went up. I told him he had to sign in and that I had to call her first because he wasn't on her list."

I'm glad I went the extra mile when I took over this place. I wanted this apartment building to feel safe for all my tenants, so I made them all fill out a paper with the names of people who could come in and out freely.

"He got angry and told me that she was his girlfriend and that he was just trying to surprise her." My body stiffens. "I told him that it wasn't possible because she was the girlfriend of a friend of mine. I didn't want to tell him you owned the building and risk him trying to take her from here. I've been watching the cameras from here and haven't seen any movement on her floor."

"Good job. I want you to call Ellis and tell him to activate our emergency team. Go to the safe room. It looks like Martin is coming around now. Can you do that for me?"

She nods. I stand up and run towards the stairs, not wanting to risk him hearing the elevator. Fuck me for putting her on the top floor! It feels like I've been running for days trying to get to her. How the fuck did I miss Alicia not being at her desk when I left? How did I not have a feeling something was wrong?

I arrive at Liza's door and quietly put my ear against it; it's quiet. Too quiet. I reach into my pocket and call her cell phone again; I can hear it ringing. I hang up and use my master key to let myself in. I inch the door open, keeping my guard up. Stepping into the room, I see Liza sitting in the middle of the living room, gagged with a cloth in her mouth and her hands and feet tied by rope.

Her eyes widen when she sees me, and she frantically shakes her head, tears streaming down her face. She starts nodding towards her bedroom, and I nod in understanding, quickly reaching her.

"Are you hurt?" I whisper. She doesn't answer me as I start working on the rope around her hands.

"I'm going to free your hands; can you do the rest?" She slowly moves her head this time, and I see blood streaming down the side of her face. I move her hair to see a gash on the side of her head. My blood turns cold; I look at her, and my jaw tenses. I remove the rope from her hands, and she quickly yanks the cloth from her mouth.

"I'm going to fucking kill him," I say, turning for her bedroom; she grabs me and silently pleads.

"Please don't leave me." I crouch down to her, cupping her face in my hands.

"I'll be right back. I want you to go downstairs and get into the safe room. Remember where it is? Alicia and Martin are already there, and my team is coming."

"But..."

"Elizabeth, trust me. I'll find you. Let me handle this."

"He was on a phone call; he has a gun."

"Go, pretty girl. I love you."

I push her toward the door just in time. Tim's footsteps start traveling toward the living room. I hide behind her couch to avoid giving up my location, but I'll have the perfect view of him.

"Oh, you got free, you fucking bitch?" He barks with his gun in hand. He lifts it and scratches his head.

"You know, all I ever wanted was for you to love me and give me a fucking chance. I've loved you since I first saw you that day in school.

I knew you being nice to me was too good to be true."

He heads for the other two rooms and starts throwing things around. "Come out, Elizabeth. It's better to come with me, or I'll kill everyone in your pathetic picture-perfect family, then still force you to marry me."

He returns to the living room and stops; he takes a deep breath and exhales. I move around the couch and launch myself toward him.

He drops the gun, just like I hoped he would. We tumble onto the floor, both of us quickly regaining our stance.

"*You.* You're the reason she isn't mine." He draws his fist back and swings; I duck and fling an uppercut. As soon as it connects, I go to hit him again, this time punching his nose, blood spewing immediately.

He turns swiftly and decks me in the jaw. I spit out some blood that gathers in my mouth.

We stand there staring at each other. "She belongs to me; she's mine," he coughs, trying to catch his breath.

I chuckle lowly and snatch him by his neck, pushing him into the wall.

"You've lost your goddamn mind if you believe that. She belongs to me, and that will *never* change, and I want you to sleep every night knowing that the woman you love will *never* love you back, you piece of shit." He spits in my face, and I tighten my grip around his neck.

"Do you know how long I've waited to watch you die by my hand for daring to touch her? For daring to touch what's mine? This is perfect, almost too perfect."

"Fuck you. She was going to marry me."

"You're delusional."

"I fucked her."

I see red and tighten my hand around his neck, the outline of his lips turning blue.

He knees my groin and launches himself to the ground, reaching for the gun. I launch behind him, catching him by his feet.

I quickly get to my feet, yanking him up. "What did you say?"

"I fucked her!" I take his head and slam it to the wall, grabbing the gun and getting in his face.

"Even if I believed you, I know she wouldn't let you touch her willingly. Which means you raped her, now there's *definitely* no chance of you living. Bye, Tim. I hope hell has a special place for you."

My finger hovers over the trigger when he rears his head back and slams it into mine. I stumble back before the taste of metal fills my mouth. He rushes after me; my grip tightens on the gun when I feel his hand around it.

I've got too much shit to live for; if he thinks for a second he's killing me before I kill him, he has no fucking idea who I am.

I'm too focused on his hand to feel him dig the knife into my shoulder. The pain hits me immediately, and I squeeze a hold around his neck. We're both on the ground, and I can't get my foot or the gun where I need it.

Fuck, it's too late.

Bang.

52

Liza

"Was that a gunshot?" *Fuck. Graham.*

Acknowledgments

I can't believe I'm finally here. I am writing acknowledgments to a book, MY book. What the actual fuck. First, I want to thank my editor, Bri, my PA, Olivia, and my ARC readers. Y'all are the bomb! I have to also thank Amber (Tilly) for answering any questions I had. Alexis, my girl! This cover is the bomb, and I can't wait to release the next one! Next, I want to thank my sister, Adriana. No matter what time it was or what you were doing, you were always there to be my sounding board and to read anything I needed you to read. Without you, there would be no book; you were my literal saving grace throughout this process. To my husband, thank you for your never-ending support. I know you're glad you no longer have to hear me pout about wanting to publish my book. To my kids, when you're old enough to read this, in many, MANY years, don't judge Mama; it's just some literary fun! To my parents, I'm sorry. Maybe you should have made me go to sleep instead of thinking, "Ahh, she's just reading." Haha! No, seriously, I hope this makes you proud of me.

To my readers, thank you. Thank you for sticking with me and trusting I could give you your "book fill." I hope this duet's second and final book will surpass your expectations.

With love,

Alaina T. Lee

About the Author

Hi, my new friends! I'm so excited that you're here! I'm a country girl who loves writing and reading in my free time. I'm a mama of two and married to a man who makes my world spin. I live in Oklahoma (Boomer Sooner!) and love traveling and making memories with my friends and family. Food is seriously the way to my heart. I can be a bit of a firecracker sometimes, especially if I'm hangry, but can't we all? I love baseball, good beer, and great vibes!

I started writing when I was about 15 years old; my imagination should have gotten me in trouble long ago. This book idea came from a dream, and I needed to get it on paper. Now that I have, I hope you love it as much as I did when I wrote it!

Also, fair warning: This was me "dipping" my toe into "dark romance writing." The next book in this duet is much darker. The fun has just begun! I have so many ideas and thoughts, and I can't wait to share them with you all to enjoy!

You can connect with me on:
Instagram: @alainatlee_author
Facebook: @Alaina T. Lee Author
Facebook group: Alaina T. Lee Reader's group
Tiktok: @alainatlee_author

Also by Alaina T. Lee

Next in this series is *Insatiable*, with a release date of June 2024! I hope you're ready for this wild fucking ride. It just gets crazier! Be a good girl, and click the link to order yours.

Love,

Alaina T. Lee

https://www.amazon.com/dp/B0D1W32R3H

Insatiable

Look at you, being a book slut and coming back for more. Click the link and order yours, babe.